WHISPERS
IN THE
LABYRINTH

KAITLYN ROSE HONG

For my first fans and helpers, Jace and Courtney,
and for those who feel they're too far
gone to start over again.

Table of Contents

Map of Sidylla Labyrinth

Prologue

"I NEED A PRINCE," A DEEP, RASPING VOICE HISSED, ECHOING throughout the dungeon chamber. A chill hung in the air, and a constant plink of moisture dripped from the ceiling into a puddle on the floor. Empty chains swung against the wall, though no wind blew, and the flickering, solitary blaze of a boy's torch illuminated the room with dim light. The boy, Everard, quivered before the looming creature he had summoned. But he wasn't alone. Leaning near the entrance a few paces away, his one and only friend kept watch.

Tightening his grasp on the cool, metal handle of his torch in one hand and the forbidden spell book in the other, Everard gathered his scattering courage and found minor comfort in the warmth of the torch's flames. "I *am* a prince," he replied, trying his best to appear so, despite his trembling. "I am Prince Everard, the fourth son of King Léon of Reudinia."

Deep chuckles rumbled through the dungeons. The immense, clouded form of the summoned spirit wavered in the torchlight, drawing closer. "Ah, but you are mistaken, young one," it whispered. "I need a *real* prince."

The words sliced through Everard like ice. He dropped his gaze, unable to bring himself to look into the spirit's face. What glimpses he had been brave enough to steal only revealed the face of death itself and blazing purple eyes which seemed to bore into his soul. Everard could almost feel its crooked grin spread when he remained silent.

The creature's form shifted and slithered around Everard like wisps of smoke.

"*You*," it said, its words biting, "do not carry a sense. I see no potential in you."

Despite his desire to appear strong and sure, Everard's insides melted. He stood still, taking in the familiar words that echoed through his past. He was no threat to this creature. If someone decided to cut Everard down, they could do so easily. He was small and thin with no magical powers or talents. The distress of his uselessness settled heavily on him as he clutched his thick spell book to his chest. Tears stung his eyes.

The spirit's focus shifted behind Everard to where his friend watched silently from the back wall. Its teeth glinted as it continued, "*He*, however, is a different story."

Everard bristled. Once again, he was overlooked, set aside, disregarded. Taking a deep breath, he steadied himself.

Not this time.

Everard stepped into the spirit's line of sight and shook his head. "*He* isn't the one who called you. This only concerns me."

"Is that so?" The summoned creature's purple eyes gleamed, but it retreated. "How unfortunate. Then what you ask of me is impossible."

Prince Everard gulped. Was this all for nothing? He squeezed the spell book even tighter. "Is there anything I can do?"

Once again, the spirit's gaze slid to Everard's friend. "If *he* is unwilling, then you must find another to take your place. Bring him to me in the labyrinth. Then—and only then—can you have your wish."

"Bring a prince to the *Sidylla Labyrinth*? I can't—"

The creature's figure filled the space, causing Everard's torch to dim and his words to die. "This is the only way!" it bellowed. The spirit shrunk again, and its voice softened once more. "The prince must be able to survive the labyrinth. Choose wisely and bring him to me within six months."

The room lightened, and the shadow faded from existence.

With a frustrated cry, Everard threw the spell book onto the dirty, damp floor and stomped on its cover.

When he had begun the spell to summon the spirit of the Sense Thief, his hope had been great. He'd thought he finally had a chance to gain his own magical power. But the hope had been short-lived—now crushed, crumbled, and tossed into a chasm.

Curse the book and its uselessness.

The creature's words rose to mind: *You do not carry a sense. I see no potential in you.* He gripped his head and pulled at his brown hair, taking in a deep, shaky breath.

Why had *he* been the only one in his entire family to miss out on the genes that allowed his brothers and parents to inherit magical abilities known as "senses"? Why only him?

Despite the fact that his father was king, Everard was 307th in line for the throne. There were 943 royals in the kingdom of Reudinia, but only the royals with senses received recognition. His father had been so ashamed by Everard's lack of one, he refused to speak about him…let alone *to* him.

Because having a sense was everything to the people of Reudinia.

"Damn it," Everard hissed, choking back tears.

His friend shifted against the stone wall behind him, a reminder that he still had company. Everard scrubbed away any tears that had surfaced and took a few deep, calming breaths.

"What are your thoughts, Everard?"

Everard faced the figure leaning against the dungeon wall, hidden in the shadows. He lowered his gaze. "It's no use. There's no way I can lead anyone through that cursed labyrinth." His shoulders slumped. "Not even the king of Niaria and his army could do it. How could I outlast an entire army?" Everard's throat burned with the effort it took to swallow his tears. "It's impossible."

His friend's slow sigh resounded through the dungeon. "Not impossible. Just incredibly difficult." After a pause, he continued. "Do you really need a sense to be happy?"

Everard hesitated and imagined continuing living as he was—being terrorized because he had no sense; running from the taunting Prince Valor; and worst of all, being ignored by his father. As if Everard didn't even exist. Thinking of his father pushed him to say, "Yes, I think I do."

Another sigh. "Having a sense is nothing special. There's nothing good about it."

Everard's brow furrowed. Since when was a sense "nothing special"?

His friend shrugged. "But…"

"But what?"

"You're certain you want one."

"Yes."

"And you will do whatever it takes to make this happen?"

"I will."

"I really mean whatever it takes. Think this through carefully."

Everard looked at the forbidden spell book lying near his feet. The idea of entering the labyrinth alone terrified him, but if doing so meant he could finally gain a sense, maybe he could do it. He had gone to this much trouble already. Either way, he longed for the neglect and torment to end; he didn't think he could stand it much longer. Everard gritted his teeth and focused on his friend once more.

"I'll do whatever it takes."

◉

1

New Spaces and Unfamiliar Faces

A SOFT RAIN MISTED SIXTEEN-YEAR-OLD PRINCESS FAVEN and the green plains around her. Squeezing her reins, she peered over her horse's dappled head and through the hazy blur at the impending gateway and the thick, stone wall rising before her. She bit the insides of her cheek and tugged her cloak closer around her. The city was quite larger than she'd imagined. Maybe the dare was too difficult for her to execute after all. It was one thing to jump off a dragon into a lake. It was another matter entirely to enter a forbidden library in a kingdom she'd never been to before.

She pictured her best friend, Ekon, and his wide smile, white against his dark skin, his black dreadlocks drooping over his shoulders. *"I dare you."*

Faven sighed, staring at the massive wall surrounding the city. She'd thought Sage, her younger brother, had been exaggerating when he'd told her the capital of Reudinia was as large as the whole kingdom of Hallon. She should've known—Sage never exaggerated about *anything*.

Oh, Sage. She wished he and their parents could be there with her. Years ago, her parents spoke about how they'd all travel together when it was time for her to take the assessment, how they'd make a family trip of it. Yet here she was—alone.

"We made it," breathed Trent. Faven glanced over in time to see her bodyguard's shoulders relax. He flashed her a relieved smile and, with a gesture of his arm, added, "Phoebus, capital of Reudinia."

Faven only nodded as she eyed the sky. It was too dark and cloudy for her liking. Naturally, the weather *would* be gloomy on such a day. She gritted her teeth and rode closer to Trent's horse. At least they'd arrive at the inn soon; she couldn't wait to get into a warmly lit room. Her mood lifted a bit at that thought. She passed the reins to one hand and used her sense to form a small ball of light in the other, brightening the blurry gloom around her.

As they drew closer, Trent and Faven slowed their horses.

Tight-faced, worn guards inspected each bag, wagon, and carriage and questioned every person passing in or out of the gates. People murmured amongst themselves as they waited to be allowed entrance.

Faven frowned, her unease returning. Why did everyone seem so solemn? "What's going on?" she whispered.

Trent's thick, black eyebrows furrowed. "I'm not sure." He straightened, his dark eyes alert as a sullen-faced guard approached them, scanning their luggage warily.

"Who are you and what is your business?" the guard asked.

Trent kept his focus on the guard. "I'm Trent, and this is Princess Faven of the Korei line." He gestured to her. "We seek entrance to Reudinia for the royal assessment."

Faven grimaced and avoided the guard's scrutinizing gaze.

While the assessment was the official reason for their trip, Faven didn't necessarily want to think about it. She was in a strange place on a gloomy day with tense people surrounding her, and her best friend's dare lingered in her thoughts. She had enough to worry about without adding the stress of where she might place in the ranking.

She brushed some of the misty rain off her face with her sleeve—though it was damp too—and tucked a wet strand of her sky-blue hair behind her ear as she squinted through the mist at the gate.

The guard deliberated Trent's words. "Do you have a royal pass as proof?"

Trent nodded and pulled out a scroll.

The guard took the scroll from him and unrolled it, shielding it as much as he could from the rain. He studied it for a moment before rolling it back up and returning it to Trent. He stepped back and bowed to Faven. "Welcome, Your Highness. You may enter."

The words *'Your Highness'* rang in her ears. Suddenly very self-conscious, Faven jerked an awkward nod in response.

"Thank you, sir," Trent said and nudged his horse forward. Faven followed.

No one had ever called her 'Your Highness' before. At home, she was Faven to everyone—except Trent and Hallon's monarch, Queen Eshe, who always insisted on calling her Princess. Since her parents were retired Reudinian royals who had moved to Hallon as envoys for Reudinia before Faven was born, it had never really sunk in that she was a *princess* in another kingdom.

One of Faven's closest friends, Queen Eshe's daughter Princess Maha, told her Eshe used Faven's title out of respect for Reudinian customs. As Hallon's queen, Eshe refused to do or say anything that might cause tension between the two kingdoms. And Faven assumed Trent titled her because her parents were his employers.

As they rode past the guards, several people eyed Faven and Trent. A few whispered, but she did her best to ignore them. Keeping her head high and her face forward, Faven exuded more confidence than she felt.

Then, as they rode through the gates into Phoebus, she forgot about the unwanted attention.

Through the dim blur of the rain, lofty orange turrets and towers rose from the royal castle. The palace stood atop a large mountain, its stonework the same shade of white as the shores of Hallon, and a waterfall tumbled from its doorstep. Orange-roofed buildings and homes crawled up the sides of the mountain and filled the city to the brim, matching the colors of the castle and making the waterfall the city's centerpiece.

Sun-rays filtered through gray clouds and several mini rainbows formed in the light spray of rain. It took Faven's breath away.

People raced for shelter, oblivious to the beauty around them. Faven could already see several differences between the people of Reudinia and Hallon, but the most striking was their clothing. Reudinian clothes appeared more restrictive and were dyed with solid colors. Contrarily, Hallon's clothing was loose, airy, and full of vibrant dyes and patterns, matching the free outlook many Hallonese had. Faven didn't necessarily dislike the differences.

Her eyes swept over the city's landscape once more. How would she find the forbidden library in such a dense place? She'd researched enough to know it was located in the Royal Academy for Princes, and that the academy was somewhere near the royal castle. But that was the extent of her knowledge.

Faven resisted sighing. Was it too risky to attempt breaking into the library? She had hoped to find the answer to her questions on healing… She clutched her horse's reins tighter and thought of the days spent nursing her grandfather. It had been three years since he'd passed. If the key to unlocking her healing abilities waited in that library, then a little breaking and entering was worth the risk.

"Reudinia has a forbidden library?" Ekon had asked, a few days before she'd left Hallon. *"Why?"*

Faven had shrugged, then fiddled with an arrow before nocking it. *"I guess they have a lot of things they like to keep hidden."*

"And you think the answer to activating your healing sense is inside?" Ekon casually leaned his back against a post and crossed his ankles.

Faven raised the bow and arrow, her gaze on the target. She'd been informed of her potential healing power by her sense tutor three years ago and yet still couldn't heal a scratch. *"I can't be sure, but Sir Aadan mentioned there were some high-profile books about manipulating senses in Reudinia's forbidden library."* She released her arrow, but it missed the target. She had always been a better swordswoman than archer.

Faven grinned at Ekon mischievously. *"However, I do wonder if the mystery of how King Heron got his sense is inside that library. Or maybe they have books carrying evil spells. Why else would it be forbidden?"*

"Well, why don't you find out?"

"Huh?" Faven stared at Ekon.

He straightened and took the bow from her before pulling an arrow from the quiver standing between them. *"You're leaving for Reudinia in a few days. You'll be in Phoebus, home of the forbidden library. Sneak in and see if they have anything about healing senses. In fact..."* Ekon aimed and released his arrow; it struck the center of the target. Then he faced her and raised his eyebrows with a grin. *"I dare you."*

Faven stared at him a moment longer before setting her face determinedly. She'd been joking about King Heron and the spells, but she *was* curious if the library held anything that could help her activate her healing sense. She thought of her grandfather. If she learned to heal, then maybe she wouldn't feel as useless as she had been when he passed.

"Fine. I accept your dare."

Faven urged her horse forward and followed Trent up the steep street. She spotted some people peering out of windows and doors or huddling under awnings, watching them ride by. They spoke to each other in hushed tones.

She would've thought they had a prejudice against foreigners if the same people weren't treating every passerby with equal suspicion.

A sudden commotion snapped Faven's gaze forward once more. Up ahead, a gathering of people, carriages, and livestock converged at a crossroad. Yelling and agitation escalated in the air.

Faven straightened and strained to see over the current of people and cattle. It looked like a fancy carriage was blocking the road. But she couldn't see enough. She would have to get closer. Without waiting for permission, Faven slid off her horse and plunged into the crowd. Her slim figure proved useful as she wove through the sea of bodies.

"Faven!"

Ignoring Trent's call, Faven shoved to the front and paused at the sight before her.

A massive, sea-blue carriage with gold wheels almost as tall as her, drawn by four white stallions, slumped amidst the turmoil blocking the way. One of those gold wheels had become stuck in a pothole filled with rainwater, and several people were heaving the carriage free. A young man with a wide, cocky grin peeked out the carriage window and waved. His dark hair was pulled into a high, tight ponytail and frills covered his coat's sleeves.

What an arrogant man. Faven crossed her arms. He wasn't even trying to help.

"Prince Archie!" a voice rose from the crowd. "What are your thoughts on Prince Tenji's and Prince Kai's disappearances?"

"Are you taking any precautions?" called another voice. "Who do you think will be next?"

This snagged Faven's attention. Missing princes? She skimmed the crowd and then studied the man in the carriage window.

Prince Archie's easy smile shifted to an uncomfortable one. He lifted a hand but failed to call silence. "There's no need for alarm. They'll turn up somewhere. Tenji usually holes up before an assessment and Kai is always disappearing." He rolled his eyes. "I'm sure it is nothing."

A chorus of exclamations and retorts erupted from the crowd.

Faven frowned. Two princes were missing? Maybe this was why everyone seemed so tense.

Trent appeared next to her and placed a firm hand on her shoulder, glaring.

"Princess, you shouldn't run off like that," he said through gritted teeth, his voice as hard as his gaze. In his other hand, he gripped their horses' reins.

"I only wanted to see what was going on." Faven nodded to the carriage just as the men finally pushed it free. Prince Archie waved goodbye, ignoring the people's cries and questions as the carriage rolled down the road.

Trent sighed and brushed back his dark, wet hair from his forehead. "Well, you've had your chance to see. Now, come. Let's get out of this rain."

Echoing Trent's sigh, Faven allowed Trent to help her climb back into her sidesaddle. While she was ready to dry off in a warm, well-lit room and get some rest after their long journey, a small part of her itched to explore Phoebus further. She wanted to learn more about how the kingdom functioned. What was daily life like for a Reudinian royal? What were the differences between the ways higher- and lower-ranked royals lived? Could there be other royals like her who lived normal lives despite their titles?

In the kingdom of Hallon, only those directly related to the current monarch held royal titles, and the one closest in relation to the king or queen was next in line for the throne. Royalty and senses had nothing to do with one another because anyone from any social class could be born with a sense. But in Reudinia, only high-ranked royals carried senses, and the people chose their next king based on sense rank rather than blood.

It was well after night had fallen when Trent led her to an inn where her parents had booked rooms for them, but Faven could still make out several columns of windows and Phoebus' token orange roof and white stone walls. After finding a place in the stables for the horses, they hurried inside and out of the worsening rain.

Warm, cozy air embraced Faven the moment she stepped through the inn door, and a golden glow lit the room. An open space full of wooden tables and chairs was on the right and a narrow staircase ascended on the left. A few travelers lingered in the dining area, drinking and mumbling to each other, while two girls hustled about the room, cleaning tables and serving guests. A middle-aged, dark-haired man with angular features came toward them. He smiled.

"Good evening, ma'am, sir. I'm the innkeeper here. How may I help you today?"

Trent nodded curtly. "A good evening to you too. We need two rooms for a few weeks. I believe Lord Jethro contacted you."

"Ah, yes, yes!" The innkeeper nodded, his eyes brightening. He scurried to a desk and dug through his documents. He pulled out a letter scribbled in her father's familiar scrawl. "Your rooms have been prepared. From what I recall, you've come from Hallon. Is that correct?"

Trent opened his mouth to respond, but the innkeeper didn't pause before he continued: "That's quite the journey…It's unfortunate you come at such a tense time." He leaned closer and lowered his voice. "In the last two days, two high-ranked princes have gone missing. Both of them in the top ten! And with the ranking assessment only two days away, the city is in an uproar."

Faven widened her eyes. Two princes from the top ten? That was a much greater deal than some random princes going missing. She fidgeted with her wet cloak, thinking back to the flamboyant man, Prince Archie, and what he'd said about the disappearances.

Maybe the princes weren't really missing. She couldn't imagine why anyone would harm those in the top ten; they were princes with the most powerful senses after all.

The muscles in Trent's neck tightened. "Missing?"

"Yes, terrible." The innkeeper waved a hand, dismissively. "Anyway, what brings you to Reudinia?"

Grimacing, Trent glanced at Faven. He didn't look happy. "This is Lord Jethro's daughter, Princess Faven. We're here for the royal assessment."

The innkeeper stared at Faven. "A Reudinian princess living in another kingdom?" His lips pulled into a slight frown. "Seems doubtful…."

Doubtful? He didn't believe them? Faven pushed back her shoulders and glowered at the innkeeper indignantly. But then she remembered her mother's warnings about not speaking out of turn—especially in Reudinia—so she bit her tongue.

"Her parents are envoys deployed to Hallon to mediate the relationship between the two kingdoms." Trent paused, tossed her a warning glance, then lifted a bag of coins. "Here is the money for our stay."

The innkeeper took the bag of coins from Trent and eyed Faven once more. His gaze landed on the long, light blue braid slipping out from under her hood. He pointed. "Do you have a sense? Or is the color fake?"

Faven winced. Unnaturally colored hair was one of the signs of having a sense. Mother had told her that before humans ever had magic, the spirits, fairies, and dragons gifted humans with abilities to reward them for assistance. Thus, gifted magic mingled with the humans' genetics and made minor changes to their features, such as abnormally colored eyes, hair, and on rare occasions, skin, depending on the strength of a human's sense. However, Faven's light blue hair *wasn't* natural.

No, her true hair color was rainbow, but she didn't want to tell him *that*.

When Faven learned she could manipulate color at the age of seven, she took immediate advantage of the newfound ability and changed her hair frequently to hide its natural state. Hallonese children had often attempted to cut strands of the rainbow colors from her head and adults petted her because they thought the multicolored strands were beautiful. While her rainbow hair meant Faven had a strong sense, she hated its bold hues.

When she didn't respond, the innkeeper continued, unfazed, "What's your rank?" He peered at her foreign, formless, dark purple dress and ragged cloak. "Not high, I imagine."

Shame like a hot blade thrust deep into Faven's chest, and a small glow emanated from her. Whenever strong emotions overtook her, she couldn't help her sense from oozing out of her. The greater the emotion, the brighter her light. She swallowed and clutched her cloak closer around her body to hide her worn travel clothes. "I've never been assessed."

The innkeeper's frown deepened. "Never been assessed? You look old enough to be courting, yet you've never been assessed?" He shook his head and poured out the bag of coins onto his desk, painstakingly counting its contents.

Faven blushed and slouched, avoiding the innkeeper's gaze as it flicked back and forth from her to the coins while he counted. Most royals were first assessed when they were seven years old—the age most senses developed—and then were assessed every year until they reached twenty-five. A royal over twenty-five could abdicate their title if they didn't want to continue being assessed—unless they were in the top ten. Those in the top ten were too close to the throne to opt out of being assessed.

Faven squeezed her fists. If only she had agreed to journey with Sage when he tested a few years ago. Maybe then she would've had a decent rank to tell the innkeeper.

"The Royal Council specially excused her from taking the assessment until now," Trent cut in.

When the amount of coins satisfied him, the innkeeper sniffed, and his eyes paused once more on Faven's hair. "Well, if you have a sense as strong as your hair color and glowing suggests, you should rank under two hundred unless you're *very* unlucky."

Neither Faven nor Trent said another word, and thankfully, a young girl materialized from around a corner to lead them to their rooms. When the girl slipped away to presumably help another customer, Trent carried Faven's belongings into her room, and she followed him.

After seeing her settled, Trent turned to her, lingering uneasily. "I'll be right next door if you need anything," he said. "Get some good rest tonight. Since we were delayed on our journey, we don't have much time before your assessment. We'll have to run a few errands tomorrow."

Faven wrinkled her nose. "Errands?"

"We'll need to pick up the dress your parents ordered for your ranking assessment and ceremony."

"That's not so much."

Trent smiled. "I did say a few, didn't I? But we should still leave enough time for the tailor to make alterations if need be." Then he frowned. His dark eyes searched hers, and his forehead creased. "Please, don't sneak off without me. Especially with everything happening. This isn't Hallon."

Faven pouted and put her hands on her hips. Her stomach flipped nervously. Did he know about her plan? "Why are you always so distrustful?"

Trent raised his eyebrows. "You do realize your parents hired me because you kept sneaking off with your friends and getting into mischief, don't you?"

Faven squinted at him. "Well, my friends aren't here, and neither are my parents." She couldn't hide the bitterness in her voice.

Trent leaned against the doorpost and sighed heavily. "Your parents wanted to come. But there are too many rumors of war with Velykov kicking up unnecessary trouble. They couldn't leave their post."

Faven knew that. But knowing didn't make the feeling of abandonment any easier to bear.

Only four kingdoms were in regular communication with Reudinia. Among those four were Shinai and Terecia, but Hallon was Reudinia's strongest ally. Terecia, home to magical beings such as elves, fairies, and dwarves, often traded their magical stones, devices, and wares with Reudinia, and Shinai often organized ties through marriage with Reudinia's higher-ranked royals.

Velykov's relationship with Reudinia, however, was remarkably hostile. The only reason Velykov hadn't declared war yet was because everyone believed Reudinia would win. Reudinia's massive collection of royals with senses made them a military powerhouse. While other kingdoms did have people with senses, most of them were peasants or field workers who were not easily wrangled into an army.

Trent stepped back. "Get some rest. We've had a long journey." He bowed his farewell and then closed the door as he left the room.

Faven turned and scanned the tiny room. A small bed mat and blankets lay against one wall. A dingy mirror hung on the same wall, and a massive wooden bucket sat in the corner of the room already filled with steaming water for her to bathe in. As she examined the gloomy room, Faven's thoughts returned to her parents and brother, Sage.

Unlike her, Sage had been ranked when he was seven and received the high rank of 22nd place. Since then, because he lived so far away, he had been excused from attending the assessment until he turned sixteen. They used his original assessment scores to assess and rank him each year. One year his rank had fallen to 23rd, but the next year it rose back to 22nd. But at least Sage had a solid idea of where he stood in the ranking. Faven had nothing.

She didn't want to think about the approaching assessment or where she would fall in the ranking. She didn't want to think about the possibility of ranking so low it was an embarrassment to her parents and herself. Since she'd never taken the assessment before, she couldn't help worrying about the difficulty or what precisely would be in such an assessment. Her mother and tutors had given her a vague idea, but that didn't ease her nerves.

Shaking her head, Faven unclipped her wet cloak and hung it on a hook by the door. Then she slipped off her dark purple Hallonese dress and laid it out to dry; the dark purple—now black from the rainwater—was covered in golden circles, swirls, and triangles. Stepping into the tub, Faven sunk into the water, allowing it to warm her as she scrubbed away the grime from their two months of travel.

As she pulled herself out of the water, dried off, and slipped on clean undergarments and a nightgown, Faven heard the sound of light footsteps edging down the hallway outside her room. Low, gruff voices accompanied the footsteps:

"...heard another prince went missing today. Prince Jovian this time."

Her breath halted in her chest. She crept closer and pressed her ear against the door.

"Another one? Do you think it's Velykov?"

"Who knows."

"How many more will go missing before this is over?"

Faven bit the inside of her cheek. Another prince missing? Unease settled in the pit of her stomach. *Could* Velykov have something to do with it? Could someone be planning to use the princes as bait to lure Reudinia into war? She shook her head and stepped away from the door. Even if Velykov was involved, what could she do about it? She was just an average girl who incidentally held a royal title.

So, Faven pushed the conversation to the back of her mind and crawled onto her bed mat to sleep. Her thoughts shifted to Ekon's dare. Her stomach fluttered nervously, and once again doubt pressed down on her. Maybe it was too risky to sneak into the library during a time like this. Should she give up and admit her failure to Ekon later? But then the memory of her grandfather's grave strengthened her resolve. Never again would she be so helpless.

2

A Borrowed Name

THE NEXT DAY, TRENT AND FAVEN BUSIED THEMSELVES with preparations for her assessment. Throughout the day, Faven's stomach churned, and she couldn't take her mind off the assessment or the dare she was planning to attempt. And, unfortunately, the best time for her to accomplish her dare was on assessment day.

Since the forbidden library was in the Royal Academy for Princes—where only princes, tutors, and the Royal Council were allowed—Faven would be immediately barred from entrance. If she wanted to enter, then she had to become a prince. Before she had left Hallon, she planned to pretend to be her brother if she was questioned, so she "borrowed" her brother's royal pass. The timeline would be tight, but royal assessments meant hundreds of other princes would also be entering the Royal Academy. A perfect time for sneaking in.

While they were picking up her dress, Faven told Trent she wanted to look around for clothes for Sage as well. Luckily, Trent didn't protest and only told her not to take too long.

Quickly, she threw together an outfit and bought it with the personal allowance her parents had given her. She even found a pair of boots.

"Those look a little big for Sage," Trent commented as he eyed the boots.

"I bet he'll grow into them." Faven squeezed the parcels to her chest. "He'll need to have some Reudinian clothes when he returns for his own assessment in a few years."

She wasn't sure if Trent had noticed her suspicious behavior, but if he did, she hoped he assumed it was only pre-assessment nerves. At the very least, Trent didn't *say* anything to her regarding her peculiarities.

After running a few more errands, they returned to the inn so Faven could "rest and recuperate" before the next day. But she wasn't so sure she could.

Later that night, two more princes from the top ten were reported missing.

Faven lay wide awake in her bed, biting the insides of her cheeks as she stared at the ceiling. The pitch-black night shrouded the room with a cloak of darkness, leaving her tense and breathless. Her heart pounded in her ears. She formed a ball of light in her palm to diminish some of the dark when something skittered across the floor. Swallowing a shriek, she leapt up and stood on her bed, ready to release some ray beams, another aspect of her sense. But she saw nothing.

By the time the sky finally lightened, Faven couldn't stand staying in a room infested with rats, imaginary or not. She pulled out the outfit she'd bought the previous day. Taking a deep breath, she changed out of her nightgown and into the dark, baggy trousers and black tunic. Then, she pulled on a purple and red princely jacket.

Luckily, she hadn't developed into her womanly figure yet, which would be helpful, but she made sure her clothes hung from her body, squaring off her physique. She put on a belt and slid her feet into the boots.

Ah, how nice to be able to move about freely again. She'd had some practice dressing and acting like a boy in the past so Ekon could teach her swordplay. Wearing male clothes now, her hands itched for the hilt of a sword and her muscles longed for the familiar burn of sword practice. Whipping on a short cape to further hide her form, Faven peered into the mirror and suddenly noticed the long, blue braid twisting over her shoulder. She groaned.

She'd forgotten to purchase a hat.

Faven's plan would never succeed with her hair like this, and there wasn't enough time in their schedule to push sneaking into the library another day. She straightened. Her rays! She formed a finger-sized ray and seized her braid. Then, she shut her eyes tightly as she cut it off. Well, she had often wanted to try wearing her hair short; now was her chance. It would grow out again anyway. She opened her eyes, looked at her reflection, and winced.

Trent was going to kill her.

Her hair was painfully short and jagged.

She didn't know if anyone knew what her brother looked like—she hoped they didn't—but Faven went ahead and altered her hair color to match Sage's. Faven did her best to style her now purple hair similarly to her brother's. When she finished, Faven nodded as she surveyed her appearance in the dingy mirror. Success.

She needed to head out before Trent caught her. Without waiting another moment, she tied her bag of coins to her belt and tucked her brother's royal pass into her jacket. Then she stole out of her room, down the steps, and out the door of the inn.

As she climbed the steep incline of Phoebus's streets, Faven searched for the Prince's Academy. Both the prince and princess academies were located near the royal castle. But she wasn't sure how close or exactly what they looked like. So she peered carefully at each building she passed.

A moment later, she peeked behind her and spotted Trent searching the crowd. Oh, no. He was already on her trail. Darting her gaze around the market surrounding her, Faven caught sight of a massive hat with a puffed feather. She raced over, threw some coins onto the vendor's table, grabbed the hat, and thrust it on her head, hoping it would hide her face. Then, she hurried up the incline toward the royal castle.

Finally, Faven came across a tall building with several blue and orange flags hanging about it. All the flags had Reudinia's emblem, the soaring phoenix. A large sign dangled between the flags and read, "Royal Academy for Princes."

She had found it.

Young men and boys came toward the building from every direction, most likely preparing to take their assessment. The princes' assessment was held early in the morning, but, thankfully, the princesses' assessment wasn't held until the afternoon.

Faven ducked behind a cart, nearly tripping over her feet. Darn these stiff boots. She wished she would've had more time to break them in. The large plume from her hat tickled her nose. Resisting the urge to sneeze, she swatted it away and fidgeted with the massive hat on her head.

She peeked over the top of the cart, only to find the owner of the cart, a chubby man with a round nose and small eyes, raising a disapproving eyebrow at her. She grinned sheepishly and waved, straightening and knocking back her feather once more.

"Hello!" she greeted shrilly. She cleared her throat and lowered her voice. "I, uh, just—tripped…and dropped my bag. Sorry. Don't mind me." She slipped the bag from her belt and lifted it as evidence.

The man only sniffed. "I don't like anyone snooping around my stuff. Even princes."

A thrill raced through her chest. Her disguise was working. The man thought she looked like a prince! "Of course, good sir." She bowed and scooted away from the cart. "Excuse me." She turned and broke into a jog. *Whew*. She needed to do better with her sneaking if she meant to succeed.

Faven glanced back half-expecting to see Trent. He'd always been an expert at finding her before she succeeded in getting into trouble. But she didn't see any sign of his tall figure in the crowded, bustling streets. She didn't want to think about how furious he'd be when he found her—especially when he saw her new haircut.

Lowering her head, Faven entered the stream of princes approaching the guarded entry, avoiding eye contact with any of the young men and boys around her. She only had until noon to sneak in, complete her dare, sneak out, and shed her disguise before her assessment began.

Faven peered up at the sky. The sun was still hiding behind the buildings around her; she had time. Taking a deep breath, she straightened her shoulders and marched up the steps as if she knew exactly where she was going.

Two guards immediately blocked her path.

"What is your name, sir?" asked a bearded guard with harsh eyes and stern face.

"Prince Sage of the Korei line." While she had planned to use his name since he was the only prince she knew who wasn't going to be at the assessments that day, guilt twisted in the pit of her stomach.

The second guard, who was much younger, pulled out a scroll. "Your ranking?"

"Oh, 22nd. I apologize."

The bearded guard's seemingly permanent frown deepened. "Where's your pass?"

She scrambled to pull her brother's pass from the random pocket where she'd shoved it and showed it to the guards.

The guard's eyes narrowed further but he stepped back and bowed. "Your Highness."

Faven rushed by them and into the building, finding herself looking at a massive staircase and a wide-open entrance. A room with several couches and cushioned chairs was on her right; a closed door was on her left. Two small hallways framed the staircase showing more closed doors leading to unknown places. How would she find a forbidden library in such a large place?

Maybe she could start at the top and work her way down? Faven followed the flow of princes up to the second floor. The staircase split and continued up on either side, and two long hallways with more doors stretched out in two directions.

She turned to her right and climbed up again, still following the crowd of princes. The princes stopped climbing on the fourth floor and continued down a hallway, but Faven didn't follow. Instead, she climbed to the fifth floor only to find the staircase ended there.

Faven looked back and forth between the hallways stretching on either side of her before she dashed to the left as quietly as she could in her stiff boots. A separate hallway branched off to her right. Peeking around the corner, she found a long hallway with a single door at the end of the hall. Cautiously, she stepped around the corner and crept down the hall. Once she reached the door, she opened it just a crack to find another set of stairs. There was a sixth floor! She glanced behind her once more before stepping inside and hurrying up the steps. Once again, no staircase met her, so she carefully stepped out of the stairwell and found a hallway with several more doorways.

As she inched her way down the new hallway, she approached a double door on the right. Both doors had massive locks. But locks were meant to keep people out—just the sort of thing she imagined a forbidden library having. She eyed each end of the hallway before pulling a pin from one of her pockets to pick the lock. Another thing Ekon had taught her that her parents would be mortified to find out she knew.

As she went to insert the pin into one of the locks, Faven suddenly realized the door was already unlocked. Had someone forgotten to lock the doors?

Faven pushed the door open a hair and peeked inside. The room was full of books. Shelves and shelves of books as well as a few tables. She grinned and a thrill of excitement rushed through her. This *looked* like a forbidden library. Stepping inside, she listened for others who might be in the room but heard nothing. Taking a deep breath, Faven walked down the aisles, marveling at all the ancient books. Their covers varied in color but were worn and covered in layers of dust; yellow and brown pages poked haphazardly out of their covers. Some of the books were even chained shut.

They looked as if they could be hundreds of years old. Maybe even more.

Oh, if only Ekon could see her now!

She could only imagine the look on his face when she told him she'd won his dare. She couldn't believe she had actually succeeded. However, she only had a short amount of time to go through the library and find something about the healing sense before her assessment.

Shaking herself from her thoughts, Faven wove speedily through the aisles, exploring the shelves and searching for anything on the healing arts.

As she pulled out books briefly to glance at their covers, her gaze happened to catch on a brown book with a phoenix image titled *The Phoenix King*. Since phoenixes regenerate, they were often used to symbolize healing. She pulled the book from the shelf and flipped it open to scan the contents. It was a historical book on some king. Not what she was looking for.

Faven closed the book and lifted it back to the shelf. Before she pushed it back into place, she spotted a small, dark blue book with a tiny symbol of a phoenix feather. Pressing *The Phoenix King* back onto the shelf, she pulled out the dark blue book and opened it. *The Healing Sense*. She blinked hard just to make sure her eyes weren't deceiving her.

No. That was truly the book's title.

Excitement fluttered in her chest. Had she actually found something? She flipped to the next page, and her excitement grew. It read: "*It has been discovered that there is a rare potential found in certain Reudinian royals to heal. There seems to be no correlation between the main sense and the gift of healing found in potential healers. However, the struggle to access the healing ability is common. Very few have successfully learned to manipulate their healing ability. However, this book shows all we have learned from those who have and have not succeeded.*"

Faven almost squealed with delight. She really *had* found it. She hadn't been certain she would find anything in this library, but she would've cut her hair a million times over if she'd known she would find such a gem.

But then, all her excitement and exhilaration morphed to terror as the mumble of voices arose *inside* the library. Faven dove to the floor between two tall shelves and stuck the book into the back of her trousers. A door creaked open, but it wasn't from the entrance she'd used to access the library. She gripped her large hat and crammed her body into one of the lowest empty shelves, hoping not to be seen. She held her breath.

"—seen the ranking, do you think your plan will work?" The first voice quivered, sounding younger than Faven would expect from someone in a forbidden library. She'd thought only old men of high status would be allowed to access such a place.

"Yes. The top ten will be enough." The second voice was cold, calculating, and quite lower than the first. Faven peeked through a crack of the bookcase to see the two speakers. She could make out one pair of legs, the other being nowhere in her line of sight.

"Are you sure?"

"Trust me, Everard. I've done my research."

Faven frowned. What were they talking about?

"Is this really the best way?" Everard asked, and the legs of the one she could see shifted. "I don't want them to die."

Faven stiffened. Die? Who was going to die? The Ten?

There was a slight pause. "If there was any other way, I'd do this without them. But we need them. Remember, we must give our all for this to work."

"Yes, I remember…" Everard murmured. "When will the rest be taken?"

"Today."

Faven's heart thumped, and a cold trickle of fear ran down her spine. Were these two behind the abduction of the missing princes? If so, she needed to warn someone.

There was a pause before the second voice warned, "We should go before the Royal Council discovers us here."

Shoes scuffled by. Faven held her breath. They didn't stop. She saw the thin figure of a young boy retreating away from her. Where was the other one? Was he going a different way? Steps faded from the room, and a door shut. After a moment of still silence, she rolled out of her hiding place and sat up.

What had she just overheard? She needed to warn someone. But how? What could she tell them? Some boy named Everard and an accomplice were going to kidnap the rest of the top ten princes today? People would only laugh at her.

Faven stood, pulled the healing book from out of her pants and tucked it into her jacket, and headed toward the exit only to stop at the sight of closed doors. Her heart dropped. She dashed the rest of the way then jiggled the handle, but the door didn't budge. A glow leaked from her and she jiggled the door harder. Oh, just her luck. She sank to the floor. Who knew how long she would be locked in here. How often did people purposefully enter a room full of ancient books? Would she miss her assessment? And how was she supposed to tell anyone about what she had overheard?

Then an even worse thought hit her: Would she make it out before dark? A glow emanated from her at the thought.

Faven eyed the few shadows in the room and imagined how dark the library would be at night; the thought was petrifying. She'd always hated the dark. What if there were rats? An image of hundreds of beady-eyed rats scurrying along the floor zipped through her mind. She turned back to the door and decided being discovered would be less terrifying than spending the night in a spooky, forbidden library.

She glowed brighter and brighter as her terror grew. She had to get out of here. She refused to stay alone in this library after dark.

Wait. The two speakers had gone separate ways.

Maybe there was another way out of the library.

Faven raced in the direction the other set of footsteps had gone and found two smaller doors in the back. One was cracked open, revealing a small room with shelves of books all titled *Ranking*. Was this where those two had come from? Why had they been looking at the princes' rankings?

Faven opened the other door. A dark room was on the other side with three bookshelves lined up next to each other. One of the bookshelves clicked as if it had been shifted into place. As she stepped inside, Faven brightened her ball of light. Was this a secret passageway? She fiddled with the books on the shelves.

Nothing happened. Oh, this was silly. Did she really think this would open into a passageway? She sighed and her shoulders sagged as she stared at the bookcase. She reached up and pulled on a black book.

The bookcase rattled and Faven jumped, taking a step back. It shifted, opening up to a long, dark hallway. Her eyes widened.

It worked.

With one last look at the ancient books in the room behind her, Faven stepped into the hallway. Her ears strained to hear any evidence of the accomplice, but no sound greeted her as she walked carefully down the hall. Sconces lined the walls, and wherever one rested, Faven saw evidence of an opening.

Faven paused before one of the sconces. Seizing one, she pulled. Sure enough, the wall slid open to reveal a lighted hallway. She stepped out and watched as the wall closed behind her, leaving no sign it was ever open at all. Looking around, she recognized the hallway as one of the many she'd seen earlier.

A wave of relief rushed over her. She had made it out of the library. Now she needed to hurry to the princesses' assessment and warn someone about what she had overheard. Maybe someone in the Royal Council.

Several male voices echoed down the hallway, steadily getting louder. Faven squeaked and searched for a place to hide, but no other doors lined the hallway. She whirled in the opposite direction of the voices and darted away. As the voices became stronger, she looked over her shoulder. A group of young boys. She slowed. At least they weren't guards.

She spotted a corner up ahead. A chance to escape from the boys' view. Eager to get away, she hastened toward it at a brisk— but not too brisk—pace and rounded the corner.

Thud!

Faven smacked right into someone. Scrambling to right her hat, she blurted out, "Sorry! Didn't see you!"

As she raised her eyes, she swallowed back a gasp. A tall, blond, blue-eyed young man stood before her, a warm smile on his face. He straightened his blue jacket, and Faven's gaze caught on the dangling gold chains crossing the front. Both shoulders had golden detailing along the pads, and his cuffs mimicked the front of his jacket. His black trousers fit him nicely and matched his shiny black boots. He met her gaze, and she was starstruck. What an attractive man.

To her embarrassment, her mother's voice whispered in her mind: *Maybe you'll find a good match for a husband while you're there!* Faven couldn't help the slight glow that emanated from her body and her cheeks flushed with a heat she had only experienced once before—when her dress tore down her back while following Ekon along the city rooftops. Most of the city saw her, and Ekon never let her forget it.

"Don't worry about it; I wasn't watching where I was going either," came the young man's deep, calming voice.

Ducking her head so he wouldn't see her red face, Faven suddenly remembered she was dressed as a boy. This prince only saw a young lad. Not a lady he might court.

Darn this disguise.

"I haven't seen you around before. Are you from the lower levels?"

"Huh?" Faven stared at him and words suddenly spilled out of her in an awkward rush, "Oh—uh, no, I just arrived from Hallon. My parents are envoys for Reudinia. I'm here for the assessment—but as I...as I was looking around, I got lost." Had she really needed to tell him all that?

"I see." He studied her, clearly amused. "Well, I'm glad I found you, then. The assessment is about to begin. I can take you there." He gestured down the hall Faven had been leaving just as another group of boys walked by.

"Oh, thank you, but you don't have to, I—"

"No, no, I want to!" He stepped after the other boys, gesturing for her to follow.

Faven swallowed a groan. How was she going to get out of this? She didn't want to take the princes' assessment. She wasn't a prince! Not sure what else to do, she reluctantly followed him.

"My name is Prince Luka. Of the Remy line." Her escort slowed his pace so he could walk next to her. "What is yours?"

"Fa—ah, I'm Sage. Prince Sage of the Korei line, 22nd in ranking." Whew. She'd almost slipped up there.

"Oh, so you're not from the lower levels! 22nd…I've heard a little about you. It's good to finally meet you." Prince Luka smiled and extended a hand.

Faven reached out and shook it, feeling like she was being electrified. He was such a good-looking prince. Should she tell him about what she'd overheard? But she didn't know if she could trust Luka, no matter how kind he seemed.

She'd just decided to ask about his ranking instead, when he gestured to a door in front of them. "We're here."

Biting her lip, Faven followed Luka inside. What she saw froze her in place and a lump rose in her throat. Young men and boys filled the large room, all sitting at evenly spaced desks with small, hovering walls on either side to prevent cheating. All eyes turned to the door and fastened on her and her ridiculous feathered hat at the same moment a tall, skinny man with a long, thin, gray beard at the front of the room said, "Welcome to your Ranking Assessment. Please remember to relax. You have only one rule—

don't cheat. If you have learned a new skill, you are welcome to demonstrate it as long as it is safe. Major ranking adjustments are rare, so there is little need to worry about losing your place."

Oh, dear, oh, dear. This wasn't good. Faven needed to abort this assessment before anyone important noticed her and forced her to stay. She turned to leave, hoping Luka wouldn't notice, but found herself eye to eye with a short man with a long, sharp nose, wrinkled skin, and billowing white robes of a Royal Council member. The councilman frowned severely at her. "And who might you be?"

3

The Assessment

NO ANSWERS CAME TO MIND. INSTEAD, SHE INTERNALLY screamed at herself. She was so idiotic; how on earth had she managed to get herself into this situation? Being spotted by the Royal Council meant she had no way out of this assessment. Either way, she was going to get in trouble for passing herself off as her brother.

Luka appeared by her side. "Lord Rufus, this is Sage of Korei, 22nd."

"Sage, is it?" Lord Rufus's wrinkles deepened as he scowled and looked her up and down. "Welcome, Prince Sage. Please find your seat between 21 and 23." The old man bowed.

Faven and Luka bowed in return and strode to the front of the room. At the back were several rows of unassigned seats full of children who must be new to the ranking system. After a few rows, seats in the hundreds began. The two of them walked further and further down until Luka stopped at a row which read "20" and pointed to an empty seat. "I believe that one is yours."

Nodding her thanks, Faven slipped down the aisle and sat in the empty chair with "22" on the back. Floating slats prevented the two princes next to her from staring. This brought some comfort. She didn't want any more attention. She was embarrassed enough.

"The intelligence evaluation will now begin," announced the long-bearded man at the front of the room, and he released a pile of papers into the air. A soft breeze—clearly a wind sense—swept through the room and the papers fanned out, floating to each prince in the room. One drifted onto her desk.

"You have until noon to finish."

Faven looked at the test lying on her desk, alarmed by the thickness of the large pamphlet. She flipped through the pages, reading a few of the questions. The questions varied in subjects such as math, science, language, geography, history, and even a little art. However, further into the test, the questions became harder. Those questions tended to be about the details of ruling a kingdom. At the end of the test were a few logic-based questions which varied in difficulty.

She took a deep breath. She had to calm down. Since she couldn't escape this situation, she would just need to continue the assessment. And since as she would be taking the assessment under the guise of Sage's identity, she also wanted to do her best not to lower his ranking. She didn't want him to lose his rank because of her rash stupidity. If she screwed up his ranking, Sage would need to travel all the way back to Reudinia to fix his score. Surely, she could at least keep his rank close to his original...right?

Most of the contents were similar to the studies she had to take as a princess. The only difference being princesses weren't tested in anything having to do with war. Instead, their senses were used to create art and beauty. Their expected conduct differed too. More differences between the princes' and princesses' assessments rose to mind and Faven trembled uncertainly, her mind racing.

Faven had studied some war tactics because she often joined her father in his meetings with Hallonese officials. She had wanted to better understand what they discussed, so she asked her father questions and read some books he recommended. If she pictured Sage and how he acted around others, maybe she could mimic a prince's proper conduct in public settings?

With a shaky hand, Faven took the quill she was given and opened the booklet to the first page. She only had until noon to finish this examination and she couldn't waste any of her time panicking. She tried her best to complete each question as well as she could, throwing in as many details as she remembered about each situation.

After working on the booklet all morning, her hand cramped and her brain felt like mush. She was beyond relieved when she finally finished the last question.

Faven put down her quill and raised a hand. No sooner had she done so than her test floated from her desk back to the platform. The wind wielder plucked it from the air and passed it to another Royal Council member to grade her work. Another councilman gestured for her to follow him. She stood and exited. Through small glimpses between the floating boards, Faven saw a few princes gripping their heads as they stared at their papers, panic written all over their faces. She wished them well.

Faven followed the council member out of the room behind one or two other princes. As they made their way down a hall, she spotted Luka striding away. Before she could say anything to the other prince, the council member paused at a door and pushed it open, ushering her inside. Why was she being led in a different direction?

When Faven stepped inside, she found herself in a small waiting room with several chairs. The other princes with them chose their seats, and Faven focused on the single open window on the far side of the room. Bright, mid-day light stung Faven's eyes and she desperately blinked back tears of frustration. The assessment wasn't over yet. She would end up missing her own assessment and still hadn't had time to warn anyone about what she'd overheard. She bit the inside of her cheek and gripped her jacket tightly around her as she faced the young councilman.

The councilman bowed to her. "Because it has been a few years since you've been assessed and we haven't seen you during that period, we have to undergo a few extra evaluations with you in addition to the one you've already finished," he informed her. "Please sit and wait until we call you."

Obediently, Faven sat, lacking the strength to remain standing. As she waited, she drummed her fingers on her legs and shifted about anxiously. She needed to get out of this somehow, but she couldn't. Other princes waited in the room with her. If she attempted an escape, a Royal Council member would surely catch her before she succeeded.

The Royal Council directed a few more princes into the room until a total of thirteen of them waited together. Finally, a councilman called one of them to follow him. Faven turned to the window once more. The princess' assessment would be starting right about now. Her parents would be penalized because she hadn't shown up, and Trent would be terribly worried.

She shifted again and something hard pressed against her side. The book on healing senses! She still had it with her. She'd forgotten in the midst of the circumstances.

Her gaze darted to the others in the room, hoping no one noticed anything. She didn't need to be caught with a book from the forbidden library on top of all this.

The sun lowered in the sky as more princes were called. What if she ended up being the last one called? How dreadful. Faven chewed on her bottom lip and squirmed.

A councilman opened the door and called, "Prince Sage of the Korei line!"

A sweet trickle of relief swept through her. Faven stood and followed the man, leaving the unpleasant room behind. She followed him down the corridor and the Royal Council member ushered her inside another door.

A pale room decorated with rich tapestries telling stories about Reudinia greeted her. One of the tapestries had an image of a king with a phoenix emblem on his coat of arms—King Heron. Before King Heron's rule, Reudinia had been a small, weak kingdom. He'd been the first Reudinian *and* the first royal to have a sense. Though how he got a sense was still widely unknown.

Faven dragged her gaze from the tapestry to the room around her. It was empty except for a table on the far side where three more council members sat. They beckoned her closer.

One of them smiled and nodded. "Prince Sage, please sit down."

"Thank you." Faven sat in the provided chair, squeezing her hands together tightly. Her heart raced. All this excitement and stress was too much.

A younger councilman smiled welcomingly at her, his square jaw becoming sharper. He had rather large ears, which she felt guilty for noticing. "We will start this part of your assessment off by informing you we didn't get the opportunity to watch your conduct and manners among others since you live in another kingdom. This may make it harder on us to assess today. However, we do have our emotion reader here to help with testing how emotionally stable you are. Therefore, we will begin with his evaluation." He nodded to a short, stubby fellow Faven hadn't noticed before. The man stood against the wall, nearly blending into the sand-colored brick surface because his clothing matched it so well. The man waddled over to her.

Emotion reader? Faven took a deep breath. She needed to calm herself before he read the fear and anxiety shooting through the turret above her. Taking another breath, she imagined flying on her green, feathered seaside dragon. In her mind, it was a calm summer evening and a purple-pink sunset spread across the horizon before her. Faven's heartbeat began to slow, and her fear eased.

Placing an odd dial in front of her, the man placed a thumb against her forehead. The dial swished back and forth while the man's finger remained pressed to her forehead. Finally, the dial paused, setting slightly off from the middle and the council members jotted down notes. The man pulled his thumb away, grabbed his dial, and waddled away.

"Now, Prince Sage, we will ask you to participate in a simulation. We will ask you to converse with us as if you're speaking with or entertaining people from a variety of different stations. We will explain who you are speaking to and what the situation is beforehand. Any questions?"

Faven shook her head, but her nerves skyrocketed again.

For the next several minutes, she spoke with the council members in various mock situations and tried her best to emulate the manners she had observed in her brother when she had watched him. When the examination ended, all the council members smiled at her—hopefully that was a good sign. She stood and walked toward the door where another council member directed her to a wide-open room. Faven held back a sigh. This princes' assessment was never ending.

She was left with another council member, but this one gave her an icy look, absent of the kindness possessed by those she'd met before. He looked at the paper he'd been handed. "Prince Sage of the Korei line?"

"Yes, sir," she breathed, straightening to her full height.

"Your sense is plasma manipulation, correct?"

Oh, dear. She'd forgotten about the sense assessment. How would she explain a sudden change in abilities? "Ah, it's not quite that anymore, sir."

Although she could mimic most of what Sage could do, the Royal Council would immediately know her abilities were not the same. "Have you developed since your previous test?"

"Yes, sir."

"Very well, please demonstrate." The council member gestured at the room and lifted a quill to scribble something on the paper.

Taking a deep breath to calm her nerves, Faven demonstrated all the aspects of her sense. She sprinted across the room, showing her light speed, then displayed her ability to change colors and glow. She manipulated some light particles to create balls of light and rainbows. Finally, she revealed her progress in her rays. An impressed smile flickered across the Royal Council's cold face.

The council member wrote something down. "Now I need to evaluate your sense potential." He lifted a device connected to a stone and pointed it at her chest. Three intertwined circles were inscribed on the stone. Elven-made.

The council man's eyebrows raised. "Your sense potential has changed; that's rare."

It hadn't changed. She just wasn't Sage.

"Can you confirm your age?"

"Sixteen, sir," Faven quipped, hoping he wouldn't know her brother was supposed to be twelve.

"Very well. Your assessment is finished. You may leave through those double doors."

It took everything within Faven not to bolt out the door.

It was finally over. How was she going to tell Trent the disaster she got herself into? But when Faven slipped out the door and heaved a deep sigh, she turned to find another council member.

"Ah, hello," the older council member said to her, smiling. "You're here pretty late. You must be an irregular. The ceremony will begin soon. Follow me, I'll take you there so you don't miss it."

Faven blinked back another bout of tears. "I know the way, sir," she lied. "You don't need to do this."

The man shook his head and beckoned for her to follow. "No, no, it would be unkind to let an irregular roam around without a guide."

With that, the council member led her outside and down the street. Soon, Faven found herself entering a massive, circular arena. There was no roof; only the wide blue sky above them. Stands sloped upward, circling around the center arena where two tall thrones stood. Twenty chairs rested beside them. As she approached more council members, Faven was directed to sit to the right with the other royals, and citizens coming to watch the ranking ceremony were directed to seats on the left.

"Go find your seat," encouraged her guide. "The ceremony is about to begin."

4

The Ceremony Swap

FAVEN FOUND HER BROTHER'S SEAT WITH A LITTLE DIRECTION from other council members and sat. Number 21 and 23 peered sideways at her, but Faven paid them no heed. She stared down at her hands silently. How could she get out of this mess? Should she try to sneak out in the busy crowd? Maybe she should fake her death and live life as a vagabond. It would be better than this mess she'd gotten herself into.

Faven tapped her pocket where she'd tucked the healing book. At least no one had caught her with it. Then she searched the crowd for any sign of Trent. She doubted he was there, but she still couldn't help looking. However, the arena had amassed so many people it was impossible to spot anyone she might have recognized.

Then the announcer called into the crowd, requesting everyone stand. "I present King Léon and Queen Osanne."

Faven had never seen the Reudinian royal family, so curiosity drew her eyes to the front of the crowd as she stood. An older man with graying blond hair, a tall stature, and a crown atop his head strode to the throne in the middle of the circular arena.

Queen Osanne approached the smaller of the two thrones. Her lovely brown hair was twisted into an elegant bun, and her face was smooth and unwrinkled. She had to be at least ten years younger than the king. She wore an olive gown with gold trimming and nodded gracefully in recognition of the crowd's cheers. Queen Eshe of Hallon was said to be a powerful woman, and she was someone Faven admired. She wondered if Queen Osanne was anything like her.

King Léon and Queen Osanne had four sons, but none of them stood with their parents. Where were they?

The king turned to the crowd. "Greetings, people of Reudinia! Another year has passed, and we find ourselves here once again for the ranking of the princes and princesses. However, before we begin the ceremony, we want to address the recent disappearances." The king's shoulders drooped, but he lifted his head high. "We are aware of the alarm these events have created and want to ease any fear you may have. We are searching for those missing and are confident we will find them soon.

"In the meantime, we ask all high-ranked princes not to go anywhere unattended. We promise we will find whoever is behind these horrid kidnappings and bring them to justice.

Please, if anyone hears anything concerning this kidnapper or the princes, contact the Royal Council. We appreciate any and all leads we can get." The king paused and gestured to several white-clad council members. "You may all be seated now. Royal Council, please begin the naming of the ranks."

Faven sat and bit her bottom lip. She should tell someone what she'd overheard in the library. Maybe after all of this was over, she could pull one of the Royal Council members aside.

A small, old man approached the center of the arena as the king returned to his throne. She recognized him. It was "Lord Rufus," as Luka had called him—the man who had prevented her from leaving the assessment. His long, pointed nose stretched out, and his short, curved body strained to appear taller. "We will begin with the princesses. When we reach the top ten, we ask each person named to please find his or her seat beside the thrones."

Rufus named the princesses and their ranking from least to greatest. The lowest ranking for a princess was currently 514th, but even the girl holding that rank received polite applause. As the names progressed, Faven suddenly wished she'd taken the princesses' assessment. She couldn't help but be curious what she would've ranked. Would it be low? Would it be middle or average? Would she possibly be considered exceptional? It was highly unlikely that she would ever know now.

After several minutes, Faven noticed the numbers nearing ten. She perked up. What would the top ten princesses be like?

"Now for the names you have been waiting for! The top ten," the old man croaked, his voice now hoarse, but his callers helped carry his words to the people. As he named the top ten princesses, Faven watched young women and girls stand and move to the chairs in the center of the arena. Finally, he came to the first princess and Faven sat on the edge of her seat.

"In first place is Princess Irabel of the Ouin line."

An elegant princess with long, white hair stood. Half of her hair was pulled into a bun at the top of her head and the rest hung loose about her waist. Faven suddenly missed her long hair. No emotions flickered across Irabel's face as she took her spot in the number one place, her head held high, revealing strength and elegance all at once.

"And now for the princes."

Faven clasped her hands and fiddled with her fingers. Now to discover exactly how much damage she may have done. She listened intently to the names of the princes as they were ranked, waiting, dreading to hear Sage's name. With each name given, a small wave of relief swirled through her. She hadn't dropped his rank too low yet.

"307th is Prince Everard of the Remy line, son of King Léon."

Everard? She couldn't help jerking her head slightly to look over her shoulder in the direction of the princes ranked in the hundreds. Could...could he be the same Everard she had overheard in the library? He was a prince *and* the king's son?

Distracted by her thoughts about Prince Everard, Faven didn't realize she'd lost track of the names being announced until the council member had already reached the one-hundreds. Oh, no. Had she missed Sage's name? Maybe not; hopefully not. They hadn't reached his current rank yet.

The council went through the hundreds, the nineties, all the way to the forties, the thirties, and the twenties. 22nd place came and passed, Sage's name still absent. Faven clasped her fingers tighter and tried to swallow down the fear and panic rising in her chest. She'd dropped her brother's rank. She knew she had. She should've confessed before taking the test. She shouldn't have given her brother's name in the first place and dragged him down with her.

Why had she not listened to all the numbers? Was Sage ranked 288th now? 276th? 291st?

"12th is Prince Romain of the Remy line, son of King Léon. 11th is Prince Michal of the Remy line, son of King Léon."

Gasps pulled Faven from her spiraling thoughts. Why was everyone shocked by the high statuses of the king's sons? Was it strange for them to be ranked 12th and 11th place? She turned to the man next to her. "What's wrong?"

The man looked at her out of the corner of his eye and huffed. "Prince Michal has been in the top ten for the last fourteen years. Him being knocked from the Ten…means someone was bumped into it."

Rufus cleared his throat and gave a little cough. "We will now announce the top ten princes in line for the throne. 10th place goes to Prince Cassian of the Roas line."

Faven waited for someone to approach the seat, but no one did. A soft murmur rose from the crowd.

"9th place goes to Prince Jovian of the Thomelin line. 8th place goes to Prince Kai of the Shao line."

Again, no one moved to the seats. Faven's eyes widened. They must be among those missing. Lost in her thoughts, Faven almost missed the next name. At least until she recognized it, and the sound of its syllables froze her insides, churning the pit of her stomach.

"7th place goes to Prince Sage of the Korei line."

5

Things Progress from Bad to Worse

FAVEN STARED AT THE SPEAKER. THAT WAS HER BROTHER'S name. Her brother was in the top ten. No, *she* was in the top ten. They were calling *her* up.

The crowd's murmurs became so deafening the speaker had to stop and wait for the crowd to quiet. The princes around her began turning in their seats to look for this mysterious "Prince Sage" who had entered the top ten, knocking the king's own son from the ranks. The speaker restated her brother's name and rank.

If she was in the top ten, Faven would have to go out to the center of the arena and sit where every eye could see her. Her secret would be blown instantly. There was no way she could trick an entire arena of people into believing she was a boy. But she couldn't just sit here either.

Faven took off her feathered hat, eased herself off her chair and out of the row. Eyes glued to her, watching her every movement as the crowd finally put a face to Sage's name. She quietly slipped down to the center of the arena and found her place in the 7th seat. Her eyes remained trained on the ground, and Faven was suddenly painfully aware she was the only one seated in the prince's section near the thrones.

The whispering quieted enough for the speaker to continue.

"In 6th place is Prince Ruben of the Dewen line. 5th is Prince Archie of the Tohaan line. 4th is Prince Tristan of the Ouin line."

Faven's breath caught. She recognized Prince Archie's name at the very least. Turning to see more of the top ten join her, she watched as a good-looking, freckled boy with curly, light green hair approached. He wore a forest green jacket with gold embroidery in the pattern of leaves climbing up it. When he approached, Faven realized two things simultaneously. First, he must've been near her own age, and second, his eyes were the same green as his jacket. The young man's forehead wrinkled for a fleeting moment before he took his place next to her—this was Prince Ruben then.

She met his gaze briefly, but Ruben didn't acknowledge her. He didn't turn to her. He didn't say a word. Behind Ruben strode the flamboyant carriage prince—Archie—with his dark blue ponytail. He took his place next to Ruben.

The fourth-place seat remained empty. Faven swallowed hard—four missing princes so far.

"In 3rd place is Prince Draven of the Sihan line. 2nd is Prince Tenji of the Tenji line."

No one moved to fill those seats. Again, the murmuring rose.

Last Faven had heard, there were only five missing princes. Were there now six?

"Our final prince, taking first place, and the current Crown Prince is...Prince Luka of the Remy line, first son of King Léon."

Luka? *He* was the first prince in line for the throne? Faven straightened and searched for any sign of his handsome figure moving toward them. But no one came. Suddenly, the crowd erupted into chaos, and King Léon stood. He gestured for a guard and Faven saw him speaking urgently to the other man. But still Luka didn't come.

Dread sank into her chest, and she knew. Seven of the top ten princes were now missing, and one of them was Luka.

The king turned to the crowd. "Due to an urgent situation, we must dismiss." He faced Archie, Ruben, and Faven and pointed a finger at them before he barked, "You three, stay with the guards and go nowhere alone." Without another word, King Léon stormed away with several Royal Council members rushing around him. The queen stared at them before following her husband.

Several guards promptly surrounded them. "This way, Your Highnesses."

As the three of them followed the guards, several of the top ten princesses swarmed them.

"Prince Archie, have you seen Luka or Tristan at all today?" asked Irabel. Her gray eyes were wide, and her forehead creased with worry.

Archie nodded. "I saw them both at the assessment! This is complete madness!"

A princess with dusky pink hair glared at him, placing her hands on her hips. "Don't worry, Archie, Ruben, and new prince. We'll make sure you aren't taken, and we'll help search for the others." She glanced at the other princesses around her. "We can save them."

Faven liked these women. She would never know where she might've ranked among the princesses, but if she had made the top ten, Faven hoped that these girls would have been her friends.

A dark purple-haired girl narrowed her eyes at Faven quietly. But before she said anything, the guards shooed the princesses away. "We must take them to a secure location. Now go."

The guards tightened their circle around Faven and the two princes as they headed for a dark tunnel leading out of the arena.

"Archie!" called a princess with strawberry blonde hair and baby blue eyes. "Be safe!"

Archie waved to her and blew a kiss. "Don't worry, my dear Aria. I'll see you later!"

As soon as the three of them and the guards entered a dark tunnel, Archie's smile dropped, and nervous lines creased his forehead. He faced a guard who was lighting a torch. "We will be safe, won't we? We're not going to be captured or killed like the others, are we?"

"Killed?" Faven exclaimed, unable to hide her horror. Could the missing princes be dead?

Archie frowned at her. "We don't know what happened to any of them. They could be captives, or they could've been murdered!"

Ruben's eyes widened.

A muscular guard with a dark beard shook his head. "We shouldn't assume they're dead."

Another guard nodded, his blue eyes piercing as he gestured for them to keep moving. "Yes, remain calm, Prince Archie."

Archie rolled his eyes. "Like I can remain calm in such a situation!"

Prince Archie continued talking, unfazed by the pitch-black halls outside the torch-light. However, Faven hated the dark. She became more aware of the noises around her, and the thought of the kidnappings only made her more nervous. She resisted the urge to glow, despite wanting to bring more light into the space to calm her jumping nerves.

Prince Ruben glanced over and leaned in. "Archie is always like this. Don't let it get to you." He offered her a kind smile and held out a hand. She couldn't help but notice it trembled. "You're Sage, right? I'm Ruben."

Faven blinked at his hand before she shook it. He neglected their titles, which no one else had done since her arrival in Reudinia.

Suddenly, a blur flashed from the shadows and knocked several of the guards down. Jerking to attention, the rest of the guards yanked out their swords and tightly circled the princes.

Faven scrambled back, her eyes wide. What was going on?

Before she even had time to scream, the blur struck once more, knocking the remainder of their guards out cold. Archie shrieked for her.

Then something sailed through the dark and struck Ruben's neck. A dart. He yelped, stumbled back against the wall, and sank to the ground.

Faven stared at him, her heart thumping, her chest squeezing as realization struck.

Whoever these kidnappers were, they had come for the rest of the Ten.

She'd never had time to alert the council.

She'd shifted her brother's rank into the top ten.

Faven had been added to their hit-list.

Archie took off down the tunnel, screaming and leaving Faven and Ruben behind. But Faven stood frozen, staring down into Ruben's terrified, dizzied face. In a spur-of-the-moment decision, she grabbed his arms and pulled him back in the dirction they'd come. It was a useless endeavor, but she couldn't leave him there. She wouldn't.

Another dart sailed out of the dark, sinking into her chest. Oh no. The world spun as Faven desperately dragged the sagging Ruben away. She shook her head as drowsiness overtook her.

Sleeping darts. She crashed to the ground, gripping the floor as if it would help keep the world from swirling underneath her. Footsteps approached and black boots stood before her, waiting as her world faded to black.

6

All In

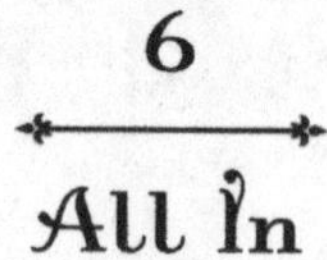

THE DAY AFTER THE RANKING CEREMONY, EVERARD HEADED to the Royal Academy for Princes, repeatedly swallowing down the bile rising in his throat. He surveyed the orange-roofed buildings, jumping whenever another person walked by. The streets were eerily silent, which only heightened his discomfort. He took deep breaths in a vain attempt to slow his heartbeat and ease his queasy stomach. However, the closer he got to the Royal Academy, the more Everard's gait slackened and the worse he felt. He didn't want to face the Royal Council or any of the other princes. He couldn't even bear to look at his own reflection. After all, how could he?

The top ten princes were missing, and it was all because of him.

Maybe this was a mistake. All the books and scrolls he'd read said the Sidylla Labyrinth was impossible to navigate. Maybe his friend was wrong to think they could make it. Maybe he should tell his father what he'd done so he could stop them before it was too late. Everard didn't want ten lives on his shoulders.

Everard paused before the Royal Academy and stared, unmoving. Young men and boys hurried in and out of the doors, whispering to each other. Guards surrounded the building, and several higher-ranked princes were attended by personal guards. Royal Council members scurried about, snapping tersely at princes as they went. Fear tainted the air.

What had he done? Everard bit his thumb as guilt gnawed at his chest. This needed to end. He shouldn't have allowed things to go this far. He turned back toward the castle. He had to go home; he had to tell them what he'd done. His father would know what to do.

To Everard's dismay, he spotted one of his long-time tormentors, Valor, down the street with a collection of his cronies. His tall, muscular body strained against his princely jacket, and his hair, unlike his friends' colorful arrays, was as black as night. Since he and his friends were ranked in the teens and early twenties, guards swarmed them.

Everard whirled in the opposite direction and sped toward the Academy's courtyard, hoping to get out of view before Valor noticed him.

But he had no such luck.

"Everard!"

Everard flinched but didn't slow his pace. Instead, he broke into a light jog. But just before he reached the door of the Academy, someone snatched Everard's arm and yanked him back. Everard stumbled and found himself face to face with Valor's smirking grin and unusual yellow eyes. With all his might, he strained to wrench his arm free, but Valor held him fast.

"It's rare to see you without your bodyguard. Oh, wait…he's missing, isn't he?" Valor teased as he threw an arm over Everard's shoulder. "Too bad."

Valor's friends laughed along with him.

Anger burned in Everard's gut. "It isn't funny to tease about those missing," he snapped. Maybe it was because he knew where they were and where they were going, but he couldn't stand Valor joking about their disappearance. He might never see them again because of his decision. Tears welled up in his eyes.

"Oh, look, he's going to cry." Valor laughed, squeezing Everard's neck so he couldn't turn away. "Feeling lonely, are we?"

"Why are you bothering me?" Everard asked, as he squirmed in Valor's tight hold.

Valor shrugged. "Oh, I just think low-ranks should stop lurking around high-ranks for protection. And I get bored easily." He winked at Everard and leaned in close. "Luckily for me, anyone who would've prevented me from having my fun is gone. Not even your father will come to your aid, as we've seen in the past."

An icy chill ran down Everard's back and his heart ached. He turned his head to search for someone—anyone—who might come to his rescue. But Valor was right. No one would come now.

Anger, frustration, and fear bubbled up in Everard's gut. All this because he didn't have a sense. He was sick of living life this way. Just a moment ago, he'd been second-guessing if his plan was worth the cost. But now, he only hoped the plan succeeded. He wanted a sense, and he wanted one as soon as possible. So the ridicule would end. So his father's disappointment would lift.

And he wished he'd trapped all these princes in Valor's pack into the labyrinth instead.

But before Valor and his friends could do anything to Everard, a Royal Council member paused by the doorway of the Academy and glared at them. "Stop lurking and hurry to your sessions before you're late!"

"We'll continue this later, then." Valor sneered, before thrusting Everard into the wall and walking off with his friends.

Everard rubbed his now-aching shoulder and trudged up the steps of the Royal Academy. That's when he noticed his brother Michal, golden hair gleaming as he stood off to the side, expression tight. Had he seen the whole thing?

Either way, Michal wouldn't have come to his rescue. He never did.

Everard jerked his gaze away and clutched his shoulder. The conversation he'd had with his friend in the forbidden library yesterday rose within him. *Remember, we must give our all for this to work.* His partner was right. He had to go all in if he wanted this misery to end. That meant he had to keep his mouth shut and trust his friend to keep his promises.

He couldn't turn back now.

7

The Long Ride

WHEN FAVEN WOKE, SHE WAS LYING ON HER SIDE WITH HER arms bound behind her and her legs tied together. The wooden floor beneath her rattled and bumped. Something wrapped tightly around her head, preventing her from seeing. All she heard was breathing, clomps of horses' hooves, and the rattling of a wagon. Then, everything came rushing back to her.

Faven's gut knotted, her chest tightened, and tears burned her eyes. Where was she? Where were they taking her? What were they planning to do with her? Would they kill her?

A hoarse voice spoke as someone kicked her. "Why'd you bring him? He wasn't on the list."

"We were asked to capture those in the top ten. He's now in the top ten," another deep voice responded. The man's thick accent sent shivers down her spine. It was a Velykovian accent. "Now shut up, they're waking."

Faven pulled and twisted at her binds, but they were expertly tied. She then attempted to use her heat rays to cut through the ropes, planning to jump out of whatever cart she was in and make a run for it. However, to her terror, her sense wouldn't work.

Then something—or rather someone—scratched and scraped against the wooden cart, thrashing.

"Let me go, bastard! I'll burn you to hell!" another voice shouted. After more writhing, the new voice hissed, "I'm sick of this nonsense."

Another voice wailed, "Please, don't kill me! Please!" Prince Archie's voice was annoyingly familiar. "I'll give you all the money you ask for. Just please don't kill me!"

The struggling ceased, replaced by heavy breathing and the angry voice scoffed. "Great. Now they've got *Archie*."

"Kai?" Archie's wobbly voice asked. "You're still alive?"

"Of course I'm alive. Bloody idiot. Think I'd die so easily?"

Faven wasn't the only captive in the wagon. How many of them were there?

Another voice Faven recognized spoke, albeit more calmly. "Why are you doing this to us?"

Luka.

Someone clucked his tongue but didn't answer. Another person shifted and stomped around the cart. "Eat up," the Velykovian's voice muttered. "Food will be sparse, so I recommend you don't skip meals."

Someone jerked Faven to a sitting position and shoved a hunk of thin, hard bread in her mouth. She did her best to consume it, swallowing her tears down with the coarse food. Her thoughts turned to her parents and Sage. Would they ever find out what happened to her? What if she never saw them again? Had Trent discovered her foolishness yet? Was there any hope she would ever be found? Her throat burned as she choked back sobs.

Somewhere in the wagon, faint sniffles could be heard, so at least she wasn't the only one with similar thoughts.

The wagon ride went on for an unknown length of time. While silence often hung over them for large portions of their captive journey, several voices did occasionally speak up to give commands, to protest or complain, or to sometimes carry on light conversation. Faven didn't know most of the voices she heard. The only voices she recognized were Luka's and Archie's.

When Archie, or "Sir Whiney" as Faven liked to call him, spoke, it was only to complain about how hard the wagon was or how bad the food tasted or how his hair was a "horrendous mess." But there were three other voices who spoke frequently, and since she couldn't keep their names straight—or didn't know them at all—Faven gave them names herself.

"The Hothead" was always yelling, shouting curses, and threatening to burn their capturer. Another voice, Faven deemed "The Jokester", always had a wry or sarcastic remark. Then there was a cool, deep voice, which Faven named "The Inquirer" because whenever he spoke, it was only to ask questions. He never raised his voice, never shouted, and never complained. Most of his questions were about where they were headed, what the capturers' origins were, how many days they'd been traveling, and what the men planned on doing with them. Their capturers neglected to answer any of the questions and only chuckled or huffed in response.

Luka sometimes called out names amongst the Ten to check on them if they hadn't spoken in a while. The most heartbreaking response to hear was from a young, childlike voice. What could they want with a child?

At the beginning of the ride, Luka frequently called on "Michal." Neither their capturers nor Faven spoke up to inform him Michal had been bumped from the Ten. No one checked on her or seemed to know she existed.

At least until one day, when something bumped Faven's shoulder, and a soft, calm voice whispered, "Who is this?"

Faven didn't recognize the voice, so she assumed he must be among the quieter captives Luka occasionally called upon. While the other captives did converse amongst themselves, their capturers didn't encourage it. Not wanting to anger them, Faven whispered, "I don't think you know me."

The silence following her words stretched for a long time. Then, his voice came back to her. "Why are you here?"

She'd like to know that herself. "I don't know."

"Was Michal knocked from the Ten? I haven't heard him speak once."

Faven nodded, then remembered he couldn't see her. "Yes."

"I see." He fell silent. He shifted before he spoke again. "What's your name?"

Faven sniffed, resisting the urge to give her real name. "Sage."

"Sage." He paused. "I'm sorry you were dragged into this with the rest of us."

Faven turned her head in his direction. "What's your name?"

"Tristan."

Then he fell silent and didn't speak to her again. However, only a few moments later, a voice on her other side whispered, "Sage?"

Faven straightened, vaguely recognizing that voice. "Yes?"

"I don't know if you remember me…"

Then the familiarity in his voice clicked. The kind boy she'd dragged away after he'd been shot with the dart. "You were captured with me…Ruben, was it?"

"Yes."

A slight smile lifted her lips. She hadn't realized how much she'd longed for someone to know she was there until this moment. But someone did know. It made this situation feel slightly less lonely and hopeless.

Ruben spoke again, "Where—where do you think they're taking us?"

"I don't know."

Their conversation ended as quickly as it had begun, but from then on, Ruben continued to make light conversation with her, which Faven always welcomed. They never could talk for too long before the capturers told them to shut up, but she didn't mind. She was thankful to have someone to check on her.

For the first several days of their journey, Faven's legs and bottom ached from the constant sitting. But the only time the capturers let them stretch their legs was during restroom breaks—and even then, their feet remained bound. The wagon would rattle to a stop, and they'd take them one by one and tell them this was their only chance to go, otherwise they'd have to wait or go in their pants. When they first took Faven out, she'd been terrified they'd discover she wasn't a boy. So, she built up her courage to speak.

"Can I have some privacy?" she asked.

"No," the hoarse one answered.

"I promise I won't try to escape," Faven pleaded. "You can lead me to a tree close by and keep both my arms and legs bound. If I take too long, you can come get me. All I want is privacy and to be able to see."

After a moment, the hoarse one grunted. "Fine. But be quick."

They shoved her against the tree and unwrapped her eyes, demanding she not look at them. She obeyed, not wanting her right to privacy to be revoked. She waited until their footsteps crunched away before she searched the space around them. A thick forest met her gaze, but she saw no one else around. After she was done, she called out to her captives and closed her eyes. They returned, strapped her head, and took her back to the wagon.

From the differences in their capturers' voices, Faven guessed there were at least four of them. Two sat in the back with them at all times and checked their binds regularly. Because they checked regularly, they caught on easily whenever someone tried to free themselves.

And they didn't handle escape attempts lightly.

The first escape attempt was made by The Hothead. It was one of their first days of travel, and he'd been especially quiet that day. The capturers were going around and doing their routine bind check when suddenly deafening shouts erupted.

Something fumbled, scrambled, tussled, and then footsteps thudded against the floorboards.

"Let me bloody go!" The Hothead bellowed as the struggle continued.

Finally, there was stillness. Faven's heart drummed in her chest. What had happened? Had they killed someone? What if they killed them one by one and dumped their bodies in some strange unknown place?

A capturer with a deep and vibrating tone spoke, "I'm going to let you all know now, if any of you even attempt to escape, there will be consequences." He paused and sniffed. "Do it."

The sounds of a beating echoed through the wagon as grunts of pain tore from The Hothead. Faven squeezed her eyes shut as if it would help block out the sounds. Because her hands were secured behind her back, she couldn't cup them over her ears. So…she heard every thud, every kick, and every cry of pain. Her lips trembled and tears pricked her eyes.

The next to try to escape was The Inquirer. Once again, Faven suffered through listening to his beating, though he was much quieter than The Hothead had been. Over the next several days or weeks, The Hothead and The Inquirer tried escaping repeatedly. Faven wished they wouldn't. She hated listening to their abuse. How could they handle being beaten so many times?

One day, the attempted escapee was Luka, but he didn't get as far as the other two had. One of the capturers merely hissed, "He's trying to escape."

Then the beating ensued.

Even The Jokester tried escaping once.

The worst one for Faven, however, was the day Tristan decided to attempt his own escape. She could feel him fidget throughout the day, but he was calm and quiet when one of the capturers came to check on Faven's ropes. After finding them secured and tight, he shifted to Tristan, who sat next to her.

Suddenly, something shoved Faven to the side and the capturer cursed. Someone scrambled and footsteps slapped the wagon boards.

"He's getting away!" bellowed a capturer. The wagon shuddered to a halt and several footsteps scuttled through the wagon.

"Shoot him with a dart!" another voice called.

The next thing Faven knew, Tristan was being dragged back into the wagon and was plopped right next to her.

One of the capturers cursed.

"Make sure to teach him well," the Velykovian called, then the wagon jolted back into motion.

The beating began but this time, it happened right next to her. Tristan's grunts and cries shook her. When their kidnappers were finished, one of them spat on Tristan before they left him lying there. A part of his body pressed against her and Tristan groaned as he repositioned himself.

Faven waited for a moment before she whispered, "Are you okay?"

"I'm fine," he rasped.

Tristan didn't try to escape again.

One day, after what felt like weeks of travel with only coarse bread to eat and little physical exercise, the wagon slowed to a stop. Faven prepared herself for another restroom break, but there was a long pause with no movement. Voices rumbled outside the wagon, but their words were hushed and hard to make out.

Someone climbed into the back of the wagon, and a metallic clink echoed through the wagon. Another person climbed into the wagon and cleared his throat.

"We're here," the Velykovian called. "This is where we part ways. Good luck!"

A chorus of male voices rose in protest of his announcement.

Part ways? Faven bit the inside of her cheek. Good luck? Where were they? What were they going to do to them? Her chest squeezed tightly and her breaths shortened.

Then, one by one, the voices of the princes hushed until something pinched Faven's arm. Immediately, drowsiness settled over her and she lost consciousness.

8

The Sidylla Labyrinth

WHEN FAVEN CAME TO, SOMETHING WAS DIFFERENT. INSTEAD of the wooden floorboards of the wagon, she lay on a hard, uneven lump. Something tickled her nose, and a slight breeze swept over her. Nothing was wrapped around her throbbing head. But the differences stopped there. Her hands were still tied securely behind her, and her legs were still bound. She lifted her groggy head and opened her eyes, almost afraid of what she would see. But only darkness and the rough outline of odd-shaped bundles piled under and around her met her wandering eyes.

One of the bundles under her budged. She twisted and squinted, trying to understand what she was seeing.

As her headache lessened and her eyes focused, she realized the mounds were actually people. She looked to her left and recognized Prince Ruben's kind face. The young man underneath her, lying face down, had cardinal red hair and was wearing muted colors.

Twisting, she tried rolling off him, but there were bodies all over and she would only end up rolling onto someone else. She paused to survey their surroundings.

All around them were trees, bushes, and vines climbing up towering stone walls which stood on either side of them and curved out of sight. In between the walls was a path so overgrown it didn't look like much of a path at all. No flowers grew, and despite the dawning sky, no birds sang. All was silent except for the breathing of those around her.

Where were they?

As Faven examined their bodies, her foreboding deepened. What was she going to do? Here she was, kidnapped, the only girl among nine strange princes, with no idea where she was. All because she'd made the idiotic decision to dress like a prince and say she was her brother. She wished she were home right now, safe in her parents' arms.

At the edge of the pile to her right, someone else was awake and sitting up. She instantly recognized him.

Prince Luka.

Despite looking ruffled due to their mistreatment, he looked as handsome as ever. Luka stared across the mound of bodies at her. Slow recognition filled his eyes and his face tightened.

Neither of them said a word. Right when she wished something would break the tension and awkwardness, the redheaded prince fidgeted, moaned, and cursed.

"What the bloody hell is on me?"

Faven faced him. His head craned back, and his opened brown eyes settled on her. His gaze hardened. "Who the hell are you?"

Faven tightened her lips. Rolling over someone else wouldn't be as scary as staying here. She twisted and rolled away and over the top of a few princes before finally crashing to the hard ground. Some of the princes jerked awake or moaned when she passed over them. She cringed apologetically. Then she dragged her knees to her chest and pushed herself onto them.

The redheaded prince rolled onto his back. He sat up, frowning at the people around him and then at her. Finally, he saw Luka.

"Arghhhhhhhh!" He slammed his feet on the ground, and his arms and legs burst into flames. The flames ate away his ties, freeing him instantly. Surprised by his outburst, Faven leaned away from the heat. Ah, he was The Hothead. His personality matched his sense perfectly. Old bruises and scabs decorated his face, evidence of his many beatings during their journey here. Her gaze flickered away.

The rest began stirring from their comatose states, groaning and complaining about being squashed underneath someone else. As the princes yelled at each other and untangled themselves, Prince Luka inched away from the pile of princes, his arms still tied behind him and his legs still bound.

Faven only recognized Archie, Luka, and Ruben. The others were complete strangers. Then her eyes landed on a child with snow white hair. Her heart tugged in her chest. He didn't look any older than Sage—maybe younger, in fact. A child in the top ten? Their capturers had no compassion.

Prince Ruben sat up, grimacing. His green hair stuck out in all directions. Squinting, he looked around. His freckled nose twitched. "What—What's going on? Where are we?"

"We've been captured," Prince Luka answered, his voice toneless and his face without expression.

The Hothead scoffed, rolled his eyes, and crossed his arms over his chest. "No, crap. We were *entirely* unaware. Thanks for the revelation."

Prince Luka pivoted to face The Hothead. He stared at him for a moment, frowning at him as if he were looking at a small, disobedient child. "Why don't you make yourself useful and release us from our bonds, Kai?"

Kai, still sitting, glared at Luka. "Like I'd want to help any of *you*. If you're so desperate to be free, why don't you use your strange wizard-y voodoo and untie yourself?"

Faven huffed. They had been kidnapped, taken who knows where, had no idea how to get back, and they were *arguing*? Her forehead wrinkled as she turned away from them. Her gaze met Ruben's and he gave her a small smile. She returned it.

Since Kai seemed to have no desire to aid them in removing their bondages, she focused on manipulating light particles in her body to create a miniature ray. Although she had become quite deft in her ability to use her rays, she'd never tried it with her hands tied behind her back. Hopefully, she could free herself without cutting off a finger.

"Oh, I forgot," Luka replied, his voice even. But when Faven looked back at him once more, the strain of the muscles in his neck revealed his growing irritation. "You don't have anything to do with the rest of us because you feel superior. My bad."

Kai opened his mouth to retort but was interrupted by a crack and a flash of light. Faven jumped, surprised by the noise, and turned to see a gray-green-haired prince with a lean figure rubbing his now-free wrists and ankles, his bangs swishing over his dark eyes. Bruises covered his face, and his lip was busted.

"Tristan," Luka began, nodding to his bound legs. "Would you mind freeing the rest of us from our binds?"

Faven jerked. This was the other prince who had been next to her in the wagon. Tristan gave a curt nod and stood to dust off his clothes.

Luka smiled. "There. Take notice, Kai. Tristan will help because he's secure in who he is and doesn't need to throw fits for attention."

"Argghhhhh!" Kai leapt to his feet, his arms bursting into flames. "You want to go at it, daddy's boy?"

He must've had elven clothes specially designed because his jacket remained untouched by the fire.

Another voice spoke up. "Challenging the Crown Prince? I don't know if that's foolish or bold." Faven turned toward the voice. A boy with long, lanky limbs smirked at Kai. His brown hair was cut short all around except for a braid swinging at the side of his head. Faven recognized his voice as The Jokester's. "Such a challenge would be interesting to watch."

Kai glowered at him. "Being ranked number one doesn't mean he's the best," he growled. "Now shut up before I cut off that idiotic string attached to your head."

The Jokester only laughed, his braid swinging as if to taunt Kai.

"Woah, woah, woah!" Archie spoke up, his dark blue hair loosed from its ponytail. Faven pressed her lips together. She'd never imagined seeing the extravagant prince look so ruffled. "I'm quite sure that's exactly what the ranking means, hothead. And you're now ranked eighth, which means there are seven of us better than *you*."

Kai paused, his brow creasing. "Who's seventh?"

Faven ducked her head, hoping they wouldn't notice her. The rest of the Ten were taking in their surroundings and working to free themselves. Some muttered to each other under their breaths.

"Does it matter?" Archie grinned, clearly delighted to have taken Kai off guard. "All that matters is you're on the lower side of the Ten."

Faven's ties dropped to the ground after her ray sliced through the last of the rope. Free at last. She rubbed her raw wrists, and then she worked on her feet. Her stomach churned. While she was glad their capturers were nowhere in sight, somehow, she knew this only meant something worse must be afoot. She chewed the inside of her cheek.

"Shut up, water wuss, no one asked for your opinion." Kai tossed a flaming ball at Archie, who narrowly dodged it.

Water rose from a nearby puddle and doused the flame. Archie smiled. "Water always beats fire, Kai."

Kai held up a fist and stepped toward him.

Faven's eyes widened. She didn't want to see anyone get hurt. She'd heard enough beatings from their time in the wagon. The words were out before she could stop them. "Let's not resort to violence! We—" her voice softened as the nine princes shifted their eyes to her, "—shouldn't fight."

Kai's eyes flickered to her freed wrists and narrowed. "Who's he?"

Archie huffed with an off-handed wave. "The boy who knocked you to eighth place."

Luka's eyebrows furrowed as he studied her. But then he turned back to the others. "His name is Sage, and he's right. We must work together."

Kai rolled his eyes while Archie wrinkled his nose, and Tristan's gaze landed on Faven. He gave her a nod.

Faven shrunk away from the attention of the princes and focused on cutting her ankles free. When the rope fell away, she smiled. How nice it was to be able to move her feet!

Ruben noticed her free hands and feet. He scooted closer and whispered, "Can you free me too?"

Faven gestured for him to turn. He did. Igniting a ray, she started cutting through the rope, but his arms quivered. She frowned and leaned closer so she wouldn't accidentally burn him. At least someone was as terrified as she was.

Archie groaned and looked down at himself. "Ugh, look at the state of my jacket! It is crinkled and *dirty*! This was my best jacket!" He puffed a strand of hair out his face and moaned some more.

Ignoring Archie, Luka turned his head to Tristan who stood near him silently. "Tristan, if you wouldn't mind?" he asked, shifting so his bound arms faced him.

Tristan nodded, reached out a hand, and snapped his fingers. With a *zap*, Luka's ties fell to the ground. Tristan then made his rounds around the group to release the rest of the princes while Faven freed Ruben.

"Thanks," whispered Ruben with a grin.

"Say," Archie said, perking up as he rubbed his wrists. "That lightning power of yours is pretty handy, Tristan."

The others muttered their thanks, echoing Archie. Tristan said nothing, but patted Archie's shoulder and nodded to the others. Kai huffed.

Another prince stood. His tall form stretched above the others as he surveyed the area around him. His cold, orange eyes and solemn face remained unreadable. "We should make a plan."

His voice revealed him to be The Inquirer. His face became more solemn as he continued to scan. He strode over to one of the stone walls and brushed some leaves and vines away from the stone, revealing drawings of odd figures. The figures looked like the monsters Faven had heard stories about but had never seen.

Luka stepped toward The Inquirer, his jaw tense. "Tenji, do you have any idea where we might be?"

Tenji was silent for a moment as he scanned the tops of the walls around them. Then he took a slow, deep breath, which only made Faven dread what he would say. "From the rough descriptions I've read, I believe we are in the Sidylla Labyrinth."

Silence met Tenji's words.

The Sidylla Labyrinth? All the scary stories she'd been told about the Sidylla Labyrinth as a child rose to mind. She'd thought it'd been exactly that—a scary story. Like the story of the Minotaur who would eat children who strayed too far from home. No one ever spoke about the labyrinth outside those stories, and she'd never read about it in any history books. Could it truly be real?

She looked around at the tall walls as eerie silence swallowed them. If the Sidylla Labyrinth truly existed, this was how she would have imagined it—only with prowling monsters surrounding them. She shivered as she mulled over the stories she'd heard, trying to remember as many details as she could.

Archie broke the silence, his voice a bit higher than before. "Sid—*Sidylla*? How—How did we end up in Sidylla?" His gaze darted to all the trees around them. "It *exists*?"

Tenji brushed his hand through his dark hair and sighed. "Yes, Archie, it exists." He gestured to the engraving of a door on the wall behind them. "My guess is our capturers pushed us through there. Once you step through the gate, you can't leave."

Faven frowned. That was the entrance? But then her mind focused on the last thing he said. *Once you step through the gate, you can't leave.* Her chest hollowed as his words echoed in her mind. She couldn't breathe. She couldn't breathe.

Tenji placed his hands on his hips. "The real question isn't how we got here, but rather, *why are we here*? And how do we get out?"

Ruben shivered along with the white-haired little boy. The child once again brought her brother to mind, and somehow, the reminder forced Faven to calm down. Panicking wouldn't help. With that thought, she hauled in a deep breath.

Yes. Rather than finding out how they got there, they should figure out why they'd been brought to the labyrinth and then how to get out.

"Maybe this will help," a gruff voice broke through the silence. Another young man stepped forward, his clothing as black as his hair. Before he stepped forward, Faven hadn't even noticed him. It was like he'd materialized out of the shadows he was standing in. A scar sliced from his left eyebrow across the bridge of his nose and ended on his right cheek. He reminded her of the dark she feared and she decided then to steer clear of him.

The shadow man tossed a yellow stone into the middle of their huddle.

Faven immediately recognized it as an elven stone known for its ability to record images or messages. Tenji strode forward and picked it up. He frowned and narrowed his eyes at the dark prince. "Where did you find this, Draven?"

"Found it in my pocket."

There was an uncomfortable shift among the group, but no one asked any more questions. Instead, Tenji lifted the rock to his mouth and said, "Release."

The stone ignited with the word and a light shot from it, revealing an image of a stooped, hooded man. Only his mouth and nose were visible under the shade of the hood. He opened his mouth with a sly smile. "Princes of Reudinia, by the time you get this message, you will already be in the Sidylla Labyrinth. Though I shall spare the formalities, I'll inform you I was hired by an unnamed source to kidnap and place you here."

His accent…this was the Velykovian. Faven's heart sped up and her stomach burned.

"I was instructed to tell you this: there is no way out but through. If you wish to leave the labyrinth alive, you must release the one imprisoned at its center."

Terror weighed down on Faven. This couldn't be real. But the message *was* from their capturer.

"I wish you the best of luck. See you in several months." The Velykovian paused, and then chuckled and shook his head. "If you can make it through alive." His mouth curled, and then his image flickered and vanished from sight. The yellow stone in Tenji's hand turned gray. The message had been received.

Kai stormed over to Tenji, pulled the stone from his hand, and then studied, shook, and squeezed it. "How do we get it to play again?"

"We can't," Tenji replied, tugging at his embellished jacket. "It can only be played once."

Kai gritted his teeth and shook the stone harder. When the stone gave no sign of replaying the message, he chucked it at the wall where the stone cracked neatly in two and fell to the ground. He cursed.

Tenji ignored Kai's tantrum, crossed his arms, and studied the brightening sky. "What bothers me is the fact a Velykovian was hired for the job," he said, seemingly unperturbed by the message they had received. "Despite their relationship with Reudinia, it's hard to believe Velykov would do something so daring. Frankly, I don't believe they would. So who is this 'unnamed source' who hired these men?"

Some of the other princes nodded, as if seeing his point. Faven thought back to what she'd overheard in the library. Should she share with the others?

As she opened her mouth to speak, Luka shook his head. "There are rumors Velykov has been gathering people with senses. Father thinks they're gearing up for war against Reudinia. This all could very well be part of Velykov's plan."

Closing her mouth, Faven blinked. She didn't know that. Neither did the other princes it seemed. They all sobered as they took in Luka's words. Velykov was gathering an army of people with senses? If so, could Velykov be behind the kidnapping? And what about Everard? What was his part in all of this? Could he be helping Velykov? Either way, if she brought up Everard's involvement, they might laugh at her or question why she'd waited so long to say something. She was already at a disadvantage since none of them knew her and she didn't know them. Maybe she should keep her knowledge to herself.

Tenji frowned at Luka. "I still have a difficult time believing this is Velykov."

Luka and Tenji stared at each other in silence. Tension hovered between them. Despite being ranked second to Luka, Tenji was a head taller than him and seemed older.

Tenji looked away. "We can't know for certain. At least not until we leave the labyrinth and observe for ourselves."

Faven hugged herself and turned away from the others. Shouldn't they be more worried about getting out of this mess than whether or not it was Velykov who had caused it?

She scanned the princes around, watching as they spoke amongst themselves. Ruben murmured to the child who nodded in return. Then Faven caught Prince Draven studying her as he leaned against a nearby tree. His gaze snapped away toward the path leading into the depths of the labyrinth and Faven dropped her gaze and bit the insides of her cheeks. Why had he been looking at her? Was something wrong with her appearance?

Draven straightened and cleared his throat. "This is getting us nowhere. We need to move." He turned his scarred face back toward the group. "Tenji, any pointers on how to get out of this place?"

Tenji sighed and pinched the bridge of his nose. "As the Velykovian man said, the only way out is through." He nodded to the wall with the gate drawing behind them. "The entrance has been sealed, which means we have no choice."

"No choice?" Archie stared at Tenji with his mouth agape. He brushed back his navy-blue hair and pointed toward the path leading deeper into the labyrinth. "You mean we have to go through the no-one-ever-leaves crazy maze? Like peasants who struggle for food and never wash? No freakin' way! I don't want to do *that*!" His voice trembled.

He turned toward the wall of the labyrinth and shifted his stance, pressing the palm of his hand upward, angled toward the wall. Water rose from the puddles and nearby plants, killing them instantly. The prince jetted the water at the wall, but it only splashed against the stone and came splattering down.

Archie crouched and put both hands over his head. "No, no, no! This can't be happening. I can't live like this!"

The lanky prince, The Jokester, laughed as he twisted his small, brown braid between his fingers. "What were you trying to do? Clean the walls?"

Without turning to look at The Jokester, Archie threw back an arm and a spurt of water shot backward and sprayed the other boy. "Shut up, Jovian."

The Jokester, or Jovian, looked down at his now-wet jacket and trousers. He chuckled. "Now I feel refreshed. Thanks." He propped his foot up on a tree root, leaning toward Archie.

The little boy with snow white hair snorted and rolled his eyes. He looked down at Archie's bent form and his nose wrinkled. "Also, this is not a maze, dullard. La-by-rinth."

Faven stared. She supposed a child wouldn't be in the top ten for no reason. He must be incredibly talented and smart. And, apparently, rather blunt.

Archie sat up and sniffed. He stood, forcing a smile on his face. "I'm fine, Cassian. I can brave this...*labyrinth*," he said to the little boy, looking as though saying it might make him braver. "And don't worry, I'll protect you."

The little boy, whose name must be Cassian, sighed and appeared far more annoyed than a child should, before he chose to ignore Archie and pointed to a cluster of objects by the entrance. "We have swords."

Faven hadn't even noticed the weapons in all the chaos. Together, the group approached the mound.

Ten intricately designed swords lay tangled in a mass together.

Bending down to pull a sword from the pile, Tenji raised a dark eyebrow. "They must want us to succeed if they were kind enough not to leave us weaponless."

The fanciest sword lifted from the pile by itself and zipped toward Luka who caught it with an outstretched hand. He eyed it and straightened taller as if holding the sword reminded him who he was. Then he said, "The sun is getting higher in the sky. Maybe we should start walking. The longer we wait, the longer we'll be stuck here and the less time we'll have to stop Velykov."

As the rest of the princes claimed a sword, Faven picked up one of the last, excited to be holding a blade once again. She tied it to her belt. Then the redhead, Kai, decided to open his big mouth.

"Woah." Kai held up two hands, his hair blazing in the light of the rising sun. "There's no way in hell I'm walking through this blasted thing with you prissy half-wits." He turned to Luka and pointed. "And who made you the leader anyway, you vain, egotistical, stiff-headed snoot?"

Faven should've known their tentative peace was too good to be true.

Jovian cackled, but Luka's only response was the tying of his sheath to his belt and sliding his sword inside.

Kai's words were harsh, but she had a feeling he wasn't the only one in the group who didn't particularly like Luka taking the lead. However, he was the Crown Prince and Faven admired that someone was trying to manage this hard-to-control group of princes. It took boldness, grit, and determination.

"You're all noisy pricks," called Draven, and Faven spotted him already several feet away from them, striding into the labyrinth. "It doesn't matter who the leader is. Just don't expect me to slow down for any of you."

And with that, everyone began walking.

The oldest-looking princes—Luka, Tenji, and Draven—led the way, followed by Tristan, Archie, and Cassian, then Ruben, Faven, and Jovian. Kai fell behind, grumbling under his breath and kicking stray rocks like a small child throwing a temper tantrum. Faven rolled her eyes, annoyed by his terrible attitude. At least the other princes had decided to stop arguing. Only Archie chattered incessantly to a silent Tristan who nodded his head in response.

Faven welcomed the silence. It helped her throbbing headache…and made it easier to listen for a potential monster attack. She shivered, and whipped her head around, suddenly terrified she might actually spot one.

Ruben slowed and matched her stride. "Quite the loving and cheerful bunch, aren't they?" he whispered with a smile and a jerk of his head in the others' direction.

Faven returned his smile. Somehow, she'd unintentionally made at least one friend among the group of princes. "They're definitely something," she replied with a quick scan at the group around them.

"How are you handling all of this?" Ruben asked, fidgeting with his jacket. His gaze darted to the tops of the labyrinth walls.

Faven grimaced, trying to decipher her complicated feelings. "I feel...I feel quite overwhelmed." She bit her lip and stared forward. She didn't want to acknowledge the rising terror filling her chest. A few of the princes turned their heads in her direction, presumably overhearing their conversation. She ducked her head.

Ruben nodded, causing a strand of curly green hair to fall across his forehead. His lips pressed together. "Me too," he mumbled, his words barely reaching Faven's ears. "About before...in Phoebus. Thanks...for not deserting me. I thought you would flee like Archie, but you didn't."

Resting her hand on the hilt of her sword, Faven dropped her gaze to the path before her as she walked. Finally, she nodded. "I only wish I could've gotten us both away." She paused. "Do you think we'll get out of this alive?"

Ruben hesitated, his face darkening before he nodded, and a reassuring smile brightened his face once more. "Definitely. Tenji will help us find the way out, and everyone here has strong senses."

For the first time since their capture, the tightness in Faven's chest eased. Ruben's confidence in the others reassured her. She pictured her family, Trent, Ekon and Maha, her home in Hallon, her seadragon; she held their images in her mind. She needed to survive this labyrinth if she wanted to see them again. Her best chance of survival would be to stay with the others. Which meant one thing: from now on, she would have to be Sage and only Sage.

Goodbye, Faven, she whispered to herself.

9
Whispers of Deception

KAI GLARED AT THE GROUP. HE COULDN'T BELIEVE HE WAS stuck in this blasted labyrinth with some of his least favorite people in the world—well, outside of the Royal Council and the king of Reudinia. Just remembering how easily that Velykovian snuck up on him in Phoebus made Kai's insides boil. He was going to hunt down the bastard and roast him.

For three days they'd been traveling down this labyrinth path with no change in their surroundings. The walls coiled ever to the left, and the dirt trail stretched on with only a few trees and bushes lining the edges—no monsters in sight. They could be walking in circles and Kai would never know. Everything looked the same.

If this was as bad as the labyrinth got, then he didn't see what all the hysteria was about. The only semi-threatening thing about it so far was the likelihood it would drive him to insanity if he had to keep walking on and on across the constantly flat, unending terrain.

To make matters worse, the egotistical snoot, Luka, had pre-decided he was the leader. Just looking at him reminded Kai of the king, which left a bitter taste in his mouth. He could still vividly picture King Léon's unforgiving face as he stood before Kai's grandmother all those years ago with five of the High Council beside him, observing. *"That means you, you little varmint,"* the king snarled as he glared at twelve-year-old Kai. The memory only made him queasy, so Kai shook it out of his head.

Once the path became too dark to see, the Snoot suggested everyone stop and rest. He organized a night watch, and Ruben located some edible vegetation from the plants lining the walls. Kai stood apart from the rest, watching as Tenji gathered wood and started a fire, the warm light illuminating his orange eyes. When they asked Kai if he would light the fire, he refused. He wasn't going to become the fire-lighting-guy. No way.

As the air cooled and night fell, everyone settled around the fire. Everyone except for Kai and Draven, at least. Draven blended into the shadows with his dark attire and sat against the wall opposite Kai. Despite being the third oldest of their group, at twenty-three, Draven didn't seem to want a leadership position. Kai didn't blame him.

The neck of Kai's jacket stifled him, so he unbuttoned it, finally able to relax. Honestly, being around the others was as suffocating as the jacket had been. They made him uncomfortable. They all knew about his past yet pretended not to. They merely tolerated him…like King Léon. Like the Royal Council.

Kai drew his attention back to the campfire. Ruben, the third youngest at sixteen years old, passed out what little vegetation he'd found, already putting his plant manipulation to use. When Ruben reached Kai, he refused the other boy's offering. He didn't want their false kindness. They never cared about him before, so why pretend to now?

Instead, Kai went to look for his own food. After locating similar looking vegetation, he returned to his post and leaned against a tree, pretending not to listen to the quiet conversation around the fire.

Eleven-year-old Cassian, his white hair blinding in the firelight, stared at the newcomer. He leaned in closer and spoke loud enough for all to hear. "You're a strange-looking boy. You kind of look like a girl."

Jovian's chuckle came from the sky. Kai looked up to find fifteen-year-old Jovian had made his bed in a tree. Kai rolled his eyes. How could he laugh so much considering their current situation?

Archie frowned at Cassian as he fixed his ponytail. "Cassian, telling him he looks like a girl won't make him like you in the slightest."

Cassian glared at Archie.

The pretty boy said nothing. He stared down at his food and continued eating. Kai was sure everyone else—though no one said it—agreed with Cassian. This new boy was too pretty. His skin and features were too soft, his eyelashes too long, his figure too petite. Kai looked away and stopped listening once Archie blabbed on and on about the state of his hair and how dirty the ground was. With every complaint, Archie reminded Kai of what he already knew—not every prince had a hard life.

"Something has been bothering me," Tenji interrupted Archie's foolish monologue. Kai's focus, along with everyone else's, shifted to him. Tenji was the oldest in the group, at twenty-six, and had always been one to command silence when he spoke. He lifted his orange eyes from the fire and looked around at them. "The Velykovian mentioned we needed to free a prisoner to leave. This labyrinth has an older legend, amidst the ones we know, about a spirit trapped in the center."

"Uh—a spirit?" Archie went still and his features became strained.

"A dark and powerful spirit," Tenji confirmed with a slight nod. "They say long ago, the spirit possessed a human with the unique sense of stealing others' senses. He became known as the Sense Thief. But he did more than steal senses."

"Like—like what?" Archie sputtered as he glanced around at the dark, looming shadows around them.

Kai rolled his eyes.

Jovian's chuckle came down from where he was sitting. "What, did he go on a murderous rampage?"

Tenji nodded. "Exactly."

Kai's heart sped up and his gaze slipped down to the dried dirt below him. However, instead of dwelling on the thought of a possible murderous spirit imprisoned in the center of the labyrinth, his mind latched onto something else. Could a spirit truly remove a sense? For a moment, an image of his mother screaming through tongues of flames flashed across his mind. Would things have been different if he had been born without a sense?

Tenji continued, "Legends say he became too powerful for any one person to restrain, and so, several people joined together to defeat him. They removed the spirit from the man's body and locked it away."

"In the Sidylla Labyrinth?" Ruben asked, his green eyes wide and his freckled nose twitching. He hugged himself and shivered.

Tenji gave another nod.

"So they succeeded in defeating him in the end," the pretty boy piped up.

Tenji sighed deeply. "Years later, after the creation of the labyrinth, the whole tribe who helped imprison the spirit was found slaughtered. No one knows why or how."

Silence fell over them once again. Kai frowned. Honestly, that story only made the labyrinth—and those who created it— seem cursed. He eyed the tall walls on either side of them. How dangerous could this place be?

The Snoot, resting one hand on the hilt of his sword, leaned closer to Tenji. "Then the legend says the labyrinth was built to keep the spirit in?"

Tenji turned his gaze to the fire as he stoked it, causing it to spark upward. "And keep people out."

Kai wrinkled his forehead and he found himself saying, "Why keep people out? It's not as if the spirit can do anything now, right?"

Tenji dropped the stick he was using to stoke the fire and leaned back. "It's to prevent someone from setting the spirit free. It's said that if someone releases a spirit from a prison, the spirit must grant said person a wish. Greed has caused many spirits to be freed who should've remained under lock and key."

"To make sure I'm understanding correctly," the Snoot interjected, "You're saying, if the spirit is freed, it would grant any single wish, no matter how outrageous the request?"

"Yes."

The Snoot's frown deepened, his face noticeably troubled. "That sounds like bad news."

"But why us?" Ruben asked.

"Isn't it obvious?" Draven tossed a stone at Jovian's tree. Without turning to face them, he continued, "We're considered some of the most powerful people in the most powerful kingdom. Getting through the labyrinth isn't an easy task, so sending the best to do the dirty work makes the most sense."

Kai didn't like where this conversation was headed. He didn't want to think about how, to leave this place, they had to free some dangerous prisoner. An action which would only accomplish what the damned Velykovian and his goons wanted. He didn't want to help those bastards, but he also didn't want to die. Not now, and definitely not here. The more he thought about it, the more agitated he became. That Velykovian man deserved the swift and agonizing end of being burned to a crisp.

Cassian leaned toward Tenji. "How will we leave the labyrinth if the only way to exit is by releasing a dangerous spirit back into the world? We don't want to do that, do we?"

"No."

Ruben scrunched his face. "Then…we're stuck here?"

"I won't accept that," the Snoot broke in. He gestured down the path they'd been walking. "We can't give up without even trying."

"I agree." Tenji's gaze swept over the group. "Let's focus on getting through the labyrinth first. We'll figure out the rest later, once we have more information."

This idea bothered Kai. What if they reached the end only to find out they couldn't leave? Would they decide to release the spirit back into the world regardless of the disaster it caused? Or would they decide to stay in the labyrinth forever?

Silence hovered over them. Kai mulled over the information he'd just been dealt, oblivious to everyone else.

A voice spoke up once again, breaking the silence:

"It still doesn't make sense." The pretty boy's forehead wrinkled. He turned whis gaze to Tenji. "Didn't you say the spirit only grants the wish of the person who frees it? If so, how would the Velykovian receive his wish if he isn't the one freeing the spirit? Wouldn't he need to be present to free the spirit so his wish could be granted? How can they be sure we wouldn't ask the spirit to wipe him—and whoever else is in on this plan—out after freeing it ourselves?"

Kai stared at him, anger suddenly churning in his chest. Looking around the group of ten, Kai scanned their faces. He couldn't be the only one to have this revelation. If the enemy needed to be present to free the spirit and have their wish granted, then they would need to be in the labyrinth with the Ten. Which could only mean one thing…

He sprang to his feet, his eyes blazing. "Which one of you did this? I'm going to kill you!"

Archie glared back at Kai and stood too. "How do we know it wasn't you? You're not necessarily a saint or anything."

"Why you—"

"Wait!" the Snoot called out, standing and raising his hands to stop them. "This is all speculation. We don't know for sure if any of us are to blame. Let's not accuse one another just yet. It would only drive us further apart and make it harder for us to get out of here."

Kai glared at him. "Maybe it was you, daddy's boy. You've been especially bossy since we arrived. And weren't you one of the last to be captured?"

"If we are going to base this off who was captured last, that would be Ruben, Archie, and Pretty Boy." Jovian scoffed, leaning back in the tree and crossing his feet out in front of him. He nodded in the direction of the three.

Ruben avoided the eyes that turned to him while the pretty boy frowned.

Kai stepped closer to them, placing his hands on his hips. "Ruben *is* behaving suspiciously."

Archie laughed scornfully and jerked his thumb in Ruben's direction. "Ruben doesn't have the stomach for something like this. It would be more likely for the traitor to be Jovian than Ruben. Jovian was only pointing out the ridiculousness of your accusation."

"No one is ever as they seem," Kai muttered. Then his gaze slid from Ruben to Archie. "But it could just as well have been you."

"Archie?" Jovian burst into a hooting laughter, holding his stomach. After he calmed down, he sniffed and flicked away a pretend tear from his perch in the tree. "It can't be Archie! He's terrified by the idea of there being a spirit, there's no way he would *purposely* plan to free it."

Archie shook a fist at Jovian. "Hey! You better watch what you say, you little twit."

Jovian only smirked and looked down at Kai, crossing his arms over a knee and resting his head on his arms. "I think it's Kai."

Kai glared at Jovian. "You're going to die."

"Or," Jovian continued, ignoring Kai and nodding in the direction of Draven who stood in the shadows of the trees, "it could be slinky, grumpy Draven over there. He's always been pretty suspicious." Then he turned his gaze to quiet Tristan who met his stare through his long, gray-green bangs, "Or it could be Tristan. As you said, Kai, no one is ever as they seem."

"Hey," Archie snapped, frowning at Jovian. "Tristan is as true as they come. Don't bring him into this." He turned and pointed at Tenji. "It could be Sir Smarty-pants over here. He already knows everything about this place, and he could have some complicated, well-thought-out plan."

Tenji frowned at the fire. "Is this my reward for educating all of you? Being accused?" He lifted his orange eyes and looked across the flames at the pretty boy. "*I* say, the most likely out of all of us is Sage. None of us know him. He just shows up one day and jumps into the top ten." His gaze was sharp. "Right after the rank adjustment, he's captured with the rest of us and put here."

When Tenji put it that way, Sage did seem the most likely suspect. Kai faced the pretty boy. Sage said nothing and avoided everyone's gaze, his back straight and legs crossed.

"No defense?" asked Tenji.

Sage lifted his gaze to meet his. "Nothing I say would make any of you trust me, so what's the point?"

Tenji narrowed his eyes, but no one questioned Sage further.

"Well," Jovian broke in. A mischievous smile spread. "I still think it's Kai."

"Argggghhh! Stop saying it's me!"

Before Kai could send a blast of fire at Jovian, the Snoot unsheathed his sword and stuck it in the ground. "Or it could be none of us! We shouldn't be like this. If we can't trust each other, one or all of us will end up dying."

Kai shot him a look that could kill. "That wouldn't stop me from believing one of you is in on this. I still think it's you."

"But Luka is right," Cassian whispered, suddenly reminding everyone there was an eleven-year-old among them. His wide, golden eyes glinted in the firelight. "We might not make it through the labyrinth alive if we don't trust each other."

Jovian snorted, his smile unshaken. "A child scolding the lot. What an amusing thought."

"Oh, shut up." Archie huffed in Jovian's direction. "You irritate me. For now, I've decided the traitor is you. At least until someone annoys me more."

Jovian laughed again. "Oh, sure. I'll confess! It was all me."

Kai rolled his eyes and returned to his spot to sit down once more. "Unbearable."

Conversations shriveled soon after as everyone settled down for the night. But Kai couldn't sleep. The idea that one of the Ten was part of the plot was still a large possibility. In fact, their capture and purpose within the labyrinth didn't make sense any other way. Someone among them was a traitor, but finding out *who* wouldn't be easy. Everyone looked suspicious when the light was turned on them. Although Kai wanted it to be Luka, he couldn't rule the others out.

Leaning against the wall, Kai crossed his arms tightly over his chest and closed his eyes. Although Jovian had only been teasing him, the boy's words still echoed in his head. How long would it take before the others turned their backs on him? If they were to base their votes on past knowledge, most, if not all of them, would vote against him. He gritted his teeth.

In that case, Kai would have to turn his back on them first.

The next morning, the group started off early. Kai hadn't had much more than a wink. It wasn't easy to sleep when the ground was hard, hunger gnawed at him, and distrust lingered.

By the time the noonday sun burned overhead, Kai started believing the labyrinth *was* going to continue on, never changing, when the group rounded a curve, and something loomed into sight. The Snoot stopped, holding up a hand. But most of the group ignored him and kept walking.

Before them lay a huge forest with a squared, stone arch over it. The walls of the labyrinth widened and disappeared behind the tall trees. A narrow, overgrown path went into the trees. A few blue flowers poked their heads through the grass sporadically, and the buzz of cicadas rose from the mass of trees, along with the soft, distant sound of running water.

This must be where things got interesting.

The group approached the wooded area, a slight hesitation hanging over them. The Snoot strode back to the front of the group, as if to seize an opportunity to wield his unnominated leadership.

"This might be a good place to find some food and water." He turned to Tenji. "Don't you think so?"

Tenji stared at him with a frown, but then nodded.

The Snoot turned to Archie. "Would you be able to locate where the water is? And Ruben, could you locate more edible plants?"

Kai grunted. Luka wasn't just vain and egotistical. He was vain, egotistical, *and* bossy. It was really getting on his nerves.

The worst part was Ruben responded as if he was *actually listening*, which would only make things worse if he allowed Luka to believe the Crown Prince really was their leader.

"Yes, I should be able to," Ruben replied.

Jovian's voice rose from the back of the group, a smile stretching across his face, "Too bad no one here can 'locate' animals for meat…" He paused and turned to the pretty boy, Sage. "Unless…Sage happens to have that sense?"

Sage shook his head. "Sorry, but no."

"Just a wild shot." Jovian shrugged, his cheeky grin still wide.

"Hey, plant boy," Draven called, waving Ruben over to him and interrupting the chatter. He pointed up at the trees. "Can you use that plant manipulation of yours and climb up? Maybe you'll see something helpful."

Ruben tugged at his collar and swallowed. "I, uh, I guess I could try."

"Draven," the Snoot called, frowning at him. "I don't know if we should let Ruben do something so risky. We don't know how dangerous the labyrinth is yet. Just because nothing has happened so far, doesn't mean it won't."

Kai gritted his teeth. If the Snoot kept opening his bloody mouth, he was going to roast him. "Ah, shut up, you bossy hen."

Luka shot him a look, but Ruben stepped in. "No, it's fine! I'll go up and see if I can see anything." He joined Draven by the forest's edge. The trees bent, wrapping their branches around Ruben's torso and lifting him into the air.

Kai huffed. What was the point of him going up anyway? These prissy half-wits were driving him insane with their stupidity and…and…and just by bloody existing!

"Where's Archie?" Cassian asked, drawing attention to him as he glanced around with his large eyes.

Kai's own eyes swept the group realizing, sure enough, there was no sight of the nitwit with the blue ponytail. What a sneaky bastard!

"The water!" the Snoot groaned, slapping his forehead. "Did he leave without us?"

Kai rolled his eyes and placed his hands on his hips. "Who would listen to you? Of course he did."

"It doesn't matter," Tenji interrupted, his gaze focused on Ruben. "If he doesn't want to stick around, let him disappear."

Amused by Tenji's bluntness, Kai watched Luka open his mouth to refute, but Tristan stopped the Snoot. He touched Luka's shoulder, gave him a look, and then disappeared into the forest.

Jovian grinned and jogged after him. "I'm going with Tristan!"

"Wait!" the Snoot called after them. But they were already gone. He shook his head. "We shouldn't separate…"

Kai took that note as his leave. "Speaking of separating," he added, as he stalked toward the forest. "I'm off. Can't stand any of you."

"Kai!" Luka cried.

He ignored them and kept walking. No way in hell was he going to stay around and listen to that bossy crap. He needed to get away before they drove him insane. He stomped through the bushes, following the narrow strip that obviously hadn't been used in a long time. Leaves and vines littered the path or were overhanging, making it hard to walk.

"Let him go," Tenji's voice drifted toward him as he marched away. "All he'd do is argue if he stayed."

With a huff, Kai lifted his head high, squeezed his fists tight, and left them behind. He didn't need them any more than they needed him. If they couldn't stand him and he couldn't stand them, then why stay? What did *he* care if he had to survive the labyrinth alone? Surely he could escape just fine on his own, especially since he could burn anything that got in his way to a crisp.

"Argghhhhh!" Kai slammed his fist into a tree. He hated them. All they'd ever done was look at him condescendingly. No one besides his grandmother had ever listened to him, believed in him. Good riddance. He was better off without them.

A vine caught his foot and he stumbled. Blasted labyrinth. Kai set fire to the vine and marched on. How long would he be alone in the labyrinth if he left the others behind? Kai suppressed the thought, but a flood of others sprang up: What if he got into trouble and had no one to call for help? What if he died, and they didn't know or care? What if *they* died, and he never knew? Kai shook his head vigorously. Why should he worry about them?

His grandmother would be disappointed in his choice to leave the others. He pictured her lying in her bed, struggling to move. Maybe he should turn around. He pivoted and paused, staring back the way he came. He shook his head. No, that would be too humiliating. He turned back around.

"Kai, wait!"

A shock ran through his body. Someone had come after him? He turned his head. The pretty boy, Sage, raced toward him, leaping over roots and vines. Complicated emotions rose within him. Unsure how to respond, Kai exploded. "Why are you following me? Leave me be!"

The pretty boy paused mid-step, his left hand resting on a tree. "But it could—be dangerous—for people to go—off on their own," he gasped, his right hand gripping his side.

"Look here, Pretty Boy—"

"My name is Sage."

"Whatever," Kai growled, his chest heaving. "I ain't going back with that up-tight, know-it-all Snoot. If you're so scared about being separated, don't follow me." Kai kept on walking, whacking a twig of leaves out of his face. Sage's footsteps crunched after him.

"I know. You made yourself perfectly clear on how much you disliked being captured and stuck here with the rest of us."

Kai whirled back around. "Why are you still following me, then? Scat! I'm not going back with you."

Sage met his gaze with a calm, stern stare. "No one is particularly pleased to be here, you know, but here we are, and we have to come to terms with that fact." He crossed his puny arms over his chest. "Stop being such a wimp and get over it."

Kai gritted his teeth. "I *have* come to terms…and I've decided I'm not doing this with you all." He couldn't stay focused on Sage's unwavering gaze, so he looked away. "Now go."

Sage gave an exasperated sigh. "Urgghhh! Goodness! I'm not here to drag you back." He pushed past Kai and continued walking. "I just couldn't let you go off by yourself, so I'm coming with you."

He stared after Sage. Who was this guy? Kai couldn't think of any response to what the pretty boy had said. He couldn't get himself to move. All he could do was stare.

Sage glanced over his shoulder at Kai again. "Are you coming, or did you decide you'd rather go back?" Then he kept trudging on through the tall grass and leaves, not waiting for a response.

"I didn't want your company either," Kai grumbled under his breath, but a sliver of relief slipped through him and he followed after the pretty boy anyway.

A little while later, they came upon a stream, and both stopped for a drink. While bending over, Sage splashed some water on his face and turned to face Kai. "Too bad we don't have anything to hold water. We don't know when we'll find any again."

"I suppose." Kai cleared his throat hoarsely. He sipped some more water. The others rarely, if ever, volunteered to hang around him so Kai didn't know how to act or how to handle this situation. It felt too unnatural.

Sage's eyes bore into him, only making him even more uncomfortable, so Kai straightened and walked away. "I'm continuing."

He didn't turn when Sage scrambled to keep up with him. However, soon after, the crunch of Sage's steps stopped. Kai looked back, unconsciously, but didn't see him anywhere. He paused. Did he decide to go back? Kai snapped his gaze forward. So what if he did? He didn't care.

Then the image of some monster tearing Sage apart flickered in his mind. What if he was in trouble and Kai ignored him? Kai turned again. "Pretty Boy?"

No response.

"Sage?"

Still nothing.

Kai retraced his steps until he found Sage standing still, his eyes trained on something in the trees. Hiding a sigh of relief, he walked over to him. "I'm going to leave you if you plan to be like this all the time, you know."

"Kai…"

Alarm flashed across Sage's face, his eyes wide and body rigid. Kai followed his gaze. Sitting in several trees were exceptionally large lizard-like creatures. Standing on four legs, they were about the size of an average man. Their yellow eyes flicked between Sage and Kai as their wingless bodies writhed through the branches of the trees. Black, slithering tongues slipped out of their mouths as they cocked their heads.

Forest dragons.

Kai drew out his sword just as one of them sprang at him. He jerked and lopped the head off the dragon. There was a second of hissing silence as the other forest dragons took in the sight of their slain brother. Then, they launched.

"Welcome to Sidylla Labyrinth."

The traitor frowned. Was the labyrinth playing tricks with his mind? It almost sounded as if the labyrinth was *speaking*. But maybe it had been nothing.

"I didn't think you were coming, but I'm glad you did. We'll be great companions, I'm sure."

Rubbing his ear, the traitor studied the hissing, rustling leaves of the trees rising above him. Maybe it was the wind. Yes, it had to be the wind.

10

Shadows of the Forest

DRAVEN STARED UP AT RUBEN AS HE MADE HIS WAY BACK down, willing the boy to hurry. The shadowy forest beckoned him. The last few days spent in the sun had given him quite the headache, and he longed to be back in the shade. But first he needed to assess their surroundings so they could decide the safest route for getting out of here. When Ruben reached the bottom, Draven stepped toward him.

"Well? What did you see?"

Ruben scanned the remaining members of their group. "I— I couldn't see the end of the labyrinth. All I could see was the forest and more towering walls swirling inward in a large spiral. Everything was covered with dense fog…" he trailed off and frowned. "Where is everyone?"

Draven waved away Ruben's question and leaned in closer. "Did you see *anything* that could be useful?"

Ruben shook his head, his forehead wrinkling. "Nothing. I could see nothing but the forest and walls and *maybe* the hint of a mountain in the distance. I couldn't even see the end of the labyrinth."

Draven grimaced. He had hoped Ruben could get a vague layout of the labyrinth if nothing else. Proceeding forward blindly wasn't safe or wise. "We could be here longer than we'd like," he muttered. He looked back to find Tenji and Luka watching him. He counted on them, the first and second in ranking, to understand his meaning when he said, "If we want to get out of here, we should keep moving."

Luka shook his head. "We can't leave without the others. If we must move, it should be toward the sound of water."

Before Draven could agree, Tenji spoke. "Draven is right. We'll lose time if we don't continue forward. I say, we keep going and forget about the others."

"No! Tenji, we can't do that!" Luka protested.

"Did…" Ruben's green eyes darted toward the forest. "Did the others…leave?"

The child, Cassian, nodded. "Yes. Foolish Archie ran off, and Tristan and Jovian went looking for him. Then Kai stormed off, and Sage went after him."

"They made their choices," Tenji continued, focusing his gaze on the forest. "It's not our job to babysit them."

Luka glared at him and clenched his fists. "It's not babysitting. It's *survival*."

Draven crossed his arms as he listened to them bicker. Ruben's lips pressed together and Cassian stared at the ground, but neither of them joined the argument. Since Tenji, Luka, and Draven were the oldest in the group, Draven assumed Ruben and Cassian probably weren't comfortable enough to share their own opinions.

Draven didn't want any part in the argument himself. Once the quarreling ended, Luka and Tenji would ask Draven his opinion and he would wait until then to give it. His goal wasn't to solve their personal issues. His goal was to keep them alive. So, instead, he stared into the shade of the forest.

It had been a while since he'd been near such a heavy, shadowy covering. It called to him. Whenever there was such a massive collection of shadows nearby, he always had to resist the urge to give in to his shadow sense. He could feel the pull now. He needed to distract his mind. However, when he turned to face the others, a chill crept into his chest. Their voices faded in and out and sounded further away than the short distance actually between them. The darkness of the forest billowed behind him, and the beckoning intensified.

Draven's breath stilled. No. He couldn't have an episode now.

Images of scratched up doors and walls shot through his mind, and his muscles tightened. This wasn't good. He'd been trying to squelch it since arriving in the labyrinth, but he'd known the inevitability of the coming episode.

Draven sucked in a deep breath, struggling to resist the pull. He plunged his hand into a pocket and gripped at a small, dark woven thread. Resist. Resist.

But it was useless. Everything was growing darker and darker. He couldn't stop it.

He wasn't strong…enough…

Then, his fingers tangled with the unfinished cords of a second thread, and he heard a small, young voice rise from his memories. *"I believe you can resist."*

Zinnia. Her sweet voice pierced through the dark clouds of his thoughts. Yes. He'd been able to find the strength enough to swallow the urge before. He could do it again. Even if just for a little bit longer. He would not, could not fail.

Focusing on her voice in his mind gave Draven renewed strength, and slowly, everything lightened again. He could breathe easier. His heart calmed.

"—stay together," came Luka's voice, reminding him they were also still there. He released his hold on the two threads in his pocket and turned his focus back to Luka as the prince continued, "We don't know what's waiting out there. If we go on our own paths and get into trouble, there will be no one to help. At least together we stand a chance."

Tenji narrowed his eyes. Finally, he nodded. "Yes, yes, I see your point. If we must, let's go toward the water. We know three are there." He faced Draven. "What do you think, Draven?"

"I say we stay together."

Tenji nodded. "Very well." Taking the lead, Tenji charged forward. "Let's move."

The five princes entered the forest. As Draven trailed behind Tenji, unease settled over him. He had always preferred to be on his own, mostly because of his episodes. Would staying with the others be more dangerous than the monsters they may come across? Maybe it was better for them if he stayed away... And yet, he couldn't bring himself to leave them.

As the group treaded deeper into the forest, the rush of water morphed and changed—like ocean waves beating against the shore. He stopped. The rest of the group paused with him.

Tenji frowned. "The water sounds strange."

Draven nodded in agreement. He stilled, focused on listening. A distant shout pierced the air followed by more wave-like crashes.

"The others..." Cassian whispered. "They must be in trouble."

Luka plunged through the trees after them, but Draven caught him by the arm. "No." He tensed and scanned the forest around them in sudden alarm. "Something's not right."

This scene was too familiar.

He pulled out his sword. The others, seeing his exposed blade and darting eyes, immediately became more observant. Tenji and Luka pulled out their weapons too, and the three of them circled Cassian and Ruben.

The forest was strangely dark and silent. No movement. No cicadas buzzing. It was all too quiet. Draven searched the tall, thick and twisting vines surrounding them. Dense bushes covered the paths, making it nearly impossible to see anything. Something shuffled behind him, and he turned. But it wasn't until Cassian pointed a trembling hand, his golden eyes wide with terror, that Draven saw what was stalking them.

A massive dog-beast with glowing red eyes and a wrinkled snout crouched before him, sharp teeth exposed, gaze watchful. The beast, if it were standing straight, was about the same height as Draven. Its fur was black, thick, and coarse, covering a lean body and skinny legs. Each paw had long, finger-like claws, stretching out. Waiting. Waiting for something.

Draven lifted his sword.

"Werewolves."

11

Forest of Monsters

TRISTAN RAN A HAND THROUGH HIS GRAY-GREEN HAIR as he stopped to listen for the gurgle of water, before allowing his hair to flop back to its place over his eyes. Jovian wasn't making it any easier to listen. He chattered nonstop, much like the monkeys he'd seen with traveling performers. Jovian could be releasing built-up tension from the silence that had hung over the group the last few days. But still.

"—I mean, don't you find it a bit odd for a forest to be sitting in the middle of a labyrinth? What person would create a place like this? Seems quite excessive. Do you believe everything Tenji said about this place is true? The fact we were brought here to release, what? A *spirit*? It's a little hard to believe. But..." Jovian smirked and manipulated two rocks into the air, twirling them around each other. "At least it's a change of pace from completing all those redundant royal duties. That's why I followed you, actually. The others were boring me with their incessant bickering. If we *are* in the Sidylla Labyrinth, then I want something a bit more exciting—"

Tristan held up a hand, unable to handle his chatter any longer.

Jovian froze mid-step and stopped talking, but only for a moment. With a wink, he smiled. "Oh my, oh my, oh my! I am *so* sorry. Was I being too noisy for you, my silent friend?"

Tristan dropped his arm and held in a sigh. Having Jovian as company was just as noisy as having Archie around. But it wasn't Jovian he was irritated with. Tristan closed his eyes and took a deep breath. That foolish Archie. Why had he wandered off? The Sidylla Labyrinth wasn't a place to take irrational and risky actions. Sometimes Archie deserved a good knock on the head.

"Fine, fine! I'll be quiet!" Jovian chuckled. Then his smile slipped from his face as he looked away and, to Tristan's surprise, he did fall silent.

However, Jovian's silence didn't bring any relief. Tristan avoided looking in the other boy's direction and focused on listening for the water once more. Why had he told Jovian to be quiet? Tristan could almost hear his father's voice in his ears. *"Shut your mouth or I'll shut it for you!"*

Tristan grimaced. He'd promised himself years ago he would never tell someone else to be quiet, and yet he'd just done so. Was he becoming like his father despite his desperate struggle not to?

Ignoring his roiling thoughts, Tristan shoved a branch out of his way and stepped over a fallen log toward the hiss of water.

Tristan watched for vines at his feet, moved or ducked under branches in his way, and cut away bushes that snagged at his clothes. Finally, he and Jovian stepped out of the forest into a clearing with a river winding through it. Archie was crouched by the water, scrubbing his jacket and face. Tristan released a sigh. At least they'd found him.

"Archie."

At the sound of his name, Archie turned to glance over his shoulder at them. He rolled his eyes at the sight of them.

The temptation to yell at Archie was *almost* uncontrollable. What had he been thinking? What would he have done if he'd come across a monster? Fallen in quicksand? Fallen down a hill and broken something? Being friends with Archie was—more often than not—a pain.

Jovian clasped his hands behind his back, strolled closer to Archie, and grinned. "Well, well, well…looks like Mr. Prim and Proper actually *did* find a place to bathe."

Archie scowled. "And it seems like you didn't need a guide after all," he muttered before standing and looking at Tristan. "Where are the others? And why did you bring the jester with you?" He wrinkled his nose at Jovian as if he were a young child. Whenever children swarmed him in Phoebus, Archie froze and an expression of pure disgust curdled on his face.

"I came to fetch you," Tristan replied evenly. He hoped he didn't have to babysit Archie while they were stuck in this labyrinth. That would be even harder than keeping himself alive.

Jovian feigned a gasp. "The mute speaks!"

"Ah, shut up!" Archie snapped at Jovian before turning back to Tristan. "If you're mad because I left you behind, I'm sorry. I was getting tired of the boss being the boss. Next time, I'll bring you with me."

Tristan pressed his lips together but said nothing. He and Archie used to play together when they were children—back when Tristan's mother was still alive—but they hadn't gotten along at all back then. Archie had always been the outgoing type; always getting what he wanted because he was bold and confident enough to demand it. He loved when the spotlight was on him and threw tantrums when he didn't get the attention he desired. Tristan never liked the spotlight, yet he was constantly dragged into it because of his rank.

Archie knew what he wanted and went after it. Tristan did not.

When Archie joined the Ten, he'd decided Tristan would be his best friend. Tristan had been appalled by his decision yet couldn't find it in himself to deny it. But, over time, Tristan grew accustomed to him. Once, Archie even helped him and his little brother, Milo, when they were in dire need. Because of this, Tristan was forever grateful to him. And, really, he wasn't so bad to have around.

He owed Archie so much, and maybe that was why Tristan couldn't bring himself to tell Archie the truth: he was in love with the very same girl Archie was courting, and he had been since he was ten years old. If he'd been more assertive or voiced his opinion years earlier, would things be different now?

Tristan clasped his hands together as he watched Archie tighten his ponytail.

"Anyway," Archie continued with no more than a slight pause, waving a hand disdainfully. "I figured you'd be able to find me. The water is quite loud. And as you know, when I'm around water, I'm safe."

Jovian scoffed. "Confident much?" He plopped himself along the edge of the stream looking entirely too cheerful.

Archie caused water from the river to swirl up and around him with a wave of an arm as he hopped onto a large rock near the river's edge. "I would say I'm self-assured." He flicked his fingers, and water sprayed in every direction, soaking Jovian and spraying the grass near Tristan's feet.

"There *is* a reason I am fifth in rank in a list that contains more than 400. I'm higher than *you*," Archie taunted Jovian.

Jovian looked down at his soaked clothes with an amused smile and shook his head. He stood and squeezed the excess water out of his jacket. "As they say, pride comes before the fall."

Tristan frowned. For once, he agreed with Jovian. He really ought to whack those idiotic, useless thoughts out of Archie's mind. That cockiness was only going to bite Archie in the back sooner than later, and Tristan didn't have time to deal with his friend's idiocy. He needed to get out of this labyrinth as speedily as possible. He had to get back to Milo.

The only thing on his mind since his capture had been the image of his little brother, home alone, with no one to take care of him other than the maid the Royal Council had hired. What would his brother do without him? Would their father come back?

That idea terrified him more than anything he could imagine existing in this labyrinth.

But was he selfish enough to release an evil spirit back into the world just so he could be free of the labyrinth? He gripped the hilt of his sword and squeezed tightly. He didn't know that answer.

Tristan opened his mouth, preparing to berate Archie, when suddenly, a slithering tentacle rose from the river, wrapped itself tightly around Archie's leg, and yanked him into the water. Archie was gone before he had a chance to scream.

Tristan dashed to the water's edge.

"Did you see *that*?" Jovian pointed to where Archie disappeared below the water's surface, eyes wide.

Tristan nodded as he searched the swirling river below, hoping for any sign of his friend. But there was none.

Please. Any trace of him. Any.

"And he's the one with the water sense," Jovian joked, nudging Tristan as if to make him laugh at the irony.

Tristan clenched his fists and glared at Jovian. "This is not the time for jokes," he said through gritted teeth. Archie could be dead or dying.

Before Jovian could respond, several tentacles holding Archie came bursting out of the river, hurling water in every direction. Tentacles wrapped around Archie's throat and his face turned purple as he strained to manipulate the water from the river to attack the beast.

"Archie!" Tristan bellowed and yanked his sword from its scabbard and sliced at one of the closest tentacles. His efforts barely left a mark, but the creature shrieked and thrashed. The tentacle Tristan had sliced smacked into him, sending him soaring back. He skidded across the ground, and his shoulder slammed into a tree trunk. Tristan groaned and gripped his shoulder with his free hand. He shook off the dizziness and pain just in time to see Jovian dance away from the beast and manipulate his earth sense to shoot himself into a tree.

Now soaked, Tristan pushed himself to his feet, brushing off the ache in his shoulder, and gripped his sword. He charged the beast. Launching himself into the air toward Archie, Tristan swung his sword with all his might, slicing through several tentacles and freeing his friend from the beast's grasp. Together, they careened toward the water below.

Archie jerked a hand. A wave of water rose and shoved them toward land. Tumbling across the grass and away from the bank, Tristan's head slammed against the hard ground. He rolled to a stop. Pain racked his body as he lay on his back, unmoving. But he couldn't stay there. With a groan, he dragged himself to a sitting position. Archie was a few feet away, pushing himself up off his face.

"Tristan," Archie sputtered, pausing to hack up water and struggling to drag in air. "That thing…it's…"

But before Archie could finish, Tristan watched as a gigantic being—whose top half was human-esque but whose bottom half was an octopus—rose from the water. The creature had long, dark hair; gray skin; and sharp, green eyes. He couldn't tell if it was male or female, but the tentacles Tristan had previously cut off had somehow mended and the beast screamed furiously at them.

Jovian's voice rose from somewhere among the trees. "How did *that* thing fit in the river?"

"The river…" Archie hissed, still gasping for air. "It has a spell on it; it's deeper once you're inside." He struggled to his feet. "It's massive down there."

Tristan stood, grimacing as he retrieved his sword. He paused as the beast rose higher out of the water and raised its hand, revealing a large golden trident. Maybe if they ran fast enough, they could get away.

"Hey, Archie!" Jovian called from his tree. "You said you could handle anything if you were near water. Now's a good chance to test that theory!"

"Ha, ha," Archie groused, pulling out his sword. "Very funny."

Then the creature aimed its trident, and a wave of water came raining down while its tentacles shot toward them.

Tristan suddenly wished he hadn't angered the creature.

12

Light It Up

SAGE GRIPPED HER SWORD, DEFENDING HERSELF FROM THE onslaught of forest dragons. Flames burned away the leaves and vines that surrounded them, repelling the dragons. Instead of blowing fire, these dragons shot black, sticky goo that extinguished Kai's flames. They hissed at the sight of his fireballs and focused most of their efforts on snuffing them out. But that didn't stop the dragons from closing in on them. Sage was covered head to toe with goo, and it was hardening. Movement was difficult, and her reaction time was significantly slower.

Kai struggled to use his flames because of the goo quenching them and the fact most of the sprays of goo were directed at him. The pair had killed several of the dragons, but there were so many it seemed as if they were always multiplying. It felt like they'd been fighting forever with no end in sight. Her muscles burned, her heart raced, sweat poured down her face and back, and her body screamed. But she couldn't stop. If she did, she would die.

Then, suddenly, the dragons retreated.

She exchanged glances with Kai tensely. "What are they doing?"

Kai gritted his teeth and adjusted his hold on his sword. "I don't know, but I don't like it!" He shot a constant stream of fire toward the retreating dragons. "Come back, you slithering beasts! Fight us square on!"

Biting the inside of her cheek, Sage scanned the burnt leaves and bushes around them. She was exhausted, but she hadn't used her sense at all. Kai, on the other hand, had been using his sense nonstop and his use of it was becoming more reckless. Surely he had to be exhausted from expending so much energy.

Whenever Sage used her light sense in great capacities for extended periods of time, she could barely walk, let alone fight. Seeing how Kai fought with increasing fervor, she could tell he was strong. Extraordinarily strong. But even strong people grew weary. Yet, aside from the steady stream of steam emanating from him and his heavy breathing, Kai showed no signs of stopping. How much longer could he fight like this?

Should she be using her sense to help? Sage shifted her weight, trying to get a solid grip on her sword's hilt despite her sweaty hands, watching the dragons crouch along the ground. She had never used her sense to attack anyone or anything. She had only used it in aid of her studies or out of enjoyment. Her sense was just another skill to explore and cultivate. Yet, here she was, faced with the need to use her sense in battle—something she wasn't sure she knew how to do. She could create heat and make it sharp enough to cut, but she'd only successfully done that on much smaller scales.

"Argghhhh! Blasted beasts! Where are you going?" Kai bellowed, letting another stream of flames loose. A raging fire spread along the forest around them, causing thick branches to collapse from the trees. It ate away all the grass and leaves and pillars of smoke streamed into the treetops and sky above them. The forest dragons continued to retreat. They hissed like snakes, crouched defensively, waiting.

What were they waiting for?

"Maybe we should attack first," Kai said.

Sage coughed against the smoke burning her lungs and shook her head fervently. "No way! You may not think so, but I know we're both tired. They're toying with us, and we shouldn't cave. If they're going to stare at us, let's wait and gather our strength."

Kai glared at her. "I don't want to wait around like prey."

"We are not waiting like prey. We should allow ourselves a moment to breathe because we need it. And strategize the best way to attack. We shouldn't rush in blindly. What we've been doing so far hasn't been working."

Kai paced back and forth like a caged beast, keeping his gaze on the dragons. Ripping his sleeves off at his elbows, he paused for a moment. "They don't like fire, but this black mush they keep squirting us with puts it out." His face wrinkled as if repulsed when he brushed his hand over some of the goo caught on his clothing and it stuck to his hand. "The flames don't burn it away easily."

"It also makes actions take more energy, like we're trudging through mud."

Kai ignored her. "They avoid their own sludge. If there was a way to get them stuck in their own crossfire, maybe it would give us an advantage." He lifted a leg, and the goo stretched, keeping his foot glued to the ground. "If they can't move, they can't run."

Sage lowered her sword a bit. "That's a good idea. We would need to get in the middle of the dragons but be fast enough to dodge the spurts ourselves," she replied, sighing. "It could work if we weren't already covered with goo."

"Unless," Kai said, glancing up at the trees thoughtfully, "we obstruct their sight somehow, and make it hard for them to see where they're shooting."

Sage's eyes widened and she smiled. "Brilliant!"

Kai's forehead creased. "We still have no way of doing that easily. Saying is one thing. Doing is another."

"No! I mean, I know how we can do it!"

"How?"

Sage turned her gaze toward the glints coming from the dragons' eyes. "I can blind them with my sense," she said.

"Your sense? What is your sense?"

"Light manipulation." Sage held out her hand and formed a ball of light.

Kai stared at her. Then he whacked her on the head. Hard.

"Ow! That hurt!" she yelped, rubbing her new sore spot only to get goo stuck in her hair. She peeled her hand from her head, ripping strands of her hair with it. She cringed.

"*Why* in the bloody hell have you not been using it? Idiot! That would've been helpful, you know." Kai huffed and stabbed the edge of his sword into the ground. "Thanks for finally deciding to bring it up."

"I've never used my sense in combat before. It's unfamiliar territory."

Kai grunted and his gaze darkened. "When it becomes a necessity, one learns quickly." Before Sage could figure out what he meant, Kai shifted his focus back to the dragons. He nodded in their direction and raised his sword once more. "Looks like resting time is over."

The dragons shifted amongst the trees, leaping from branch to branch, releasing chirping calls into the air.

"Or what they were waiting for is finally here." She had a bad feeling. "We should act fast."

"Then let's *go*!" Kai's arms burst into flames, and he poised himself to run. But they couldn't easily charge the dragons because their feet were fixed to the ground by the "sludge," as he called it. Sage closed her eyes and allowed her light energy to fill her. The energy ebbed through her arms and legs. It was worth a try, wasn't it? She opened her eyes, and her body oozed a slight glow. She bent down and released a foot-long, consistent ray from her finger and sliced the goo away from the bottom of her boots, then turned to Kai and freed his feet as well.

Kai peered down at her. "Nice!"

"*Now* let's go!"

Kai didn't hesitate. He took off, full force, toward a cluster of dragons. Sage easily sped after him. The dragons hissed and spat spurts of sludge at them, but as Sage pushed past Kai, she wielded rays of light with her free hand and sliced the streams of goo away, causing them to melt and drip to the forest floor. Kai dove into the cluster of dragons, slashing his sword.

"Sage! Your sense!"

Sage released all the light she had been storing inside and screamed, "Kai, close your eyes!"

In an explosion of light, Sage sliced through as many dragons as she could while they were blinded. Kai fought with an arm over his eyes, releasing blasts of fire. The dragons nearest to him disintegrated into ash. Sage was surprised by how easily her sword swiped through the dragons' scales, as if they were pudding. It wasn't until her sword sliced through a large oak tree's trunk and the entire tree tilted and crashed to the ground that she realized why—somehow, her sword had become a ray, ignited with white light.

The rest of the dragons scrambled away, disappearing into the shadows of the forest. Sage panted as the light around her faded and stared down at her blazing sword. As the energy in her chest dissolved, the glow on the blade also dimmed. Steam rose from the blade. She tapped it, her fingers stinging from its heat, but she was surprised by how firm it still was.

"What was *that*?"

She turned to find Kai staring at her. Her chest squeezed, her lungs struggling against the smoke, and exhaustion weighed down her muscles. Her arms trembled and ached as she held out her sword. She coughed. "I don't really know. I didn't know I could do that."

Kai stuck his sword in the ground, shifted his weight to one leg, and laughed. "I mean, you did say you had never used your sense in combat."

Startled by his laugh, Sage giggled with him. She had only heard his sarcastic laugh so far, but this was a genuine one. His laugh was deep, warm, contagious. And he had a really nice smile. He should use it more often.

"And you said when it becomes a necessity, one learns quickly," Sage added.

"Ha! I'm impressed. I suppose I should've known your sense would be strong if it got you into the top ten." Kai sheathed his sword, still grinning. "I'm actually more surprised it took you so long to rank in the Ten with that sense."

Sage's cheeks warmed as she sheathed her now cool sword. It was the first time any of the princes had complimented her sense. But she supposed he was the first to see it in full force. It made her feel better that Kai thought she deserved her placement, even if she was only pretending to be her brother. Luka's face flickered through her mind. He'd been ignoring her since their arrival in the labyrinth. Would he be impressed if he saw her ability too?

Sage returned Kai's grin.

Kai's smile melted instantly, and he looked away. He coughed. "We should move somewhere safer in case the dragons decide to return." He stepped in the direction of the path, the fire around them sizzling out as he walked away.

Sage cocked her head as she watched him go. Why did his moods swing so rapidly? One moment he was surprisingly pleasant, and the next he was back to his grumpy self. Suppressing a sigh, she followed after him.

Despite his grumpy side, Sage didn't regret her decision to chase after him. She shuddered when she imagined Kai having to fight those dragons alone. He might not have survived.

A rustling noise quivered in the brush behind her. Sage paused and looked back but saw nothing. Just the fire fading from the blackened trees and the ashy bodies of the dragons left behind. Had the dragons been waiting for something? If they were, she didn't want to stick around to find out. Sage turned and ran in the direction Kai had disappeared, not wanting to be left behind.

On the other side of the trees, though, Kai stood waiting for her. Sage bit back the smile that tugged at her lips.

"You brought an interesting collection of sense wielders with you," the whisper hissed. *"Though I only asked for one."*

The traitor narrowed his eyes. Could the creature Everard summoned in the dungeons be speaking to him somehow? He didn't like this at all.

"You may not like it, but my help is necessary for your survival."

I don't need you, the traitor thought back. He could do this without help from the creature. That's why he had insisted on bringing the others, after all.

"Time will show just how much you need me."

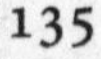

13

Coward

RUBEN TURNED TO SEE CASSIAN POINTING AT A MONSTROUS beast that crouched growling before them. A huge, horrible werewolf twice Ruben's size. A menacing growl rumbled from its throat and its red eyes focused on him. All the time Ruben had spent telling himself to be strong and brave and not to give in to fear was instantly forgotten. Icy terror ripped through him, halting every muscle in his body. His heart thumped deafeningly. He couldn't breathe. Only one thought rang through his mind:

Run.

He spun and sprinted in the opposite direction, ducking between Draven and Luka and running as fast as his feet would let him.

"Ruben!"

The werewolf howled and several more appeared, surrounding them. Two of them blocked his path. He skidded to a stop, trembling so much he fumbled as he pulled out his sword and almost dropped it.

"Ruben!" came another cry, but Ruben didn't dare tear his eyes from the beasts towering over him.

A werewolf pounced at him and knocked him down before he could react properly. A scream tore from him as he pressed his hand against the flat of his sword with all his might to push the wolf's teeth away from his neck and face, a sob rising in his throat. He didn't want to die. He didn't want to die.

A burst of ice exploded to his left, and snarls and the gnashing of other wolves mixed with grunts and thuds. The others...the others were too far away. They couldn't help him. Ruben's eyes blurred with tears, and he cried out again.

The wolf's claws dug into his chest and arms like knives as it strained to snap at his throat. Ruben's chest and arms burned from the scrapes and from using all his might to keep the wolf's mouth away. He couldn't hold out much longer. He was going to die. He was going to die.

Just when Ruben couldn't hold the beast back any longer, a heavy thud vibrated through the werewolf's body and into his sword. The creature yelped. Then, somehow it was off him. Draven stood over him, bleeding, fighting against two more vicious, violent werewolves. He stepped onto their shadows, and the werewolves halted, as if they couldn't move. Luka slid over to them and, with a wave of a hand, used his telekinesis to send the two werewolves sailing through the air. Draven bent and pulled Ruben to his feet before turning to block another attack.

"Get it together, Ruben, or they'll kill you!"

Ruben gripped his sword, but his legs puddled underneath him. Why couldn't he move? Why couldn't he fight? Why was he such a coward? He stared at Luka and Draven. They were ferociously defending him...and he just stood there uselessly. Ruben's gaze swept the battlefield around him. He counted ten werewolves and only three of them were dead so far. His gaze paused on Tenji and Cassian.

Cassian.

The child looked especially tiny alongside the massive werewolves, yet he didn't flee. Shame mixed with Ruben's terror. He was five years older than Cassian, yet here he was, cowering and watching as the younger boy shoved icicles through the werewolves' hearts. He hated being like this.

Get it together, Ruben, or they'll kill you!

Ruben focused on the vines and roots around him and willed them to move. The vines obeyed, scrambling up the legs of four werewolves. Snarling and snapping, the werewolves squirmed frantically against the vines. *Come on, Ruben,* he hissed to himself. *You can do this. You can fight.*

Draven took advantage of the seized werewolves and sank his sword deep into an imprisoned werewolf's heart while Ruben struggled to maintain a grip on their wild, thrashing bodies. He strained every single muscle in his body, hoping to strengthen the vines and keep the werewolves contained. But then, one werewolf slipped from its entanglement and dove toward him. In a panic, Ruben manipulated a thick, tree branch to slap it, but the branch only smacked the werewolf into the earth near his feet. The werewolf lunged and took hold of Ruben's right leg, yanking him to the ground. There was a sickening *snap!* and pain raked through his body.

Ruben screamed.

He released the other two werewolves from their plant prisons, unable to concentrate on holding them anymore. The werewolf who had seized his leg dragged him across the ground and didn't let go. Pain blazed through Ruben's body and made it hard to focus. Ruben clung to his sword and looked down toward his leg, preparing to hack at the werewolf in the vain hope it would free him. But when he saw his leg bending and twisting in a way it shouldn't, he gagged.

Another werewolf turned to face Ruben and stalked closer. Tears spilled from Ruben's eyes and he squeezed them shut. They were going to kill him, and this time, there was no one there to help. He didn't want to die; he wanted to go home and see his parents and sister again.

Then, a bright flash shot through the air, and several simultaneous yelps and howls pierced his ears. Silence fell. Ruben looked down at the werewolf at his feet and found it impaled by several sharp icicles. He sat up slowly and surveyed the battlefield. All the other werewolves were similarly impaled.

He was still alive.

Ruben dropped his sword and pressed a hand to his scraped-up chest to double check. Yes, he was truly alive.

Luka and Draven picked themselves up from the ground and stared at the dead werewolves. Then everyone's gaze settled on the younger boy, who stood panting, his arms making an 'X' in front of him, palms facing outward. He stood like that a moment longer before he lowered his arms. Besides the sweat coursing down the eleven-year-old's face and dampening his white hair, the only evidence of the fight was a slash on his left arm.

He had saved all of their lives.

"Cassian," Luka murmured, then fell silent.

No one else spoke.

Cassian trembled violently before dropping to his hands and knees. His quiet sobs echoed through the silent forest. Only Luka dared to move, kneeling by the young boy's side and resting a hand on his head.

Ruben sat there listening to Cassian's cries, fighting to swallow his own sobs, until his breathing calmed, though his heart took much longer to slow.

The throbs of pain reminded him of his leg. Grimacing, Ruben bent forward to pull the werewolf's jaws open. Then he leaned closer to examine his wound. Tears pricked his eyes. His leg bent unnaturally, and blood spilled from deep gashes in his flesh, making the skin and muscles twist. The world spun about him, and Ruben's head swam. He vomited. He couldn't look at his leg again. If he did, he might faint.

How was he going to get through the labyrinth with this kind of injury? There was no way he could manage it. Ruben gritted his teeth. No, he wouldn't think about how bad this situation was. Staying positive was the only way he would make it out of here alive. Ruben closed his eyes and forced himself to think of things he was grateful for.

He was alive, not dead.

He still had one functioning leg.

If only he could become braver.

Ruben had never enjoyed the sparring lessons required of the princes. He couldn't care less about carrying a sword and preferred to use his plant sense to create beautiful things. However, despite his dislike, Ruben had been quite decent with the sword. He should've been able to hold off the werewolves better than he had. But when he'd looked into the eyes of those beasts, it was like all his training was scrubbed from his mind. All he could think of was running.

Did that make him a coward?

Draven stood, walked over to a tree, and punched it. Everyone looked at him, but no one asked for an explanation, nor did he provide one. Tenji knelt by Ruben's side, grimacing at the sight of his broken leg.

A shiver ran down Ruben's spine. They were only at the beginning of the labyrinth, and he already had a severe injury that would slow the group down and make his chances of survival slim. Would they leave him here to die? Tenji hadn't seemed very keen on staying together so far; Draven and Luka had been the ones to step in and rescue Ruben despite his attempt to flee. Would they decide he was too much baggage to haul around?

Ruben thought of Sage. Despite being a stranger, Sage hadn't deserted back in Phoebus like Archie had. But like Archie, Ruben had left the others to their fate when danger came upon them, almost killing himself in the process. He wished he could be more like Sage, resisting fear and facing danger to save and protect others.

Ruben's mouth was too dry to swallow. He stared at Tenji, dreading what the prince might say.

However, Tenji said nothing. Instead, he pulled off his jacket, spread it out on the ground, and carefully lifted Ruben's leg onto it. Ruben gripped the root of a nearby tree and winced, a tight cry escaping his lips. Tenji wrapped Ruben's leg with the jacket.

Finally, Tenji turned to Cassian and said, "We would've died if it weren't for you. Cassian, we are indebted to you and your bravery. Thank you."

Cassian cried a bit harder, and Luka patted his back.

"Let's continue toward the river. We'll wash our injuries and re-hydrate; let's hope we're not attacked again."

He faced Ruben once more, expression grave. "I know it will hurt to move, but I need you get onto my back."

For once, Ruben didn't care how much it hurt. Tenji wasn't suggesting leaving him behind. His chest trembled, but Ruben shifted his good leg, and, with Tenji's help, pushed himself into a standing position, careful not to put weight on his broken leg.

He slung his arms over Tenji's shoulders, and the older prince hooked his arms under Ruben's legs.

Ruben whimpered, his leg aching. He couldn't bring himself to meet anyone's gaze. It was humiliating, hanging from Tenji's back like a little child, but he couldn't stand on his leg, and he didn't want to be left behind. He tightened his arms around Tenji's neck as they proceeded toward the sound of water.

Ruben stared forward. In the future, he would prove himself. He would show the others he wasn't a deserter. He wouldn't be someone who ran in the face of danger; he would face it straight on. Like Sage. Like Draven. Like Tenji. Like Luka…like Cassian. He would make it up to them—for saving his life, for helping him, for not leaving him to be consumed by the werewolves despite his foolish decision to run. If he pushed himself, he could be bold and brave too. Right?

14

Elements for a Perfect Storm

ARCHIE STRUGGLED TO STAND AS THE OCTOPUS-MONSTER'S immersive waves clobbered him and Tristan. Water choked him and obscured his view, despite his attempts to deflect the waves with his water sense. Tristan stood behind Archie during the surge of waves and then circled in front to block the monster's thrashing tentacles. Archie could think of no easy way to defeat it, even with his water sense. To make matters worse, his hair was a disaster, his skin was wrinkling, and the state of his clothes was beyond horrific.

That foolish scamp, Jovian, leered out of sight in a treetop, chuckling and calling out jokes, not helping whatsoever. Most of his jokes were at Archie's expense.

Archie raised his hands and managed to ward off an overpowering wave, still gagging on water. "Jovian!" He deflected another wave, but water still sloshed down on them. Coughing, he tried shouting again. "Jovian! We need your help, you twit!"

"Water-you worried about? Shouldn't this be easy for you?"

Archie glared in the boy's general direction. Jovian was lounging on a branch, smirking. His stomach curdled. There couldn't possibly be another person in this world who irritated him as much as Jovian did. How could such a young rascal infuriate him this much?

"Jovian!" he bellowed. "This is not a joke! This is the farthest from a joke, you stupid, idiotic jester!"

Jovian's laugh was almost drowned out by the crash of waves. Almost. "I highly doubt that, Archie. It could get much, much, *much* worse."

Diverting another wave, Archie channeled his frustration at the monster. He truly wanted to snag that scamp of a boy and drown him himself. "Argh! That Jovian!"

He glared at the monster and fired a jet of water at the creature's face, but his sense was useless against the monster. They would have to find another way to defeat it. Archie paused, almost forgetting to fend off the oncoming wave. Another way. That was it. Lightning.

"Tristan! Use your sense!"

Tristan only grunted as he continued swinging his sword and cutting through the regenerating tentacles. He spared a look back at Archie.

Another plummeting wave caused Archie to lose his footing and a sharp rock sliced across his leg. Archie hissed. His best trousers had a good-sized rip at the knee, and watery blood flowed down his leg. Yes. Actual *blood*. He was sick of this. "Tristan! Do *something*!"

As if on cue, the sky darkened to a gray-green color. Thunder boomed, and it started drizzling. Flashes of lightning colored the clouds with bright blue strains. While Archie deflected another wave, he watched as Tristan sliced at the tentacles, then angled his sword at the beast. Lightning darted down from the sky and into the octopus-monster, but with the strike of the bolt came electricity that shot through the water, shocking both Tristan and Archie.

Archie flopped onto the soggy ground, convulsing.

"Dammit, Tristan!" he cursed, his body buzzing from the pain. But the monster also writhed, and the waves halted. It worked. Now if they could do the same thing without shocking themselves in the process. That would be preferable.

Jovian howled from somewhere in the trees, grating on Archie's nerves.

Archie scrambled to his feet and glared at Jovian as Tristan struggled to stand. "Is this funny to you?" Archie demanded. He faced the creature once more. "See if you still feel like laughing after watching us die."

The monster straightened, its green eyes glaring, and attacked with another onslaught of waves. Archie jerked to block them.

"Oh my. So dramatic. Very well, my fragile friends."

Right when Archie was about to send another jet of water at the beast, the ground vibrated and a large boulder came out of nowhere, smashing into the monster's gut and scattering into a million pieces. Stray rubble shot back toward Archie and Tristan; they ducked. Some bits struck Archie's skin, but before he could curse Jovian for the sting of the rock, the creature staggered back and tumbled onto the opposite bank.

Archie glanced back at Jovian, who was leaning against the tree calmly, arms folded.

He winked at them. "I guess I could help clean up your mess."

"You scamp!" Archie couldn't resist smiling in relief. He could almost consider forgiving Jovian for cutting his immaculate skin. "*Finally*. That's what I'm talking about!"

Tristan pulled Archie away from the water before directing his hands at the octopus-monster. A torrential flood of bolts came charging down on its body. The creature convulsed once more, but this time, there was no reverberating shock.

Archie grinned. "Let's finish this!"

He puffed up his chest and pulled the water away from the monster so it couldn't use it to defend itself; the water rose like towers on each side of the monster's body. While he pulled the water away, Tristan and Jovian worked together, firing lightning bolts and boulders at the creature. Several small rocks rose from the ground, molding into sharp, dagger-like points. Then, they pelted the beast. It screamed as the rocks cut through its slippery skin and electricity wracked its body. Its wounds weren't healing as quickly as before.

Sparing a glance at Jovian, Archie's stomach dropped. Jovian stood in the tree, smiling wildly, manipulating stones in an intricate, complicated, effortless manner. Archie had forgotten how powerful the other Ten were. Even currently ranked ninth, Jovian used his sense with great ease and control. And Tristan could create an incredible force out of nothing.

Archie needed to be around water to use his sense, and he could only use it at this extent for a brief period of time. His muscles trembled with the effort it took to keep the water away from the beast. He didn't think he could hold it back much longer. Heaviness sank into his stomach. Could he, *the* Prince Archie of Tohaan, the handsomest and most popular of all the princes, actually be the weakest in the Ten?

He hadn't entered the Ten right off the bat at seven years old like most of the others had, gradually working his way into his current ranking. For two consecutive years, he'd jumped forward three spaces. Tristan, on the other hand, entered the ranking right at fifth and soon moved up to fourth, keeping his place solidly for the past ten years. Archie wasn't as smart as many of the others were, and his combat skills were lower than most of them—except for maybe Ruben. If Archie was honest with himself, several of those ranked lower than him could probably easily unseat him if they were older or didn't have such a rude, crappy attitude.

No, he didn't dare think such a horrid thing.

With another rain of rocks and lightning, the octopus-creature crashed against the bank. It was still moving, jerking with electricity and covered in wounds. Tristan shifted his weight, his hands charged with a large ball of electric waves that sent kinetic energy into the air, making some of the hairs on Archie's arm stand on end. Tristan fired the ball at the monster and it convulsed. Then a large rock pierced through the air and struck the creature in the chest with a tremulous *crack!*

The monster didn't move again.

Rocks lowered to the ground, the thunder softened, and the clouds lightened. Archie released the water towers and they crashed down, taking his confidence with them. He used his sense to remove the last of the creature's tentacles from the stream so its dead body wouldn't sit and decay in the water.

Then he sank down on a rock, taking slow deep breaths, his muscles screaming, and his energy depleted. His mind reeled. No, it wasn't true. He deserved his spot in the Ten. Anyway, even if he couldn't match the other members of the Ten with his sense abilities or smarts, he could at least act like he could. Archie brushed his soaking hair out of his face. So much for his ponytail. "I never want to do that again."

"Don't worry," came Jovian's cheerful voice. "It's fish-cabobbed." He jumped down from his tree, and the ground seemed to soften, his feet sinking into the earth, light and silent. He grinned and strolled over to Archie.

Archie promptly gathered his energy and wrestled the younger boy into a headlock. "You twit. I really thought you would desert us back there." After a moment of tussling, Archie released Jovian and allotted the other prince a singular smile.

He had saved their lives, but Archie still hated his guts for taking so long.

Jovian smoothed his hair and touched his swinging braid. "Yes, well, you looked like you needed the extra help. You were getting pummeled."

Archie's ears reddened. "It was a giant octopus-monster, for crying out loud! What was I supposed to do? Drown it?"

"Good point." Jovian chuckled.

Even Tristan smiled as he brushed wet hair back from his face and sat down. Tristan's hair always hung over his forehead, so it was a bit strange to be able to see his forehead clearly.

Then Tristan stiffened and his smile slipped away. He stood, looking back at the forest. Someone trudged toward them.

Archie shot to his feet. "Luka? Draven...what happened?"

Luka, Draven, Cassian, Tenji, and Ruben stumbled out of the trees covered in blood and dirt. Luka carried a trembling Cassian while Tenji carried Ruben whose leg was wrapped with a jacket. Archie's mind scrambled for words, but their battle with the octopus-creature paled in comparison to whatever they had endured. The three of them had walked away from the battle with only a few scrapes and water-soaked clothes; the others' clothing was in shreds and stained with blood. Ugly gashes ripped through their skin in too many places to count.

The beaten group only staggered toward them.

"What did this to you?" Archie asked again, before noticing two people were missing. "And—and where are Sage and Kai?"

Tenji grunted as he helped Ruben lower next to the stream, his own body raked with large slashes. "Werewolves."

Cassian trembled and hugged himself tightly as Luka set him down.

Luka nodded at the dead beast on the other side of the river. "Looks like we're not the only ones who met a creature of the labyrinth."

Archie ignored Luka and gaped at Tenji. His heart quaked in his chest. "Werewolves? Wait—do you mean Kai and Sage…" He couldn't bring himself to finish. Were they…dead? Even if he hadn't ever liked Kai because of all the trouble he caused and his touchy personality, Archie still didn't like thinking of him lying dead somewhere in the forest.

Luka shook his head as he sank down by the river. "No. We don't know where they are or whether they're alive. They left long before the werewolves attacked. But I wouldn't be surprised if they come across something themselves. Hopefully nothing like what we experienced."

Archie swallowed hard. What if they were dead? This was the first time since entering the labyrinth that it occurred to Archie that people could die here. *He* could die. He had been so concerned about living like a poor vagabond that the possibility of death had never even crossed his mind. Guilt and terror slipped into Archie's gut. He shouldn't have run off on his own. What if he'd come across the werewolves first? He would've died instantly. And because of him, the group had separated into smaller, easier to pick off groups.

Frowning, Archie watched as Tenji untied the jacket that was wound tightly around Ruben's leg. Torn flesh, blood, and deep gashes twisted into a gory wound. His leg—or what was left of it—was swollen three times larger than normal, and mottled purple, and bent in a way no appendage should ever bend. Archie cringed. Ghastly.

Ruben shut his eyes tight, crying out. Tristan grimaced and Tenji cursed. Despite being covered in his own deep lesions, Tenji tore Ruben's pants away from the wound and dipped the fabric into the river. He scrubbed away the blood on the fabric, then used it to gently clean Ruben's wound. Ruben hissed in pain.

Archie couldn't watch anymore. He crouched down, gagging as he looked away. "I think I'm going to be sick."

Then he remembered he had a few of his own cuts. He examined his arms and legs. He didn't dare look at his reflection in the water. He feared he'd see a beggar looking back.

"We don't have any bandages," Tristan said.

"Except for the clothes on our backs," came Jovian's solemn voice.

Archie glanced at Jovian, and for once the jester wasn't smiling. Even Jovian could be serious, apparently. A side of him Archie never thought he'd see.

"Keep your clothes," Luka said, shaking his head. "We'll use any herbs we find, the moss from the river, and our own clothes. We will be fine as long as we don't have many more experiences like this."

"Ruben," Tenji's voice was tight, rigid. "Do you know what plants are best for preventing infection?"

Ruben's voice became labored, his words spread between gasps of breath. "…garlic…or ginger…will help."

Archie groaned. He'd forgotten they didn't have doctors or even *bandages* here with them. They would have to take care of their wounds some other way.

Tenji nodded. "I'll go look for one of those." He faced Tristan. "Can you cover me?"

Tristan nodded and they disappeared into the trees. Archie spotted Draven crouched by the edge of the forest, gripping his head. He didn't move for a long time.

Movement from Ruben drew Archie's attention back to the two younger members of their current group. Ruben laid back against the wet grass, throwing an arm over his eyes, and Cassian shuddered. Luka pulled his jacket and shirt off, exposing the deep cuts across his torso.

Archie stared between the three of them, his stomach still churning. He couldn't rid himself of the guilt slinking around his gut. "This is my fault, isn't it?"

Luka looked up at Archie. He stared for a moment and then sighed. "We're safer in a larger group. But those beasts would have attacked no matter what." Luka waved Cassian over to him and the eleven-year-old obediently joined him. Luka pulled up Cassian's sleeve, revealing a long cut. Otherwise, Cassian seemed untouched. "We were lucky Cassian was with us this time around. He saved our lives."

Archie blinked. "Cassian?" The youngest and lowest ranked of them all? *He* was the one who had saved the top three?

Cassian scowled at him. "Just because I'm young doesn't mean I'm weak, dullard."

Archie held in a huff. The little rat. Even though he'd set aside his disgust for children and had been trying to get on Cassian's good side for the past year, it was proving to be a harder challenge than he'd expected. Why did the little twit refuse to like him?

Archie turned away and clenched his teeth, forcing down several nasty remarks.

BOOM!

A far-off explosion echoed through the forest and Archie jerked toward the sound. Smoke billowed above the trees, creating a thick cloud in the sky.

Cassian's voice broke the silence: "Kai and Sage."

Luka nodded. "They're alive."

"But for how much longer?" Jovian asked.

Luka's jaw clenched. "That's a good question."

When Tenji and Tristan returned, Tenji held several long stems with bulky roots. Archie had no idea what they were. All plants looked the same to him.

"We found some garlic," Tenji said. "We'll keep our eyes open for more later." With that, he tossed some of the plants at Luka and walked over to Ruben. "We need to tend our wounds and head out first thing in the morning. If we stay too long, we're sitting prey."

Tenji eyed the river and continued, "We should stay along the river until we can find the path. It's too dangerous to wander in the woods."

No one refuted him.

With Tristan and Tenji's help, the five of them cleaned up and bandaged their wounds. Tenji eyed Archie. "I don't plan to chase after you every time you disappear. However, your sister will never forgive me if I return without you. So, don't be a pain."

Archie wrinkled his nose. "I'm quite capable of taking care of myself." He crossed his arms over his chest. He didn't need their forced relationship to get any more awkward than it already was. Why did his older sister have to be engaged to *Tenji* of all people?

Archie helped Jovian build a fire away from the water-sopped ground, and then Archie caught fish from the river for them to eat. The only distraction from their work was the enlarging stream of smoke rising from the trees in the distance. At one point, Kai's unmistakable yell echoed through the forest.

Tenji shook his head. "Kai brought it upon himself when he decided to go on alone." His gaze met Archie's briefly before he turned back to study the cloud of smoke once more.

Archie pulled at the collar of his jacket. Tenji never failed to make him feel inferior. "Ah, well, he probably realized his mistake. We shouldn't judge him too harshly." Archie let out a nervous laugh. "Who knows? Maybe we'll get to see a mellow Kai later?"

Tenji frowned at him, then grunted. "A mellow Kai? I'll believe it when I see it."

Ruben's weak voice interrupted them, "If he's been fighting all this time and burning down the forest, it must mean the adversary is strong." Ruben laid with his swollen and bleeding leg straight out before him, his arm still slung over his eyes.

Jovian chuckled, stretching his arms behind his head. "Kai would burn down the forest for a lizard. He's probably overreacting."

Luka sighed. "I just hope he didn't desert Sage."

A sudden crack and thud came from the direction of the fire, and the trees shifted with the noise.

Ruben sat up, looking in the direction of the rising flames. "It's something bigger than a lizard, Jovian."

15

A Hostile Reunion

SAGE TRUDGED ALONG THE PATH, THE GOOP FROM THE forest dragons still covering her. Kai and Sage had traveled in silence for a while, both worn out. With only the two of them, they had alternated who rested throughout the night. But even when it was her turn to rest, the fear of the monsters lurking in the forest prevented her from falling asleep. She didn't think Kai got any sleep either because he fidgeted restlessly whenever it was his turn. Sometimes when she'd look at him, his eyes would be open and staring at the branches above them. The longer she was alone with Kai, the more she realized the benefit of being in a larger group.

At last, they spotted a river up ahead. Kai took off toward it and slid to the river's bank before viciously washing the goo from his arms and hands. He cupped his hands and splashed water on his face. "Finally. I thought I'd never be able to clean off this dragon sludge."

Sage joined him by the river and washed her own hands and face, scrubbing vigorously at the stubborn goo. But it felt so nice to be able to remove it from her body. As she cleaned, Kai pulled off his jacket and began scouring the goo from the cloth. Then, he pulled off his shirt.

Alarmed, Sage looked away. She didn't want to see a half-naked man. She closed her eyes. Please let him not be planning to remove any more clothing. She shuddered and her neck and cheeks flushed.

"This stuff is nasty!" Kai scrubbed at his shirt before pulling off his boots to wash them. After that, he cleaned his belt and sword. Finally, he stood and dove into the water. "Ah! This feels amazing. You should try it, Sage!"

"Ah, uh…No, I'm good where I am, thank you."

"Suit yourself."

Sage focused her attention on removing the goo from her clothes without taking anything off. Brushing the water toward her, she splashed it over her shoes while she ignored the sounds of Kai splashing about the water. Somehow she'd forgotten she was stuck in a labyrinth with princes who thought she was a man—which meant she would be forced to experience many similarly awkward moments. She took a deep breath.

She couldn't act like a girl would or they'd discover her.

Kai looked in her direction, his red hair like fire over the water, and watched her brush the water onto herself. "That's very inefficient. It'll take ten times longer the way you're doing it."

Sage frowned and swished the water onto her sleeves. "Let me do it how I like."

He splashed water in her direction and turned away. "Sure, whatever."

Just then, voices echoed in the distance.

Kai moaned. "Ugh…they caught up to us."

Sage stood, a relieved smile flickering across her face. The others were fine. She looked down the river bend and made out vague silhouettes coming their way.

"It *is* them!" For Kai's sake, she tried not to sound too excited.

He only groaned again and swam back to shore.

As the group came closer, her smile fell. They looked ruffled and messy and very un-princely. Jovian caught sight of her first.

"Well, if it isn't Number Seven!"

The others noticed her, and Ruben waved and smiled, his expression strained. Luka, despite looking beat up, was as handsome as ever. His blond hair was messy—but in a cute way—and his determined face and angular features made her heart flutter. She hadn't realized how good it would be to see him again.

The group stopped when they reached her, catching sight of Kai grumpily squeezing the water from his shirt and jacket. However, no one greeted him, and he didn't greet them in return.

"Is now really the time for a bath, Kai?" Jovian smirked.

Archie grimaced at the river. "I wouldn't be doing that if I were you…"

"I do what I want," Kai muttered.

"You don't look too banged up considering the explosions we heard yesterday," Archie added, looking him up and down.

Sage blinked. "You could hear us?"

Archie made a face when he turned to her. "You, on the other hand, look terrible. *You* need a bath. What's all this gross stuff on you?"

Pulling on his wet shirt and jacket, Kai glanced over at her. "Something worth washing off."

Looking past Jovian and Archie, Sage couldn't help but stare at each of them. While Archie, Tristan, and Jovian looked ruffled but unharmed, the rest were bandaged with bloody shirts and jackets. If their shirts or jackets weren't being used as bandages, they were blood-stained and shredded. Even little Cassian had a bandage around his arm. Draven blended in with the shadows of the trees, and Tristan supported Ruben who wasn't putting any weight on one of his legs. The leg was securely wrapped, and Ruben's shredded shirt and jacket exposed several bloody bandages all over his chest and arms. He looked the worst out of them all.

"What—What happened to you?" she asked faintly.

Tenji looked in the direction they had come, crossing his arms over his chest. "We were attacked by creatures of the forest. I assume you were also." He turned his orange eyes back to her.

She nodded. "Forest dragons."

Luka's expression hardened and his gaze locked onto Kai. "I'm glad you didn't desert Sage as well."

Kai said nothing, busy pulling on his boots. "I'll be on my way then."

Sage's heart dropped to her boots. "No! Don't!" she cried, turning and reaching out to stop him. "We—we should stay together. It's our best chance for survival."

Kai paused but said nothing. She hadn't meant to sound so desperate, but the idea of Kai disappearing into the forest alone meant he would definitely get into trouble and may actually die. She couldn't let him go. Especially after seeing the condition of the other five princes. Who knew what other beasts the labyrinth had?

"Sage is right," Luka agreed, stepping closer. "Several of us almost died yesterday. You'll never survive on your own."

Still refusing to face them, Kai clenched his fists. "Fine, whatever. I guess I'm stuck with you nitwits."

Sage let out a breath of relief. She really didn't want to strike out alone with him again—it was too dangerous and too exhausting. But she also didn't want Kai going on by himself.

Tenji stepped to the front of the group. "We should keep moving. There are many dangerous creatures lurking in this forest and in the river. We can't afford to be attacked again."

"In the river?" Sage studied the ripples of the water's surface. There didn't seem to be anything dangerous in it. At least, not that she could see.

Archie side-stepped away from the bank. "Ah, yes…I'd rather not wake another beast of the river."

"Of course, *you* wouldn't," Jovian smirked. He cocked his thumb at Archie, turning to Sage. "Water-boy here was almost drowned by a giant octopus-monster."

Both Sage and Kai stepped away from the river just as Archie tackled Jovian, pulling him into a headlock. "You little twit!"

Ignoring Archie and Jovian's rough play, Draven strode out of the shadows and along the river's edge. "We should move."

Sage flinched and stepped away from Draven as he passed by. Draven glanced at her. Ashamed of her reaction, Sage's cheeks flamed and she dropped her gaze. But he said nothing to her.

Draven and Tenji led the way with the group trailing behind. Sage stood still, waiting for Ruben to reach her. Ruben, his arm slung over Tristan's shoulders, limped toward her.

"Ruben, are you okay? What happened?" she asked.

"I'm fine," he replied, breathlessly. The pained expression interrupting his smile told her otherwise. "We were attacked by werewolves."

She gasped. "Werewolves?"

He grimaced and nodded. "Big ones. It was horrific." He shuddered as if reliving the horror of the experience. "But we're all alive, only one of my legs is injured, and we've reunited with everyone." He turned to face her and flashed a smile that told Sage he was genuinely happy to see her.

Warmth spread through Sage's chest. She smiled back. However, as she scanned Ruben's injuries, her smile faltered. How she wished she could help him heal all his injuries. Yet, despite having the potential to heal, she still didn't know how to. Maybe if she practiced while she was here, she could get to the point where she could help heal the others.

Suddenly, she remembered she still had that healing book, hidden inside her jacket. She unconsciously reached up to touch the outline of the cover through the fabric of her jacket. She'd forgotten about the book in the wild chaos of their kidnapping and the labyrinth. Maybe the book would be able to help her understand how to access her healing powers.

Tristan adjusted his grip on Ruben and gave her a polite nod. "You don't look too banged up. The forest dragons…were they difficult?"

Sage looked down at herself. Other than the black goop that had refused to come off her clothes, she had nothing to show from her earlier battle. No doubt thanks to Kai. "Yes, very. They shot black sludge that slowed you down and made you stick to everything." She glanced toward Kai, who walked a little bit ahead of them near Cassian and Archie. Even his back looked grumpy. The moment the others showed up, he'd morphed right back into his usual sullen self. Why did he dislike them so much?

"I can see that," Tristan replied.

Then Sage realized she had been staring at Kai too long and darted her gaze to Ruben. Her battle with the dragons couldn't quite compare to the disaster the werewolves had left behind. "How did you defeat *werewolves*?"

"I didn't. If Cassian hadn't been there…" Ruben shuddered. "I would be dead." Sage turned her gaze to Cassian. His white hair contrasted sharply against the green of the forest, and his shoulders curved as if beneath a great weight. How had this child saved them?

Cassian turned his head toward them, probably overhearing their conversation, and their eyes met.

Once again, Sage's brother came to mind. When she imagined him going through a similar experience, her throat burned. Unable to resist, she sped up and pulled Cassian into a hug.

At first, Cassian stiffened and held his head away from her. He didn't say anything, but stared at her as if she was crazy. And honestly, she probably was. But she couldn't stop thinking about her little brother, the real Sage.

Then Cassian moved. Sage thought he would push her away, but he clung to her arms and his shoulders trembled. Faven's heart tugged at her, and her eyes welled with tears.

The group was forced to stop walking, but for once, no one complained. No one shamed Cassian for crying. Instead, they all looked away and let him cry.

"Something is following you. Be wary. I can't have all of you dying."

The traitor scanned the forest around them but saw nothing. As much as he hated that the spirit was the one providing the warning, he wasn't stupid enough to ignore it. He would need to be cautious.

16

Discord and Some Berries

ONE MORNING, SEVERAL DAYS LATER, SAGE SAT BY ONE of the campfires, sharpening her sword with a wet stone she'd retrieved from the riverbed. Cassian sat on her right, busy cracking nuts, and Ruben lay to her left, his injured leg propped up on a rock as he laid back with his arm thrown over his eyes. Most of the others had just woken and were preparing for another long trek.

Jovian lounged in a tree—which seemed his favorite place to be—avoiding as much responsibility as he could while munching on a random apple. Faven had no idea where he'd gotten it, and Jovian didn't seem inclined to share. Archie, Tristan, and Tenji sat around another campfire, cooking fish Archie had caught for them but refused to catch for others—because he wasn't everyone's "slave."

Archie's voice carried over the campsite as usual, "I smell wretched. I never thought I'd see the day I would look and smell like a beggar."

Tristan sliced open and gutted a fish, saying nothing, while Tenji closed his eyes, pinched the bridge of his nose, and took in a deep breath. "Please be quiet, Archie."

On the other side of the camp, Luka stoked his own fire, alone. Sage had offered for him to sit with them, but he'd ignored her and built his own. She wasn't sure how she'd gotten on his bad side. She must've done something because he refused to speak to or even listen to her. But she was working to remedy it.

As for Kai, he crouched near his own fire, forcing himself to eat something that looked less than edible. He usually gathered his own food, lit his own fires, and did everything on his own. The only way he ever participated with the group was by walking with them or arguing with Luka.

"Do you want some, Sage?" Cassian asked, bringing her wandering focus back to him. He held out a handful of cracked nuts.

Sage smiled at him. "Only if you've had enough."

Ever since their hug, he must've decided he liked her, because he'd followed her around ever since. He even taught her a few easy tracking techniques as they traveled. She scraped the rock against her sword, allowing the achy burn in her arms to hide the painful squeeze of her stomach. Since Archie refused to provide everyone with fish and Ruben was down because of his injury, finding food hadn't been easy. Though Ruben *had* been teaching her how to identify certain plants.

Cassian reached over and poured the nuts on a rock near her. "You can have it." He cracked another one and popped it in his mouth.

"Thank you." Sage put down her whetstone and tossed the nuts into her mouth. Maybe it would ease the intensity of her hunger.

"My sister hates nuts," Cassian continued. "She always gives her share to me." He grinned, and it wasn't hard to see how much he adored his sister.

"You must be close to her." Sage eyed her blade, finally satisfied with her work. When she raised her head to look at Cassian, she lowered the sword hastily at the sight of a quiet and withdrawn Cassian. He turned his face away and hugged his knees to the chest. Had she offended him somehow? "What? What's wrong?"

"Nothing," Cassian mumbled, resting his chin on a knee. "I'm fine."

Unconvinced, Sage bit her lip, and her forehead creased. Was it because of what she said about his sister?

Draven chose that moment to stride into camp and slump beneath a tree, busying himself with braiding a multicolored thread. Faven frowned. A few nights ago, Draven vanished during the night and didn't return until dawn. When asked about his reason for his disappearance, their questions were met with a cold stare and a brusque: "It isn't your concern."

This odd behavior had continued each night since. Faven eyed the small colorful strands he intently braided—a hobby she hadn't expected from a moody, shadowy man like him.

Ruben groaned and Sage turned her focus to him. Even with the sticks bracing his leg, he couldn't walk by himself, and several members of the group traded off helping him. Despite the help, Ruben needed frequent breaks and slowed them down drastically.

At first, he had maintained a positive outlook and would offer light encouragement to others despite the pain he was in. However, his smile had become stale and drained, and he kept to himself more, taking advantage of any moment he could to rest.

She studied his bloodied bandage. "How's your leg?"

Ruben sighed before removing his arm from his eyes and staring up at the branches above them. "It hurts."

"Did you check it today?"

There was a pause. "No, not yet." Ruben turned his face away from her. "Tenji said he would help check it before we continue on."

Although Tenji seemed to know a great deal more than anyone else about taking care of injuries, he was far from a doctor.

Sage's grandfather rose to mind and she tightened her grip on the hilt of her sword. The days leading up to his death were still fresh and raw in her mind. The stench of his aromatic medicine, his stillness, the long periods of spooning him soup and water, the days of wondering if any of their attempts were helping him at all, the hopelessness of seeing no progress. She hadn't learned about her healing ability until after his death, but she'd vowed she'd learn the skill so next time she'd be able to do something. She never wanted to fail someone she cared about again.

Sage's gaze dropped to a dead plant near her feet. She'd been flipping through the healing sense book whenever she could find time, or when others weren't paying attention to her. According

Ice manipulation. Sage scanned the others in their group. She knew Kai's, Ruben's, Tristan's, and Archie's senses, but the others' senses were still a mystery. Maybe Cassian could tell her. She leaned in and lowered her voice, "What can everyone else do?"

"Why don't you tell us yours?" Tenji asked.

Sage jumped, whirling to face Tenji who was standing behind her. He frowned down at her, his orange gaze piercing into her soul.

"In fact, I don't think I know anything about you, Prince Sage."

Several of the other princes turned their attention to them.

A chill seized her heart. She shouldn't have been so nosy. Now she'd brought the focus of the other nine toward her and her suspicious appearance and behavior. Surely, they'd noticed odd differences between her and them.

"My sense?" Clearing her throat, Sage hastened to squash her panic. They were only asking about her sense. She could answer that. "I can manipulate or imitate light."

Archie burst into a fit of laughter, but Tenji and Luka only frowned. Immediately, heat crept to her cheeks, and Sage fidgeted with her hands. Tristan, Ruben, Draven, and Cassian looked at her, as if waiting for a deeper explanation, but she couldn't bring herself to meet their gazes.

"Light?" Archie snorted. "What kind of sense is that?"

The heat amplified and light emanated from her.

Jovian's smirking voice could be heard from the trees. "What do you do? Turn into a lantern?"

Her light brightened and she clenched her fists. "No—"

Archie laughed harder. "Look! He's lighting up like a firefly! How do you get into the Ten with a sense like that? There's no way—" He paused, and his face contorted into mock astonishment. "Unless…you *did* something! What did you do? Bribe them? How much money did it take?"

"I didn't—"

Tenji turned away, suddenly disinterested. "How useless."

Sage trembled, her insides burning, and tears pricked her eyes. But she couldn't find any words to refute theirs. Anything she said would only fall flat. Instead, her gaze darted to Kai, the one person who had witnessed her sense, and then Luka, hoping one of them would jump to her defense. They only avoided her gaze.

They were all jerks. All of them.

Standing, Sage glared at Tenji and Archie, before she spun around and marched away from the group, tears threatening to spill. While she didn't want to cry at all, she definitely didn't want them to *catch* her crying. It would only show them how much their words had hurt her.

Her feet sped up as the tears spilled. But as she hurried away, she overheard Tristan say, "If the Royal Council put him in the top ten, then they believed he deserved the spot."

Those words held her together. As she walked, her mind cleared, and she was able to swallow her tears. At least someone had defended her instead of cowering in fear or pride. She remembered how impressed Kai had been when he'd seen her sense before. He'd thought she deserved her high-ranking spot.

She'd just have to prove it to the others.

Sage waited for the evidence of her tears to fade when a sudden, mortifying thought struck her. What if they left her behind? She turned and raced back toward camp, even though she wasn't ready to face them again. Dealing with those jerks would be less scary than being left alone in a forest of monsters.

A distinctive rustle brushed the leaves above her. She stopped and searched the branches. Nothing. But then, a strange sensation oozed over her, and she jerked, half-expecting to find a pair of eyes watching her. Again, nothing. This was disturbingly similar to the feeling she'd had after the battle with the forest dragons. She hadn't been able to shake the sensation since and here it was again. Was there something following them?

She searched a moment longer, but when she couldn't find anything, she shook her head. Maybe she was just spooked.

When she returned to camp, everyone was still there and Sage relaxed slowly. They hadn't left.

Though no one spoke to her, Tenji announced it was time to head out. He'd taken over leading most days. He also organized night watches. It was Tenji who finally said they only needed to stick together, not like each other—much to Luka's distaste. But in that moment, Sage agreed. She didn't have to like them, but she *did* need to stay with them.

Ruben offered Sage a friendly smile as Tristan helped him stand, and Tristan nodded in her direction. He didn't speak to Sage often and seemed to be more comfortable with talking to Cassian or Archie, but she would never forget how he'd been the only one to stand up for her. So she smiled and nodded back.

As they headed out, Cassian slipped close to her side. "Can you make light out of nothing?" he asked.

Sage considered his question. "In a way. I can feel the energy inside me and use it to create light."

Cassian stared at the ground as he walked, his face scrunched in thought. "I create ice by gathering the water in the air and freezing it."

Somehow, in that simple exchange, Cassian erased any of Sage's remaining irritation. It made her want to hug him again. But she didn't.

The group trekked along the river, following every curve, only stopping when they had to. Eventually, they came across what looked to be a trail leading through the forest.

Tenji surveyed the riverbed and then the trail. "I say we move to the path. That's what will lead us out of the labyrinth."

"The path?" Luka's head snapped toward Tenji. "Are you sure? The river is the best source of food and water we have right now. If we move away, we'll lose that resource."

Kai rolled his eyes, crossed his arms, and leaned against a tree. "Blah, blah, blah. Just do as the old man says. He knows more about the labyrinth than all of us put together. What do you know?"

Jovian cackled and muttered, *"Old man,"* but Tenji didn't even blink.

Luka glared at Kai. "I know that we need food and water."

"Actually," Archie interrupted, fidgeting as he looked in the direction of the path. "I'm with Luka on this one. The path doesn't seem safe."

"Pfft," Jovian sneered, fingering his braid and flashing a smile. "The only reason *you're* on Luka's side is because you're scared to be without a water source for your sense."

"Shut up, twit!"

Archie swung a fist but Jovian nimbly dodged it.

Tenji held up a hand, immediately commanding silence from the group. "The path is the quickest way out of the labyrinth," he said, gesturing toward it. His voice was cool and calm despite the opposition he was receiving. "We'll find food and water along the way. It's better than wandering blindly in circles."

Luka, still not fully convinced, looked away. "If you think that's for the best. I just want to be sure we're making the right decision. The goal is to get through *alive*." Luka took a careful step toward the path.

"You're such a wimp, Luka," Archie moaned, slapping a hand over his face. "The one time I back you up, you chicken out just because Tenji is a better leader than you."

Luka stiffened but continued toward the path, his knuckles turning pale as he tightened his fists. Sage searched for something reassuring to say, but Kai spoke before she had time.

"He's just afraid that if he stands against Tenji, no one will follow him." Kai turned to face Luka as the crowned prince halted. "Your father being king doesn't instantly make you a leader, daddy's boy. You're more like a flower trying to stand tall but shifting whichever direction the wind blows. A weakling who does whatever gets him the most attention."

Sage stared at Kai. Why did he hate Luka so much?

Luka didn't turn. He stood there as silence fell on them. Finally, he faced Tenji, ignoring Kai. "Which way, leader?"

Tenji stared at Luka and didn't say anything for a moment, then his eyes darted away. "This way."

The rest of the day passed in awkward silence, though Ruben did try breaking it from time to time by making passing comments. Sage did her best to respond, and Tristan, who was helping him that day, would offer a small smile. No one else even pretended to listen.

They tramped downhill, further into a vale in the forest. Sage shivered at the sight of the hills surrounding them. They better not stay in the vale too long. She hated being on low ground.

That night, they set up camp and Tenji organized the night watches as usual. Luka remained silent, just as he had the rest of the day, which was very unlike him. Sage watched him carefully. Why was she worrying about him when he'd ignored *her* when she needed defending? But if she said nothing, she wouldn't be any better than the others. Before she could talk herself out of it, Sage trudged over to him as he busied himself building and stoking a fire.

"Luka..."

He looked up at her, then away.

"I just wanted to say that I think you're a good leader. Don't listen to the others."

He stilled, but didn't look up.

She paused a moment longer and bit her lip. This was a mistake. "That's all I wanted to say." She turned to leave.

"Sage…thanks. And…I'm sorry."

She turned back to find Luka standing, looking down at her, the fire illuminated his blond hair like a golden crown on his head. "For what?"

Luka ran a hand through his hair and his gaze dropped. "For earlier…and actually for everything else too. I haven't been the nicest to you since…well, since we came here." He stared down at the flickering flames. "I'd been expecting Michal to be with us the whole journey here. When I discovered you were here instead, I didn't know how to process it. I was upset that you knocked him from the Ten, but glad he wasn't in the labyrinth…" Luka trailed off, then shook his head. "I've been taking my frustration out on you." He met her gaze again. "You had no choice in the Royal Council's decision, and I should've been more welcoming." He paused. "The labyrinth is hard enough without isolation."

"Oh," Sage breathed, biting her lip. Was that why he hadn't spoken to her since their arrival? "Well, yes, I didn't have a say, but I accept your apology. Thank you for that…few people admit their wrongs easily." She frowned in the direction of the others, many of whom she was sure would have a terribly tough time apologizing.

Luka smiled. "Thank you, then. For not being like the others."

Sage returned his smile and went back to her campfire, her insides warmed by his acceptance and kind words.

It was then Archie exploded into the campsite holding a branch of what looked like blackberries.

"Look what I found!" he exclaimed, looking proud of himself. His lips and fingers showed evidence that he had already eaten some. He held it out to Tristan who picked a berry from the branch and popped it into his mouth after a quick examination. "Berries!"

Tenji jumped up. "Don't!"

Archie and Tristan both paused and looked at him. Archie's grin melted into a scowl. "What now?"

"You can't eat whatever you find!" Tenji snapped. "You don't know what could be in it."

Ruben sat up straighter. "Let me see them."

Archie sighed and walked over to him. He held out the branch. Ruben picked one berry and examined it. As he studied the fruit, his forehead creased and his lips thinned. He looked back up at Archie.

"It's poisonous."

17

The Stalkers Strike

POISON? SAGE STARED AT ARCHIE'S BLACKENED FINGERS and the residue around his mouth. Dawning horror spread across Archie's face.

"What?" Archie squeaked, taking a step back.

"It's a rare poisonous berry called Black Venom. I've never seen one in person before now," Ruben continued, looking down at the berry in his hand.

Tenji snatched the branch from Archie and tossed it into the fire. "What did I tell you?" he snarled. Closing his eyes, he pinched the bridge of his nose and moaned. "Ah, such idiots…"

Archie stared at the fire as the branch, leaves, and berries burned. "But—but I already ate some!"

Tenji scowled and whacked Archie on the head. "That is why you don't eat everything you see!" he barked, then looked back at Ruben. "Do you know the side effects and intensity?"

He returned Tenji's gaze. "It starts with abdominal pain, nausea, and vomiting. Then fevers and body aches come a little while later. Lastly, your throat closes, and you have difficulty breathing. Most of the time, it ends with death."

"Wait, wait, wait!" Archie cried, holding up his hands and taking another step back. "*Death*?"

Luka stood and gestured for Archie to sit. "Don't panic. We'll figure this out."

"Panic?" Archie laughed, his hands shaking. "No, no, I'm not panicking. Just mildly concerned about the fact I could be *dying*!"

Releasing a slow sigh, Tenji rubbed a hand over his face. "Is there a cure, Ruben?"

"I'm not entirely sure. My books never specified one."

"I'm doomed!" Archie wailed, dropping to his knees and gripping his head. "I'm going to die! I don't want to die!"

Sage's chest deflated. If only she had figured out how to heal, then maybe she could fix him. Why was it so hard to revive dying plants? Did she really have the capability to do that? If only the book had clearer instructions. She reached for the book in her jacket, ready to search through it again.

Ruben shook his head. "No, no, don't give up yet," he reassured Archie. "I can go scavenging and see if I can find something with strong combating or healing properties. My sense allows me to understand the makeup of plants. I'm sure I can find something."

Luka nodded. "Okay, we can assign a group to go with Ruben and a group to stay and watch Archie. Tristan, you had one as well?"

Tristan gave a slight jerk of confirmation.

Tenji sighed. "Very well. Luka, you should stay here with them. If trouble comes and they're unable to move, you would be able to get them to safety with the greatest ease." He turned, pointing to the others as he called more names. "Kai, Jovian, Draven, you stay behind and help Luka look after Archie and Tristan. I'll go with Ruben to look for an antidote. Sage, Cassian, you come with us."

Sage started when Tenji called on her. He wanted her to come with them?

Kai stepped closer to the group, crossed his arms, and rolled his eyes. "I don't want to babysit people who were idiotic enough to eat something they shouldn't have."

Pivoting to face Kai, Tenji's expression became icy. "Correct me if I'm wrong, but are you saying if you happened to eat something you shouldn't have, we have permission to leave you behind? This is helpful information. I'll keep it in mind for the future." He paused, giving room for Kai to object. When he didn't respond, Tenji shot a glance at Jovian and Draven. "Are you two good?"

Jovian smirked. "I'm great."

Draven didn't argue. Instead, he looked up from his haphazard attempt to braid the multicolored threads in his hands and studied the growing shadows. "Be quick."

Archie gave a noisy groan as he crouched down. "Oh, I feel woozy."

"Stop being so dramatic, water wuss," Jovian snickered, fingering his braid. "Do you see Tristan having a meltdown?"

Tenji waved Sage, Cassian, and Ruben after him, and he moved away from the fires. "Let's go."

Not wanting to be barked at for moving slowly, Sage scrambled up and helped Ruben stand. She supported him as best she could as the four of them left the campsite. Her lips pressed into a thin line as she studied Tenji's broad shoulders. Since he'd said she was the most likely to be the traitor and called her sense useless, she'd been under the assumption he didn't like her. So why did he want her to tag along?

Sage looked back at the campsite one last time before it vanished from view. Then, from the corner of her eye, a shadow brushed through the branches of the trees. Sage jerked her head toward it but found nothing. She frowned. Had she imagined it? She scanned the lining of the trees once more to no avail. Her nerves must be getting the better of her. She shivered in the dimming light and turned her focus back to following Tenji.

The more the sunlight faded, the harder it was to identify the plants, and the jumpier Sage became. She glowed, casting a soft circle of light over and around them. Tenji, Ruben, and Cassian glanced in her direction, but she said nothing and neither did they.

The forest grew darker outside her sphere of light, and Sage imagined countless monsters hiding inside those shadows. Part of her wished Tenji had let her stay by the bright fires. The others—particularly Kai, Archie, and Jovian—could be rather boisterous, which surprisingly pacified her terror whenever the sun went down. However, the silence stretched with Tenji, Ruben, and

Cassian. And with the silence, the darkness only buzzed louder and towered higher, as if ready to suffocate her. Her grip on Ruben tightened.

Ruben led the way as best he could. He told them which direction he wanted to look, and they helped him move. If he asked to stop or be lowered down, they listened.

After a long while, they were still empty-handed. They were forced to stop and rest since Ruben's leg made it difficult and painful for him to walk, and he had already spent most of the day walking.

While they rested, Sage crouched next to Ruben and noticed Cassian's gaze continuously dart toward even the slightest rustle. The shadows were longer, and a cool breeze blew from the tops of the trees causing them to shiver. Even Tenji seemed tense. He remained standing and stared back in the direction they had come.

"We should head back," he said finally. "We've looked as long as we can in the dark." He paused before adding, "I have a bad feeling."

Sage nodded in agreement, ready to get back to the fires and more people. She studied Ruben. He was breathing heavily, sweat dripping from his curly, light green hair, and wasn't speaking much. She could tell how much pain he was in by how ashen his face was and by the way he gripped the grass beneath him. He couldn't keep doing this. It was too taxing on his weakened body. But Ruben shook his head.

"No, I can find it. Let's go just a little bit farther."

"They could already be dead." Tenji gestured to him. "Ruben, you're barely making it. If we're attacked by a monster or more of those werewolf-beasts, we'll be slaughtered. Even if I used my sense, I'm not sure I would be able to help. It was a miracle Cassian was able to save us last time."

Ruben looked Tenji in the eye. "I can find it," he said, heaving heavy breaths. "Just a bit farther…please."

Tenji shook his head, but before he could object, Sage stood. If Ruben wanted to keep looking to save Archie and Tristan's lives, then he would, even if it meant she had to keep wandering in the dark.

"I'm here too. I can help if we are attacked. Let's try going a little farther. For Archie's and Tristan's sakes."

"Not against those werewolves, you won't," Tenji scoffed. "They're too powerful for mere sword play. A light sense won't stop them."

Sage clenched her jaw and gripped the hilt of her sword. "You don't know what I can do, and yet you judge so harshly."

"I don't need to see to know what light can do. Honestly, I think the fourth son of King Léon would be more useful to the top ten than a candle." His orange eyes were brutal as he glared down at her. "Do you think I've forgotten you're the most likely among us to be the traitor? I won't entrust anyone's life to you."

Sage felt as if she'd been punched. Her heart stopped, her breath stilled, and she couldn't focus. Acid boiled in her stomach.

She was tired. Tired of being doubted, pushed around, and looked down on. She was tired of pretending to be a prince. She was tired of shrinking into the shadows to avoid the piercing gazes of the others.

She. Was. *Tired*.

Sage's fingers tightened into fists and she met Tenji's unwavering glare. "I can see why you think I'm an easy target to dump all the guilt on. Go ahead and think whatever makes you feel better about the fact you were captured and deposited here. However, I'm not going to sit by quietly while you mock me." She jabbed a fist to her chest. "Do you think I want to be here? Have you stopped to consider that I don't want to be in a dangerous labyrinth with a bunch of spoiled, obnoxious princes who only know how to argue and bicker and put others down? Yet here I am. And I'm not going to be treated like dirt just because I'm the new one. Leave me and my sense alone."

Something flickered in Tenji's eyes as she spoke, and he leaned back. Crossing his arms over his chest, he studied her and didn't say a word. His stare made her uncomfortable, as if he was seeing right through her and her disguise. So, she bent down and helped Ruben stand. "Let's keep looking, Ruben."

Cassian shrugged at Tenji and followed them. "The obnoxious ones are Jovian, Archie, and Kai," he offered. His eyes narrowed as he added, "*Especially* Archie."

Ruben laughed despite the sweat dripping down his freckled face. "We know who *your* least favorite is, Cassian."

Those two brightened her mood and a small smile slipped onto her face. Sage gave a quick glance back at Tenji whose brow furrowed as he stared at the ground, as if deep in thought. Had she said too much? She'd been unable to keep the words from spilling out; she'd been too angry. However, she'd also believed he wouldn't be affected by anything she said. He was too stubborn and single-minded to listen to anything that came out of her mouth. Maybe he was thinking of a way to quietly dispose of her…

A few moments later, Ruben pointed to a nearby bush. She brought him over to it and he released his grip on her, tumbling toward the bush. He beamed. "This is it! This is what we need!"

Tenji pushed Sage aside and crouched next to the bush. "Which part of it?"

"The roots and leaves are both helpful in combating poison. We should take both."

Tenji broke off several branches and handed them to Ruben, who then handed them to Sage.

Tenji sat back and said, "You can get the roots, correct?"

Ruben nodded and before Sage could ask how he would manage that, the roots climbed out of the dirt and into his hands all on their own.

"Incredible," Sage breathed, and Cassian nodded in agreement, his eyes wide. Then Cassian pulled the branches from Sage's arms.

"I'll carry these since you're helping Ruben walk."

Tenji cut the bush from the roots and stood. "Let's hurry back."

They rushed through the forest as quickly as Ruben's injuries would let them. After they'd been walking for a while, Cassian halted and pointed upward. "The sky!"

The group came to an abrupt stop. An orange glow illuminated the darkness over the trees and Sage's stomach twisted.

The others.

Tenji drew his sword and raced in the direction of the glow, leaving Ruben, Sage, and Cassian fumbling after him.

As they drew closer to camp, the orange glow outlined the trunks of the trees and a distinct crackling hissed and sputtered before them. The all-too-familiar smell of smoke choked the air; Sage shoved down her rising alarm. What scene would meet them?

When they burst into the campsite, broken, flaming trees surrounded the camp and the uneven, busted ground was littered with arrows and spears. A large branch tumbled to the ground from one of the flaming trees, sending sparks. In the middle of the wreckage stood Tenji, surveying the destruction.

He faced them. "Gone. They're all gone."

"Gone?" Ruben squeaked.

Another quick scan of the site showed no sign of any bodies, not even charred ones. Just arrows and spears. "How can they be gone? Were they taken?" Sage's heart pounded, and she forced herself to draw in several deep breaths despite the thick, choking smoke that burned her lungs. Were they dead?

As she picked up an arrow, a thought occurred to her. These weapons weren't something dragons or werewolves used. "Could there be humans in the labyrinth?"

Cassian bent to pick up a small dart and held it up. He sniffed it. "This is coated with a sleeping potion."

Tenji joined them and pulled the dart from Cassian's grasp. "He's right."

"A sleeping dart?" Sage frowned. "What else could be living in the labyrinth that has enough brains to create weapons?"

"Goblins," Tenji muttered. He gestured to the litter of weapons around the campsite. "Look at the size, the rough design. These are goblin-made."

"Don't goblins live in the mountains?"

"There are mountains not far from here," Cassian said, gesturing vaguely into the distance. "I saw them earlier."

How had Sage missed seeing an entire *mountain*?

"What are we going to do now?" asked Ruben, leaning most of his weight on his good leg. His free hand squeezed the hilt of his sword.

"We're going to rescue them, obviously," Sage declared. They stared at her, and she stared back, daring them to protest. "We can't survive the labyrinth without them, and I refuse to leave them behind."

To her surprise, Tenji nodded. "Yes, we'll need to rescue them."

"How?" asked Cassian. "There are only four of us. The goblins took down six of them. Four of whom are the top five highest-ranked princes. We need to know how many goblins there are or where they're at before we can even hope to come up with a good plan."

Tenji eyed the weapons around them once more. "Yes, but they had sleeping darts, not to mention the element of surprise."

He held up the dart as if to make a point. "This time, *we'll* be the ones to take *them* by surprise."

"How?" Sage asked. How on earth could they surprise an unknown number of goblins who most likely had a lair filled with guards and scouts? Not to mention the fact that the native goblins knew this forest a million times better than the princes did.

Tenji twisted the dart in between his fingers. "I have the beginnings of a plan." He nodded to the floor. "Let's gather some of the darts they left behind."

Ruben pointed to the branches in Cassian's grasp. "What about Tristan and Archie? They still need an antidote for the poison. It might already be too late by the time we reach them."

"In the best circumstances, how long do you think they could last without the antidote?" Tenji asked.

Ruben picked up a long stick from the ground, his forehead wrinkled with worry. "Two days at most, less than a day if they're unlucky."

"Then we should hurry."

18

A Fiery Challenge

A DARK SHADOW ROSE BEFORE SAGE, MARKING HOW CLOSE they were to the mountain. Her legs buckled, and her eyelids drooped from exhaustion. They had spent the whole night heading toward the mountains, following the few tracks the goblins had left behind. Fortunately, Tenji announced they would stop and rest in the shadow of the mountain before attempting their rescue. Sage dropped to the ground.

"I'll take the first watch," Tenji said, settling himself by a tree.

Sage didn't object. Even if he had asked her to take the first shift, she didn't think she'd be able to stay awake. Her eyes barely stayed open as it was. Not taking any time to make a fire or clear the ground of sticks and rocks, Sage curled up and fell asleep.

After what seemed to be only a few moments, Tenji shook her awake. "We need to keep moving."

Sage sat up groggily. The sun filtered through the leaves of the trees and shadows no longer covered the mountains. How long had she been sleeping? Did Tenji get *any* rest? A ray of sunlight blinded her and she winced. The beginnings of a headache throbbed against her temple, but the fear of the others dying dragged her to her feet.

After a quick breakfast, the group progressed alongside the mountain with Tenji in the lead. Sage still wasn't good at tracking, despite Cassian's lessons, but she kept an eye out regardless. After walking a while, Cassian pointed up the mountainside.

"There are goblin tracks this way," he informed them, and, as if to prove it, he lifted a piece of fabric from a bush and then brushed some leaves aside to expose an oddly shaped, small footprint.

"You can track?" Tenji asked.

"Some," Cassian replied with a shrug. "My father used to take me hunting. He taught me how."

Tenji studied Cassian and then the mountain as if debating. Then he nodded. "Very well. Lead the way."

Cassian took the lead as they climbed the gradual steep incline. A few rocky areas among the trees they passed had cave openings, but Cassian kept trudging upward. Finally, he paused, holding up a hand. Sage, Ruben, and Tenji halted, waiting for guidance. Carefully, the boy waved them closer, crouching low to the ground as he pointed. Crouching next to him, Sage followed his pointing finger.

A very short, ugly creature, which Sage easily believed was a goblin, exited a narrow cave opening in the distance. It called, and several others appeared outside the entrance speaking in whiny, high-pitched voices that only intensified Sage's headache. Their wrinkled skin varied between shades of sickly green, gray, or brown. Some goblins only wore a loin cloth, while the others wore a mix of armor, fur, and human-looking clothes.

Dragging a freshly killed deer with them, the scraggly group plopped down around a fire pit. Well, they'd found one clan at least, but how would they find out if these were the goblins responsible for kidnapping the others?

Ruben lowered his staff to the ground, easing to a crouch beside them. The boot of his broken leg snagged on a stone, and he pitched forward. One hand reached out to soften his fall; the other seized his injured leg. Tenji lurched and caught him before Ruben accidentally signaled their arrival to the goblins. Then, carefully, he helped Ruben sit down.

Ruben's face contorted in pain, and he gripped his thigh with both hands, but he didn't cry out. Instead, his face softened and he reached down and lifted a dirtied strip of what used to be a Reudinian jacket lying on the ground near his injured leg.

Sage's heart flipped. The others. They had to be nearby.

"Okay," Tenji whispered, staring at the goblins by the cave entrance. "We'll need to get to the others before the goblins slaughter them, assuming they haven't already." He shot a look at the three beside him and continued, "Cassian, Ruben, I need you to take care of the goblins already in sight, while I go in and gather information. When I return, we'll work out a fully functioning plan to rescue the others. Do you think you can handle that?"

Ruben looked unsure, but Cassian nodded. "No problem."

For a moment, Sage thought Tenji had forgotten about her until he said, "Sage, help them as best you can."

Acid burned her gut. Did he seriously think that lowly of her ability? "How will you get in without being seen?" she asked, forcing herself to not sound too irritated.

Tenji narrowed his eyes at her. "I suppose you know nothing," he said, before turning to face the goblins again. "Watch and see."

Before her very eyes, his large form—as well as his clothes—shrank and morphed until he became a teeny, tiny, pesky fly. He buzzed around her head before dashing toward the cave. Sage stared after him, her mouth hanging open. Tenji had turned into a fly. What else could he change into?

"He can morph his clothes as well?" she asked after a moment.

Ruben smiled through his exhaustion. "No. He just has specially designed elven-made clothing. They cast a spell on them that allows them to morph with him."

"Ah." She turned her attention back to the goblins. "Should we move closer?"

Cassian nodded and the three of them slipped closer to the cave.

"We can split three each," Cassian whispered, pointing. "If I freeze three, Ruben can use his sense to capture or entangle three, and then we can help Sage with the final three." He paused to look at her questioningly before he added, "If you need it."

This was her chance to show Cassian and Ruben that her sense wasn't useless. Although she wanted to say she didn't need their help, Sage kept silent. Because honestly, she didn't know. She could need help depending on the goblins' skill level. Instead, she faced Ruben and said, "You should stay back, especially since you can use your sense at a distance. We'll wait until you're ready."

Ruben's face relaxed and he nodded.

Ruben limped further away, leaning on his stick, while Cassian and Sage inched closer to the cave opening and waited for Ruben's signal. Sage gripped the hilt of her sword and bit her lip. Battling with Kai—a strong and reliable ally—was one thing. Battling with a child and a severely injured person was something completely different. A slight flutter quivered in her stomach. What if…

No, she wouldn't allow herself to think such thoughts. They could do this. They would be fine. Somehow, she'd make sure of it.

Without warning, vines broke from the earth and tangled around three goblins on one side. The other goblins leapt up, their shrill voices screeching, and hurried to aid their comrades or search for the perpetrator.

Sage tightened her grip on her sword and eyed Cassian. The boy nodded determinedly. Together, they charged.

Sliding along the muddy earth, Sage used her sense to zip through the group and slashed all three of her goblins across the chest before they even saw her. With horrid shrieks, they toppled to the ground, blue blood oozing from their bodies. She whirled around and faced Cassian. His three were frozen and the boy stabbed through each of their icicle bodies with his sword. He met her gaze across the space between them, and then they rushed to end those being held captive by Ruben.

Once they finished, Sage scanned the area, making sure no goblins had slipped past them, but all nine of the goblins were dead. She flashed Cassian a relieved grin. They'd successfully accomplished what Tenji had asked them to do. But now what?

"Should we hide the bodies?"

Cassian nodded slowly. "Maybe. In case more goblins appear."

Ruben appeared near the edge of the trees, beaming victoriously, and Sage and Cassian trotted over to meet him.

"Do you think you can drag their bodies away with your vines?" Sage asked, gesturing over her shoulder.

Ruben straightened a bit taller, shifting his crutch. "Yes." He focused on the goblins once more, and several vines snaked across the ground, wrapped around their bodies, and dragged them away. Then Cassian gathered leaves to spread over the patches of blood, and Sage collected the goblins' weapons and hid them behind some bushes.

"Will it work?" Ruben asked, his forehead creasing as he studied the piles of leaves.

Cassian shook his head. "Not for long."

"Let's hope Tenji gets back before they discover us," Sage said, fidgeting with her jacket. What if someone had heard the goblins' screeches? What if a whole army of goblins came out? "For now, we should hide."

The three of them retreated into the woods and kept a watchful eye on the entrance as they waited. How much longer would Tenji be gone? It shouldn't be taking him this long, should it? Unless he got lost, or captured, or…killed.

Ruben adjusted his broken leg, his face tight. Sage studied him silently and pressed her lips together. Ruben couldn't keep on like this in such a dangerous place. He was pushing himself too hard.

Ruben cleared his throat and pulled at the collar of his tunic. "How—How many goblins do you think are in there?"

Sage wished she knew. It had never occurred to her to pay attention during her studies on creatures. She hadn't known she'd be trapped in a labyrinth full of monsters, after all.

"We can't be sure," Cassian answered. His young voice wavered as his wide golden eyes met hers. "But they say clans can range anywhere from fifty members to hundreds of thousands."

Sage clutched the front of her jacket and swallowed a gasp. "Hundreds of thousands?" She didn't want to think about the possibility of there being that many goblins inside the mountain.

The three of them sat in silence for a long time.

The sun hit its height before, finally, a whirring buzzing drew closer, and they spotted a fly circling a nearby tree before it transformed back into Tenji. He crouched by them, face grim.

"There are more goblins than I had anticipated," he informed them. "We'll need to distract them long enough to get in and out without being noticed. We won't succeed otherwise." His eyebrows furrowed and he zoned out for a moment, as if deep in thought. "I can pass as a goblin with my sense. However, the problem will be successfully getting you three in and the others out."

Sage shared an uncertain look with Ruben and Cassian. How would they get in and out unnoticed if there was an alarming number of goblins inside?

Tenji massaged his temples wearily before he said, "I'll come up with something." But even he seemed uncertain.

Sage leaned back against a large stone, racking her brain for a way to help. She clenched her fists, her frustration building and swirling in her chest the longer she debated. There *had* to be some way she could help.

Suddenly, Cassian straightened, his gaze focused on the clearing near the entrance. Sage followed his gaze but saw nothing. He stood and stepped out into the opening. What was he doing?

Then he bent over and picked up something that glittered in the sunlight. He returned to them and held out a sparkling necklace. "Don't goblins love pretty things?"

Tenji, who must've decided to perfect his goblin-transformation-technique, morphed into a rather hideous shape. He nodded without looking in Cassian's direction. "Yes, they are especially fond of gold."

"Then they should have some sort of stash, shouldn't they?"

Nodding again, absentmindedly, Tenji morphed into another, not-quite-right variation of the oddly shaped, green-tinged creatures. "Yes, I did see something like that inside."

Cassian flipped the necklace up into the air and caught it. "Wouldn't they want to protect their treasure? If we can somehow mess with their hoard, they'd be so occupied with saving it, they might not even notice us."

Tenji reverted to his normal self and stared at the younger boy. "You might be onto something, Cassian." His next transformation succeeded in finally taking the shape of a goblin. The Tenji-goblin snapped his fingers and turned to face them. "I have it. There was a large pit in the middle of the cavern. We could distract them by sending the treasure into it. Ruben, Cassian, both of you can use your senses to push it in. I'll go ahead as a goblin to make sure the path is clear and find good places for you to hide. Once they're good and distracted, we'll rescue the others."

Ruben swallowed hard and clutched his staff tightly; Cassian nodded and Sage couldn't help but notice him squeeze the hilt of his sword. Sage looked between the members of their small group and pressed her lips into a thin line. She didn't like the idea of injured Ruben and little Cassian getting involved in the escape plan. But she didn't like the idea of leaving them out here alone any better.

So she nodded, biting the inside of her cheek.

Meanwhile, Tenji had left her out of the plan once again, and this time, even *she* didn't know what part she could play. Light would only bring attention to them rather than keep them hidden. But that wouldn't stop her from doing everything she could to save the others.

Kai pulled at long chains, only for one of his ribs to give a sharp twinge, throbbing incessantly. Dammit! He burst into thin, small flames. The metal chains didn't budge. If he had been at his usual strength, he would've been able to make his flames hot enough to melt the chains and break free. But his head was still swimming from the drugs the goblins kept giving him. He couldn't focus.

Blasted creatures…blasted labyrinth.

"Argggghhh!"

"Quiet down, will you?" the annoying Snoot said. "Wasting your energy won't help us." Luka stared out of the cage he was in, his own hands and feet clasped in similar chains. A deep slash sliced across his right eye, evidence of their attack. It made him look different and very *un*like his father.

Each of them was in their own cell, long chains shackling their hands and feet—except for Draven, who didn't have a cell at all. Instead, he was chained by his hands, feet, and neck. Both Tristan and Archie lay shivering in their respective cells, covered in vomit. Except for the occasional moan, they were still and quiet. The stench from the vomit made Kai gag. If he had to hear one more person heave, he was going to start his own vomit pile.

Kai didn't know how many days had passed since they'd been in this place. With no sunlight for guidance, and a few blanks in his memory from the sleeping darts, he couldn't be sure. But no matter how long it had been, he didn't want to spend another *moment* in this hellhole.

"*You* shut up! I don't need your annoying, meddlesome, bossy voice adding to how damn sucky this situation is!" Kai's head thrummed as he glared at Luka. He gagged reflexively when someone else hacked and spewed. He was so done with having sick members in their group. He found himself muttering, "Archie better not die. I'm gonna sock that stupidity right out of his body. And Tristan can stop being such a copycat. Maybe we should just let them die to rid us of their idiocy."

Luka's one-eyed stare was still piercing. "What if it had been *you*? Would you want us to leave you behind? Or would your opinion change because it's you?"

Grunting, Kai turned his head away and glared at the damp cave floor. He didn't want to look at Luka's irritating face anymore; he didn't want Luka to know how close he'd hit home. A painful memory zapped through his mind. His grandmother—the only person who had ever stood by his side—quiet and motionless on her bed. No, he didn't want to be left behind. Not in the slightest.

Draven sighed. "Kai's just taking out his anger on Archie and Tristan. He doesn't actually want them dead. Direct your anger at the goblins instead. They're the ones who did this to us…or direct it at me. It's my fault we got caught."

Kai frowned at Draven, ignoring the intensity of his ribs' throbbing. What did he mean this was his fault?

"How is this your fault?" Luka's confusion echoed Kai's annoyance.

But Draven just shook his head. "It just is," he muttered tersely, glaring darkly at the stone wall.

What in the world was Mister Gloomy rambling about now?

"This isn't your fault, Draven," Luka said. "And neither was the werewolf attack. This labyrinth is dangerous. No one can predict what is going to happen."

Draven said nothing and continued to glare darkly at the wall. Not that it was anything new. He'd always been pretty dreary.

Kai thought back to the attack. One moment, everything was normal. Water-wuss Archie was wailing about his possible death while Tristan patted his back; the Snoot watched over his fire while Jovian, Draven, and Kai were in their respective corners. Tenji and the others had left not long before. Then the next moment sleeping darts were raining from the night sky, followed by the goblins' attack.

By the time Kai came to, he was in these blasted chains.

The goblins, unfortunately, weren't thoughtless monsters, though they looked the part. The creatures had stripped the princes of their weapons, coins, and what was left of their jackets and belts, not to mention that they'd found some way to weaken their senses. The goblins came occasionally to fire some potion at them—Kai figured that was what was draining their abilities.

After a long stretch of silence, Luka spoke again: "I wonder where they took Jovian. I hope he's alive."

Kai sniffed. Jovian. Not long after they'd awoken, the lucky bastard escaped from his chains, despite having a dislocated shoulder, and had started fumbling with Draven's chains. Before he could free Draven, Jovian was caught. The goblins had dragged him out of the prison, and they hadn't seen the kid since.

A sharp bang came from the tunnel leading out of the cavern. Kai scowled, listening to the approaching steps. The shrill, aggravating voices of the goblins echoed around them, grating on his already short nerves. Were they coming to shoot them with the sense-sucking potion again?

Three ugly goblins stepped into view. Two of them carried spears and one a bow and arrows. Their wrinkly green-gray skin distorted their hideous faces. One of them sniffed from his large, pointed nose as he poked the dull end of his spear at Draven. The gloomy prince glared at them, the same way he'd glared so ferociously at the wall.

"Which one-sy did he says to bring?"

The one with the bow and arrows walked past Draven and pointed a long, crooked finger, his face twisting into a sneer. "The fires one."

Kai gritted his teeth and tensed as the other two goblins turned their beady eyes toward him. Whatever they had planned, it wouldn't be anything bloody good—but he didn't plan to go down without a fight. Kai strained and twisted at his chains as the three advanced toward his cell. He struggled to light a flame, but one of them shot him with another dart. Immediately, his sense melted away and the only flame he could manage was the size of a candle. He grimaced. Blasted goblins.

One of the spear-wielding ones opened the cage, and the other dumped water over him. The candle flame went out. Anger flickered hot inside Kai, but then the one with arrows grabbed his hair and pushed his face into the ground, causing his ribs to scream in pain.

He was going to roast these imps.

"Such red hair. We should scalps him. It would sells very nicely to the Dazuit clan. They loves hairs."

Kai wriggled, but the goblins' painful, rock-hard grips only tightened, pinching his skin. The rattle of the others' chains clattered and scraped along the stone floor.

One goblin placed his spear point against Kai's back, still clutching Kai's hair tightly. Kai winced, growing angrier the more humiliating their treatment became. The other two chained his hands and feet together before releasing him from the chains on the wall. The point of the spear pressed harder when he squirmed; Kai clenched his teeth so hard, his jaw ached.

He longed to send these little imps to bloody hell.

Pulling him up by his hair, they forced him to stand, still pressing the spear into his back. The three of them were too short to hold him by his hair any longer, so they gripped his arms and shoved him from the room. Kai refused to meet any of the other princes' gazes as he stumbled past. He was already humiliated by the fact he couldn't resist three little goblins; he certainly didn't want to admit anyone had witnessed it, especially not Luka.

The goblins dragged him through a dizzying maze of cave tunnels. Eventually, they pulled him into a large cavern where the ceiling hung low. However, what he saw made his stomach plunge. He almost preferred the bloody cells.

The cavern was full of hundreds—no, thousands—of goblins. Kai gritted his teeth and suppressed the instant panic that rose in his chest. How was he ever going to get out of *this*?

To his right, the ceiling rose higher, and below it spread a large, still lake. Over the middle of that lake—dangling from a rope—was Jovian.

So that's what they'd done to him.

The goblins jerked Kai toward the center of the cavern and into the middle of a crowd of chattering goblins. Goblins cackled at the sight of him; some leered, others spat, others cheered. One goblin splashed some sickly smelling liquid over him and the turmoil inside him became more like lava.

They tossed him in front of a large hole, and his heart sped up as he gazed down into nothingness. A piercing chortle pulled his gaze away from the dark abyss. A goblin, perched on a throne chiseled out of rock, peered down at him. He wore Jovian's jacket and was decorated with various gaudy bits of jewelry. On his head sat a tall, oversized crown. Golden coins spilled from his throne onto a vast pile surrounding the throne. On either side of this crowned goblin rested a forest dragon.

These imps had been following them for a while.

"It's rare for humans to visits us anymore. Especially rich-y ones," the crowned goblin sneered, elongating his 's's. The goblins around them screeched in laughter. "It's even more rares to come across humans with a sense. Me thinks your group is the first of those who have entered the labyrinth."

Kai glared, too furious to respond.

"They says you have the sense of fires, is they rightsies?"

When Kai didn't reply, the goblin held his hand out and a flame unfurled, dancing merrily in his palm. The two forest dragons winced away, as if they had experienced those flames firsthand. The goblin smiled his ugly smile and cackled. "Me have the fires sense too. Therefore, me thinks you must be the leader of these humans."

Kai gritted his teeth. Although he didn't want to be thought of as the leader of these pricks, he wanted to admit to Luka's leadership even less. And he didn't want to remind the goblins of Tenji and the others who hadn't been captured.

The goblin leader jumped down from his throne. "As king of the goblins, me is curious whether the fires of a human or of a goblin is stronger." The goblin king smirked, holding the flame close to Kai's face. Kai winced. "So, before me kills you, me decides to finds out."

The goblin waved to his goblin subjects. They split, forming a path to a makeshift arena. The goblin king handed his crown to one of the other goblins and sauntered over to the arena, pulling jewelry off and casting it aside as he walked. "It has been a whiles since we have had funsies. You humans are uniques. It makes it a funsies game."

The goblins dragged Kai after their leader. Was he really going to have to fight the goblin king? His fire sense wasn't back yet. His power trembled in his chest: dim, faint, and feeble. At this rate, the goblin king was going to burn him alive.

The goblin horde unchained his arms and legs and shoved him into the arena. Kai tumbled and landed hard, jarring his broken ribs and knocking the air out of his lungs. He gasped for breath, writhing in pain, while listening to the swirls of goblins' screeches, cackles, and leers. Once the air came rushing back into his lungs and the pain in his ribs eased, Kai pushed himself up onto his knees and surveyed his surroundings, raking in shallow breaths to prevent upsetting his ribs. The walls of the arena were too tall to jump over and lined with thousands of jeering goblins.

The goblin king strolled around the arena. "Don't worries. We shots you with a smaller dose of the power-stripping potions a while ago." He smiled crookedly. "Me will waits until your sense is back before we begins."

Kai clutched his knees, his mind racing for a way out of this. But the situation seemed too bleak. If he started winning against the goblin king, the other goblins wouldn't hesitate to end his life. All the goblins surrounding the arena were well-armed. On top of that, he couldn't stand without the room swirling, couldn't make more than a candle-sized flame, and could barely move without severe pain from his cracked ribs. The probability of getting out of this alive was slim. Should he refuse to fight? Should he let the ugly creature kill him?

His grandmother's withered face floated into his memory. Even when he resisted thinking about her, she always insisted on being remembered—no matter how painful his memories might be. Despite his struggle to block it, the image of her lying on her bed during her last days jolted his mind. Even with how frail she'd been then, her eyes still held their usual sharpness, her face as kind as ever when she said, *"My dear Kai, promise me you won't give up, no matter how desperate your situation is. Keep going, keep doing your best. And know that I'll always love you. I'll always be on your side. Promise me."*

Kai lifted his head and breathed through the pain. Even though this situation wasn't at all what his grandmother had been referring to when she'd said those words to him, if she were here, she would've said the same thing. And if there was one thing his grandmother had drilled into his head as a child, it was to always keep his promises. Even though he couldn't see a way out of this, he would keep himself alive as long as possible. He refused to go down without a fight. And anyway, he had to get revenge on these cave maggots for how they'd treated him. Anger coursed through his veins, waking his lethargic muscles.

"The abilities to control elements is rares among humans and goblins." The goblin king strolled along the edges of the arena, eyeing Kai curiously. "This makes us differents than others of our kind. Goblins may be able to use minuscules magics, but it's nothing to the extents of me fires sense."

Kai's strength sluggishly seeped back into his body. The goblin king hadn't lied; a little bit more, and he would be able to use his fire sense to the magnitude of his ability. He clenched his fists repetitively, checking his muscles and mobility before he stood. The room didn't swirl, and his legs remained strong and stable.

He might have a chance to do some damage after all.

Closing his eyes and taking a deep breath, Kai calmed his mind and tuned out the pain. Growing up, Kai's fire sense had been tied to his temper—at least, that's what the Royal Council had told him. When someone made him angry, he tended to use his sense. Back then, he hadn't known how to control his ability, and the fire often went berserk.

The Royal Council never succeeded in teaching him; Grams taught him the most. Even so, as much as he hated the Royal Council and their attempts to control him, their enforced practices had enabled him to put to use what Grams had taught him: separating his emotions from his sense.

Kai opened his eyes and fixed his gaze onto that grimy goblin. It was time. The goblin king paused and faced him. Judging from the goblin's expression, he was aware of the changes in Kai's countenance.

Kai burst into flames.

He was bloody ready for his revenge.

"You need me."

No, I don't, the traitor replied. He hadn't come here to befriend some murderous spirit. He'd come here for Everard, and for himself. *Leave me alone. You're getting what you want either way.*

"Not if you all die," the spirit hissed. *"I can help. Just let me in."*

Was the creature right? Would they die if he didn't give in?

19

Battle of the Goblin King

SAGE AND THE THREE PRINCES SLINKED DOWN THE CAVE tunnels together, as quietly as possible. They'd been winding through tunnels a lot longer than Sage preferred, but she tried not to think about it too much. Goblin-Tenji briefly transformed into a hunting dog and sniffed around before morphing back into a goblin. He then led them down a smaller tunnel. Following a few steps behind him, Sage jumped at every sound she heard.

Cassian's golden eyes darted around the dark tunnels and Ruben breathed heavily as he limped behind them.

They entered another tunnel which had several diverging paths that led to a massive cavern. A chorus of goblin screeches echoed from it, and Sage caught a glimpse of a large crowd. Tenji gestured for them to hide in a divot as he sped down the path toward the crowd.

He returned a while later, face tense. He waved for them to follow him away from the crowd before he spoke. "It looks as though we might not need a distraction after all. Something is already distracting them, though I had trouble seeing what it was." His goblin-forehead wrinkled, somehow more so than it was already. "I don't like it. Let's move carefully."

Tenji morphed into a dog once more and sniffed the ground before leading them back into the depths of the tunnels in his goblin-form. Eventually, they came down a narrow corridor, and Sage jerked to a stop at the sight of two goblins standing guard before another smaller cavern. Cassian lifted a makeshift tube to his mouth and shot one of the goblins with a sleeping dart they'd taken from the campsite.

Sage gaped at him. His aim was incredibly accurate. She didn't think she could do that. Ruben and Tenji didn't even blink. The other goblin snapped to attention and spotted them, but before he could give a cry of alarm, Cassian shot him too.

Tenji led them toward the opening as the goblins drifted to sleep.

When they entered the room, Sage's heart leapt. Inside the room were several cells, and inside those cells waited Draven, Luka, Tristan, and Archie. They were, to put it bluntly, in terrible shape—Draven and Luka bearing bad wounds, and Tristan and Archie pale from their sickness. But they were alive.

Draven and Luka spotted them immediately, but their eyes went to Tenji's goblin form. Their foreheads creased.

"Where are Kai and Jovian?" Tenji demanded.

Sage searched the cells but saw no sign of either. She bit her lip. Could they be…?

"Tenji?" asked Luka, standing. He studied Tenji's goblin form in confusion. Tenji chose that moment to morph back into himself and both Draven's and Luka's faces relaxed.

Luka stepped forward as far as he could in his chains. "How did you get here?"

Sage couldn't help staring at him, cringing unconsciously. Blood covered his face and a nasty laceration slashed across his right eye, which was swollen shut. He looked so different.

Tenji peeked out into the hall, then stepped further inside. "The goblins left a mess of a trail behind."

Ruben limped over to the cages holding Archie and Tristan and pulled at Archie's door. It was locked tight. "Are they alive?" he asked, studying their pale, slumped figures.

"We think so," Draven replied. "Archie heaved recently, and Tristan was moaning earlier."

"How did you get past the goblins?" Luka asked.

"They are distracted by some commotion," Tenji responded, jiggling the cage doors as he studied their chains. He frowned. "Do you happen to know where Jovian and Kai are?"

Luka shook his head. "We haven't seen Jovian for a while. Kai was taken recently."

Were they too late? Sage bit the inside of her cheek. Were Jovian and Kai already…dead? Anxiety rose up in her gut, but she shook her head. She didn't know what had happened yet. No use panicking over something unknown.

Tenji cursed. "Either of their senses would've been helpful in breaking the chains."

Luka sighed. "The goblins have been keeping our senses sedated by injecting us with some potion."

Sage thought back to the battle of the forest dragons. She had sliced through an entire tree trunk as if it were butter. If she could do it once, maybe she could do it again. "I can do it," she piped up, pulling out her sword.

Everyone turned to stare at her. Their foreheads creased and eyebrows furrowed. Sage stared back at them. They didn't believe her. She squeezed the hilt of her sword. She was sick of them looking down on her. She wasn't really sure if she could execute the same ray sword again, but she was determined to do her part in getting them out of here. She *had* to prove she wasn't useless. So, instead of dwelling on the others' doubt, she focused on channeling her inner light, building it up on the inside.

"What makes you think you can free them?" Tenji crossed his arms over his chest and his frown deepened.

"Light can do many things," Sage retorted. "One aspect of light sense is heat energy. Now get out of my way." She sounded more confident than she felt, but Cassian and Ruben moved out of the way. Tenji stared at her a moment longer before he too stepped back.

Sage directed the warming energy out of her core, through her arms, and into her sword. She approached Archie's and Tristan's cages, causing Ruben to stumble further out of the way. Gripping her sword tight, she feigned confidence and chanted to herself.

Like butter. The cage was butter. Then, she shifted her stance and slashed her sword at the lock on the door. To her delight, her blade ignited just like before and slid through the metal as if it were air. The door swung open.

There was a moment of silence.

Sage fought to conceal a delighted smile. Then she stepped inside Archie's cell and her joy immediately sobered.

Vomit covered the floor and Archie's clothes, and his face was deathly pale. He didn't respond when she approached. She wasn't sure if he was aware she was there at all. She swallowed her horror, holding in the urge to gag, and sliced off Archie's chains, careful not to cut him while also trying to avoid stepping in his vomit. Then she left him and hurried to Tristan's cell, repeating the same actions.

While Ruben hurried to check on Archie and Tristan, Sage went to free Draven. Draven jerked his face away as if it hurt to look at her. Sage frowned as she sliced through his chains, and the moment he was free, Draven retreated as if she had burned him. Was her light too bright?

She then sliced through Luka's chains before retracting her light energy, and she faced Tenji.

"Not too bad for a candle, huh?"

Tenji only turned away. "Let's find Kai and Jovian. We need to get out of here." With that, he transformed back into a hunting dog and sniffed.

Cassian grinned at her; Sage grinned back.

Archie couldn't stand, so Draven and Luka got on either side of him, and Sage supported a semi-steady Tristan. Then they left the cells behind, retreating down the tunnel with Tenji in the lead.

Jeers and cheers reverberated ahead of them, gradually growing louder. Once they reached the end of the tunnel, Sage barely suppressed a gasp as she stared out over the sea of goblins who swarmed around an enormous arena.

Sage bit the inside of her cheek again and shifted Tristan's heavy arm over her shoulders, struggling to hold him up. While he was more conscious than Archie, he didn't speak. Sweat dripped down his forehead, and his face strained and contorted with pain. How were they going to find Kai and Jovian like this?

"What do you think they're watching?" Ruben whispered.

Cassian rose on his tiptoes and scanned over the goblin heads.

Tenji transformed back into a goblin and pointed away from the crowd. "Let's go while they're distracted. There are a lot of supplies. We should take some with us. I can go in disguise, but first, we need to get Tristan and Archie out of here. We can worry about Kai and Jovian after."

Draven shook his head, his eyes set determinedly. "You're our best chance at finding Jovian and Kai. I'll go. I can take Archie and Tristan too."

Tenji studied him, then nodded. "Fine."

Sage didn't know how Draven would carry both Archie and Tristan on his own, but he and Luka only set Archie down and Draven gestured for Sage to do the same with Tristan. Sage helped Tristan lower himself to the ground. Then Draven stood between the two and, before her very eyes, the three of them melted into the shadows and vanished. Cassian's eyes widened. He waved a hand over the space.

Sage gaped. "How?"

Ruben blinked, then faced her. "Shadow manipulation?"

"Let's find Kai and Jovian and get out of here," Tenji said. Luka agreed and their leader once more assumed the form of a hunting dog.

The remaining group slipped along the edges of the large cavern, keeping to the shadows. Sage pressed her hand against the wall as she walked, almost forgetting to breathe. Dog-Tenji halted and pointed with his paw. To their right, over a great lake, dangled a bound figure.

Jovian.

Sage couldn't tell if he was dead or alive from where they stood, but at least they'd found him. But where was Kai?

They crept toward Jovian as inconspicuously as they could, pausing whenever a goblin came too close, ready to yank it into the shadows and subdue it if they were spotted. Sage squeezed the hilt of her sword, her heart hammering in her chest.

Just before they reached the lake, a blast of flame surged from the arena. Sage's eyes widened.

Luka barely muffled his groan. "Kai is the distraction."

The goblin king grinned in delight before Kai surged a tornado of flames at him. When the flames crackled away, the goblin stood unaffected by his blast. The goblin king's crooked grin stretched wider.

"This wills be a good battle." Then he shot a return blast at Kai.

Kai, who had never been trained to fight against another fire sense, had never learned to block directed flames. He tried his best to deflect, but his block flung him to the other end of the arena. He skidded across the rock floor and rolled violently. His shoulder twinged and his ribs screamed in pain. Kai moaned, straining to ignore the pain, and forced himself back onto his feet. He was barely up before the goblin was flying at him with a stream of flames.

Kai stared and tensed. This impish king could use his flames to *fly*?

The goblin king blasted him with another fire tornado, and Kai attempted a block again, but failed. Fire knocked him back.

Kai hissed, his ribs screaming. He climbed to his feet. Forcing himself to focus on the fight, Kai tossed various flaming balls at the king, ribs aching with each throw.

"What's wrong, fires human?" The goblin king sneered. He blasted Kai again. "Is this alls you have? Me knows you has more yous not using. Quits holding back and fights me!"

The flames around him gave Kai a strange sense of déjà vu. A vague memory of his old home immersed in flames rose within him, and his heart sped up. Kai tried to block the king's blasts as if he was blocking those memories. This time, the flames successfully diverged, and Kai gathered the flames into a massive ball and returned it to the goblin king.

The goblin waved away Kai's flaming ball with ease, and flaming tornadoes spun to the ground as he snarled, "This is pathetics, reallsies. Is this the true extents of yours abilities? Maybe me was wrongs to thinks this battle would be worth anythings."

"Arghhhh!" Kai lurched out of the way of the tornadoes, his ribs throbbing agonizingly. He bent over and seized his knees, breathing through the immense pain. Damn these cracked ribs. He couldn't focus.

The king strode across the arena, closing the space between them, forcing Kai to stumble back and surge another torrent of flames toward the king. This time, the flames rippled out of control, tinged with his frustration and fear. The uncontained flames tugged at his memory again, stronger this time. Why now? Why was this memory rising now of all times?

The goblin chortled as he waved away Kai's attack once more. "Weaks. So weaks."

The goblins around the arena cackled and jeered, filling the cavern with deafening noise.

Another one of the goblin king's blasts threw Kai back. Kai was going to be killed if he couldn't focus and figure out how to fight with his injuries. Flames danced around the arena and around the goblin king's body. He was genuinely terrifying, walking through the flames unharmed. Was that how Kai had looked back then?

Before he could resist the memory again, it came flooding back from the recesses of his mind. In his mind's eyes, flames surrounded him, swallowing the house that had been Kai's home so long ago. Through the tongues of fire, his mother screamed at him: *"Stop the fire, Kai!"*

His father appeared behind her and pulled her away, fear staining his face. A baby's screams drew four-year-old Kai's gaze to the crib in the corner. Flames curled around it.

Then his father's voice came through the flames: *"A monster, you're a monster."*

Voices that had once been lost somewhere deep inside suddenly pierced Kai's soul.

Don't use your sense.

When you use fire, you become dangerous.

Bury it down within you.

Another blast of organized flames from the goblin king slammed Kai to the ground. Pain from his ribs and shoulder seared through his body, but all he could focus on was that memory. He had almost killed his parents and baby sister that day. No one had blamed them for abandoning him; especially since their child walked through the very fire he had begun, untouched. He looked every bit the terrifying demon they believed he was.

Kai's fingers gripped the stone ground and tried to steady himself, but the pain and his rising memories only made it difficult. He raised his head to stare through the flames at the laughing goblin king. Was he really any different from this creature standing in front of him? Kai curled his hands into fists. Maybe Kai's death would mean the removal of one more monster from the world.

Then his grandmother's sharp voice reverberated through him, *"You're not a monster, Kai."* He pictured her small, strong figure standing before him, her eyes staring firmly into his. *"Never say that to me again."* She placed a hand resolutely on his shoulder, her grip solid. *"You may feel as if your sense brings only pain and that the world would be better without you, but it isn't true.*

"No mistake is too big. You can always turn around and go a different route. Remember that. I know you'll choose the right path when the time comes. Don't be discouraged."

Kai pushed himself unsteadily to his feet and glared at the goblin king as the creature sauntered toward him. Kai had always held back to keep himself from hurting others. But if he held back now, he would die.

He dodged another blast by rolling across the ground, grimacing in pain. Searching deep within him, he found where he had buried his deepest emotions and that wild, primal part of his sense that had swallowed his home in seconds. Kai shook away the anxious feeling rising in his gut. It was okay. These goblins were just ugly imps who were planning to kill him and then the others.

The goblin king soared through the air using his flames. He dropped to the ground in front of Kai. "It's a shames… me thinks this fight would bes good. But it seems yous sense is unable to combats mines after all. Goodbyes." He raised a hand and released another stream of flame.

Kai jerked back, releasing the full power of his sense, and everything exploded.

When the flames cleared, the goblin king was sprawled several yards away. Scrambling up, he shot Kai a vicious grin. "Yous finally decides to fight, eh?"

Kai fired himself into the air and flipped, exploding the area where the goblin stood. The goblin king struggled to block it.

"You try fighting with broken ribs, bastard!" Kai landed a few feet away from him and slashed his flames like a whip at the king, spinning to then throw a flaming kick at the goblin's head. In his efforts to block the whip, the king never saw Kai's kick coming. He went flying.

Rising to his feet once more, the angry goblin created a large ball of fire above them and pelted Kai with small balls of flames. Waving a flaming blockade over his head, Kai returned the wave of fire to the king.

The goblin king pulled up a wall of flames to defend himself, and flaming ropes suddenly sprung from the ground and wrapped around Kai's body. He struggled to free himself as the ropes tightened. The goblin king stamped toward him, calling a flame-like sword to his hand. The goblin king paused in front of Kai, his gaze severe. "Thanks you, fires human. This has been a stimulatings match, buts now it's overs."

Just as the king raised his fire sword to strike, a sudden commotion arose outside the arena. Both the goblin king and Kai turned toward the uproar. Kai's eyes widened. A non-goblin group was bringing Jovian down from the middle of the lake. Some of the goblin crowd had noticed the attempted rescue and rushed in their direction.

A hint of a smile flitted across Kai's face. The others—they had escaped their cells somehow. Maybe he had a chance to get out of this after all.

"The humans are escaping!" bellowed the goblin king. Kai temporarily forgotten, the king built a massive ball of flames in his hand and poised to throw it in Jovian's direction.

No.

Kai reacted without thinking. Closing his eyes, he felt the flaming ropes melt away. He gripped something that rippled like water in his hand. Imagining it was like Sage's ray sword slicing through that whole tree during the forest dragon attack, Kai slashed his weapon toward the goblin king.

Silence.

When he opened his eyes, he was standing over the king's body, holding a blazing spear in his hand, covered from head to toe with tall, hot flames. A large, deep gash sliced across the goblin king's chest. He didn't move again.

He'd bloody done it.

Kai, not fully believing what had happened, turned toward the stunned silence of the observing goblin subjects. They hovered between the arena and the escaping princes, as if unsure what to do. They must've eventually decided avenging their king's death was more important than the escaping prisoners because they all turned back to Kai.

In a flurry of anger, the goblins flung their weapons at him. Kai dodged some and burned others to a crisp before they ever had a chance to touch him.

The goblins' shrill cries rang in his ears and Kai glanced back just in time to see Draven grab Ruben and melt safely into the shadows. Kai tightened his grip on his spear.

They were leaving without him.

Of course. His distraction was the only thing allowing them to escape. There was no way they would come after him, no way they would stay with him now, even if they *had* liked him. He turned back to the goblins, gaze hardening.

Who cared if they left him behind? They would've rejected him eventually anyway. Like his parents. Like the Royal Council. Like the king. Kai drew in a deep breath. It didn't matter. He didn't need them any more than he needed anyone else.

The least he could do was keep the goblins' attention on him so they could escape.

Kai leapt from his place, blasting himself out of the arena and into the crowd of goblins, detonating the ground beneath him. Flames enveloped the goblins, and they squealed in pain. The goblins swarmed around him, but Kai slashed through them, drowning out his thoughts with their screams.

20

The Escape

KAI FOUGHT WITH FERVOR, SWEAT POURING DOWN HIS face, refusing to dwell on being left behind. He couldn't. Not if he wanted to survive.

A goblin bore down on him with a sword and Kai jerked his spear to block the attack, but before the goblin's sword could slice through him, a blazing sword jutted through the goblin's gut. The goblin froze, then slumped to the ground, revealing Sage, face grim but shining brightly.

"Let's get out of here."

Kai blinked at Sage but didn't have time to react because another goblin bore down on them. Kai blasted the maggot, then whirled around to slash down another. Between swings, he squeezed out, "What are—you doing—here?"

Sage grinned as he stabbed and hacked at the imps. "Rescuing." He grunted as he blocked a swinging ax. "You."

Kai almost stopped when he heard those words, a flicker of complicated emotions sputtering in his chest. But it was too dangerous to stop.

Suddenly, Tenji dropped out of nowhere and one of his arms turned into a huge octopus tentacle. The arm enveloped a group of goblins and tossed them away. "Let's go!"

"I got our swords!" Luka shouted over the chaos as he tossed several more flailing goblins into the deep hole in the middle of the cavern. When Kai looked up, Luka could be seen sailing on a piece of rock he was levitating. Jovian appeared on Kai's left, pulling a jacket over his shoulders. One of Jovian's arms hung uselessly at his side, but that didn't seem to slow him down as he pulled boulders up from the ground with his feet and kicked them at the goblins. He flashed Kai a grin.

"Nice abilities, my flaming brother! Releasing some pent-up wrath?" Jovian winked, braid swinging, before turning his gaze back to the goblins, expression darkening as he said, "I need to do a little of that myself."

Finally, the pipsqueak, Cassian, slid into view, turning the whole floor behind him into ice. He slashed a sheet of ice at the goblins' huge pile of treasure, freezing the floor in front of it. Now on the precipice of a slippery, icy slope, the treasure tumbled toward the hole Kai had stood before earlier. Several goblins shrieked and ran for their gold and jewels as it disappeared into the dark chasm.

"The exit!" Luka called.

Kai pressed his lips together, confusing emotions twisting up inside of him. They...came for him? He darted after Tenji, following him toward one of the many tunnels.

As the six of them rushed for the exit, the cave rumbled and vibrated. The few goblins still pursuing stopped and retreated in alarm as massive boulders fell from the ceiling and the floor cracked under the impact, creating fissures Kai had to leap over.

Tenji transformed into a huge monstrous wolf-beast and barked, "Hop on!"

Kai didn't particularly want to, but he wasn't quick enough to keep evading the falling bits of cave. Jovian flung himself onto Tenji's wolfish back, and Kai blasted flames, shooting himself up to join him. He looked back to see Sage and Cassian lagging behind them. But then, Sage sped up and dashed past them so fast he was there and gone like a flash of lightning. Cassian created a ramp of ice and flipped through the air, landing hard next to Kai on Tenji's back. Sage was now ahead of them.

Tenji took off after Sage, away from the disintegrating cavern. Luka struggled to keep up with them on his levitating rock, their swords swirling behind him. But, for a moment, Kai thought he saw the cavern ceiling bend away from Luka. As if the cave didn't want to crush him. Kai eyed Jovian.

"Is this you, boulder-boy?"

Jovian gave him another wide grin and winked.

Finally, they reached the entrance.

It was dark out, but Kai welcomed the fresh air. Tenji slid to a stop directly before Draven who stood over a pile of bags. Several slain goblins lay at his feet and next to him sat Ruben, who was forcing sick Archie and Tristan to drink something from a flask. Kai furrowed his brow. Where had he gotten a flask?

Jovian launched himself off Tenji while Kai and Cassian dropped down more carefully. Luka lowered himself to the ground behind them and dumped the swords in the middle of the group with a resounding clatter. Sage collapsed next to Ruben, panting heavily, and Cassian promptly joined them.

Tenji transformed back to his normal, overbearing state. Looking exhausted, the man huffed and looked at the bags Draven had gathered. "What did you manage to find?"

Draven tossed one of the bags to Tenji. "I stole a few things off the goblins."

Tenji immediately rummaged through the bag in his hands before crouching to look through the other bags. "This is good stuff," he said with a satisfied nod. "Nice, Draven."

Kai leaned over Tenji, trying to catch a glimpse without being too obvious. A few flasks, cloaks, and some other clothing filled the bags.

Tenji pulled out some of the material. "These are human. Where'd they get these?"

Draven shrugged as Luka came forward to examine the supplies.

Kai turned away and crossed his arms cautiously over his aching ribs. Somehow, his mood had greatly improved. He paused. Did he actually like being around these nit-wits?

"The goblins mentioned others entering the labyrinth," Kai told them.

Tenji said nothing but began tossing tunics to Draven and Luka, who had nothing but torn shirts as bandages around their torsos. They pulled on the new tunics.

Ruben limped to Jovian's side. "What's wrong with your arm?" he asked, nodding to Jovian's left shoulder which hung in an odd way.

Jovian laughed and gestured with his good arm. "Those annoying goblins dislocated my shoulder during their kidnapping attack."

Without a word, Tenji joined Ruben and, with a quick jerk, popped Jovian's arm back into place. Yelping in pain, Jovian danced away from them. He rubbed his shoulder and then cautiously rotated his arm in circles. He huffed. "A warning would be great next time, old man."

Kai took in a deeper breath on accident and a sharp pain shot through his back and side. He flinched and clutched his side. Damn ribs. It was like breathing shattered glass. But he dropped his arm and relaxed his face the moment Ruben peered his way. Kai didn't want them poking into *his* business.

Luka looked back at the cave with his good eye as he bent to pull his fanciful sword from the pile. "I don't feel comfortable staying near the cave entrance, but Archie and Tristan will have trouble moving far."

Tenji paused, considering, before he nodded. "I agree. We shouldn't stay. I can transform, and they can ride."

Jovian turned to the entrance, raised his good arm, and the entrance crumbled to pieces, blocking the goblins' exit. Everyone stared at him, but the jokester only smiled. "It'll be hard to come after us now."

Kai raised his eyebrows. Why hadn't he bloody done that *before*? "Impressive."

Tenji only transformed back into his wolf-beast form once more. "Help them get on."

Kai didn't budge. He didn't want to have anything to do with the sick. Instead, he stood on the sidelines and watched Sage, Draven, and Luka help Tristan and Archie onto Tenji's back. Ruben manipulated vines to wrap around Archie and Tristan since they were too weak to hold themselves, and Luka cut the vines free from the ground once they were ready for travel.

"Ruben should ride too," Draven said. "He'll just slow us down."

No one, not even Ruben, protested.

Using his telekinesis, Luka lifted Ruben onto Tenji's wolfish back and then grabbed a bag from the pile Tenji had left behind. "We should grab whatever we can carry."

Sage picked up two bags, then tossed Kai a third. Kai caught it and sighed. He slung it over his shoulder and strode over to the pile of swords. He pulled the least extravagant sword from the pile and put on the belt still attached to the scabbard.

Cassian, Jovian, and Draven grabbed the rest of the bags and swords. Then they all left the foot of the mountain and headed back into the dark forest. When Sage began to glow, brightening the area around him, Luka suggested he led the way.

As Kai tramped along with the others, his gaze kept returning to Sage's light, and he found himself picturing Sage's expression when he saved him from the goblin back in the caves. Kai shuddered. He had known Sage was a pretty boy since the first moment he saw him, but now he wondered if he was a bit too pretty. His feminine voice didn't help much either. Was his voice just naturally higher pitched? Whatever the cause, Sage's puberty needed to hit soon. His girlishness was beginning to weird Kai out.

21

A Change of Clothes

THE DAY AFTER THE RESCUE, WHILE THE GROUP WAS PREPARING for another long day of trekking, Ruben lay unmoving by a tree with his injured leg stretched out before him. He closed his eyes and focused on taking deep, quiet breaths to keep his mind off his leg's constant throbbing. And though his throat burned with tears, he swallowed them down. He couldn't let anyone know how much it hurt. It would only put more pressure on them. He didn't want to become an even greater burden than he already was.

The crunch of footsteps approached, and someone squatted nearby. Ruben opened his eyes to find Sage staring down at him with large eyes. His stomach flipped and Ruben jerked to a sitting position.

"I want to help change your bandages and treat your wound," Sage said with a slight smile.

Ruben, unable to hold his gaze, turned his head away and only nodded in reply.

Ever since Sage had ranted at Tenji two days ago, he hadn't been able to see Sage quite the same. A rather uncomfortable and seemingly impossible thought persisted in his mind, refusing to be ignored. Sage's words echoed repeatedly in his mind, *"I don't want to be in a dangerous labyrinth with a bunch of spoiled, obnoxious princes."*

He'd said it as if…he *wasn't* a prince.

And something about the way he'd said it, something about the way he'd looked at them, something about his eyes, *something* about him screamed "*woman.*"

At first, Ruben thought it was only because Sage was one of those boys who had a pretty face. But the more Ruben dwelt on it, the more certain he was there was more to it than that. The long restroom breaks, the way Sage wouldn't even unbutton his jacket despite the heat, and even certain gestures, words, or expressions.

Ruben pressed his lips together and leaned back so he didn't have to watch as Sage unwrapped his wound. Could Sage actually be a woman? Ruben didn't dare bring himself to ask. It seemed ridiculous and crazy, and he'd never hear the end of it if he was wrong. Sage would be terribly offended, and Ruben didn't want to ruin their friendship.

As Sage busied himself—or herself—with cleaning his leg, Ruben's throbbing eased. For whatever reason, whenever Sage helped him walk or treated his leg, the wounds felt the tiniest bit better. It didn't ache as badly, and the swelling reduced a bit. Whenever he walked with Tenji, Tristan, Luka, or Draven, he became more easily exhausted and his leg ached so much he often felt faint.

"There," Sage said as he—or she—wrapped his leg once more and refastened his makeshift brace. Ruben slowly sat up and peeked at Sage out of the corner of his eye, but Sage was scanning their campsite. For now, Ruben decided to ignore his own questions.

Sage sighed. "Everyone looks horrible."

Ruben followed Sage's gaze. Archie lay unmoving, still pale and unresponsive, while Tristan sat propped up against a tree, head leaned back and face scrunched. Jovian fidgeted with his sore arm, Draven had some new wounds mixed with his old ones, and Luka's eye still bled sometimes and needed to be regularly cleaned.

Ruben wasn't sure about Kai. He didn't *look* good, but Ruben couldn't see anything wrong with him other than a few bruises.

Only Cassian, Sage, and Tenji remained in decent conditions.

Sage was right. They needed help. They needed a doctor.

Then, Ruben made up his mind: he needed to do something to compensate for his uselessness. He did know a few things about treating wounds, as well as what kinds of plants helped fight infection. Ruben dragged his leg to the side, grimacing as he shifted his good leg under him.

Sage lurched to his feet to help him stand. "What are you doing? You should rest."

Ruben shook his head. "I can treat the others." Then he reached for his crutch and hobbled over to Archie and Tristan to give them another dose of their antidote. Cassian lingered around Archie and Tristan, frowning, and quickly volunteered to help crush more leaves for the antidote.

Ruben's forehead wrinkled in confusion. Why was Cassian suddenly so eager to help Archie? Didn't he hate him? Then his gaze slipped to Tristan. Maybe *he* was why Cassian was willing to assist with their treatment. Whatever the reason, Ruben didn't object to the young boy's help.

Afterward, Ruben helped create a sling for Jovian's arm.

Luka's eye was among the worst of the other princes' injuries though. As Ruben examined it, his lips pressed together. "I—I'm afraid there's no hope that you'll ever see from your eye again."

Luka nodded, but squeezed his thighs, and Ruben shifted uncomfortably. It couldn't be easy to accept being partially blind for the rest of one's life. Ruben turned toward Tenji who stood nearby, allowing Luka some time to process. "His wound needs to be sealed."

Tenji nodded. "A hot blade should do it. And for that, we'll need you, Sage." Tenji didn't mention any of his previous doubts in Sage's sense; he only acted as if it had never been an issue.

Sage bit his lip but joined them when Tenji held out one of the knives Draven had snagged. His face strained as he reached for the knife. Ruben searched the ground for a stick for Luka to bite on, then Tenji and Draven braced Luka's arms. Luka didn't speak; he only complied and peered at Sage with his good eye.

Sage's jaw clenched and he shifted his stance before igniting the knife with a white blaze. Luka stared at the blade and Draven flinched away. Sage dimmed the blaze before pressing the hot blade to Luka's wound.

The stick in Luka's mouth only barely muffled his bellow, and his face contorted in pain as he thrashed against Draven and Tenji's hold. Ruben's cringe mirrored Sage's. When Ruben couldn't bear to watch any longer, he turned away.

After they finished sealing Luka's wound, Tenji announced that they should head out soon. Ruben gathered the antidote for Archie and Tristan into a bag and slung the strap across his torso. Sage appeared next to him.

"Can you—can you check on Kai? He keeps grunting, so he must be hurting somewhere."

Ruben peeked in Kai's direction. Kai sat on the other side of the campsite, shoving things into his bag with his eyebrows knit. Ruben couldn't hide his grimace as he faced Sage again. "I don't think he'd let me."

Sage's forehead creased with concern. "At least try?"

Ruben sighed and limped over to Kai. He paused a few feet away, not wanting to get any closer, and cleared his throat.

Kai glanced up at him and huffed before glaring down into his bag.

"Do—do you have any wounds that need to be treated?"

Kai scowled but winced as he stood. "No," he snapped.

Ruben clutched his staff tighter, eyeing the twitching hand that hovered almost defensively near Kai's chest. There was definitely something wrong.

"Well, if you change your mind, let me know," Ruben told him, gesturing toward Sage. "I only came over here because Sage asked me to check on you."

With a snort, Kai crossed his arms and leaned against a tree. "Sage needs to stay out of others' business."

Cassian, who happened to walk by, paused and frowned at Kai. "I'd thank Sage, if I were you."

"And why's that?" asked Kai, rolling his eyes.

"Because Sage was the one who insisted we didn't desert you yesterday." Cassian looked Kai in the eye.

Kai said nothing to that, and, if possible, only looked more cross than before. Sensing Kai's growing irritation, Ruben quickly followed Cassian as he walked away.

Tenji transformed into a werewolf once more. "Time to head out."

Luka and Draven helped the two sick people back onto Tenji's back. To Ruben's immense relief, they had him get on Tenji's back as well. He'd done enough walking to last him a lifetime. He wished he could be home in his bed and never walk another step again.

As he rode on Tenji's back, he kept an eye on Tristan and Archie and thought of home and his parents and the plants he helped manage around their house. He thought of his older sister, Raelynn, who was pregnant and due to give birth any day now. Ruben missed them more than he wanted to admit.

Would he ever make it out of this place alive? Would he ever see them again? An image of him being eaten by werewolves struck his heart, freezing it in his chest. What if he died from running away like he'd done before? He hurriedly shook the idea from his mind.

Whether he made it out or not, Ruben didn't want to leave anyone with the impression he was a coward. If he did end up dying a gruesome death, he wanted to die bravely. He didn't want to cower anymore. He wasn't going to be the same boy who had run from the werewolves or who stood by when someone was picked on. He would overcome his fears.

With that thought in mind, Ruben set his gaze on the path ahead, clenched his teeth, and swallowed back a grimace. Even though Tenji's gait jarred his injured leg and walking was excruciating, he would bear the pain if it meant they could get home sooner. He could bear it. He could fight.

Several days after the goblin debacle, Sage inspected her clothes as the group settled in for the night. Cuts and rips tore through her tunic and trousers. She bit her lip. This wasn't good. Her gaze darted toward the bag that held some of the extra clothing Draven had found and then toward the darkening sky. She squeezed her hands into fists. She *had* to change her clothes or else they might end up exposing her. And even though the darkness would be a better covering than the daylight, she didn't want to be out alone in the forest when it was dark. That idea terrified her more than the others discovering she was a girl.

Sage waited until the others busied themselves with cooking or gathering food before darting over to the bag of clothes. Snatching a change of clothes out of the bag, she checked to see if anyone was watching. No one seemed to care what she was doing, so she tucked them into her jacket and hurried over to where Ruben and Cassian sat around their fire.

"I'll be back in a bit. Taking a restroom trip," she told them with a wave before slipping off into the trees.

Sage trekked into the forest until she was a good distance from the others. Not too far, but not too close. Then she ducked behind a tree and surveyed the area carefully. No princes. But the shadows had grown longer and deeper. Her heart sped up and she resisted the temptation to glow. The sooner she changed, the sooner she could return to camp.

Sage stripped quickly, pulling off her jacket, belt, shirt, and trousers. Then she pulled on the new set of clothes. However, before she had time to finish tying the laces on her shirt and pull on her belt and jacket again, she heard Luka's voice.

In a panic, Sage grabbed her things and darted farther into the forest. But in her haste, Sage tripped over a vine and tumbled down a steep incline. She had no time to think, barely keeping herself from crying out as she slid down the ravine. When she finally stopped sliding, Sage lay still, her heart pounding. At least she hadn't smacked her head on a rock or tree. Finally, throbbing in her ankle, knees, and elbows forced her to move.

Sage sat up and examined herself as best she could in the growing darkness, but she couldn't make out anything with any amount of clarity. Her breath stilled in her chest and her eyes darted to the trees looming above her, black, eerie, and silent. She was alone, far from camp, and it was dreadfully pitch-black. Her heart pounded wildly, and her breath grew shallow and haggard as fear's icy fingers closed around her heart.

She needed to calm down. Sage crossed her arms over her head and forced herself to take several long, deep breaths. She squeezed her eyes shut, refusing to look at the blackness enveloping her.

Flashes of memory zipped through her brain, chaotic and incomplete, and she hunched over, squeezing her eyes shut tighter as tears pricked her eyes. Her body trembled violently. She couldn't breathe. She couldn't breathe.

She could almost hear Ekon's voice calling to her. *Let's go play hide and seek in that abandoned house over there. It would be spooky and fun!*

Ekon and a six-year-old Faven clambered into the house, Maha hesitantly following after. The gloomy house reeked of mildew and the wood rotted with age.

Ekon's voice echoed in the rafters. *Faven! You count first. Maha and I will hide.*

Sage could almost see the old, gray house falling to pieces around them.

In another flash, six-year-old Faven wandered around the deserted home, stepping over fallen beams and rubble, listening to the creak of the wooden boards beneath her. It was dark, so she lit a small halo of light around her. She couldn't do more than a simple glow at that point, but as she stepped into what used to be the kitchen area, inhaling the stinging scents of mildew and rust, she heard a rustle.

The cabinet. It was coming from there. Faven ran and sprang around the corner of the cabinet door. However, what she found wasn't Maha or Ekon. Instead, a horde of giant, mangy rats stared back at her with their beady red eyes. They hissed.

Faven stumbled back and shrieked before she tripped over a broken stool. Crashing to the ground, she cried out as the floorboards cracked and crumbled away. She fell into a dark cellar, suddenly surrounded by hundreds of rats.

Sage jerked out of the nightmarish memory as something soft brushed across her arm. She squealed and lurched away, trembling so hard she knew she wouldn't be able to defend herself from anything. When she realized it was only a plant brushing against her, Sage couldn't help it…she sobbed, too terrified to think and uncontrollable light oozed out of her. She clutched her head, pulled her knees to her chest, and huddled as close to the earth as she could get, as if that would help the darkness go away.

She heard something crunch to her left. Whirling in that direction, Sage threw out her arms, ready to release her rays. What she saw wasn't the monster she was expecting.

Holding an arm over his scarred face and wincing in her light, stood Draven.

The wave of relief that ran through her was overpowering and Sage's light flickered, dimming of its own accord as she bent over, sobbing. Although she didn't want to cry in front of him, she couldn't hold the tears inside any longer.

Someone was there. She wasn't alone…even if it was Draven, the one who reminded her of the darkness she so feared.

Once her sobs subsided, silence draped heavily over them. The silence went on so long, Sage was almost afraid Draven had left her in the dark. But when she looked up, she found him staring at her. He looked away.

"Sage…what are you doing so far from camp? It's not safe, especially alone."

Sage couldn't bring herself to respond. She was still trembling.

Finally, Draven crouched next to her. "Are you alright?"

Still unable to speak, she nodded.

Draven was silent for a moment longer. Then, slowly, he pulled off his dark jacket and draped it over her shoulders.

"Let's get you back to camp," he said softly, then paused. "But…before we do…you should clean up a bit. I assume you don't want the others to know."

Sage looked up and met Draven's dark eyes. "What?"

Looking away, Draven put a hand on the back of his neck. "Well…I mean…how do I put this?" He sighed and dropped his arm. "If you don't want the others to find out you're a woman, you should fix yourself up a bit. You can wear my jacket. I assume you lost yours?"

Sage's eyes widened. She was too flustered by what he'd said to know what to do. Instead, she blushed and turned away in alarm. Quickly, she finished tying the laces of her shirt, and slid her arms through the sleeves of Draven's jacket. She buttoned it all the way up and folded up the too-long sleeves before staring down at the bulging jacket. The others were going to question why she was wearing Draven's clothing, but she couldn't go back without it.

Then she sat there, still facing away from Draven, her face, neck, and ears warm. Finally, she had the courage to speak.

"Are—are you going to tell the others?"

There was a pause. "Do you want me to?"

She shook her head, her eyes watering.

"Then I won't."

She sat there, hugging Draven's warm jacket around herself. She almost couldn't believe her ears. "Why are you helping me?"

"Why shouldn't I?"

Sage turned her head to look at him. Draven was still crouched next to her, his dark hair hanging over his scarred face, arms dangling over his knees, eyes on the ground. He lifted his gaze to hers and smiled slightly. "Come, let's get back."

He stood and held out a hand. Sage awkwardly grabbed it and stood, wincing at the sudden twinge of pain in her ankle.

"Are you hurt?"

She shook her head and released his grip. "Not anything serious."

Draven nodded toward the hill she'd toppled down. "Camp is this way."

With that, the two of them began carefully picking their way back up the hill. Sage didn't know what to think about the fact that someone in the group knew her secret. She watched Draven's dark silhouette traipse ahead of her, and he politely paused to help her when there was a tricky step. Why wasn't he demanding answers? Why wasn't he asking why she was dressed like a prince?

Finally, Draven spoke: "What happened? To upset you." He paused, before adding, "You don't have to tell me if you don't want to."

That was what he decided to ask?

Looking down at the dark jacket around her, Sage sighed. "I was trying to change clothes, but I heard Luka's voice. I thought maybe he was coming, so I ran away. That's when I fell down the hill and I...I..."

Draven didn't push her to continue or even seem to care if she ever finished her sentence. He just kept walking, waiting silently.

She took a deep breath. "I'm scared of the dark."

Draven eyed her thoughtfully. "Ironic," he muttered as he turned his gaze forward once more.

Sage frowned in confusion. What was ironic about that?

Then Draven grunted and said, a little louder, "I'm the opposite. I often hate light." He looked back at her, expression amused.

That explained his reaction whenever Sage used her sense. A small smile crept across her face. "Really?"

"Really."

Then Sage remembered the healing book. Oh, no…it was still in the inside pocket of her now-lost jacket. Just her luck. She pressed her lips together tightly and snuck a look at Draven, but she didn't dare mention the book. She'd had enough secrets discovered for one day.

Before long, they were stepping into camp, the firelight bright and warm around them. Everyone turned toward them. Ruben sat up, and Cassian and Luka stood.

Stepping closer, Luka studied Draven and then looked Sage up and down, his gaze searching hers. "What happened? We were about to send out a search crew."

Sage's mood lifted a bit. Luka looked like he had been worried. But before she could think of an excuse for both her sudden disappearance and her current appearance, Draven said, "From what he told me, he ran into some angry wasps and had to run away. Ended up getting lost. Luckily, I happened across him."

He lied so smoothly—mixing bits of truth with untruth—that his story seemed completely believable. Sage had to hide her amazement.

Jovian chuckled. "Guess we better keep an eye out for wasps as well." He leaned forward over his criss-crossed legs. "But what happened to your jacket? Isn't that Draven's?"

"Oh, I—um—took it off as I ran away hoping it would help deter them…and lost it." Sage could feel herself cringing under Jovian's regard.

Draven folded his arms over his chest. "He wanted to go looking for it, but I told him he could have mine. I don't want it anyway." He turned to Jovian. "Did *you* want my jacket?"

Jovian laughed. "Nah, thanks. I'm happy with mine."

Sage quietly let out the breath she'd been holding. She turned back to Draven, ready to thank him, but he was already retreating into the woods. She would have to thank him later.

As she joined Ruben and Cassian at their fire, Sage avoided Ruben's stare and noticed Cassian peering after Draven before turning back to the fire.

"Are you alright?" Cassian asked, eyes wide with worry.

Sage nodded. "I'm fine."

"Did you get stung?" Ruben asked, eyeing Draven's bulging jacket.

"Nothing bad happened to you other than the wasps?" Cassian asked, clutching his knees tightly.

She shook her head. "No. I'm okay, really." She smiled at them.

Finally, both Ruben and Cassian relaxed.

Warmth swirled in Sage's chest. It was so nice to have others worry about her. She blinked back a surge of tears, not wanting to cry in front of everyone, and glanced toward the forest again.

Draven knew she was a girl.

She didn't know if that was a good thing or not, but at least there was one person she didn't have to hide it from anymore. A small weight lifted from her chest.

Hugging her knees to her chest, Sage rested her head in her arms. Draven hadn't even acted a little disturbed. He'd just accepted her as she was. Why had he been so calm? Could he be trusted? She stared down at the dirt. She would just have to wait and see. Hopefully he would continue to keep her secret.

"Why do you persist in resisting me?" the spirit whispered. *"If I hadn't muddled the minds of the goblins, all of you would've been captured a second time. Then where would you be?"*

The traitor gritted his teeth and glared at the ground. The only reason this *spirit* had helped them was out of self-preservation. But...*did* they need its help to succeed?

"You came for my power. Remember that."

22

The List and the Gate

"CASSIAN!" SAGE CALLED, SQUINTING THROUGH THE BLINDING sun rays that pierced through the leaves. They'd just had a quick lunch and were setting off once more on their seemingly never-ending trek. Normally, Cassian trudged beside Sage since Ruben still needed to be carried, but instead, the boy lagged behind the group, staring at the ground.

When Cassian didn't respond, she called his name again.

Still unresponsive.

Sage frowned and, with a quick glance at the departing group, jogged over to him. "Cassian, is there something wrong?"

Cassian bent down and picked up what looked like a letter. Sage recognized Reudinia's crest pressed into a broken seal. He opened the letter without responding to Sage's question, eyes widening as he read the contents.

"What's that?" Sage shifted so she could read the contents too, but before she could get a proper look, someone snatched it from Cassian's hands.

Tenji frowned at them. "Stop slowing the group down." Then he seemed to notice the seal on the letter and held it up to examine it closer, his brows tightening. "Where did you get this?"

"The ground." Cassian's face was unreadable. "It's our ranking assessment averages."

The muscles in Tenji's neck tightened as he scanned the page. Then he folded the letter and slipped it into his bag.

"What are you half-wits doing over there?" Kai called impatiently. "Let's go!"

Tenji's gaze flickered between Sage and Cassian. "Don't tell anyone else about this," he muttered before striding back toward the head of the group.

Sage trotted to keep up with him and Cassian followed behind her. "But why? What does it mean?" she hissed.

Tenji stopped and looked at her, forcing her to skid to a stop so she wouldn't run into him. His gaze was sharp. "It confirms someone among us really is a traitor. Now quiet."

Sage stared after him. She couldn't move. Instead, her mind returned to the forbidden library and the voices she'd heard all those weeks ago. *The top ten will be enough.* The traitor had said that…not Everard. Even the kidnapper had mentioned some other person being involved.

Cassian touched her arm, drawing Sage out of her spiraling thoughts. "No one ever sees the official scores for the assessment except the Royal Council and the king. We only see the final ranking."

Sage blinked. Then Everard and his friend had been looking at something they shouldn't have. "Is that why Tenji wants to keep it a secret?"

"It might start an uproar among the others, but I don't think that's why Tenji is keeping it a secret."

He spoke so seriously, so mature for his young age. It was rather cute. But Sage couldn't bring herself to smile, not when discussing something so serious.

"Because sharing it will let the traitor know we're onto him?" she asked.

Cassian crossed his arms over his chest and looked up at her. "I think the traitor knows we have it. He let it be discovered on purpose."

"To create further division?" The group already had too many regular disagreements and arguments. Why did the traitor think they needed something more to drive them apart?

With another shake of his head, Cassian's serious eyes focused on the group ahead of them. "No." He looked up at her again and their eyes met. "The list…Tenji should've been first in the ranking. He had the highest score. If he had the highest score, then why is Luka ranked number one?"

Sage stared at him. "That's what you saw on the list?"

Cassian nodded. "The traitor's too smart to just leave something like this lying in the middle of our campsite. Anyone who can devise a successful plan to bring us all here and deceive us this long isn't an idiot." He paused. "Sage…this is the ranking scores from last year."

"So maybe Luka scored better this year?"

Cassian shook his head. "Highly unlikely. What I was trying to say is…since it's last year's score, you aren't on the list. Which looks suspicious." He gave her a meaningful look. Oh.

"I see," she murmured. Sage fidgeted. "If everyone sees this, they'll suspect me even more."

Cassian nodded.

Sage's shoulders drooped. "But why? Why—" she lowered her voice farther. "Why would they change the scores? Why make Luka number one if he's not?"

Cassian shrugged. "Because the king is his father."

Sage fell silent. Too many thoughts were running through her head, making it hard for her to process. Luka shouldn't be in first place. Tenji should. The Royal Council—and maybe even the king himself—were manipulating the scores. There really was a traitor among them. And whoever the traitor was, he knew a lot about each person here. Except she wasn't on this list…. Did the traitor plan to dump all the blame on her? Who could this traitor be?

"Why would he want us to know about Luka's misplacement? Is he playing some sort of game with us?"

"Cassian!" Luka called, waving them over. "Sage! Come on, before you get left behind!"

Cassian stepped after the group. "I don't know. But Tenji has been vying for first place for a long time. He's confronted Luka about it in the past. Maybe the traitor wanted Tenji to know he's been cheated."

The two of them raced to catch up with the others as Sage's mind whirled. She eyed Luka. Did he know his ranking was incorrect?

Over the next several days, the group continued onward, following the path at Tenji's lead. Tenji didn't bring up the list again, and neither did they. But Sage couldn't help thinking about it. Throughout their trek, the list and the interaction in the library remained at the forefront of her mind. Who was the traitor—the other voice in the forbidden library? No one here had quite the same voice as Everard's accomplice had. Out of everyone in their current group, Tenji's cold, calculating tone was the closest to the traitor's. Yet, Tenji's voice was deeper, huskier.

Should she tell someone about what she had overheard? But she didn't know who she could trust. She didn't know who the traitor could be. Maybe Tenji had been right to keep the list a secret. Here she was, comparing everyone's voices to the one in the library—even Cassian's.

To help distract her mind from those wandering thoughts, Sage busied herself by focusing on her "possible" healing ability. As of yet, she'd seen no evidence that her tutor, Sir Aadan's, inkling had been correct. She'd read and reread that healing book several times before she lost it with her jacket, but no matter how much she looked at, handled, and imagined making the dying plants she came across whole, nothing ever happened. Maybe she didn't have the capacity for such an ability.

While Archie and Tristan had fully recovered from the poison after about a week of treatment and were back to walking on their own, Tenji continued to give Ruben rides at Draven's insistence. But whenever Tenji transformed back into his human form, his forehead dripped with sweat and the tension in his face rarely eased. He was using his sense too often. Sage didn't think he'd be able to keep this up much longer.

Bickering amongst the group occurred daily over the smallest things—like who got to sip water from the flasks first. Despite Tenji's knowledge about the ranking error, he and Luka had stopped arguing almost completely, but Tenji was still very cold toward Sage.

Every day, the group came across new forest monsters: forest dragons, goblins, river creatures, bears, jaguars, and giant snakes, ants, bees, cockroaches, and spiders. Fewer monsters attacked when they remained together; it was the smaller groups who had to be wary.

Adjusting to the harsh environment of the forest was only one of the ways the princes changed. Each of the princes—except Sage and Cassian—had grown varying lengths of facial hair, some fuller than others. They used the knife Draven provided to trim or shave their beards. Everyone's hair was longer, their bodies skinnier, and they looked more like beggars than princes. It felt as if they had been in the labyrinth for an eternity, even though Tenji said it had only been a month and a half.

After three solid weeks of carrying Ruben, Tenji nearly crumpled beneath the other boy's weight. He transformed back into a human and staggered. "I—can't carry Ruben anymore," he gasped through heavy drags of breath.

Draven studied Tenji before turning to Ruben. "I'll carry you instead."

Ruben shook his head. "I'm fine. I can walk," he said with a smile. As if to prove it, he put some weight on his leg and limped around.

Draven's forehead wrinkled. "You'll be too slow. Just let me carry you."

"No, no." Ruben shook his head again and smiled reassuringly. "I'll keep up."

Despite Draven's obvious protest, no one pushed Ruben about it again. Draven checked on him regularly and often offered to carry him, but Ruben always refused. And he *did* keep up, though he trailed in the back, so Sage kept pace with him, making sure he wasn't left behind. Ruben's eyes set on the path determinedly, and he didn't complain about his leg once.

A week after Tenji's collapse, Sage stepped through another line of trees to find a large grassy opening amidst the forest. To the right stood the goblins' rocky mountain home, and to the left were more trees. However, no one looked in either of those directions. Sage, as well as everyone else, stared forward.

The tall, stone labyrinth wall towered before them, blocking the path they'd been following. Sage's eyes followed the wall until it disappeared into either the trees or the mountains. This was the first time she'd seen any part of the labyrinth wall since they'd entered the forest.

The path led right up to the wall, and it took Sage a moment to recognize intricate engravings decorating its surface. Sage studied the engravings. Eight different symbols formed an octagon on the wall. She deciphered only two images: One was the sun; another was a human skull. The rest confused her. In the very center of the octagon was an engraving of a phoenix.

Then Sage focused on something lying near the path, and a shiver ran down her back.

A large mass of human skeletons lay strewn across the ground. Sage followed the others closer, clutching the front of her jacket. Silence hung over them as they stared at the carnage. All the bodies were clad in armor with a jaguar on their coat of arms.

They were soldiers. Soldiers from a kingdom she didn't know.

Tenji knelt to study their coat of arms.

"Niaria…they're from Niaria," Tenji muttered, as if to answer the unasked question.

Sage pressed her lips into a thin line. Niaria. Legend said that five hundred years ago, Niaria's king and his entire army marched into the labyrinth in hopes of saving their kingdom. None of them were ever seen again, and Niaria had fallen to a neighboring kingdom.

Luka stepped closer, his face tight. "So the story is true."

Kai kicked a helmet and glared at the wall in their path. "What is this anyway? A dead end? Is the labyrinth just a farce of death?"

Standing, Tenji examined the wall once more. "It seems to be a doorway."

Archie brightened. "A doorway out of the labyrinth? Is this the exit? Did we make it?"

Draven's dark laughter surprised Sage. "The exit? We aren't even out of the first section yet. Why would this be the exit?"

"First section?" Kai repeated, staring at Draven. "You've got to be bloody kidding me! There are *sections*?"

Tenji eyed Draven, his eyes narrowing as he nodded. "This must be the entrance to the next section of the labyrinth."

Sage's shoulders sagged. How many sections were there?

Ruben wiped some sweat from his forehead and leaned all his weight onto his good leg. "We finished one section?"

"Not yet," Jovian replied, cocking a coy smile. "There's still time for us to die before making it through."

Kai slapped Jovian on the back of the head.

"Despite the morbid description, Jovian makes a fair point." Luka gestured to the bodies on the ground. "We need to figure out how to open this door before we can assume we've made it. And considering the bodies, that's not an easy task."

Archie dropped to his knees and wailed. "Why? Why did they have to make multiple sections?" He gripped his head. "Haven't we suffered enough? Look at these awful clothes we have to wear and the state of our hair! We eat badly cooked fish, raw vegetables, and unflavored plants. We walk all day and hardly sleep at night. We're attacked and wounded by monsters…" He paused, only to moan. "It would be better to die now rather than continue through this murderous labyrinth which makes us look and act like beggars instead of princes. Oh, let me die and—"

"Oh, sure," Jovian cut in, rolling his eyes. "Go ahead! Give up and die. Your skeleton will make a nice addition to the pile. Though, I must say it would be strange to see you without all your precious hair." A hint of a smile tugged his lips.

Dropping his arms and standing, Archie glared at him while dusting off his pants. "Oh, shut up, twit." He pouted but didn't mention dying again.

Draven approached the door and placed a hand on it, examining it up close. His action broke the tension and everyone else felt comfortable enough to do the same.

"Is it a puzzle?" Sage found herself asking.

"I think so," Luka replied. "It looks strangely familiar."

"I thought so too," Tenji added, his eyes distant. "If only I could remember where…"

Then, something crashed behind them. Sage turned to find Ruben passed out on the ground, his face pale and dripping with sweat. Her stomach plunged. Tristan dropped to a crouch next to him and pressed the back of his hand to Ruben's forehead. He looked up at the rest, face tight and eyes wide.

Sage joined him and placed her own hand on Ruben's head. "He's burning up!"

How long had Ruben been in this condition? Why hadn't he said anything? Why hadn't she noticed the signs earlier?

"Is he sick?" Archie asked.

Tenji joined Tristan and Sage. "Exhaustion."

However, as Ruben lay shivering and unconscious before them, a sinking feeling settled in Sage's gut. She pushed her bag under Ruben's head as a pillow. "No, it's his leg."

Without hesitation, Tenji knelt next to Ruben and unwrapped his bandages. Everyone crowded around, but Luka shooed them back. Sage gasped when Tenji exposed the wound.

Green-yellow puss and fresh blood covered the gory lesions, and Ruben's leg, blackened and swollen, had red streaks running all the way up to his thigh. Although parts of the wound had succeeded in healing, the constant walking, battles, and lack of ability to stay properly clean prolonged healing in others.

Sage squeezed her hands into fists. Every time Ruben had smiled and said, "I'm fine. I can walk," it had been a lie.

Tenji's face showed no emotion. "How did his leg become this bad?" He turned an accusatory glare toward Sage. "You were with him the most. Tell me. How did this happen?"

His accusation infuriated her. "This environment isn't necessarily the best for healing, first of all. Second, he's been walking on it all week. It probably escalated because of that."

Draven groaned and walked away, kicking a tree stump and gripping his head. "I knew this would happen. I knew he shouldn't have been walking."

"Why did he push himself so much?" Luka asked, looking incredibly stressed. "He should have said something!"

A small voice broke through their distress: "He was afraid of holding the group back." Sage turned to look at Cassian. "He didn't want to be baggage, so he pushed himself and kept quiet."

No one said anything. They had been traveling at a ruthless pace for weeks, hardly taking enough time to rest. Especially after Archie and Tristan recovered from their poisoning. Sage squeezed the folded edges of her jacket sleeves. She should've insisted they slow down. Why had she been so careless?

Tenji put his face in his hands, then brushed his dark hair back. "Amputation is risky. It will make Ruben's chances of leaving the labyrinth slimmer." He paused. "Before we commit to an amputation, we should try to attack this infection more aggressively and hope for a miraculous recovery."

Sage's stomach twisted. If only she could heal…then maybe Ruben would have a chance. Her grandfather's face rose to mind and she squeezed the jacket's cuffs even tighter. She refused to let Ruben suffer and die.

Sighing, Luka studied the door that stood between them and the rest of the labyrinth. "There are ten of us. Some can focus on treating Ruben, some can work on opening the door, and others can gather more food and supplies." He looked at Tenji, as if waiting for him to disagree.

Instead, Tenji nodded. "We should try our best to keep progressing while we try to save Ruben. No use in wasting time on one thing if we can accomplish multiple."

Before long, Luka and Tenji had determined who would do what. Sage, Tristan, and Tenji—when he was available—would focus on healing Ruben. Tenji, Draven, and Luka would work on solving the door. Jovian, Kai, Cassian, and Archie were tasked with gathering food and wood from the surrounding forest, much to their obvious displeasure.

The day passed with no luck on either of the main tasks. No one understood how the door's puzzle worked or how to open the gate, and Ruben remained in fitful sleep despite their efforts to clean, treat, and combat his infection. When no more supplies were needed for the day, Kai, Archie, and Jovian joined the others in deciphering the puzzle while Cassian remained with Ruben, Sage, and Tristan. At one point, Kai exploded in anger and tried to burn down the wall before he finally stomped off.

During all this, careful not to draw attention to herself, Sage focused all her energy on healing Ruben. If she could activate her healing ability, she could save Ruben's life, and maybe even his leg.

Archie plopped down by their fire next to Tristan, having long given up on helping figure out the door. "Ugh! What if we're stuck here forever? Those soldiers could've died from waiting for all we know."

Tristan said nothing. Jovian joined them, squatting with his arms dangling over his knees, and grinned his usual wide grin. "Don't be a baby. Tantrums don't look good on twenty-somethings."

Twenties? Sage hadn't realized he was so much older. He didn't act his age.

"You make me sound so old." Archie frowned. "Anyway, why do you always act like you're more mature? You're the second or third youngest here—depending on how old Sage is." Archie blew a strand of his blue hair out of his face and picked at his nails, which had long since lost their cleanliness.

"Because I *am* more mature. More than you are at least."

Archie punched him in the arm. "Twit."

Jovian chuckled and rubbed his arm, then flicked a finger. A rock came sailing out of nowhere and smacked Archie in the arm—hard. "Pay back for the punch." He smirked as Archie yelped.

Before Archie could chase him, Cassian sighed, "Archie, even *I'm* more mature than you. An eight-year-old could be more mature than you."

Archie immediately sat down to sulk. Sage glanced between him and Cassian. Over all their weeks in the labyrinth, she had never heard Archie berate Cassian for his remarks the way he did with Jovian. Instead, Cassian seemed to have the opposite effect on him.

Archie looked back at the wall. "Can't we just go over the top? It might be easier than opening the gate."

Kai stood nearby, his arms crossed, refusing to join their group. He rolled his eyes at Archie's comment but didn't join the conversation.

Jovian scoffed. "If we could go over the top, don't you think we would've done that in the beginning and left the labyrinth behind?"

"It couldn't hurt to try," Archie muttered. He picked up a rock as he stood and poised his arm to throw. His gaze locked onto the top of the labyrinth wall and his grip tightened on the rock. With a yell, he threw it.

The rock arched and landed five feet in front of him.

Jovian burst into a fit of laughter, holding his sides, and Kai joined him. Shaking her head, Sage sighed and placed her chin in her palm.

"What was *that*?" Kai asked, still laughing. "You throw like a girl!"

Sage stiffened and for a moment she forgot herself. "I know many girls who could throw better than the whole lot of you. You shouldn't say such things. It negates an entire gender, regardless of how well they actually throw."

All the princes around her turned and stared. Jovian's eyes narrowed as he studied her and Sage's cheeks warmed. Oh, what had she done?

A mischievous smile slid across Jovian's face. "You're one to talk, boy-who-*looks*-like-a-girl."

"You make it sound like you're better at throwing than us," Kai commented, his eyebrows raised. "Let's see *your* throw."

Jovian tossed her a rock.

Staring down at the stone in her hands, Sage bit her lip. She hadn't meant to exclude herself while defending her gender, but she had. Tightening her grip on the rock, she stood. She'd just have to prove she could throw decently. She needed to prove them wrong—even if just for herself. Taking a deep breath, Sage locked her gaze on the top of the wall. It was high, but she didn't have to make it. The whole point of this was just to prove she could throw. Not to prove she could make it over the wall.

Oddly, she felt energized and powerful—as if her determination had strengthened her. She drew back her arm, pivoting her body. She felt the pressure of their watching eyes, but she couldn't allow her nerves to affect her throw. With all her strength, she released the rock. It sailed up in a large arc and slapped the top of the wall with a satisfying *thwack!*

Sage turned back to look at the others just in time to see Archie's mouth drop open.

Jovian shot her an approving look. "Not too bad, pretty boy." Picking up another stone, he tossed it up in the air and caught it. Then he winked. "My turn."

With an air of confidence, Jovian took no time in sending the stone flying. The instant it left his hand, Sage knew it would make it over the wall. However, just when the stone reached the top, it exploded into thousands of pieces with a sizzle of charged energy. Several bits of stone hit the mountainside, causing more rocks to tumble down the hillside with it.

Everyone, including Tenji, Luka, and Draven, stared up at the explosion in silence before Jovian turned to Archie and said, "I don't think going over is an option."

Luka glared at them. "Now isn't the time to fool around! It's hard enough trying to figure out this puzzle without all of you bickering and playing in the background. Do something useful!"

Shrinking back, Sage stared at him. This was the first time she'd seen Luka this irritated. Was the stress of the puzzle getting to him?

Archie glared back at Luka before walking off without another word. Jovian shrugged and squatted down once more, picking up a stick to draw in the dirt. Kai huffed and kicked a rock, but then walked off in the opposite direction of where Archie had gone.

Sage hesitantly met Luka's gaze. She shouldn't have taken the bait the others had tempted her with. She should've kept her focus on taking care of Ruben.

As she turned back to Ruben, she straightened. More sweat dampened his hair and face. Was his fever breaking? She knelt and switched out the wet bandages on his forehead and used a fresh cloth to squeeze water into his mouth. Cassian watched her quietly while Tristan busied himself making a simple soup in a flask.

That night, everyone—except Tenji and Draven, who were still hard at work on solving the gate's puzzle—gathered around their own fires, eating what they had found or caught for their supper.

Tristan helped her clean Ruben's wound again. Cassian even came over and lightly frosted the cloth on Ruben's head to help with the fever. Hardly anyone spoke that night.

As Sage sat there surveying the sulking princes around her, the list they'd found returned to her mind. She peeked at Tenji from the corner of her eye. He had one hand on his hip and his head in the other. Then her eyes flickered across the fire to Luka, who was finishing up his dinner so he could join Tenji and Draven again. Had he really been given first place because his father was the king? Even though she'd never heard many good things about King Léon, she found it hard to believe he would manipulate the system to force his son to the top.

Did Luka know?

Regardless, the answer wouldn't be pleasant.

23

Denial

THE NEXT DAY WAS JUST AS DISCOURAGING AS THE PREVIOUS two had been. The puzzle continued to puzzle, tensions continued to rise, the gate remained closed, and Ruben existed in a fitful, unconscious state. Yet, despite all of this, Sage found comfort in having Tristan as her partner. He had a calming charm about him. He smiled at her frequently, gestured for her to rest while he kept watch, and somehow knew when she was worrying too much.

Once, when she was really stressed about Ruben, Tristan placed a hand on her shoulder, looked her in the eye, and smiled as if to say, *don't worry. He'll be all right.*

Tristan got along well with everyone, never fought, always helped when needed, and never complained. Of course, he never said much of anything, but still, it was a pleasant change from everyone else's sharp tempers and snappy responses. Sage found herself increasingly fond of him, especially after he'd defended her and her sense to Tenji when none of the others had. And though she hadn't spoken to him much since then, she'd always meant to thank him for it.

That afternoon, half the group hovered over the gate puzzle and the other half roamed the area restlessly.

"Tristan," she found herself saying. "I meant to thank you… for standing up for me all those weeks ago."

Tristan looked up at her through his gray-green bangs, pausing briefly as he cleaned Ruben's leg to meet her gaze. Until that moment, Sage had never noticed how beautiful Tristan's dark eyes were. He shook his head. "No need to thank me."

Sage studied him silently for a moment. "If you don't mind me asking, what do you think about all this?"

Tristan's eyes darted away from hers and scanned the area. Finally, his soft, deep voice replied, "None of it makes sense."

Sage stared at him, unsure if he would continue or not.

But then, Tristan drew in a short breath and said, "Why does someone want to free the prisoner of the labyrinth? If one of us is behind it, why would they risk their own life to free a dangerous, power-hungry spirit? What are they hoping the spirit will give them?" His eyebrows drew together tightly. "And how can we leave the labyrinth without releasing the spirit? Will we be forced to stay here forever?"

Sage stared at him, stunned. She hadn't known he could speak that much, much less that he'd been worrying over all these things.

"Yes. It doesn't make any sense." She chewed the inside of her cheek, her mind churning with his questions. She thought of the list. "I wish I knew the answer to even one of those questions."

Tristan nodded and dropped his gaze back to Ruben's leg. "So do I."

Sage gathered some courage before she asked, "Why does everyone seem to dislike Luka so much?"

Tristan stilled and stared unseeing at the ground. Slowly, he straightened. "Luka's father…He's not the…kindest king."

Sage lowered her eyes to the dirt. The others were taking their hatred for the king out on Luka? What could the king have done to make the others so bitter toward him?

She watched Tristan gather dirty cloths together. "Do you hate the king, Tristan?"

He stiffened and his eyes swept back to hers. Then he stood abruptly.

"No." His voice was so gruff, it surprised her. And with that, he turned, picked up an empty bag, and walked away.

Oh, dear. Sage hadn't expected him to react that way. Was she too nosy? Should she apologize?

A moan interrupted her thoughts. Sage dropped her gaze to Ruben. He was stirring!

Ruben's eyes fluttered open, and she couldn't help but smile.

"Ruben?"

Ruben's hazy eyes wandered until they found her. He moaned. "How—How long was I out?"

"Over two days."

"Two *days*?" Ruben struggled to sit up. "Ugh, I feel terrible."

Placing a firm hand on his shoulder, Sage shook her head. "Stay down," she insisted. "Rest, please. You've been fighting fevers and infection."

Reluctantly, Ruben obeyed and she helped him lay down once more. "Is it bad?" he asked, his voice hoarse.

Sage involuntarily glanced at the twisted skin and bone that made up his leg and searched for the right words. She didn't want to alarm him, but she also didn't want to lie.

"It's bad, isn't it?" he said, more as a statement than a question. "I know it is. I know." He closed his eyes, then opened them again to stare at the sky.

Sage looked down at her hands. "Why didn't you tell us before it became so bad? Tenji would've slowed our pace; Draven would've carried you."

Ruben sighed, his expression tired and heavy. "That's why. I could tell how tiring it was for Tenji to carry me and the same thing would eventually happen to Draven. I didn't want to be more of a burden than I already was." Ruben strung an arm over his face. "And I didn't want to cause everyone to slow down more. The slower we walk, the longer it'll take to get through the labyrinth and the less likely we'll ever be able to leave… I don't want that any more than anyone else does." Ruben's face contorted and his voice grew wet with emotion. "I'm already a failure and a coward—why would I want to be baggage too?"

Sage remained silent as Ruben pressed his arm tightly over his red eyes and turned his head away. She shifted and asked gently, "Why do you think you're a failure and a coward?"

For a moment, Ruben didn't respond. Then he sniffed a few times and swallowed.

"I ran," he finally whispered. Again, he fell silent.

Sage waited and didn't push him to explain.

Ruben swallowed again. "I ran. I deserted the others and ran when the werewolves attacked…and yet…they—" his voice broke and he paused again. "They still saved me. I couldn't fight. I couldn't even stand my ground. I was weak. I was a coward. I'd be dead right now if it wasn't for them." Ruben rubbed his arm over his face, wiping away his tears, and hiccuped.

For a long while, Sage said nothing. She didn't know what to say. How could she comfort him? Finally, she stared up at the clear, blue sky. "It's not easy to face our fears. To be honest, I find my own fears difficult to face." She took a deep breath and shuddered. She remembered shedding her own tears of terror at the bottom of that dark hill—before Draven had found her.

She continued, "And I'm sure if the others were honest, they would say the same. But, Ruben, I don't think you're weak or a coward at all. It takes a lot of guts to keep such a positive outlook on our situation, but you always try your best. You pushed through your pain without ever complaining once. Facing werewolves is a different kind of courage. Just because you couldn't face them doesn't mean you're any less courageous than anyone else here."

Ruben sniffed and his body trembled.

"Don't call yourself a coward or a failure. In my eyes, you're far from that."

It was a long time before Ruben removed his arm from his face or looked at anyone, but when he did, he straightened his clothes and accepted everyone's greetings with a smile, his eyes red and puffy.

That evening, Tristan brought four rabbits back for dinner, avoiding Sage's gaze despite her attempts to catch his eye. Draven slipped off into the woods as per usual and Sage stared after him before turning back to the fire. What did he do every night? Why did he wander so far from the rest of them?

Tenji—who had scarcely budged from the gate since they'd arrived—came over to check on Ruben. Though he said nothing, his face said it all. Ruben's leg was beyond hope. Her eyes flickered to Ruben's briefly, but Ruben's hands gripped the earth and avoided their gazes. If only she could do something, do anything to help Ruben. If only she could *heal*.

"Ruben…if you weren't here, if you could rest for several months, you might have a small chance of saving your leg." Tenji's voice was as cool and calculating as ever. "However, we're in the labyrinth. There's danger around every corner. We can't risk stopping. But if you keep up the pace with your leg in this condition…I don't know if you'll make it. It's either the leg or your life. You can choose."

Sage grimaced, her heart sinking after she watched Ruben's face. She wished Tenji had delivered the ultimatum a bit less callously. Ruben said nothing.

"I'll let you think it over," Tenji added, standing. His gaze swept the forest around them, looking a bit unsettled. "We've remained in one place for too long," he muttered, mostly to himself, then more loudly, "I'm going to take a look around."

No one protested as their leader disappeared into the forest.

Tenji traipsed through the forest, his eyes combing the branches of the trees. He jerked at every twig that snapped and every leaf that fluttered. But he found nothing. It was abnormal for them to go more than two days without a monster incident. Why hadn't they been assailed by anything the last few days? There had to be an explanation. He paused, considering. Should he return to camp? If he went deeper into the forest, he might be able to discover the reason behind this anomaly, but would it be worthwhile to walk into possible danger unaided?

Undecided, Tenji instead pulled the list of the ranking averages from his bag. Ever since he'd discovered it, he hadn't been able to concentrate. He stared at the seal before he unfolded the paper once more and read his name at the top. He'd done it after all.

He had the highest score.

His older brother's voice echoed in his mind, *"You can try, Tenji, but you'll never make it to first. Never."*

Tenji had only been twelve when his brother had told him that, but it had struck him in a way nothing had since. If only he could present this list to his brother and prove to him that he had been wrong.

Then again, his brother *had* spoken the truth.

Tenji thrust the list back into his bag and strode onward, deeper into the forest. Knowing his brother had been correct only left him vacant, hollow, empty, worthless. All his time spent consuming knowledge had been futile.

Although part of Tenji wanted to be angry—no, furious—and bitter, he couldn't be. Because deep down, he'd already known what would happen—when his brother had first told him, when Tenji excelled over everyone else, when his place in second was momentarily taken away by a seven-year-old. He'd cornered Luka and demanded he reveal how he'd managed to outdo him over and over and over again even though Tenji surpassed Luka in all their sessions. But Luka was naive to the betrayal surrounding them; his eyes told Tenji that Luka truly didn't know. Yes, Tenji had known he'd never be first. Yet, he feigned ignorance.

You'll never make it. Never. Until now, Tenji had assumed his brother was being spiteful, challenging him. Now he understood what his brother had meant. The king wouldn't allow anyone except Luka to reach the top. No matter how high another scored.

His thoughts were disturbed by a shifting shadow. Draven. Tenji stopped and stared at Draven who was hunched over, clutching his head. In one hand he held a dark woven thread— different from the multicolored one he braided repeatedly. Tenji frowned. "Is this what you do when you go off on your own?"

Jolting, Draven raised his head. He hadn't even heard Tenji approach.

"Tenji." Draven stood and thrust the thread into his pocket. "What are you doing out here?"

His question ignored, Tenji raised an eyebrow. "Scouting the area. And you?"

Draven turned away and gripped a nearby tree. "Just getting some alone time. Excuse me." With that, he walked away. He paused a short distance away. "Be careful, Tenji. The labyrinth is dangerous. Even the highest-trained prince can die out here."

Tenji stared after Draven as he disappeared. Highly suspicious. He turned and continued through the dark woods until he heard something snap in the distance. After pausing briefly, Tenji treaded in that direction.

24

Cracking the Code

SAGE SQUINTED ACROSS THE FIRE AT TRISTAN—WHO ignored her—before returning to the nuts Cassian had collected. She was helping Cassian crack them while Tristan and Luka built a fire to cook the rabbits on. They had already skinned and gutted Tristan's kill. Archie, who still hadn't gotten used to watching meal preparations, had scooted closer to Ruben and away from the blood. The wind blew harder than usual, causing the fire to sputter and falter.

Luka's brow furrowed. "We may need some more firewood."

Sage stood. She hadn't budged from her spot next to Ruben in a while, and she doubted anyone else would listen to Luka. Plus, the sun was still out. "I'll go get some."

Sighing loudly, Kai stood and began walking away. "No, you stay. I'll go." He paused and turned back, pointing a finger at her. "But don't get used to this!"

What? Sage blinked. She sat down once more and stared after him, her brow furrowed. What was that about?

Everyone looked at Sage and then back at Kai's retreating figure.

Jovian grinned. "Who knew the stiff-head could actually volunteer to go get something in someone else's place?"

Archie, who was lying down with his arms crossed behind his head, sat up and stared at Sage. "Seems Kai doesn't hate *you*. And I thought Kai hated everyone." He leaned in her direction, squinting at her. "Are—are you secretly in league with him?"

"Huh? No!" Sage felt her cheeks growing warm. "Who knows? Maybe he just wanted to get the firewood."

Jovian chuckled. "Oh, sure. That's why."

Luka frowned in Jovian's direction before he said, "Well, whatever the reason, you've gotten Kai to pull some weight for once. Something no one else has succeeded in doing so far."

Sage didn't respond; she only busied herself once again with cracking nuts. She didn't entirely agree with the others' perception of Kai. She still remembered how he'd waited for her in the forest after the forest dragon attack and how he'd conversed with her when it had been just the two of them. He did care, though he pretended not to. But Sage chose not to mention this to the others since she was positive Kai would hate her for it.

"Well," Cassian broke in. "Out of everyone here, Sage has been the kindest to Kai. I wouldn't blame him for hating the rest of us. After all, it was Sage who refused to desert Kai back in the goblins' cavern."

Everyone shifted awkwardly beneath the weight of Cassian's words, and Archie grumbled, "Well it's his fault for having such a bad attitude." He sniffed. "*I* hardly remember our time in that dreadful goblin cave. So, you can't blame *me*. The only thing I remember is how hideous those goblins were. Oh, how horrid it would be to be one of them!"

Jovian stood abruptly; his face hidden from the light of the fire. "I'm going with Kai."

Archie didn't bat an eye as Jovian stalked away and continued rambling. It wasn't until Tristan finally placed a hand on Archie's shoulder and gave him a look that Archie quieted down.

After the rabbit meat had fully cooked, Tristan and Luka handed out food to the people still lingering around the fire. Then, Draven strode out of the forest and headed directly to the gate.

Sage straightened. This was her moment. She grabbed a piece of rabbit meat and hurried over to him. She slowed as she drew closer, approaching cautiously.

"Draven," she called timidly.

He startled and glanced at her briefly before turning his focus back to the gate and its odd symbols. He said nothing to her.

"I brought you some food." She held it out to him, expecting him to refuse it and tell her to go away.

To her surprise, Draven accepted the food, his gaze focused on the door. His free hand brushed the figures he could reach, and he stared up at the others.

Sage bit her lip as she gathered courage to speak again. "About before...I never got to thank you."

Draven grunted. "No need." He took a bite of the meat and his roaming gaze halted over one of the images. "It's the same one," he whispered to himself. He studied the other symbols and then turned and strode slowly around the campsite, his eyes searching the ground, rocks, and trees. He dug through a few bushes.

What was he doing? Sage followed him curiously.

Finally, Draven paused and dug dirt away from a stone. On the stone was the symbol of a skull. A skull identical to the one on the gate. Sage's eyes widened as Draven marked the area with a large stick before continuing his search.

Draven circled the area and marked other random spots. Finally, he returned to the gate and counted the symbols before he continued his hurried searching.

Sage slipped over to one of the places he marked near the foot of the mountain.

"Careful!" called Luka. "You don't want to be buried in an avalanche."

Heeding Luka's warning, Sage cautiously trod around the base of the mountain, avoiding the small sprays of falling rocks. She searched the area Draven marked until she found a symbol on a nearby tree—a sun. She turned and ran to the gate, searching the images there. Sure enough, there was a matching sun symbol at the top of the octagon.

Her heart quickened and she whirled to look for Draven. He'd returned to the tree, muddy and ruffled, prodding at the sun symbol. Suddenly, a pillar rumbled out of the ground, and the figure on the gate glowed. Draven's expression brightened as everyone leapt up from the fire, their mouths gaping.

Draven returned to the gate as the rest of the group crowded around him.

"It did something to the gate!" cried Archie.

"Do you think this is the key to the puzzle?" Luka asked.

Draven stiffened but nodded and pointed. "The symbols. A little while ago, I found a symbol on a tree and recognized it from the gate. I thought if there was one, there might be more. I was able to find all the symbols in the surrounding area. So yes, I think they have something to do with opening this gate." He paused as he studied the signs. "It occurred to me yesterday that the symbols could be telling a story—if placed in the right order. I decided to try the sun first because I remembered that same symbol on top of the labyrinth's gate entrance."

"Any ideas on what story it could be telling?" Luka asked.

Draven shook his head.

Sage didn't know any stories that had to do with the sun. Plus, most of these symbols were random and hard to make out. She shrunk back from the group, watching as they studied the figures and argued over their guesses.

Ruben hobbled up next to her, leaning on his staff. She almost urged him to lie back down, but then realized that if they continued onward, he might lose his leg soon. Her words died in her mouth.

Luka pointed to the phoenix in the middle of the octagon. "Reudinia's emblem is the Phoenix. It's sometimes associated with the sun—"

"But this is the labyrinth, not Reudinia," Ruben interrupted. "If it was a story about anything, I think it would be about the labyrinth. Does anyone know the story of the labyrinth?"

No one spoke. Ruben made some very valid points. This was the labyrinth. Why would the puzzle be about anything other than the labyrinth?

"Doesn't Tenji know the story?" she found herself asking.

Draven's face jerked toward her. "Tenji's not back yet?"

Everyone shook their heads.

A worried wrinkle lined his forehead. He turned his focus back to the gate. "I don't know the details as well as Tenji. He said something about a tribe. A tribe that made this labyrinth under the order of their leader. Tenji mentioned them when we first entered, saying they locked a spirit away in the center. That's all I remember."

"The tribe was called Kyndrie," Cassian spoke up, standing near the gate with his arms crossed over his chest. "I vaguely remember reading about them. They were found slaughtered; no one knows how they were killed. Those kinds of facts tend to stand out."

Cassian pointed to an image of a man holding a triangle with an 'X'; generally, Sage knew that such 'X's symbolized dark magic. He continued. "If I remember Tenji's story correctly, there was a man who used dark powers." Cassian pointed to an image of a man with waving lines around him. "They say he could take away senses." He nodded to the image of a man holding a large boulder. "He became too strong.

"The leader of Kyndrie gathered an army," Cassian continued, pointing to an image of warriors, and then moved his finger to an image of chains. "They captured the man and separated his spirit from his body." Cassian reached up and brushed the figure of the larger man coming out of the smaller man. Then his hand hovered over the swirling circle. "Then they locked him in the labyrinth."

Sage, along with everyone else, stared at him as they processed his story. She smiled. He was so young, but so brilliant.

Cassian slowly faced them. "It makes sense, doesn't it?"

After a moment of silence, Luka nodded. "It does. Why don't we try it?"

Brief chaos ensued as Draven showed the princes where each of the symbols were. Cassian stayed by the gate to call out the order while the others rushed to take places near each of the symbols. As he called them out to the others, each of the princes pried at their symbol until a pillar shot up from the ground nearby and the matching symbol on the gate glowed. Finally, he called out the last one.

"The labyrinth."

Sage turned to the swirling image carved onto a rock near her. She tugged and pushed at it until a small pillar rose from the ground next to the stone. As the last symbol on the gate glowed, the whole wall shone and the ground trembled.

A large pedestal emerged from the earth in the center of the mass of dead bodies. As the pedestal rose, the glowing symbols, which made the shape of an octagon on the gate, began to rotate. From the center of the pedestal rose a glowing orb. When it finally settled, the trembling subsided, and the group shifted closer to examine the globe.

"Nice work, Cassian!" Archie exclaimed, clearly excited to be making progress toward escape.

Luka reached out, like a fly drawn to a fire, and touched the globe's surface. He winced, but his hand remained on it. Finally, avoiding their gazes, he said, "I can't move my hand…It's—It's stuck."

Archie took several hurried steps backward. "Is this how all those other people died? Because if something is going to happen, I'm getting as far away as possible."

Draven crouched by the pedestal and pointed to an engraving on its side. "It says, 'Only those who are worthy of following in the footsteps of Sigeberht the Great may pass through. Solve the conundrum on the door to prove your worth and continue. If you fail, the shadow of death is swift and stealthy." He grunted and stood. "It seems you're stuck there until you solve the puzzle."

"They need to work on their poetry," Cassian muttered, rolling his eyes and shaking his head.

Luka shifted his stance, but his expression was unreadable. "Solve the puzzle," he muttered as he studied the maze-like design on the door in the center of the octagon.

"Sigeberht?" Ruben's pale, pain-stricken face twisted in confusion. "Who is that?"

"Yeah, who is he?" Archie demanded, still leaving a fair amount of distance between himself and Luka. "I have never heard of this Sijerbertie."

Sage bit the inside of her cheek and wrung her hands. Did it matter? Luka's life was on the line.

Cassian rubbed his palm on the hilt of his sword. "He's the leader of Kyndrie."

The puzzle on the door shifted again and Luka's lips strained. "I can control the gate. But I'll need some help deciphering the new puzzle…Tenji might know how."

Eager to be helpful, Sage shot her arm in the air. "I'll go find him!" Then, before anyone could object, she took off in the direction Tenji had disappeared a while ago. Why hadn't he returned yet? It was growing darker, and Tenji normally discouraged late night adventures. Climbing over tree roots and tripping over vines, Sage brightened the darkening area to calm her nerves.

She shouldn't have volunteered.

It was getting darker, and she already knew how useless she was in the dark on her own. What on earth had she been thinking?

As she walked deeper into the forest, her anxiety grew. Where had Tenji gone? Why did he come out so far alone? He should know better, especially since he'd been the one to organize their safety system, insisting others didn't roam this far from camp alone. A rustle to her left made her jump and stumble back and she tumbled hard to the ground.

"What are you doing out here?" Tenji's gruff voice came from above and Sage looked up to find him staring down at her. "It's not safe out here for you."

"And it is for you?" she snapped as she climbed back to her feet and rubbed her sore bottom. A wave of relief flooded through her. She'd found him.

Tenji's face tightened, and he looked away. "I can change form if necessary; I can confuse the monsters. You, however, will die swiftly. And your death would be an inconvenience."

Sage wasn't sure if she should feel angered or touched by his words. He'd never shown any signs of caring whether she died before, but his harsh and superior tone angered her. He'd always looked down on her. She wouldn't be surprised if he still believed she was the traitor, even after six weeks together. "Haven't I proven myself to you?"

Tenji didn't face her. "Proven yourself? No. Though I'll admit, your sense is more useful than I originally expected."

Sage frowned. "I've kept the list secret. Shouldn't that gain me some trust?"

Tenji faced her suddenly and met her gaze, staring into her as if doing so would enable him to see into her soul. "Sage, if there is one thing you are good at, it's keeping secrets. This isn't the only secret you've been keeping. Why should keeping this small one gain you any trust?"

Her breath halted. "What—what do you mean?" Alarm swirled in her gut. What was he implying? "What secrets?"

Tenji eyed her up and down silently. Finally, he shook his head. "Did you really think no one would notice, Sage? You're with us all day, every day."

Sage's heart froze. Oh, no. No, it couldn't be. He couldn't have found out. Maybe he still believed she was the traitor. Maybe it was only that. She truly, truly hoped that was the truth. "I'm not the traitor."

Tenji laughed, a genuine but short laugh, which was weird to hear coming from him. "Traitor? I'm well aware you're not the traitor, Sage. Yes, in the beginning I was quite convinced it was you. Something didn't sit right with me when I looked at you. But I realized what it was over a month ago. Do you really not understand what I'm saying?"

She couldn't breathe.

"I know about you, Sage," Tenji said, and, after realizing he would have to spell it out, continued, "I know you're a woman."

The moment his words sank in, everything spun around her.

Tenji had found her out.

"Danger is approaching," a whisper suddenly slipped through the traitor's mind. *"It won't be long before someone dies. How long will you hold out?"*

The traitor stiffened, suddenly more aware of everything around him. What was coming this time?

25

Round Two

HE KNEW. TENJI KNEW. WOULD HE TELL THE OTHERS? Would they leave her behind? Would they think she was the traitor because she wasn't a prince? Her heart pounded in her ears, and she became painfully aware she was alone with Tenji.

"Before you go on and try to convince me otherwise or persuade me not to tell the others, let me inform you," Tenji continued, crossing his arms. "Your difference in gender will only cause an unnecessary amount of drama that I don't wish to deal with on top of everything else. They can figure it out on their own. But what I do want to know is why you pretended to be a prince in the first place."

Sage struggled to fight her drowning thoughts and focus on Tenji's words. Wait. Did he just say he wasn't going to tell the others? "Who else knows?" she found herself squeaking.

He sighed. "I haven't told anyone if that's what you're implying. But that doesn't mean they haven't figured it out themselves already. Though I'm quite sure Kai, Jovian, and Archie don't know. They would've definitely voiced it to the rest of the group."

Her legs wobbled underneath her. They didn't all know yet, and Tenji wasn't going to blab about her. "How did you find out?"

"How could I not? Everything about you only made sense if you were a woman. Your behavior. Your interesting choice of words. And various other things." He leaned in closer. "But I still want to know why. Why are you acting like a prince?"

Sage bit her lip. Could she tell him? But what if he was the traitor? If she told him she pretended to be her brother to go into the library the day of the assessment, he might realize she'd overheard him. He could kill her right where she stood and say a monster did it. No, she would have to keep it to herself.

"I don't want to tell you."

Tenji said nothing for a moment as he studied her. "Fine. But I'll find out one way or another." He took a step closer to her.

She had to get the focus off her. But how? Then she remembered the gate. "Oh, uh, I forgot to mention…Draven figured out the gate and Luka needs your help solving the puzzle we've unlocked."

Tenji straightened and stared at her. "He did?" With a twist, he looked in the direction of the gate. "Why didn't you say so earlier?" He frowned at her. "We'll continue this conversation later." He turned and headed back toward camp.

Sage relaxed her shoulders and took in a sigh of relief. Then she trotted to keep up with his long strides. She glanced up at his face. For the first time, a small smile lifted the corners of his mouth.

Then something glinted to her right. She turned her head toward it unconsciously and what she saw made her reach for her sword. With a yank, she pulled the sword from its scabbard and screamed, "Tenji! Look out!"

Tenji turned as a large, dark shadow leapt at him. Sage jumped, energy warming inside as she whipped her sword forward. A nasty snarl and sharp yelp sliced across the dark woods as her ray sword pierced the creature. Unintentionally, Sage lit up the entire area around them, revealing several large, black creatures with red eyes and bared teeth. She had seen this creature before.

With a jerk, Tenji pulled her back, pushing his bag into her arms, and transformed into the same black, towering creature.

Werewolves.

"Sage, run!"

Instantly, the werewolves launched, attacking Tenji. She stumbled back, the urge to run rising in her chest. It was one thing to see one terrifying creature and know it had Tenji somewhere inside. It was entirely something else to see seven of them with the intent to kill. She quaked where she stood, her hands gripping her sword, and she could understand why Ruben ran before. Any sane person would run if they weren't already fighting for their life.

Shoving several werewolves away to one side, Tenji transformed his tail into a large tentacle that he used to throw several of them off him. "Sage, warn the others! Go! I'll hold them off as long as I can."

Sage didn't want to leave Tenji behind, regardless whether or not he was the traitor, but the others needed to be warned too. She recalled the blood-stained shirts and jackets. The bandages on the backs, arms, and torsos of those attacked by these beasts. And Ruben and his chewed-up leg that was eating away at his life. If they could barely hold them off before, there was no way Tenji could do it alone now. She slung Tenji's bag over her torso. "Tenji! Let's go together!"

Brandishing her sword, she lit it with her sense and swung the sword at one of the wolves. It slashed through one of its legs and the wolf howled, collapsing to the ground. Sage's body quivered. But she couldn't allow these creatures to hurt the others like they had before. She thrust her sword deep into its chest. The squeal of the wolf echoed through the woods, turning the attention of the other wolves to her. Several of them leapt.

Tenji swept a tentacled-tail and knocked them away. He bit Sage's jacket and threw her onto his back, galloping back to camp. She scrambled to hold onto the coarse fur of Tenji's wolfish back before she glanced back. The werewolves bounded after them. She blasted a bright light behind, and the werewolves skidded to a stop, yelping and howling.

When they reached camp, several more howls bellowed, resounding through the forest. Archie, Tristan, Ruben, Draven, Luka, and Cassian were all staring at the forest, still crowded around the gate. Tenji slid to a stop by them, and Sage hopped down and threw Tenji's bag toward the wall.

Turning to face the trees, Tenji bared his werewolf teeth. "It seems the whole pack is here."

Archie pulled at his collar. "Werewolves?" he squeaked.

Ruben and Cassian involuntarily shuddered in response. Tenji nodded his wolf-head, right as some werewolves emerged from the trees to their right, growling. Some more appeared by the mountains on their left. Finally, six werewolves ran in from the direction Tenji and Sage had just come. They crouched as if ready to attack, but none of them moved closer.

Draven pulled out his sword and grimaced. "Round two."

Everyone joined in suit and pulled out their own swords, though four out of eight of them trembled at the sight of the beasts. Ruben could barely stand, let alone fight. His cheeks were red, showing signs of another fever. He could barely hold up a sword, but he looked at the wolves dead-on despite his trembling body.

Luka, his hand still stuck to the globe, glanced around them. "How many are there?!"

Without a glance back, Tenji responded, his tail swishing behind him, "At least twenty. Double how many attacked us last time."

Archie swallowed, his legs wobbling underneath him. "Double?"

Luka grimaced and turned his gaze back to the gate. "I can't move. I'm stuck until I figure out the puzzle."

With those words, Tenji risked a look back. "You'll be sitting prey."

Ruben limped between Luka and the others. "Don't worry, Luka. I'll protect you."

Archie scoffed. "How? You can barely stand."

As if to respond, plants sprouted from the ground and enlarged to an impossible size. Everyone stepped away, even the werewolves. Soon, the entire area surrounding Ruben and Luka was covered in living, moving vines, leaves, and thorns. Ruben, sweat rolling down from his green hair, braced his leg with a vine that crawled up him. "I said I will protect Luka. I won't fail this time."

Tenji nodded and turned back to the werewolves. Sage looked around the group, bracing for the dreadful fight to come, and realized something terrible. "What about Kai and Jovian?"

Tenji didn't respond. The werewolves crept closer. Trembling, Sage lifted her sword. Were Kai and Jovian dead already? They'd been gone way longer than a trip of gathering firewood should take, which meant they should assume the worst. But she couldn't. Not yet.

Cassian trembled violently as he lifted his sword.

"Cassian."

Cassian turned his head toward her, his eyes wide.

"I'm here with you," Sage assured. "We will get through this together. Alive."

He nodded, then stepped closer to her and gripped his sword a little tighter.

One of the wolves howled and the pack launched. Tenji met them with the same force, waving his tentacle tail around. Lightning lit the sky, striking four of the werewolves simultaneously. Then Sage, calling as much intensity as she could, dug her blazing ray sword into the gut of the first to meet her and slashed at another. To her left, Cassian froze the werewolves, causing ice to pierce their hearts like a knife.

For just a moment, she had hope. They were attacking with such fervor and meeting them with strength. But then she noticed the wolves were barely affected, just thrown off a bit. Their wounds healed before her eyes instantly after receiving the wound. A werewolf she had pierced deep with her sword attacked again and scratched her across the arm. It then knocked her to the ground. Just as it was about to bite her neck, ice shot through its body.

She didn't have time to thank Cassian as she scrambled up to block another attack. The werewolf Cassian struck didn't move again. Maybe it had something to do with where they were hit. Maybe striking them through the heart was one of the few ways to defeat them. But their speed made it hard to accurately aim.

Another wolf charged for her. She blocked its attack and sliced across its chest.

She risked a glance toward the others when a werewolf sprouted from nowhere and closed its jaws on her shoulder. She screamed, and it dragged her to the ground.

Was this it? Was this the end?

26

Nine

KAI GROANED WHEN JOVIAN APPEARED NEXT TO HIM IN THE forest. He really didn't want extra baggage on this lame errand. Kai's arms were full of loose, dry sticks and branches he'd found lying around. He bent down and picked up another. How many of these things did they need anyway? This wasn't really a task for two people.

Smiling, Jovian leaned his shoulder against a tree. "I've decided to join you. The others were boring me with their needless chatter."

"You sure *you're* not the one spouting needless chatter?" Kai rolled his eyes and continued walking, hoping Jovian would go away. "I don't need help. Why don't you scamper back to camp?"

Chuckling, Jovian trotted to catch up and then kept pace with him. "I'm quite aware you don't need help. I merely came along to tease you."

Kai gritted his teeth and clutched the sticks he'd gathered. He'd roast him.

His smile unfaltering, Jovian dodged the flaming ball Kai tossed his way. "Oh, my. Savage."

"Don't follow me. Go away."

"You know," Jovian continued as if he hadn't heard Kai at all, "it's interesting to see you working with the group for once. Is this your first time?" Jovian strolled up ahead and spun around to face him.

Kai took a deep breath. Jovian sure knew how to irk him. Kai glared as Jovian continued to smile that grating smile of his. He sure was full of crap.

"I don't see *you* ever doing any work. You just follow people around," Kai said as he resisted the urge to throw down his pile of wood and pummel the other boy. He scanned the forest for an escape and caught sight of a small shadow darting past in the treetops. He returned his gaze to the more immediate nuisance.

Jovian leaned against another tree, crossing his arms once more, and smirked. "True." He straightened and strolled up ahead before he faced Kai again, walking backward now. "I consider myself a free bird. I do what I want." He grinned wider, then turned around and kept walking.

Kai frowned as he picked up another piece of wood. *He'd* said those same words before, but they sounded arrogant coming from this jokester. If that's what it sounded like, he'd never say those words again.

With a sigh, Kai gave up hope of shaking Jovian off and instead focused on his search for firewood. Once again, he thought he saw something flutter by in the branches above, but then Jovian leapt onto a tree stump and drew Kai's attention back to him.

"So, tell me, Kai," began Jovian as he squatted on the tree stump and cocked his head. "How does it feel to have a wild, powerful sense like yours?"

Kai blinked. How did it feel? He'd never been asked that before.

Shifting his wood in his arms, he turned away. "I never asked to have this damned sense. Do yourself a favor and be happy with the one you have." He strode away from Jovian.

There was no sound for a moment, but soon Jovian was at his side again, chuckling. "Of course, who wouldn't want to have a sense like mine? And I mean, wouldn't the world be boring without any senses? No one to set fire to homes or crush entire cities!"

Kai stopped walking and stared at Jovian. His gaze hardened as Jovian's words washed over him. "Never joke about that again."

Jovian stared back at him. He raised his eyebrows. "I apologize. Didn't realize you'd take it so *seriously*." He took a few steps away, sticking his hands into the pockets of his trousers. "I'll remember that next time I try to joke with *you*." He grinned.

What kind of a sick joke was that? Kai forced himself to relax the tight grip he had on the wood pile. Someone needed to teach Jovian when his jokes went too far.

Then Jovian straightened, his smile dropping from his face, and searched the trees to his left.

Kai followed his gaze. "What?"

"Shhh…" Jovian placed a finger to his lips. Then he crouched down and motioned for Kai to follow him. "Something large and fast. Weaving through the darkness."

Dropping his wood pile, Kai obliged and crept after Jovian.

Jovian skulked with surprising stealth, as if he was walking on an entirely different ground than Kai. His steps made no sound, finding spots without crunching leaves and sticks; Kai, however, accidentally stepped on anything possible. He cringed with every crinkle and crack.

A moment later, Jovian jerked to a stop and yanked Kai behind a tree. Kai scanned the trees around them. Suddenly, the ground bent underneath them and launched them both into the branches above. Wind whirled past Kai and he strained—harder than he'd ever want to admit—to contain a shout of alarm. He landed awkwardly on a branch, scrambling for purchase, while Jovian landed gracefully on his feet nearby. Kai glared at Jovian and lifted a threatening fist before looking down below. Large, black shapes flashed by, pausing to sniff the air.

The shapes looked oddly familiar. Like the creepy wolf-creature Tenji often transformed into. Kai's breath stilled.

"It seems the werewolves have reappeared," Jovian whispered grimly.

Kai nodded. Then he gripped the tree branch tightly, staring after the creatures. "They're too close to camp. The others."

"I bet they can smell the food cooking."

That was all Kai needed to hear. Clenching his fists, he prepared to jump into the midst of the wolves, but then Jovian's arm struck out, catching him in the chest and stopping him short.

"Don't. You might die," Jovian whispered. "The five attacked last time barely made it out alive. Cassian told me there were only ten of these beasts then. This pack is close to thirty."

"How can you tell?" Kai hadn't counted more than a handful.

"When I focus, I can sense vibrations in the earth." Jovian's gaze remained focused on the werewolves passing beneath their hiding place.

"But we can't let them attack the camp!" Kai hissed, shoving Jovian's arm away. "I'd rather die taking out as many as possible than stand on the sidelines and watch them slaughter the others."

For the first time since they'd seen the wolves, Jovian turned to meet Kai's gaze and raised his eyebrows. "That's news to me. Didn't realize you cared so much about the others."

Kai maintained Jovian's stare long enough to say, "I'm going. Are you coming or not?"

Without waiting for Jovian's reply, Kai leapt from the branches, landing in front of four werewolves that had trailed behind the others. The snarling beasts encircled him and soon there were five more joining the four. He stared right into the blood-red eyes of the first. "You're going to die today, you blasted creature."

Body erupting into flames, Kai attacked. Claws grazed his shoulder, but the werewolves leapt away as soon as the fire touched them. A wave of flames sent several of them skittering back. Then Jovian landed next to him and showered a gush of large rocks at the wolves creeping in from behind.

Kai nodded to Jovian before turning to block a pounce from another werewolf. "These things are huge," he muttered as he set one ablaze. It yelped and ran off, rolling furiously on the ground, only to finally collapse dead.

Jovian responded with a cry of pain. The ground trembled, a werewolf barked, and Jovian cursed. "I really didn't want to get bloody."

Setting a few more of the mangy beasts on fire, Kai swiveled to help Jovian. He threw another wave of fire and the werewolves around Jovian backed away.

Jovian's expression darkened and he gripped a bleeding arm. "They're weak to fire. Take them out." The ground began to shake beneath them and crumbled inward around the wolves. Two giant pieces of earthy rock smashed one of the wolves with surprising viciousness. That must've been the one that had clawed Jovian.

Gritting his teeth, Kai spun, releasing a fire tornado to envelop the remainder of the werewolves. Soon, nine flaming, smoking, lifeless werewolf bodies littered the forest floor.

Pulling off his jacket, Jovian inspected the wound on his upper arm. "Aisshhhh. It hurts." Distant howling echoed through the trees and Jovian's gaze snapped in the direction of their camp as he pulled his jacket back on. "Let's smash the rest of those damn creatures. They ruined my mood."

Kai raced back toward camp as fast as he could, his vigilant gaze catching on anything that shifted in the trees and tangled vines, keeping a lookout for more of the hideous beasts. Kai's feet, however, found every branch, root, or vine tangled on the forest floor. Jovian soon caught up with him and then darted past.

Jovian looked back at him. "Guess we won't need firewood now," he joked with his usual infuriating smile.

Unbelievable. Kai grunted in reply, too annoyed to even think of a response. Then, once again, Kai saw something flutter past in the treetops. This time when he looked up, a small creature skittered through the branches above. Then another form appeared, running alongside them.

Kai and Jovian skidded to a halt. Staring down at the creature who also slid to a stop beside them, Kai frowned and gave the creature a quick, calculative scan. It came no higher than their calves, had a lizard-like scaly body, but stood upright on two feet. Instead of arms, the lizard had wings. The creature cocked its head, watching them curiously.

"What is that?" asked Kai, frowning.

Jovian shook the ground under it, but the creature only fluttered briefly and landed back down. He furrowed his brow and bumped the ground under the creature once more, but again, it easily evaded. "I think it's a wyvern."

Ah. Wyverns were similar in appearance to dragons but didn't blow fire and had two legs instead of four. Yet, they were said to be quick. They *looked* like carnivorous chicken dragons.

"Just ignore it. It's too small to worry about anyway. We need to hurry," Kai muttered and continued toward camp.

Jovian followed, looking back at the creature. A few minutes later, he tapped Kai's shoulder. "It's still following us."

Kai peered back. Sure enough, the wyvern stared at them and cocked its silver head. He sighed, annoyance crawling up his throat. He didn't have time for this. "Just ignore it," he bit out.

"I don't know." Jovian was still looking back at the wyvern. "I have a bad feeling about this."

As if his words had opened some sort of floodgate, Kai turned back in the direction of camp and found about fifty more of the creepy little chicken lizards staring up at him. For the first time since seeing the creature, anxiety began to swirl up in his stomach. Maybe Jovian was right…

The wyverns cocked their heads back and forth repetitively, staring up at them. Neither Kai nor Jovian budged. The creatures' heads continued their rhythmic twitching until Kai couldn't stand it anymore. One more twitch and he'd roast them for supper like the chickens they were.

"Any ideas, jokester?"

Jovian's gaze flickered around. "You wouldn't happen to be carrying any food on you, would you?"

Shaking his head, Kai glared at the little beasts. "Of course not. Arghh, these creatures are really bugging me with their twitchy little lizard heads! Why don't we just burn them?" Without waiting for a response, Kai launched a fireball straight through the crowd.

The wyverns scrambled out of the way of the flaming ball before turning their attention back to Kai and Jovian. Then, almost as one, they hurled themselves at Kai.

Kai blasted fire at them, and Jovian rained down rocks, but the little chickens were too fast and small for either of them to aim well. Wyverns swarmed Kai, their bites and needle-like claws stinging. He flailed about, brushing, pulling, and kicking them off, blindly burning everything in his path. He even ignited the ground around him with fire, but only a few of the chickens were deterred by the flames.

A few paces away, Jovian gracefully dodged their attacks by jumping up and around, showering rocks over the crowd of beasts. But he was no match for the wyverns' speed.

When Kai finally set fire to one of the tiny pests, it only angered the rest, and they all attacked him simultaneously. He stumbled back and fell to the ground, covered with the little creatures nipping and biting. "Arghhh!"

He exploded. The blast catapulted several pesky chickens away.

But he still had too many on him to get out from underneath them, much less fight back effectively.

Then shrill howls, snarls, and yelps rose in the distance.

"They're attacking the camp!" Kai yelled. He called his fire spear and whipped it around, sending several more wyverns flying. "I can't get these blasted creatures off me!"

Something crashed and Jovian laughed victoriously. "Finally! Got some of them!"

Kai fought to get up, dragging himself to his feet and struggling forward. He huffed, knocking more back with his flaming spear and using his free hand to wrench one from his dominant arm.

His muscles screamed with exhaustion, carrying the extra load of surprisingly heavy wyverns. They were never going to make it back to camp in time at this rate.

Then the wolves quieted.

Kai clutched his conjured spear. Were the others dead already? Or had they won after all? He unfurled another volley of flames with his free hand, consuming a few of the wyverns.

Jovian leapt over their heads, smashing several more. "These things are harder to beat than those werewolves were."

With a grunt, Kai pulled another one off him and threw it. "And much more annoying."

Howling arose once more, louder this time. The others must still be alive! Or at least some were. But since there were sounds of a fight, it meant *someone* was still alive.

"Jovian, jump!"

After Jovian disappeared into the trees, Kai released a massive wave of flames in all directions. He watched as the wyverns scurried off or were consumed by the blazing fire. When Jovian dropped back beside him, the grass, trees, and bushes were all on fire. Jovian opened the ground around them and swallowed any remaining wyverns like quicksand.

"Finally," he breathed, panting as he flashed a grin Kai's way. "I suppose that's why there's the saying 'kill two wyverns with one stone.'"

Kai didn't have time to be annoyed. He turned and ran, calling over his shoulder, "Hurry!"

The two of them leapt over logs, vines, and roots, weaving through the bushes and trees, leaves and branches. When they finally emerged from the trees into the clearing, Kai scanned the scene before him.

Ruben stood near the gate and manipulated vines and tree roots, throwing off or deterring any werewolves coming close to him and Luka. He had three snarling werewolves trapped in vines. Archie was knocked down and had surrounded a werewolf's head with a bubble of water. Tristan, taking on four werewolves at once, alternately electrocuted the beasts and slashed at them with his sword. One werewolf was fighting off three others, so Kai assumed that werewolf must be Tenji.

A scream pierced through the night and Kai's eyes flew toward the source of the sound. One of the werewolves had Sage's shoulder in his teeth and dragged the struggling boy across the earth. Sage weakly swung his sword at the wolf but couldn't hit it because of his position. Crying out, Cassian ran after Sage but other wolves sidetracked him.

Kai dashed after Sage. The werewolf shook the other boy violently and threw him hard enough for Sage to rebound and skid. Sage curled up on the ground.

Why couldn't he run faster?

The werewolf stalked toward Sage as he struggled to stand and hold up his sword, but stumbled, keeling over once more.

With a yell, Kai hurled himself through the air with a blast of fire, landing hard in between the wolf and Sage just as the wolf pounced. He blasted the werewolf with the hottest flames he could form. The werewolf shrieked, stumbled back, then crashed in a charred lump. The werewolf's shriek called the others' attention, and several deserted their current prey and came rushing toward Kai.

Bleeding from the wyverns and werewolves he'd fought earlier, Kai blasted himself into the air and set the ground ablaze in an explosion of flames. He punched one beast with a flaming hand, slashed another with his conjured spear, spun and kicked a third with a flaming leg, and stabbed the next.

Kai whipped his head around, searching for the others. Jovian propelled himself between a werewolf and Ruben and Luka, easily knocking it away with a rock. Ruben crumpled to the earth at the sight of them, and his vines sagged, releasing the werewolves he'd captured.

Sending a volley of flames at the falling wolves, Kai sprinted toward Archie and Tristan, flipping over a wolf, slashing it with his spear, and released a torrent of flaming balls down on the werewolves. Kai breathed heavily, muscles trembling and watched the final three run back into the forest, yelping shrilly.

Without hesitation, Jovian took off after them and disappeared into the trees.

Tenji, transforming back into his human-self, stumbled, and then hurried to Luka's side where the Snoot still stood by the gate. Maybe it was all the adrenaline but seeing Luka doing nothing and letting injured Ruben fight for him bloody irritated Kai. He propelled himself over to the gate, landing near Luka.

"How could you just stand there the whole time the werewolves were attacking and do nothing? You made everyone protect you? That's pitiful and sick."

Luka, sweat dripping down his face, glared at Kai. "I have no choice. This bothersome globe is keeping my arm captive until I finish the puzzle."

Kai dropped his gaze to the glowing blue orb resting on a pedestal. A pedestal that hadn't been there earlier. Where did that come from?

Shooing Kai away, Tenji's eyes locked on the gate. "We need to unlock this gate and get out before more creatures come." He gripped Luka's shoulder. "I know why this puzzle looks familiar." He studied the puzzle for a moment longer. "To the left, Luka. Go to the left. Down. Down. Right. To the right!"

The puzzle shifted with Tenji's instructions and Luka looked on, tense and strained. Finally, the bricks aligned into an intricate design, and there was a flash of light. Luka's hand dropped from the globe, and he sank to his knees. The gate stayed where it was, unmoving.

"What now?" Kai asked. If that bloody gate didn't open, he'd throw something at it.

Tenji approached the gate and pushed his finger into a small hole. The gate quivered and the ground trembled. Then the gate creaked and groaned and slowly opened. Dust and rock cascaded from the gate as it slid, moaning as if it hadn't opened in hundreds of years. And probably, realistically, it hadn't.

When the gate finally stood wide open, a dark tunnel greeted them. Kai scanned their group as they gathered around. Only two were missing. Jovian and Draven.

Kai creased his forehead. "Where's Draven?"

Right as the words left his mouth, Draven emerged from a shadow, gasping for air. Four werewolves fell from a shadow cloud next to him, their eyes wild. Then before Kai could react, the werewolves rabidly darted toward the first person they laid eyes on. A person who just happened to be Archie, pulling his hair back in a neat ponytail.

Tenji lunged, transforming into his wolf form and knocked Archie back. The four rabid werewolves tackled wolf-Tenji in a wild tussle of claws, teeth, and fur, and bashed him backward toward the mountain. Kai snapped to attention and raced to help Tenji.

But he didn't know which one was Tenji and which were the wolves. If he burned them, he could accidentally hurt Tenji.

Luka, Draven, and Tristan joined Kai and circled the werewolves. But all they could do was stand and watch as the violent brawl slammed against the mountainside.

The mountain trembled and an avalanche of rocks descended. "Watch out!" Kai cried.

Luka levitated as many rocks as he could away from the werewolves, and Draven dissolved more into clouds of shadow, but it was too late.

The rocks buried Tenji and the four werewolves.

Kai, Luka, Draven, and Tristan dashed to the pile and began digging through the rocks. Kai pulled stone after stone away, but there were too many to dig through. Kai looked over his shoulder and searched the forest edge.

Where was Jovian?

Archie lay where Tenji had knocked him, staring. Cassian, covered in the werewolf blood, and Sage, holding his injured shoulder, stood close by.

Luka took a step back and struggled to elevate a large quantity of the rubble with his telekinesis and tossed it to the side where it scattered across the dead. Underneath, they finally found Tenji's human head. Draven reached out and checked his neck for a pulse and his nose for breath. Then he dropped his hand and curled it into a fist. "He's gone."

Stunned, Kai sank back on his heels. Dead? He gritted his teeth and clenched his fists. How could Tenji just be…dead?

However, before he even had time to fully process what he was seeing and hearing, the gate groaned and started creaking closed.

"The gate!" Cassian cried.

Everyone stared at the gate, unsure what to do, until Draven bellowed, "Through the opening before it closes!" He yanked Tristan and Luka away from Tenji's body. Dazed, Kai followed, turning to see Sage, Cassian, and Archie not far behind. Where was Jovian?

Luka stopped and looked back at Tenji a moment longer before he ran to the gate. Tristan stooped to throw a passed-out Ruben over his shoulder while Draven created a massive shadow under all their belongings. Kai watched as their bags sank down into blackness, as if a sinkhole of sorts. Then they rushed past the closing gate and into the dark tunnel. The gates were about to close when, suddenly, Jovian vaulted through the sliver of an opening, barely tumbling through before the gate closed tightly behind him, leaving Tenji and the forest behind.

Kai stared at the dark side of the gate, hands scraped and raw from digging through rock, Tenji's death hanging hollowly over him.

No one spoke until Jovian, covered in werewolf blood and breathing heavily, smiled a cheeky grin and cocked a hip.

"That was a close one!" he chuckled, then looked around at the group. His eyebrow arched. "What's with the doom and gloom?"

Draven stood, rubbing a hand over his tired face. "Tenji... didn't make it."

Jovian's smile slid from his face. He turned and stared at the doors along with everyone else. Kai lowered his gaze.

They were no longer a group of ten.

"Don't be discouraged by the death of your friend. You knew this was a possibility when you came here."

The traitor lowered his head and tensed. He had. He'd always known death was a possibility. For any of them, even himself. Even so, he'd hoped he could find a way to keep them alive. Suddenly, the other princes' lives were a crushing weight against his chest, a squeezing fist around his conscience.

"I know why you came."

Yes, yes…to get Everard's sense.

"No…I know the real reason you came."

The traitor lifted his head.

"You came to ask me to remove your sense…but I know you have an even greater wish than that. One you can't even begin to dream. Let me start by telling you: it's possible. It's all possible if you allow me to help you. Success will make all this worth it, yes? Death is just part of the process of achieving your greater purpose. Just focus on that—the greater purpose."

The traitor's eyes widened.

"I can give you the power you need to make it possible. All you need to do is listen to me."

27

Broken Family

EVERARD'S STOMACH CHURNED AS HE STARED DOWN AT HIS rolls, venison, and potatoes. He refused to look at the big cake sitting in the middle of the table, afraid that if he looked, he might vomit all over the rich tapestry rug below. His navy jacket, full of golden buttons, chains, and ruffles stifled him, trapping him in unwanted heat.

"Why aren't you eating, Everard?" his mother's voice broke into his thoughts.

He pushed a piece of venison around his plate. It had been two and a half months—ten weeks and two days, to be exact—since the top ten princes, including his eldest brother, went missing. Reudinia was in an uproar as the news of the missing princes swept through the country. Even Velykov, Shinai, Hallon, and Terecia knew about the missing princes.

Some assumed Velykov had kidnapped them to start a war. Others said it was a group of rebels from the east who were against the royal ranking. Some even said the kidnappings had been happening for years. A few other princes had disappeared in the past such as Prince Cyprian, the first ranking prince before Luka, or Prince Talon, who was once second. But in truth, Prince Cyprian had died during a riding accident and Prince Talon had been banished.

No one ever thought to consider Everard had a hand in the princes' kidnapping. And why would they?

Finally, he answered, "I just don't feel well today."

"Again?" His mother's voice was full of worry as she reached over from her seat beside him and touched his forehead. "You haven't been feeling well for weeks. Maybe it's something serious. We should call a doctor."

"No, I don't need a doctor," he blurted out. As if to prove his point, he picked up a fork, swallowed the acid boiling in his throat, and took a bite of venison.

"He's just throwing a fit to get attention," Romain, the third eldest, retorted with a roll of his eyes. "It's what he's best at."

Everard looked across the table at his brother. A few strands of dark hair fell over Romain's forehead, his pinkish-brown eyes glaring. It was rare for the whole family to eat together, but today was Michal's twenty-first birthday so Father had allowed Everard and Mother to join the family meal.

Everard's gaze slipped to Michal who ate his meal without saying a word. Unlike Romain, not a single strand of his blond hair was out of place. Although it was his birthday, Michal hadn't smiled once during the meal and stared vacantly down at his plate. Occasionally, he'd look across the table at Mother, who would smile at him, but they'd both glance at Father and neither would say a thing.

Something sharp poked Everard's rear and he jumped, whirling just in time to see the retreating end of a wooden branch slip under the rug. Romain. He never stopped being a jerk, did he? He avoided his brother's eyes as he took another bite.

"Enough!" their father's booming voice echoed through the near-empty room. He turned to Mother, gaze sharp. "You've raised that boy with no manners. Jumping at the table." He huffed and turned his attention back to his food.

Everard flushed, feeling the indirect rebuke as strongly as if it had been said to him.

"Father, have you heard anything about the missing princes?" Michal asked, his eyes flickering in Mother's direction.

Their father dug his knife into his venison until it scraped loudly on the porcelain plate. Everyone winced, even the servants standing along the walls. Father smiled coldly, his eyes brimming with fury. "No." He leaned back against his chair and stared at his plate. "Whoever did this left no trail." He shoved another bite into his mouth and chewed it aggressively. Then he banged his fist onto the table, startling them all. "How did they manage to take so many powerful princes without a single trace? I'll kill whoever took my son from me."

Shrinking back in his chair, Everard began to play with his food again. Kill? He swallowed the lump in his throat, his heartbeat rising suddenly. He kept his eyes on the plate full of food he didn't have the stomach to eat. Would his father kill him if he found out? Surely not.

Father banged the table again and cursed; Everard flinched. "I will find him."

Mother eyed Father silently, as if debating whether to say something or keep her mouth closed. Finally, she replied, "He will be found."

Father glared at her. "How is it, after two months, we've still heard nothing? We have no messages or threats. No one asking for a ransom. No one taunting us. Just silence. They took the Crown Prince and then did nothing. What does it mean?"

No one responded to his rhetorical questions. Instead, Everard made himself as small as possible, and no one moved. Even Mother sat frozen, her face pale and tight as she watched Father carefully.

Father snapped his gaze to Michal and Romain. They both flinched. "You should know, the Royal Council has even suggested it could've been someone lower in the ranking system. An attempt to get ahead."

Michal's lips tightened, and his knuckles whitened as he clutched his silverware, refusing to meet Father's accusing eye.

Everard hunched over and clenched both hands together in his lap. That wasn't true. He hadn't wanted to be in the top ten. He hadn't even really wanted to get ahead. He'd just wanted to have a sense like the rest of his family.

Romain's brow furrowed, and he shook his head. "But that idea doesn't make sense. That would make Michal next in—" He faltered and went unnaturally still.

Father raised an eyebrow. "Yes, that would be outrageous, wouldn't it?" He stood, pressing his palms to the tabletop as he continued to stare down Michal and Romain. "If it's true, don't expect any sympathy from me just because I'm your father." Then, without another word, he abandoned the table.

Mother waited until Father left the room before she leaned over the table toward Romain and hissed, "You must be careful what you say, Romain. Watch your tongue before you find yourself on the gallows for something you didn't do." Her forehead wrinkled with worry and she raised a trembling hand to rub it.

"You—" Everard started, then swallowed hard. "You don't really think he'd put Romain or Michal on the gallows for this, do you?"

Mother met his gaze, then Romain's and Michal's before biting her lip. "I don't *think* so, but your father has never had the best temper. He can make illogical, *scary* decisions sometimes. *Don't* get on his bad side. This is more than just a kidnapping. Your brother and the other princes were considered the most powerful men in the kingdom. Next in line for the *throne*. Whoever did this either wanted to start a war or wanted to become king."

When Everard had concocted this scheme, such a thought had never occurred to him. Had his partner considered the consequences of what would happen in the kingdom—not to mention in Everard's family—while they were gone?

"Everyone will begin to suspect other princes. And the first ones they will suspect are you, Michal and Romain." Mother's voice was sharp and serious as she stared at them. "Watch your backs, especially around your father."

Romain stood, gritting his teeth, and threw his knife at the stone wall. It hit the stonework with a loud clang and clattered to the ground. No one spoke as they stared at Romain who glared at the knife on the floor, huffing and puffing. Then he spun on his heel and marched out of the room, slamming the door behind him.

Michal put down his silverware, straightened his jacket, and cleared his throat. He raised his eyes to Mother and his tone was hushed as he said, "Thank you for having dinner with me, Mother. Please excuse me." He stood, and turned to go, but paused and looked back at Mother. "Don't worry. Father always finds a way to blame us for everything. We've been expecting it for a while." Then he too left the room.

Everard pushed his plate back and lowered his head to the table. What had he done? He hadn't meant to cause his mother extra tension and stress, much less put his brothers in possible danger. He really hadn't.

Say something, he hissed to himself. But his confession stuck in his throat.

Mother brushed her fingers through the hair at the back of his head. His head still on the table, he turned it away from his mother. What would she say if she knew? How would his family react? A fear greater than his guilt mounted. Everard didn't want to find out. He didn't want to feel his family's wrath. *Especially* his father's.

Maybe everything would turn out fine on its own.

Or maybe it wouldn't.

28

A Bitter Farewell

WHEN LUKA FINALLY CALLED FOR THEM TO STOP AND REST for the night, Sage sank to the tunnel floor, dimming her light. They'd been trekking in the darkness for what seemed like hours. No one spoke about Tenji or his death, though Sage couldn't stop thinking about him. She leaned back against the tunnel wall, neck stiff. Her left shoulder throbbed and she could almost still feel the werewolf's teeth embedded in it. Sage shuddered. She hadn't had time to inspect her injury before now, but she needed to clean and wrap it. Sage eyed the others. She wouldn't be able to tend the wound easily on her own, but she couldn't ask for help either— for obvious reasons.

Cassian sank to the floor next to her, crossing his arms over his knees and lowering his head on top. If her shoulder didn't hurt so much when she lifted her arm, she'd do the same. Instead, she turned to the others.

Tristan lowered a still-unconscious Ruben to the ground and rubbed his own shoulder. Sage stared in weary fascination as Draven released their supplies from the shadows he'd been carrying them in, and he and Luka examined what was left. She'd never quite been sure how Draven's sense worked. Did he have little pockets in his shadows?

Kai kept his usual distance, and Jovian and Archie dropped to the stony ground. Finally, Draven announced he would walk a bit farther and disappeared into the dark.

What did Draven do during his disappearances? He never brought back any food or water and never said anything about scouting for threats. On the night he'd helped her, Sage discovered just how far off he typically went on his own and she was rather surprised he hadn't died yet during one of his adventures.

Died.

For a moment, Sage listened to the silence that hung over the group. One thing was for certain: no one had been ready for a death. Especially not Tenji's. Everyone had been relying heavily on his understanding of the labyrinth to lead them out of here. He had seemed so sure, so brave, so confident. And now he was gone.

The echo of whispers brought her attention back to those around her. Luka and Tristan attempted to treat wounds, but Jovian, Kai, and Archie resisted help. Finally, Tristan crouched beside her and Cassian. "Here's some cloth we can use as bandages. We don't have anything to clean your wounds with, though."

With a soft word of appreciation, Sage accepted the cloth and tucked it into her bag for later. Cassian was still covered in blood but refused the cloth offering.

Settling down to sleep, Sage closed her eyes, the heaviness of the day baiting her to rest. But before she could fall asleep, a finger poked her arm. She cracked an eye open. Cassian stared back at her through the dark. "Cassian?"

He looked away for a moment, then down at the ground, fidgeting with his sleeves. Finally, he opened his mouth but mumbled in such a way, she had to lean closer to hear what he said: "Is your shoulder bad?"

Shifting her shoulder slightly, Sage winced. "It hurts. What about you?" She couldn't tell what blood was his and what was from the werewolves.

"I have no injuries," he whispered as he hugged himself. Cassian's eyes glittered with tears in the dim light of her glow. "I thought—I thought you were going to die…when that werewolf had you. Then Tenji died." He buried his face in his arms once more. His voice came out muffled, "I could've done better."

Sage patted his back with her good arm. "No, Cassian, you were amazing. My shoulder and Tenji's death aren't your fault. Please don't blame yourself. And don't worry about me. I'm not dead, and I don't plan on dying any time soon, okay?"

When Cassian sniffled and buried his head deeper into his arms, Sage raised her hand to brush her fingers through the hair at the back of Cassian's head. "It's okay to cry, Cassian. A lot has happened to us since we got here. But don't worry, we'll make it out of here one day."

Nodding, Cassian kept his head down and sniffed.

"Now try and get some sleep."

Cassian lay down, huddling nearby her, his sniffles quiet but constant. "Sage?"

"Yes?"

"Could you call me Cass?"

Surprised by his request, Sage paused. "If that's what you want. Now get some sleep, Cass." Sage resisted the urge to brush her hand through his white hair once more before she settled down herself.

Sage stared up into the darkness, her lips pressing together. Her head still ached from slamming against the ground. At the time, the world had swirled around her. She could barely focus on the spinning image of the werewolf stalking closer, the echoes of snarls and growls filling her ears. Sage had accepted she would die. But then—then there was Kai.

He had appeared out of nowhere, a blazing sun lighting the darkness of the world around her. The werewolf had seemed impossible to kill, but with a single strike, he'd burned it to a crisp. Although the world had still swirled, Kai's blazing figure remained steady and clear. There had been a glow about him— probably from the flames—and he was angry, ferocious, and— strong. Really strong. He'd saved her life and, without hesitation, moved on to rescue the others despite how much he disliked them. Despite how much they disliked him.

Looking over to where she thought Kai might be, she looked for his spark of red hair. But even with her dim glow it was too dark in the tunnel to make out who was who. She sighed, wishing she could thank him for saving her life. Because, despite his angry and rough exterior, he did care about her, about the others. At least enough not to let them die.

Sage closed her eyes and slowly drifted off, giving in to the temptation of sleep.

She woke to rustling. Sitting up, Sage released a faint glow and squinted. Luka and Draven were organizing their bags and speaking in low tones. Tristan sat up and watched them silently as well.

After a moment, Luka noticed them and nodded. "Let's head out."

Those who were still sleeping were woken, and Kai and Archie snapped angry, sleep drenched protests. Sage took that time to hurriedly wrap her shoulder as best she could without removing her shirt. Shortly after, the group headed down the dark tunnel once more, Draven and Tristan carrying Ruben, who still hadn't woken.

Once more, no one spoke of Tenji's loss, but as Sage studied their faces, she could see a heaviness hanging over them all. She turned her gaze on the path ahead. The further down the tunnel they ventured, the warmer the air around them became, and a faint light glimmered in the distance. It didn't take long before they reached the opening and peered out.

Sage's heart dropped.

On either side towered the tall, impenetrable walls of the labyrinth and as far as the eye could see, in the expanse between each wall was dry, sandy desert. Few plants, no trees, and no water in sight.

Sage was suddenly painfully aware of the small amount of water in their bags. Monsters didn't seem so bad—at least in the forest they'd had enough vegetation and meat to eat and places to gather water.

Everyone stared across the hot, grainy land without a word or movement.

It was Archie who broke the silence, moaning and falling to his knees: "You've got to be freaking kidding me." As if his first words unclogged some sort of faucet on his tongue, Archie spilled into his typical, rapid-fire complaint routine. "A desert? A freaking desert in a labyrinth? I can't handle this heat! I'll melt into a puddle and dry up. We'll never be able to clean all the sand off us. It'll be etched into our skin forever. This heat will turn me into an ugly, old prune!"

"Ah, shut up, water wuss," Kai muttered, massaging his temples. His gaze darkened as he glared down at Archie. "If I hear one more of your bloody complaints, I'll kill you myself."

Shooting up off the ground, Archie gaped at him. "Did you all hear that? He said he'd *kill* me." He pointed at Kai, stabbing the air aggressively with his finger. "*Kill* me! I knew you were the traitor. I knew it was you all along!"

Luka's shoulders slumped and he looked away, heaving a deep sigh.

"Hold up...*traitor*?" Kai snapped. "Who are you calling a traitor? I ain't no bloody traitor."

Jovian jabbed Kai with his elbow and grinned at Archie. "Your wussy attitude is enough to drive anyone mad."

"Well, I'm sorry I'm not blooming with positivity. Tenji is *dead*." Archie turned on all of them. "Freaking *dead*. How are we supposed to get out of this place without him? He's the only one that seemed to have *some* sort of a plan."

"Says the bloody one who caused Tenji's death," Kai muttered, darkly.

Archie pressed his lips together and glared at the ground.

Sage stared between them, the terror of losing Tenji fully sinking in. She clutched the hilt of her sword and squeezed tightly as she stared out at the desert. How were they going to get through this place without Tenji? Before, it had already seemed highly unlikely considering there was a spirit at the end who they didn't want to release. But without Tenji…leaving the labyrinth seemed almost impossible. If releasing the dark spirit into the world was the only way out, what would they do? Would they be stuck in the labyrinth forever, never to see friends or family again?

Her eyes blurred with tears.

"We can't lose hope." Tristan straightened and placed a hand on Archie's shoulder. "We might not know everything, but we can keep moving forward. We'll find our way. One step at a time."

Luka nodded. "Losing Tenji *is* an unexpected blow." He gritted his teeth. "But we can't accept dying here. Not yet." He paused. "Archie, we'll have to rely on you quite a bit to locate water as we move through the desert."

Archie didn't respond.

Sage drew a careful breath and nodded. If she dwelt too much on the impossibility of leaving this place, she'd lose all hope. So, instead, she pushed all the swirling thoughts and emotions away. She would follow Tristan's advice. One step at a time.

With a grunt, Draven said, "Let's go then."

The nine fell silent once more as they headed into the shifting desert sand.

About half-way through the day, Ruben woke from his coma and broke out in another fever. Since he was weak and unwell, the group traded off carrying him. Even Sage helped once. But as her shoulder hurt too much, and she wasn't strong enough to hold him—especially in the deep, sliding sand—she volunteered to carry extra bags instead.

Her shoulder ached ceaselessly and the bandage held nothing, and her wound still needed cleaning. She rubbed it, drawing Cassian's attention.

"You should have someone look at your shoulder," Cassian whispered. His white hair clung to his forehead and sweat dribbled down the sides of his face.

Sage pressed her lips together. She couldn't. She couldn't ask for anyone's help. Except…

Her gaze darted to Draven who glared at the sand as he walked, wincing in the sunlight. Would it be too awkward to ask him? But there was no one else…

Another sharp pulse of pain from her shoulder decided for her.

That night, after they settled down, Sage approached Draven. He sat still and silent, staring up at the starless night sky. His forehead creased when he noticed her, but he didn't speak.

"Draven," Sage whispered with a glance over her shoulder at the others. "I need help."

Draven adjusted his position and eyed her. "With what?"

"My shoulder. It was injured during the werewolf attack, but I can't check it easily on my own." Sage felt herself blushing and bit her lip. She tossed another look at the others. "I'm sorry to ask, but…you're the only one who knows."

Draven closed his eyes, grimacing, and released a slow sigh. "Fine."

Sage flashed him a weak smile. "Thank you." She sat down beside him, and with another quick glance, unbuttoned her jacket, and slipped her arm carefully out of the sleeve. Then she paused and she stared at him again, unsure. "But…how?"

Draven scratched the back of his head looking pained—much to Sage's chagrin. He sighed again. "I can't check it like this unfortunately."

Oh, this was absolutely mortifying. Sage grimaced as she untied the string on the front of her tunic and slid the tunic off her injured shoulder, careful it didn't fall any further. She turned her head away, unable to look at him as he leaned in to check her wound.

"It's pretty chewed up," he said. He dug in his bag and pulled out a flask.

"Wait," Sage hissed, reaching out to stop him. "We don't have a lot of water. We can't waste it."

"It's not wasting." Draven ripped a corner off the bottom of his own tunic and pressed the cloth to the flask's now-open mouth and tipped. Draven cleaned her wound as best he could and then dug in his bag again and pulled out some herbs.

"Where'd you get those?" Sage asked.

"The forest. I figured we'd need them for Ruben." Draven crushed a few in his hand, mixing them with a little water to make a paste. He spread it carefully over her shoulder before wrapping the wound with the cloth Tristan had given her last night. "That will have to do for now."

Sage pulled up her tunic, re-tied it, and donned her jacket once more. She didn't bother to ask what *for now* meant. "Thanks."

Draven turned his attention back to the night sky. "It's better than you falling sick like Ruben."

Sage didn't reply. She only hurried back to where she'd been sitting beside Ruben and Cassian. Ruben lay passed out on the sand, shivering, sweat dribbling down his forehead. Worry twisted in her gut as she studied him. How would he survive this desert?

The next few days, they trudged through endless dunes, sand blowing into Sage's eyes, nose, and mouth. The dry heat made it hard to breathe, and they had little food or water. Ruben came in and out of consciousness. The blowing sand made it impossible to keep his already infected wound clean, and the lack of water prevented them from giving him the hydration he needed. He wasn't doing well—not in the slightest. But Sage avoided allowing herself to dwell on the fact Ruben was failing.

One freezing night, Sage sat by Ruben's side and focused all her energy on channeling her powers to heal him. She still hadn't even revived a plant like the book had said to, but she *had* to try.

Good intentions and desperation aside, nothing seemed to be happening. Sage stared at Ruben's pale face and the dribbles of sweat along his skin. His still form reminded her too much of her grandfather, and she didn't like it at all.

As she imagined Ruben's leg healing and his infection dissipating, Ruben woke suddenly. He lifted his head slowly to scan the campsite around him before his eyes landed on Sage. He lowered his back into the sand and turned his gaze to the sky. "Sage…am I going to die?"

Shaking her head firmly, she blurted out, "No, Ruben. You won't die. You'll pull through this. Just keep fighting."

Ruben coughed, wincing in pain. He didn't respond and kept his gaze on the sky instead. After a moment of silence, he shifted. "Sage? If I asked you a strange question, would you blame it on the fever?"

"Do you want me to?" Sage shifted closer to better hear him since his voice was low and hoarse.

"Maybe." He smiled wearily, green eyes flickering toward her. He strained to sit up, but Sage eased him back down. Ruben gestured for her to lean closer, so she did.

"You're a princess…aren't you?"

Sage stared at him, her heart speeding up. How did he know? She whipped her head around to see if anyone else had overheard, but everyone was too busy tossing coarse remarks at each other as they tried beating sand from their shoes and clothing. Returning her gaze to Ruben, she pressed her lips together. She couldn't seem to think of anything to say. Why couldn't she respond? How was she going to convince him to keep this quiet?

"I guessed right," he whispered as he studied her. "I know I did."

Sage resisted the urge to ask how he found out. She couldn't risk anyone else overhearing. How long had Ruben known? Was he upset that she was a woman? Did he hate her?

"Are you—mad?"

Ruben shook his head and gifted her another tired smile. "No. And don't worry. Your secret's safe with me."

Early the next morning, when the sky was still dark, a small moan woke Sage. She lay still, listening until she heard the sound again. Ruben. Sitting up, she crawled to Ruben's side. He was shivering, more than he had been last night, and his face contorted in pain. She pressed a hand to his forehead. Burning heat met her palm and alarm shot through her body.

"Luka!" she shrieked, waking half the group with a start.

Luka joined Sage at Ruben's side a moment later. He pressed his own palm to Ruben's head and cursed. "Someone hand me a flask with water," he demanded.

Archie scrambled to toss him one while Draven and Tristan appeared on either side of Sage. After Luka poured some water, Draven pulled out his herbs and pushed some sort of paste into Ruben's mouth.

Tristan tore off a piece of his tunic and wet it, pressing it to Ruben's face and neck.

Cassian lingered nearby, peering over their shoulders at Ruben. "Is—is he going to make it?" he asked, voice tight.

No one answered him.

Sage squeezed her eyes shut, forcing down tears. Ruben had to make it. He had to.

"We can't move him while he's like this," Luka said, his face drawn and tight. "It will only make his condition worse."

As the sun rose and blue and purple colors painted the sky, Kai, Archie, and Draven set off to look for more water, while the rest of them stayed with Ruben. But with the rise of the sun came the blistering heat.

Jovian struggled to use his sense to keep Ruben from being buried in the blowing sand while Tristan and Luka worked to bring down his fever. Sage didn't budge from her place at Ruben's side and spent every moment laboring to instigate her healing capabilities. But none of them succeeded.

Ruben was still dying.

Tears slipped down Sage's cheeks, despair drowning her. Supposedly, she had the ability to solve this problem, to save Ruben, but she couldn't figure it out. Her healing power refused to budge. She was a failure. Ruben was going to die, and it would be all her fault. She was going to fail him the same way she'd failed her grandfather.

By the time Archie, Draven, and Kai returned with filled flasks of water, Ruben's breathing had become labored.

A sickening feeling churned in Sage's gut.

Night fell once again and everyone hovered around Ruben in silence, listening to Ruben's struggling breaths. Jovian bent the sand into a cozy bed and Luka hand-fed Ruben what little they could get down him. Cassian placed cooling cloths over his forehead, and Kai lit a fire to keep them warm during the chilly night. Archie manipulated water to help him drink, and Tristan laid their cloaks over him. Draven stood solemnly nearby, watching carefully, occasionally feeding Ruben more herbs.

Sage's body trembled beneath the strain of the energy she'd spent trying to heal Ruben all day. She'd cried on and off, despite her best attempts to hold her tears back. Why couldn't she do this?

Then Ruben's labored breaths disappeared and his fidgeting quieted. Terror seeped into her gut and Sage gripped Ruben's arm tightly, staring at his pale, still face.

Luka reached over and touched his fingers to Ruben's neck, then looked away. "He's gone," he announced, hands clenching into fists.

"No," Sage whispered. Tears spilled from her eyes, and a sob escaped her throat as she pressed her hands against Ruben's shoulders and urged her dormant "healing ability" to revive him. He couldn't die. Not like this. She couldn't fail him.

"Ruben." She shook him gently, squeezing his shoulders. But his face and body remained unresponsive. "Ruben, stay!"

It wasn't until Tristan dragged her away that Sage finally crumbled. Sir Aadan had been wrong. She couldn't heal a thing. She'd failed Ruben, just like she'd failed her grandfather.

Sage wept until her lungs ached and her eyes were raw.

Eventually, Jovian separated the sand with his sense and buried Ruben. None of them spoke for a long time, staring down at the mound of sand that was once their friend. After a while, Luka suggested they should sleep.

But Sage couldn't. Not a wink.

29

Archie's Shortcomings

AS DAYS TURNED INTO WEEKS, THE REMAINING EIGHT struggled in the desert terrain. Trudging and sliding through the sand drained all of Sage's energy. Her feet lugged as if carrying weights, and her chest ached. Ruben's death had wiped out any vigor she'd had before. At different points, she, Archie, Cassian, and Jovian buckled from exhaustion and the group was forced to rest.

Sage was constantly parched and tired—freezing in the night, but blistering during the day. Archie signaled whenever he sensed water nearby, but sometimes they had to dig for it.

One day, Cassian became so delirious, he tripped and fell face first in the sand and mumbled incoherently. Sage wouldn't lose another person. She wouldn't. Especially not Cassian. So she gave him all the water in her flask.

"We should take turns carrying Cassian," Luka suggested as he knelt on Cassian's other side.

Cassian came out of his delirium long enough to shake his head. "No…I can…do it."

Draven huffed, gripping his head and glaring in Cassian's direction. "You can't. Do you want to die like Ruben?"

Ruben's name hung in the air, stinging Sage's heart.

Cassian didn't reply, pressing his palms over his eyes. He didn't protest about being carried again.

Sage, still smarting from Ruben's mention, glowered at the sand. She'd avoided mentioning Ruben because she couldn't trust herself to speak without crying. She couldn't even *think* about Ruben without tears pricking her eyes and a burn rising in her throat.

She missed him. She missed his positivity; she missed his companionship. And her failure to heal him only made her feel worse. Her regular practice to access her healing ability had dissolved after Ruben's death and she hadn't bothered with it since.

Sir Aadan had been wrong. She wasn't a healer and it was time she stopped trying to pretend she was.

One day, the group stopped to rest by the only tree they could see for miles. They hadn't had any water for two days, and it took all Sage's will to keep placing one foot in front of the other. While the group rested, Luka and Archie broke off in search of water.

Sage plopped onto the ground with a moan of pain. She removed her boots and beat out the sand before examining her bleeding blisters. No matter how much she worked to prevent sand from seeping into her boots, it always found its way in. She bit her lip and squirmed, holding back hot tears. Her legs and feet ached, her stomach twisted in hunger, and her tongue stuck to the roof of her mouth. When would this misery end?

Cassian slumped beside her, eyes dark with exhaustion.

Sage reluctantly pulled her boots back on, cringing in pain as she did.

"How's your shoulder?" Cassian asked as he pulled a slice of dried meat out of his bag and chewed on it.

Sage cautiously rotated her shoulder, wincing. "Still sore." Then she dropped her gaze to her feet. "But less painful than these blisters." She leaned back against the tree, thoughts of her family filtering through the pain. How long had it been since she'd last seen her parents and her brother, Sage? Days had blurred together, and Tenji had been the person to keep track of the passage of time in the labyrinth. Since then, no one—that she knew of—was keeping track.

It had been a few weeks since they entered the desert at least. Maybe even a month. Sage looked around at the others, covered in layers of dirt, each with varied lengths hair. Sage's hair was longer too, but not quite at the length where she could pull it into a decent-looking ponytail.

Sage longed for a refreshing dip in the fresh waterfalls back home in Hallon and a bath. She hadn't had a proper bath since before the kidnapping. Mostly because she couldn't undress to any degree.

When Sage noticed Cassian was staring at her, she turned her attention to him.

"What is it, Cass?"

"What were you thinking about?" he asked, cocking his head. "You seemed sad."

"Oh." Sage brushed back a strand of hair that fell into her eyes and looked out across the desert. "Just about how long we've been here."

Hearing a soft sigh from Cassian, she turned to study him. The skinny boy leaned back against the tree next to her and pulled his knees up to his chest. "I think about that too, sometimes," he murmured.

Sage placed a hand on top of his head and smiled. "Don't worry, Cass. You'll see your parents and sister again. I promise."

Cassian looked at her. "You know, Sage?" He hugged his knees a bit tighter. Then he looked away and mumbled, "You remind me a lot of my older sister."

Sage's heart thumped. Sister?

Nearby, Kai scoffed. "It's a little weird to be telling guys they remind you of sisters, pipsqueak."

Standing, Jovian flicked Sage's head as he walked by. "It's because Sage looks like a girl."

His comment made Tristan finally glance her way too. Draven acted as though he heard nothing, braiding that multicolored thread again, like he did during the times he sat with them.

"I don't look like a girl," she retorted. Heat rose up her neck to her ears. She didn't want to be compared to a woman. Not by them. It was too risky, no matter how flattering Cassian's compliment was. "Do you have any brothers, Cass?" she asked.

Cassian shook his head.

Sage turned toward Jovian. "See? He just doesn't know what a brother is like. That's all."

Cassian shook his head again. "My friend says older brothers are mean. He says they like to pick on little brothers. Sometimes they'll be protective, but only if they feel like it. Kind of like Kai."

Jovian burst out laughing and Kai huffed, turning his back on them. "I'm no brother of yours, pipsqueak. Put that out of your head right now."

Cassian cracked a chapped smile at Sage. "See?"

Sage couldn't help but chuckle in response.

After swallowing his laughter, Jovian turned to Cassian. "Can't older sisters be mean too? I've always heard they were just as bad." A mischievous grin slid across Jovian's face, his eyes slipping to Kai. "Because then that would make Kai a big sister instead."

Kai sprang up and chased Jovian around, tripping through the sand.

Ignoring their rough play, Cassian shook his head firmly. "Not my sister. Aria is the kindest person I know." He gestured to Sage. "She'd like you, Sage."

Aria. Cassian had never said his sister's name before.

Skidding to an abrupt stop, Jovian's eyes widened. "Oooooh, it sounds like you're saying you would approve if Sage courted your sister." Kai tackled Jovian to the ground.

"Woah!" Archie exclaimed, appearing out of nowhere. Luka came up behind him and sighed, brushing a hand over his face. They'd come back empty-handed. Archie marched over to them. "No one is courting Cassian's sister except me. I'll kill anyone who thinks about trying it. Now, who's trying to take her from me?"

Cassian's sister was courting *Archie*?

"Sage is!" Jovian knocked Kai back and pointed in her direction.

Her stomach dropped as Archie turned his gaze to her. Sage frantically waved her arms in front of her and shook her head. "No, I'm not!" she protested in alarm. What if she got on Archie's bad side because of Jovian's joking? "Jovian's just saying that."

"But Cassian told Sage he was sure his sister would like him," Jovian added, twisting his head just enough to hide his wink from Archie. "It's hard to win Cassian's approval. What else could that mean?"

Archie puffed out his chest and stood taller. "Let's duel this out and see who's really better, Sage. I'll show you, Cassian. I'll show you."

Cassian rolled his eyes. "I would pick any of you over Archie," he said, with a dismissive wave in Archie's direction. Then his eyes widened, and he blurted out, "But I'm not saying I would want any of you to court her! Don't misunderstand. But if I had to choose one of you, I'd pick Tristan."

"Tristan?" Archie gasped, his eyes wide and mouth gaping at the same time Tristan blushed and whirled around to stare at Cassian. "But why Tristan? What does Tristan have that I don't?"

Cassian held up a fist, cleared his throat, then lifted fingers as he listed: "He's the most well-balanced out of everyone here. He behaves well, never gets in fights with others, is always helping, has great manners in public settings, is emotionally stable, is academically smart and popular, and has a great sense ability. And that's just to name a few things. Whereas you, water wuss, may be popular—but that is where your positive qualities end."

All Archie could do was stare at Cassian, mouth hanging open in surprise.

Finally, Luka spoke up. "Since all of you seem to have a burst of energy all of a sudden, we should keep moving."

Kai gave his usual glare, but no one argued and they all gathered their things and traipsed across the sandy landscape. Archie appeared near Sage and Cassian's sides. "What can I do to get on your better side, Cassian? I really do love Aria more than anything."

"You love her more than yourself?" asked Cassian with a snort. "I highly doubt that. Everyone likes my sister, but 'liking' is quite different than 'loving,' Archie. Even if I'm younger than everyone else here, I'll protect my sister like my life depends on it. And I don't think there's anything you can do to change my mind about you unless you make a complete personality change."

"A complete personality change? Brutal, Cassian." Archie's shoulders slumped. "My feelings for your sister aren't mere interest. I really do love her. If you don't believe that, then why do you think I'm with her? To have fun?"

Cassian shook his head. "I think you want her because everyone else wants her. It makes you feel important when you're the one to succeed in claiming her." He paused and looked at Archie. "My sister isn't something to be claimed, and she's not an object you can use to make you feel better about yourself."

Archie's footsteps halted for a moment before he trotted to keep up with them. "That's not true at all! I love Aria because she's Aria. Yes, I'm aware everyone likes—or has liked—Aria at one point or another, but that only shows how wonderful Aria is! I don't like her just because everyone else does." He huffed, sticking out his bottom lip as he pouted.

For a moment, Sage thought he'd come off as slightly admirable. Until he'd stuck out his bottom lip and reminded her what an immature baby he was.

"What do you mean *everyone* likes Aria?" she asked.

Archie looked across Cassian at Sage. "Maybe you're un-aware, but my fiancée is a beautiful jewel. It's hard to resist her charms."

When no one replied, Sage couldn't stop her jaw from dropping. "You mean…*all* of you liked Cassian's sister at some point?"

Archie, looking proud, puffed out his chest. "Of course! Right, Kai?"

Kai's face flushed as red as his hair and glared at Archie. "Of course not!"

Jovian laughed. "Look at his face! It must be true!"

"I'm going to kill you."

Kai dashed after Jovian again, who ran away laughing and singing, "He's not denying it!"

For some reason, it struck Sage funny that a person like Kai with such a brusque attitude could like a girl. Then, again, Sage had never personally known any of the top ten princesses and had only briefly encountered the first ranked princess. "Well, what about the top-ranking princess?"

Archie laughed and raised his eyebrows at Sage. "Um, you mean Princess Irabel...Luka's betrothed?"

Sage didn't know Luka was betrothed, and especially didn't know he was betrothed to her. She grimaced when Luka turned to look back at her. She gave a nervous laugh. "Ah, I didn't realize you were betrothed, Luka. Congratulations."

Luka sighed and turned forward again. "It was an arranged engagement."

Oh. Sage studied Luka's back. It sounded like he wasn't entirely pleased about the arrangement. But why? Princess Irabel seemed beautiful, strong, and serene when Sage had seen her, even if she'd never really known her.

Jovian came closer to Sage and whispered, "Why? Do you like Irabel?"

"No!" gasped Sage, alarmed. "I just thought, since she was the highest-ranked princess—"

"Why are we talking about girls?" Kai asked, brushing a hand through his hair since he'd successfully finished pummeling Jovian. "Let's stop before I get a headache."

"I agree with Kai." Sage peeked back to see Draven trailing behind them, looking dark and angry. Draven's attitude had gotten worse each day they'd been in the desert. He'd withdrawn more than usual since he couldn't go off on his nightly disappearances. "We should save our breath for walking."

A wider smile spread across Jovian's face. "Draven, did you like Princess Aria?"

"No," Draven responded without hesitation, expression growing darker. For some reason, Sage believed him.

"What about Irabel? Oakina?"

Draven glared at Jovian. "Don't even try."

Jovian stopped harassing Draven and leaned closer to Sage to whisper, "Such a crank. It's never fun to tease him."

"Water!" Archie jerked to a stop and then darted past them, running toward a large mound of sand on their right.

The rest of the group didn't hesitate to follow after. Sage's heart lifted when she saw insects buzzing the area and a strange rabbit-rodent creature scurrying by. After they climbed the mound of sand, slipping and sliding their way up, they halted. A small rocky mountain rose up from the sand a short distance away.

Archie raced toward the mountain, and Sage followed close behind.

As they drew closer, the rush of cascading water grew steadily louder. Sage clambered over the rocks, circling the small mountain and doing her best to keep up with Archie. Then they stepped past a large boulder, and she halted. *Water.*

A narrow river ran alongside the mountain, curving and disappearing into a distant labyrinth wall. Clearly some sort of fairy magic. Sage turned her gaze to the small, glittering waterfall that gushed over the side of the mountain. Several tall trees stood around the river and an antelope creature was drinking from it. When it heard them, it lifted its head and took off.

Sage couldn't hold back a smile.

Without waiting, Archie threw down his bag and plunged straight into the middle of the river, immersing his whole self, clothes and all. "Water! Oh, beautiful, wonderful water!"

"You're drawing closer to the town and the next gate," the spirit whispered to the traitor.

The traitor raised his eyebrows. They were finally nearing the end of this hell? What sweet news to his ears.

"You must bring the jewel with you when you leave," the spirit continued. *"Forget the jewel and you can forget our deal."*

The traitor frowned and clenched his fists. *I won't forget.*

30

The List Dispute

SAGE JOINED THE REST OF THE GROUP AT THE EDGE OF THE pond and dropped to her knees, plunging her hands deep into the water and funneling it to her mouth. Wonderful, sweet, quenching water. Oh, how she missed being around so much of it.

Jovian pulled off his boots, climbed up the mountain side, and splashed down into the water with Kai not far behind.

"Come in!" Archie called, splashing around like a child and waving to the others. "It's not every day we get to clean ourselves of all this sand."

Cassian and Tristan waded in at Archie's beckoning, followed by Luka. Sage lingered outside, gulping down as much water as she could. As much as she wanted to dive in with the rest, she couldn't. If she did, they'd know she wasn't a prince. She'd already struggled enough hiding her gender in the desert, though Draven had done his best to help.

The first time she came up with an excuse to go to the restroom far off, Draven announced he too wanted to go a distance on his own for restroom breaks, making her seem a little less odd. She longed to thank him for his help, but he evaded her when she tried.

Sage looked in Draven's direction. He remained out of the water, gazing into the trees. "I'm going to sit in the shade instead," he said.

"You're such a grumpy gnome, Draven!" Archie called.

Draven paused and looked at the sky, his face twisting into a sour expression. "Let's not stay too long," he stated before plunging into the trees.

Sage stood along the river watching the others enjoy the cool water. Maybe if she only waded in a little ways, it would be okay. She pulled her boots off, climbed into the water, and splashed her face. It was the best feeling she'd had since arriving in the labyrinth. Refreshing water. For a small instant, the stress of the last few months eased away.

Her tranquility was short-lived, however. Jovian splashed water at several people, and Archie and Kai chased him. But worst of all, Luka pulled off his shirt. Oh, no.

Ducking her head, Sage climbed back out of the water and pulled her boots back on, trying to ignore the flush crawling up her neck. "I'll be back," she called, hurrying toward the trees and away from the others' voices.

Sage's chest deflated. She hated this secrecy and constant awkwardness. She'd long grown tired of this façade. All she wanted was to have a nice bath in the cool water. How much longer would she have to pretend to be someone else?

Finding a shaded spot under a tree and away from the others, Sage settled down and leaned back against the trunk. She closed her eyes and envisioned Hallon, with its many sparkling lakes and waterfalls, wide-spread ocean, and best of all, a warm bath waiting back at her house. How much she missed it and her family.

She missed her mother's warm hugs, her father's riveting stories, and her brother's playful pranks. Her eyes misted as she pictured their faces. Would she ever make it out of here? Would she ever see them again?

A rustling noise made her jump, scattering her thoughts. She turned to see Draven lurking in the shadows not too far away. She pressed her hand to her heart and gasped. Then she closed her eyes and took in a calming breath. "Oh. It's you. You startled me."

"Sorry," came his reply. She had expected him to avoid her like usual and leave, but instead he leaned against another tree and crossed his arms over his chest.

Since he wasn't the easiest person to approach and had been especially grumpy during this desert trek, it took a great deal of courage for her to speak. "I meant to thank you, by the way, for helping me maintain my secret these last several weeks."

Draven met her gaze. "Why are you so desperate to keep it a secret?"

Sage paused. "Well...I don't want to receive hate and suspicion because of my gender. And I especially don't want to be left behind."

Draven studied her silently as he took in her words. Finally, he looked away. "I don't think any of them would do that. They aren't that cruel." He sat down, leaning back against his tree and pulling the multicolored thread from his pocket once more. "Anyway, some of them may have found out already."

Sage hugged her knees to her chest. It wouldn't be easy to confess to her lies after keeping them for so long. She raised her shoulders. "Tenji and Ruben found out. They told me."

Draven looked at her. Then, after the news seemed to settle in, he nodded. "And did they throw you out?"

His question left her speechless. "Well, no..." she said at last. "I suppose not."

They were silent for a moment, listening to the hum of bugs in the trees and the distant splash of water. She eyed the thread in Draven's hands but didn't dare ask what it was for or why he braided it over and over. And since, for once, Draven didn't seem majorly grumpy, Sage didn't wish to upset him. She looked up into the trees giving them shade and suddenly remembered what he told her about not being fond of light. "Is the desert hard for you since there's no shade for you to hide in?"

Draven stiffened. "I suppose I haven't been the kindest lately, have I?" he asked. When she didn't respond, he sighed. "Not always, but sometimes the light gives me a headache if I'm in it too long."

"I see," murmured Sage. Was it a side effect of his sense? "So, being in the shade helps?"

He gave another slow sigh. "It depends. Sometimes it helps, sometimes it makes it worse. My sense…can get a little out of control when I'm deprived of the dark." He avoided her gaze, the shadows around them morphing briefly into various images before they faded back to their original shape. "It's a bit harder to control it on my own. But there was one person who always helped."

"What did he do to help?" She didn't understand what Draven meant by 'out of control' but she wasn't sure she wanted to know, and even if she did, she wasn't sure she wanted to risk asking. What if he didn't like talking about it?

Draven paused, hesitating. Then he looked at her. "She helped me focus on something else."

She considered his words. "This person must be special to you."

"She is," Draven murmured as he looked out among the trees. "She's someone I always want to protect."

"Well, hopefully we'll leave this labyrinth soon and you can see her again," Sage said, offering him a small smile.

When Draven finally looked at her, his expression had a heaviness to it. "Hopefully." Then he stood and headed back toward the water and the others, tucking away the thread. "I think they're done."

Sage jumped up and hurried to follow him, but then he paused. Draven's stillness gave her the impression he still had something he wanted to say. "What? What is it?"

Draven turned to face her. She could feel his hesitation. "Do— Do you ever hear a voice in the labyrinth?"

A voice? Sage stared at Draven. Whatever could he mean? She frowned, puzzled. "No…I haven't heard anything. Why? Do you?"

With a firm shake of his head, Draven turned. "No, I don't," he said, and then walked off.

Sage wasn't sure if she believed him. His answer had been too rushed, too brusque. If Draven was hearing a voice, that couldn't be a good sign. Not in this place.

When they reached the others, the sun had set. They were all out of the water and had already built some fires to keep them warm during the cold desert night. Sage joined Cassian, and Draven sat on a rock a little distance away.

For once, everyone seemed to be in a rather good mood. Archie was demonstrating some tricks with his water sense. "I used to do stuff like this to impress the princesses," he said proudly—and then, after a side glance at Cassian, added, "Before Aria."

"I don't think it impressed as many girls as you thought," Tristan said, a slight smile spreading across his face. Sage clapped a hand over her mouth to hide a surprised giggle. She didn't think she'd ever heard Tristan joke with anyone.

Jovian cackled. "What girl would be impressed with that splashing water show?"

Even Luka smiled.

However, the pleasant moment was ruined when Sage spotted Luka rummaging around in a bag and then pulling out a piece of paper with the familiar torn red stamp of Reudinia. The List. Luka had found Tenji's stash. Sage reached out and grasped Cassian's arm, gesturing with her head toward Luka.

Cassian stood. "Luka, don't read that!"

But it was too late. Luka had opened it.

Archie, Tristan, Kai, Jovian, and Draven turned to eye Luka.

"Don't read what?" asked Kai, standing up to investigate. When Luka didn't answer or even look up, Kai snatched the paper from his hand and looked at it.

Sage clenched her fists as Kai's face darkened.

"What is it?" asked Archie. Tristan and Draven stood also.

Jovian jumped up and ran to Kai's side, peeking over his shoulder. "Woah! It's the ranking list with our average scores on it!"

Archie didn't hesitate to join them and Tristan eventually followed.

Draven turned his gaze toward Cassian. "How did you know about it?"

Sage fidgeted with her jacket and bit the inside of her cheek. If she told them, would they think she was the traitor?

"We found it, several weeks ago," Cassian replied, gesturing to the list. "It was lying on the ground after we packed up camp in the forest."

"We?" Draven asked.

Cassian shot a look at Sage and Sage nodded before answering, "Yes, we did."

Luka remained seated and continued to stare at the ground. Kai didn't say anything either, but Archie's eyes widened, and he pointed at the list. "Hey, why does Tenji have the highest score if he's second?"

"You're right, water wuss!" Jovian exclaimed, pulling the list from Kai's hands as Tristan stepped closer.

Archie frowned. "Why did someone have this list with them anyway?"

Draven scowled, his bad attitude seemingly back. "Because someone here is a traitor."

Finally, Luka looked up at Cassian. In a quiet voice, he asked, "Why didn't you tell anyone about the list before, if you found it so long ago?"

Sage stood to join everyone else, knowing she needed to speak. Otherwise, she would appear more guilty than she was. "Tenji told us not to say anything."

"Wait, Tenji knew about it too?" Archie said, looking up from the list.

Sage nodded and Cassian pointed to the bag Luka had found it in. "Tenji was the one holding onto it."

Luka covered his face with his hands and sat there without saying a word. Kai finally turned to Luka, snatching the list from Jovian and waving it at Luka. "Did you know the ranking system was rigged?"

Luka swatted the list away and stood, glare chilling as he stared at Kai.

"Did you bloody know?"

"No," said Luka, his voice cracking. "I didn't know. I honestly didn't know...and Tenji died knowing...knowing he was cheated." Luka combed his blond hair out of his face and looked up at the darkening sky. Then he turned and walked off into the trees, refusing to look at anyone. No one went after him. No one ridiculed or yelled at him. Not even Kai.

But the fires the list caused weren't put out.

Archie pulled the list out of Kai's hand and stared at it. "Tristan, your scores and mine actually aren't that far apart! See? You're 108.4 and I'm 107.2. Do you hear that, Cassian?"

Cassian rolled his eyes before he strolled over and pointed at the list. "You're forgetting age has a part in the overall score. Tristan is younger than you, which means he had to score quite a bit higher for him to still rank above you. Look at the top three: Tenji, Luka, and Draven. They're also the oldest."

Kai frowned at Archie. "Cassian is better than you in most ways, water wuss, yet he's ranked tenth. It's obviously because of age."

Archie opened his mouth to retort, but then paused. His forehead wrinkled as he eyed the list again. "How do you think they add the age in?"

Jovian laughed. "Try subtracting your age from the number and see what happens."

Archie gave Jovian a blank look before he squatted down, squinting hard. "Minus twenty-one...minus twenty-one..." He began mumbling random numbers.

After this went on for an unbearable amount of time, Tristan pulled it from Archie's grasp and looked at it. "Your score would be 86.2, Archie."

Archie stood and sniffed, glancing toward Cassian. "Math was never my strong suit," he explained, then faced Tristan. "Tell me yours, Tristan."

Tristan looked down at the list but didn't say anything.

"What? What is it, Tristan?" Archie squinted at the paper. "Tell me what it is."

Tristan shook his head.

"I already know it's higher than mine, so you don't need to be so modest."

Jovian yanked the list from Tristan's grasp and ran, Tristan chasing after him. With a laugh, Jovian yelled back, "How old are you, Tristan? Eighteen or nineteen?"

"Nineteen!" called Archie.

"Archie, Tristan's score would be 89.4."

"It's a little more than before, but still not that far off," Archie said contemplatively.

Jovian scanned the list, eyebrows furrowing. "Actually, Archie…I see why he didn't want to tell you. Everyone is close in scores. And when you subtract everyone's age, Tristan has the second highest score out of everyone."

"What? Where am I then?"

Jovian counted. "You would be…ninth."

Archie said nothing, staring blankly at Jovian.

Sage had known this list might cause unnecessary chaos, but this was beyond petty. She couldn't hold in her annoyance. "What does it matter what everyone's score is? And you're not even sure if that is how the age thing works anyway."

Jovian smirked, waving the list at her. "Says the one who isn't on the list, Pretty Boy."

Sage grimaced. She shouldn't have said anything.

To her surprise, Cassian said, "They probably do just add age to the overall score. Before they added age as a factor, it was possible for several children to be in the top ten. For instance, wasn't Kai ranked second when he first entered the ranking?"

Archie nodded, perking up. "Yes, Tenji was upset because Kai bumped him out of second rank for two years. I mean who wouldn't be upset if they were sixteen and a seven-year-old knocked them to a lower ranking."

Kai avoided everyone's gaze. "They were mistaken about me. I never should have ranked that high. It was only because my grandfather was king before Luka's father."

My grandfather was king before Luka's father. Sage gasped. "You're King Darian's grandson?" She had always heard wonderful things about King Darian growing up. Her parents told her Darian had been a good king—wise, selfless, and generous. However, he'd died suddenly a few years before she'd been born, passing the throne to King Léon. Her parents had told her King Darian had a son, but... "But wasn't King Darian's son sense-less?"

Some of the others frowned at her, and others looked away. Cassian waved his hand by his throat as if to say: *Stop! Abort! Abort!* But he stopped as soon as Kai looked back at them. Had she said something wrong?

Kai scowled. "What? Think I'm going to blow up just because my bastard father was mentioned?" He turned his gaze on Sage and an immediate uncomfortableness shifted over her. He'd called his own father a bastard. "He has no sense. Neither does my mother. Any more nosy questions?"

"N-no," she stuttered, embarrassed. Why was she so foolish sometimes? Of course King Darian's son would be Kai's father. And it seemed Kai didn't like his father. Not even a little.

"Just dandy, then," Kai muttered. Then he sat down, his back to all of them. Everyone dropped the discussion about the list after that, turning back to their own conversations and nightly routines. But Sage couldn't focus. Instead, her gaze slipped to Kai's back, and she bit the inside of her cheek. It had seemed as if everyone knew about Kai's relationship with his father except her. And, shamelessly, she wanted to know more.

Later that night, Luka returned to the fires, but he said nothing to anyone. Archie bit his knuckle as he huddled over the list, telling Tristan to leave him alone, while Jovian lay across the ground and stared up at the sky. Draven and Kai kept their usual distance from the others. Cassian sat with Sage, sipping water from a flask.

Sage chewed on her lip, fidgeting with her own flask, unable to stop wondering about Kai. Finally, she broke. "Do you know about Kai?" she asked the young boy beside her. "What's his story?"

Cassian didn't reply at first. "I really only know the rumors. Someone older could tell you better what happened. Like Luka or Draven."

Sage peered in Luka's direction, taking in his slouched posture and sullen expression. She couldn't speak to him. Not tonight. She turned her gaze to Draven. "I'll be right back."

At first, Draven didn't notice her approach. He was busy grilling some small creature he'd caught, his back toward her. Then he must've sensed her presence because he twisted and looked up at her. He stiffened and returned his focus to his food.

"Do you need something?" he asked, gruffly.

Sage hesitated. "Well… I…" She paused. How could she ask him? She didn't even know where to begin.

He waited for her silently, eyes glued to his food.

"I was wondering…if you could tell me Kai's story." Sage stood awkwardly behind him and waited for his reaction. Would he chase her away? Chastise her?

"I don't usually like to talk about peoples' pasts. Go ask someone else."

"But Cassian told me to ask you or Luka, and Luka isn't really in the best mood," Sage explained with a gesture at Luka's sullen figure. She crouched next to Draven. "Everyone seems to know except me. I don't know anything." She sighed. "I know I shouldn't ask, but…I'm afraid I brought up some painful memories because of my cluelessness."

Draven eyed her, then sighed. "Fine." He shifted in place, looking away. "Kai was abandoned by his parents at an early age. He doesn't like talking about it."

Unable to stop herself, Sage peeped over her shoulder at Kai again. "Why?"

Draven shook his head. "He kept igniting fires in all the houses they moved into. His sense would erupt every time he was upset about something. And babies get easily upset. Eventually, his parents grew tired of it. After their second child was born, Kai accidentally set fire to the house again. They say he almost killed his sister. His parents decided they'd had enough and handed him over to the Royal Council."

Something tugged in Sage's heart. "How old was he?"

Cocking his head, Draven lifted his eyes to the dark sky. "I don't know. Four or five? It happened a few years before he was ranked."

"And the Royal Council has been raising him all this time?"

Draven shook his head again. "His grandmother took him in. But in doing so, estranged herself from her son and grand-daughter."

"So Kai got his grandmother, and his sister got their parents? How awful." How had she never heard about this? She couldn't imagine being neglected by her parents or separated from her brother.

Turning back to his kill, Draven pulled it from the fire. "That's all you need to know."

"Thank you for filling me in."

With a nod, Draven bit into his food, letting her know he was done. Sage stood and returned to Cassian to settle down for the night.

That night, she had trouble sleeping, thinking about the events of the day and Kai's story. After tossing and turning for too long, Sage finally sat up and decided to have her bath. She could get away with it as long as she kept her clothes on. She retreated to the far corner of the pond near the waterfall, hoping the sound would drown out any noises she made. She rinsed off her boots and left them on a rock to dry, then she waded into the waterfall, letting the water rinse away all the grime and dust that covered her body. Although she longed to bathe fully, it was much too risky. She would just have to make do for now.

She washed her face, neck, and hands. Then, with a quick scan of the sleeping piles of other princes, decided to risk slipping off her jacket and ducked under water to scrub her hands through her hair.

Satisfied, Sage crawled out of the pond and squeezed water from her shirt, pants, and jacket before throwing the jacket over her shoulders.

"You could've cleaned up earlier, you know."

Sage jerked and whirled around. Kai stood nearby, looking at her, perplexed. His gaze swept to the waterfall and returned to her. "Why didn't you? The way you were sneaking around, I thought you were a monster."

Sage rolled her eyes and continued to squeeze the water out of her clothes as best she could, pulling her jacket closer over her body. "I like to be alone sometimes. Don't pretend you don't understand that." She shook the water from her hair, an imaginary image of a young, neglected Kai popping into her mind. She turned her face away to hide her grimace.

When Sage didn't hear an immediate rebuttal, she turned back to find him staring at her, forehead furrowed. Kai turned away abruptly when she faced him and said, "I don't think that's the real reason though."

Sage's heart sped up. Was she being too suspicious? Her mind raced for another excuse. "Everyone always says I look like a girl, so you can't say I'm necessarily confident in my appearance, if that's what you mean." She sniffed, picking up her boots.

Kai shifted his stance and looked her straight in the eyes. "The only way to overcome that is to not care a damn bit what others think. So get over yourself." He started walking back to camp before pausing. "And just so we are clear, I don't give a damn what you do. As long as you're no traitor."

31

Tenji's Shadow

LUKA LAY AWAKE. HE SAW SAGE GET UP IN THE NIGHT AND heard murmurs between him and Kai, but Luka didn't want either of them to know he was still conscious. So, he lay still and stared out into the dark, feeling as if his world had become as black as the night. He could still visualize the list in his mind's eyes—with Tenji's name first and his name second. He wasn't number one. And he hated how the moment he'd seen the list all the confusion in his life suddenly made sense.

A tangle of emotions twisted in his gut. Anger, betrayal, frustration, shock, shame, guilt. However, the deepest and loudest of those, filling every corner of his body, was fear. He was too afraid to ask how this had happened. Too afraid to admit several things—things he knew deep down but had continually denied until now.

Closing his eyes, Luka pictured his father sitting at his desk last year after the Ranking Ceremony, busy signing papers. His father stopped what he was doing when Luka entered the room. He stared at Luka in silence for a moment, a look of disappointment on his face. Finally, he broke the stillness.

"Luka," he had said. *"Follow me."*

His father led him to the balcony where they looked over the city of Phoebus and beyond. *"Do you see all of this? The kingdom of Reudinia is one of the greatest kingdoms in the world. Unlike other kingdoms, not just anyone can rule. Only the strongest and smartest of royals are given such an honor."* His father turned to face him. *"Luka, you must become that person. You must become stronger, greater, better than all the others. You must."*

"But, Father," Luka had said. *"I am already number one among the princes. What else must I do?"*

His father was quiet as he looked out at the city below. *"It's not enough. I want to see excellence, not idleness."*

At the time, Luka had been flustered and frustrated. Why had his father always pushed him so hard and continually berated him about his studies when he was already number one? He had lived his life trying to live up to his father's expectations and the expectations of those around him, but he never could. Now he knew he never had. Luka had never truly earned anything, and his hard work was for nothing.

A failure. He was a failure.

Kai and Sage settled back down to rest and Luka shifted onto his back and stared up at the starless sky. Did his father know about the list as well? The moment the question flitted through his mind, he shook it out. His father was innocent in this, clueless, just like Luka had been. But even as he tried to convince himself of this, his heart sank. If he was honest with himself, Luka's father undoubtedly knew. After all, he was the only one who could enforce such a change. Why else would Tenji get second place when he had bested Luka in all their sessions and beat him in every test outside the Ranking Assessment? Why else would his father insist he do better constantly? Why else would this list find its way through several Royal Council members without one of them protesting the changes? It must have been an order. One they could not disobey.

As his heart reluctantly accepted the obvious truth, other things Luka had been denying slowly rose within him. His thoughts shifted to his younger brother Everard and how poorly he had been treated by their father. He thought of the way his father locked their mother away, as if he were afraid she would say something the king didn't want anyone to hear. He thought of the way his father restricted Luka and his siblings from regularly seeing her.

Luka slung an arm over his eyes and gritted his teeth. He struggled to resist the other thoughts about his father that were crowding into his mind. The evidence against his father continued to stack and grow, proving just how terrible of a person, a king, and a father King Léon was. It was too much for Luka to take in.

And yet, even though he'd heard the rumors about his father and had seen for himself how much the other princes hated him,

Luka still wanted to believe in his father. He wanted to trust that his father was good.

His father's legacy would be quite different from that of King Darian. Luka had only heard good things about King Darian and the more he read about him, the more Luka had wanted to be like him. He had hoped to emulate the character, charisma, power, and virtue the prior king had shown. Luka had hoped others would be able to see similar aspects of a great leader and king in him, rather than seeing his father. But now…he couldn't even get a single prince in the labyrinth to want to follow him. Especially not the grandson of King Darian himself.

What would Tenji do in this situation? How would he encourage and rally the others to keep progressing through the desert? How had he handled the revelation of being cheated?

Even though it had been several weeks since Tenji's passing, his absence only grew deeper and loomed larger with each passing day. Tenji had been confident, demanding, and had easily spurred the others to follow him. He'd known the most about the labyrinth and had been determined to get them out of here. While the older man had been too abrasive in the beginning, Luka had seen him become more team-oriented over their time spent in the labyrinth. Tenji had become their pillar, fighting to keep everyone alive and together.

Maybe Tenji would've known a way to prevent Ruben's death.

His heart squeezed. Ruben had been so quiet over the years Luka had known him, but his energy was always cheerful, always bright. Now he was gone. Tenji was gone. And they had been left leaderless.

Luka only pretended to hold the confidence and assurance Tenji had exuded. Truthfully, the others followed him only because Draven supported him. To be blunt, Luka was a speck in Tenji's shadow.

What would happen if he couldn't keep them together? What if he couldn't find the way out of the labyrinth? What if they lost more people because of the choices he made?

Picturing Tenji and King Darian in his mind's eye, he wished for both their personalities, wisdom, and characters to sieve into him and help keep him from giving up. At least long enough to get out of here. A good leader didn't give up on himself or on others. A good leader faced danger and remained steadfast and bold. A good leader treated everyone equally. A good leader didn't allow his weaknesses to affect others.

Even if he could never live up to his father's expectations, and even if he would never meet the expectations of the others in the Ten, he had to keep moving forward.

A good leader didn't give up when things became difficult.

32

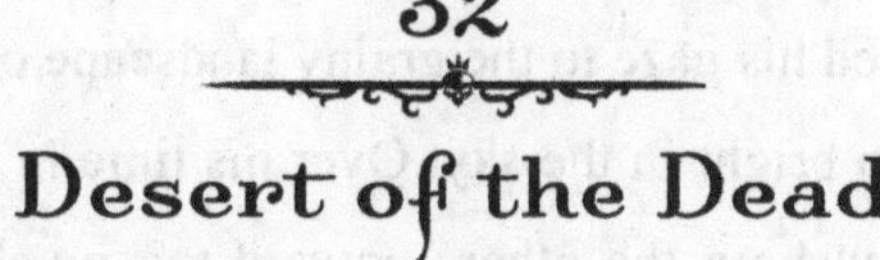

Desert of the Dead

DRAVEN STOOD ON THE ROCKY LEDGE OVERLOOKING THE waterfall, staring across the swells of dunes. The sky lightened, and yellow, orange, and pink splashed across the horizon. He frowned at the ascending sun. Another day of unbearable brightness and headaches. Yet, as he squinted at the sunset, a wistfulness twisted in his gut, and the image of the little girl waiting for him back home rose to his mind.

Over two months. Two and a half months spent in this dastardly place with the others. The outside world might think they were lost forever. Was anyone still looking for them, or had the king and his Royal Council simply replaced them with other princes? He couldn't care less about whether or not they had forgotten him, but he did care about his family. And he cared about Zinnia.

He closed his eyes and pictured Zinnia holding out a dark woven thread to him. *"I made this for you! You can hold it when your episodes come. Maybe it will help a little."*

Draven fingered the woven thread he'd recently tied to his belt. It was easier to reach there. Then he pulled out the multicolored thread he'd been braiding and re-braiding, in an attempt to make it perfect. The thread still looked a bit lopsided, but it was better than his first attempts. One of these days he'd get it right. And someday, hopefully, he would be able to give it to her.

Draven raised his gaze to the grainy landscape once more, the sun already too bright in the sky. Over his time in the labyrinth, he'd resisted pushing the others onward too much, even when they trudged at their slowest. But ever since they'd entered the second section, his patience waned. He couldn't stand being in this aggravating desert any longer.

Turning back to camp, Draven tucked the multicolored thread away. He sighed as he climbed back down. Several of the others were still sleeping, so he kicked them awake. "Get up. It's time to head out."

He waved them after him and waited at the top of the waterfall as they filled their flasks and stuffed their packs with edible food. Draven scowled at the landscape. He couldn't tell if the labyrinth was shifting or if it really was this large. He had read some legends that said the labyrinth was bigger on the inside than it appeared from the outside and others that claimed its walls shifted, making one believe they were making progress when really, they weren't.

But those were speculations, not facts. Whether or not those legends were true, the labyrinth felt endless. It had been four weeks since they had left the forest of monsters behind, and he had hoped they would be out of the desert long before now.

Draven winced as the ache in his head increased. The unforgiving sun left no room for shade or shadow. No room to hide. How much longer would they be stuck in this maddening place? He didn't think he could last another week.

"Let's head out," Luka called, his face and tone heavy with exhaustion. He didn't look anyone in the eye as he tramped onward.

As the group plodded across the endless desert, Draven held back, maintaining separation between himself and the seven others. Being forced together in dangerous terrain, constantly surrounded with each other, didn't mean he wanted to be friends with any of them.

Sage turned and smiled at him as she walked with Cassian. Draven furrowed his brow and his scowl deepened. He adjusted the strap of his bag uncomfortably. From the beginning, something about Sage had made him nervous, and now it only made him want to avoid her at all costs. But somehow, she seemed to have mistaken him for a friend.

A sharp ache pulsed in his temple, and Draven gripped his head. Darn migraine.

They stopped to rest, maintaining their silence, when the sun beat down on them from the highest point of the sky. Draven brushed a frustrated hand through his hair. The silence must have something to do with the list, despite its current meaningless-ness. The others were so absorbed about their places and past that they'd become fixated on the list. If they remained in that mindset, it would only create more problems later.

A ruckus of murmurs caused Draven to lift his gaze to the land before them. A large, spread-out structure-like shadow stood in the far distance.

"What's that?" asked Kai, his face twisting into his usual scowl.

Archie beamed and shook Tristan's arm, as if last night's affairs had long slipped his mind. "It looks like houses! Are my eyes deceiving me? Is this an illusion?"

"I doubt it's an illusion since we're all seeing the same thing." Kai rolled his eyes and crossed his arms over his chest.

"Maybe there are people living there!" exclaimed Archie.

"People living in a desert in the Sidylla Labyrinth?" laughed Jovian, shaking his head. "Sorry, kind of hard to believe. In this place, civilization could be a sign of danger."

Luka nodded. "We should remain wary. But the only way to be sure is to check it out for ourselves."

The group abandoned their rest to lumber closer, and Draven followed slowly. His headache worsened and his steps became more reluctant with each stride.

This was it. This was the place. One of the places he had been most dreading.

As the structure solidified and became more defined, Draven could make out a city. But all the buildings were of an ancient design. The group paused briefly outside the outskirts.

Luka exchanged a grimace with Draven and Draven turned his gaze away, gripping the hilt of his sword tightly. He didn't like this.

The group entered the eerie, silent streets, climbing over the stones littering their path. Even Archie found it in himself to remain silent. Parts of the one-to-two-story buildings had caved in, spilling piles of rubble along the roads. Cobwebs hung from doorsteps, windows, and roofs. Tapestries hung from some buildings—some torn, others still partially intact. Shredded baskets sprawled sporadically along with turned-over dinnerware or shattered clay and glass. A small, rodent-looking creature scurried across the street from one empty house to another. Draven's sobriety only deepened the further into the city they went.

Eventually, another type of rubble lay in doorways and littered the streets. Draven tensed and gritted his teeth. Bones. Human bones.

Luka paused in front of one of the bone heaps. He bent down and picked up a small, wheeled toy horse lying next to it. Sage joined him and whispered, "What do you think happened to this place?"

Cassian, his eyes wide, pointed up ahead. Draven looked.

Before them lay a massive pile of skeletons.

"Whatever happened to them happened suddenly," Draven muttered. Something dark and powerful seemed to loom before them. Sharp pain throbbed and tightened in his head. He winced.

Archie gripped his sword at his hip. "I have a not-so-good feeling about this."

Standing, Luka looked down an alleyway leading away from the pile. "Let's go cautiously."

As they progressed through the ruins, large plants and vines tangled over the buildings and rubble, growing thicker the farther into the town they went. Then a stone from one of the houses tumbled and whacked Archie hard on the top of his head.

"Ahhh!" he wailed, jumping and whirling around. Archie calmed and rubbed his head with a grimace. But not much farther in, he tripped over a vine that tangled the sand-covered cobblestoned streets and smacked his knee on some rubble. He howled and hugged his knee to his chest.

"Oh, would you shut *up*, water wuss!" grumbled Kai, slapping Archie on the back of his head. "Why are you being so loud?"

Archie glared at him and the tension that had followed them collided with the stress of the spooky town. "This place hates me. I'm telling you; it hates me!"

"You're such a wimp!"

"No, I'm telling you. One moment there's nothing in front of me, and then suddenly I'm tripping. This place is trying to kill me!"

"Drama-fanatic," Jovian teased with a laugh. The laugh echoed, sounding especially chilling in the deserted ruins.

"Maybe if I burn that tongue of yours, you'll finally shut up," Kai hissed. He and Archie glared at each other, their irritation fizzling almost tangibly in the air between them.

Draven's eyes darted down the street. The shadows elongated and the unforgiving sun dimmed. But no relief came. Something wasn't right.

"The one who needs to have his tongue burned is you, Hothead," Archie retorted. "Everything that comes out of your mouth is garba—"

Draven hushed them sharply, the hairs of his arms standing on end. He scanned around them again, searching for something, though he didn't know what. "You're both too loud."

But before Kai or Archie could respond, a toothy plant darted from one of the homes. It wrapped around Kai's body, clamping him in its jaws. Kai's eyes widened. "What the—"

Draven drew his sword and lunged for him, but the plant yanked and Kai went soaring through the air, disappearing into the house the plant had come from with a shout.

Draven dashed to Kai's rescue with Sage and Tristan a step behind. But as Draven turned the corner of the doorway, he saw the plant and Kai vanish inside a trap door.

The door slammed shut behind them.

Draven raced over to the door, but several other plants dove out of nowhere and crowded around and over it. That didn't stop Draven from slicing through them with his sword and kicking at the door. But it wouldn't budge.

Sage burned away as many plants as she could with her light rays, and Tristan yanked at the trap door.

Archie, Luka, Jovian, and Cassian peered in through the doorway.

"Did that plant just kidnap Kai?" Archie asked, eyes wide. "I told you something was off!"

Before anyone could respond, the houses around them shuddered and shook. Stone walls shot up from the ground, ripping the house and trap door in half. Draven, Sage, and Tristan stumbled backward and out of the house. More walls rose all around them, leaving only one direction to move in: forward.

"It's—it's a maze," Tristan murmured.

Jovian sighed. "Another twist in the labyrinth. Why am I not surprised?"

Draven's gaze darted and scanned the new walls around them. Then he gripped his aching head. What should he do?

"What about Kai?" Sage asked. "We have to help him."

Jovian's voice answered, "How? He vanished."

Draven forced himself to draw in a slow, deep breath. Kai wasn't dead yet. He would find him. Turning, Draven advanced in the only direction he could.

Someone clutched his arm and he flinched. Whirling around and yanking his arm free, Draven found Luka hovering behind him.

"Where are you going? We shouldn't go traipsing farther in without thinking," Luka scolded. "And Kai is still missing."

Archie, looking very much terrified, pointed at Luka. "This was your fault, Luka. If Tenji were here, he would've helped us avoid this situation. He would have an escape plan by now."

Draven turned back to the path.

Again, his arm was seized. "Wait, Draven! We should plan first."

Draven yanked his arm from Luka's grasp. "Don't touch me." He glowered at Luka. "I'm going after Kai. We don't have time to plan. Are you coming or not?" Without waiting for a response, he strode on. Steps scratched against stone, following after him.

Draven didn't care to lead, but all he could think about was what *she* had shown him. He couldn't lose another person. He had to save Kai.

The group weaved through the maze. Whenever the path forked, Draven chose the opposite path of the one that beckoned him. Sometimes they hit a dead end and had to turn around, but everywhere they went, living plants rose from the ground and swatted or snapped at them.

Sometimes Draven sensed the shadows of the plants before he was attacked and halted their movement, Tristan electrocuted any plant that came near, and Archie yelped occasionally from getting hit. Cassian turned plants into icicles, Sage cut with her rays, and Jovian—without a look to the right or left—blocked the plants with a rock or smashed them when he caught sight of one. Luka trailed in the back, helping where he could.

Draven paused. "This is too easy."

"What do you mean *too easy*?" Archie wailed as he tripped over another vine. "Nothing about this is easy. This place gives me the creeps."

Striding to the front, Luka studied Draven. "Do you think something is doing this to us intentionally?"

Draven nodded and stared down the path in front of him. "Whatever it is, it's taking us where it wants us to go."

"Then how do we get to Kai?" asked Sage, fidgeting with her fingers and peering back in the direction they had come. "What if we can't find him?"

Jovian snorted. "Kai won't go down easily. Whoever is doing this is going to realize he picked the wrong person to isolate."

Luka turned his head in the direction they'd come. "Well, we don't have much of a choice. If this place is leading us somewhere, we'll end up going there no matter how much we fight. If we can find out who or what is doing this, maybe we can force it to let Kai go."

Unsure, Draven eyed the squirming vines as they writhed against the walls. Whoever it was didn't seem like the "letting go" type. An ominous presence, full of strength and power, pressed over and crawled inside of him. And Draven wasn't particularly good at resisting anything forcing its way in. He closed his eyes and gripped the woven thread Zinnia had given him. Her words drifted back to him. *I believe you can resist. Maybe if you focus on why you're resisting, it will give you the strength to fight.*

Why did he want to resist?

Because he didn't want to hurt others.

And he didn't want to be alone anymore.

"Let's go then," Draven grunted.

After a long, tiring trek through the winding maze, they finally reached an opening.

A large temple with massive round columns holding up a curved roof stood before them. Despite having no walls, the inside of the temple was particularly dark. On one side of the temple stood a well. Woven braids hung from another small building next to it. The whole area was almost unaffected by the destructive touch of time. The temple looked as if it had been built only the night before, gleaming like the pinnacle of the desert.

Yet to Draven, it arose as if out of a nightmare. It was exactly as *she* had shown him.

As the princes filed out into the open air, the maze walls surrounding the temple's courtyard shuddered closed, confining them to the temple's space and preventing their way out. Draven held back as the group approached the building.

Cassian pointed through the temple. "Look, the second gate!"

Sure enough, standing not far behind the temple was the gate to the third section of the labyrinth.

"Finally!" Archie cried. "We're almost through this awful desert! Is this the end of the labyrinth?"

Draven shook his head. "No, the labyrinth has five sections."

Luka and the others turned to face him. He flinched. He shouldn't have revealed what he knew.

"How do you know so much about the labyrinth, Draven?" asked Jovian, his smile absent for once.

With a shrug, Draven passed them and headed toward the temple. "Books," he lied. The group silently followed him. Inside the temple stood a throne, and on the throne sat a skeleton wearing a crown and armor.

"Niaria," Cassian murmured, nodding to the jaguar emblem on the king's armor. The emblem *did* match the one found on the bodies in front of the first gate. "It seems some of them made it through the second section."

Luka stared at the corpse. "This must be the king," he whispered almost sadly.

"Do you think…" Sage scanned the landscape around them. "Do you think the king and the rest of the army made this town? Or do you think they stumbled across it like we did?"

Cassian shook his head. "No, I think this city was here long before the labyrinth existed." The boy jabbed his thumb behind him. "Unless the army brought children with them to the labyrinth."

"What's this?" Something cracked, and Draven turned to see Archie pulling a jewel from the king's hand. A light flashed from inside the jewel and the ground trembled. Draven stumbled and braced himself, body tense, the others stumbling and scrambling behind and around him. The maze walls jolted with the quake, causing parts of it to crumble and cracks splintered through the ground around the temple.

Draven's stomach twisted as the vibrations rattled his bones. What was happening? Were they about to be swallowed into the earth? He should've paid attention. He should've stopped Archie.

"Archie!" Luka bellowed furiously.

Then, the quakes quieted and Draven cautiously relaxed, looking first over the group and then over the landscape around them. Besides the destruction caused by the earthquake, nothing had changed. He took a deep, calming breath.

Tristan thumped Archie on the head, and Jovian whacked the jewel from his grasp.

Cassian joined in the glares that were tossed in Archie's direction. "Didn't you learn anything from the poison berries?"

Archie, his face as red as strawberries, didn't respond.

The ground shook violently once more, and Draven braced himself again. An ominous laugh rose out of the crumbling of the city. Then a deep, vibrating voice spoke from behind them. "Finally…I've been released! Years! It's been years."

Draven's pulse quickened. Turning slowly, he faced the voice and watched as the skeleton king stood from its throne. Its gleaming, purple eyes searched their group and settled on Archie. "For a buffoon, you do your part nicely, Prince Archie."

Archie stumbled back, his eyes wide, an expression of terror twisting on his face.

How did the skeleton know Archie's name?

No one moved, not even Draven. He searched for an escape.

"Who—who are you?" asked Luka. "Are you the king of Niaria?"

Draven wished he wouldn't talk to it.

The skeleton laughed and looked down at himself. "King of Niaria? Hmmm…I suppose that is what I used to be called."

"Um, everyone?" Cassian's voice wavered. Draven glanced at the boy to see him staring outside the temple columns. Draven followed his gaze. Hundreds of skeletons rushed toward the temple, crawling and clambering over the crumbling houses and broken walls of the maze.

"Oh, crap, oh, crap, oh, crap!" shrieked Archie, clutching his sword.

Draven grimaced and pulled his own sword free of its scabbard. How were they going to get out of this? And where was Kai?

The skeleton king chuckled. "Don't mind me—I'm just debating whether to spare or kill you." Its purple eyes flashed. "Though maybe, since you've freed me, I'm feeling generous."

Luka tightened his hold on his sword. "The king of Niaria had no sense. He couldn't do any of this. He was a kind, gentle soul. You can't be him."

The skeleton brandished its own massive, golden sword, swinging it lightly, as if testing his reach. "Maybe I am, maybe I'm not. But you're right about one thing—I'm no merciful god." The king stepped back and lifted his sword to point at them. "Kill them."

Hundreds of skeletons responded to the king's demand and charged, scuttling, clattering, and clicking. Their jaws and bones chattered noisily. Half of the skeletons wore the same Niarien emblem on their torn clothing and dull armor and clutched an array of weapons. The other half wore shreds of cloth and used old pots and bricks as weapons.

Several skeletons reached Draven, swinging swords, scythes, and axes at his head. He ducked, blocked, and evaded each swing. However, when he swung his own sword at them, he couldn't seem to hit them.

He sliced again and again, blocking blows. Finally, he broke through the mishmash of armor and swung at a skeleton, but its bones only broke apart and reformed after his sword passed through its body, missing his blow entirely. Then, without a break in stride, it jabbed a knife toward Draven's gut.

Draven lurched backward, narrowly dodging the strike. He frowned and stepped on the skeletons' shadows, constraining them. He swung his sword once more and finally connected with bone. The shattered skeletons crumpled in a heap on the ground.

Draven stepped over the heap and angled his sword to block the next onslaught.

As he fought, something rattled behind him. Draven shot a glance over his shoulder and gritted his teeth. The skeletons he'd fragmented shook and jittered toward each other, slowly mending back together.

Stepping back, Draven shoved the reformed skeletons away with his sword, and knocked a head off another skeleton. Out of the corner of his eye, he spotted Archie sticking his sword into the ribcage of a skeleton, only for it to get stuck.

Draven leapt out of the way of a mace and whipped around to knock through several more skeletons. How could they win against enchanted bones? He propelled himself through the throng and collected a mass of shadows beneath the skeletons, weaving and knitting them together. Then he sucked the skeletons down into the depths of the shadows, creating a pocket of darkness to trap them in.

Manipulating the shadows, Draven heaved up a massive piece of broken ground and kicked it toward a crowd of living corpses, trapping several underneath.

Luka used his telekinesis to send several skeletons soaring and raised clumps of buildings and walls to smash them. Cassian shot a wave of ice through several more, freezing at least ten of them.

A skeleton's sword slashed Draven across his torso and he clutched his chest, wincing at the burn. His muscles ached and sweat dripped from his face and back. He longed to rest, but he couldn't.

Forcing himself to keep fighting, Draven kicked the creature who had cut him, spun, and slashed through a whole row of skeletons behind him.

His legs trembled and Draven stumbled back, his sweaty hands struggling to keep a grip on his sword. His lungs heaved for air. Draven cursed, and stepped on the shadows of his attacking skeletons, halting them mid-movement.

Then, a massive, ax-wielding skeleton came toward him. Draven jerked his sword, bracing for impact. But the impact never came.

Lightning split down from the sky and fried the giant and several others. Draven shot Tristan a grateful look before swallowing more skeletons into the shadows.

Then, a low and dark voice slithered into his thoughts. *Don't send bones. They're not as juicy and tasty as flesh. Send me some meat. In fact, why don't you let me in, and I'll take it myself? Your companions have been nothing but trouble to you anyway. You'll be much happier without them, I'm sure.*

Draven clutched his head, his migraine worsening. The voice was louder than usual, which only meant one thing: another episode. It was coming. Draven stumbled, his world becoming dark and faded. He struggled to fight off the skeletons, but another sword nicked his cheek, another jabbed his leg, and another his arm. He couldn't focus.

The ground cracked and split before him, consuming several skeletons, and Jovian slid in front of him, kicking a leg high into the air, only to slam it down into the ground. The earth trembled and rolled, knocking several skeletons into crevices opening in the ground. Jovian spun, shifting his stance, and forced his arms up. Large rocks rose into the air and rained down on their enemies.

"Thanks," Draven muttered, struggling to shake the voice from his head. Jovian gave him a wink and vaulted off.

Then Sage's cry echoed through the courtyard. Draven twisted. The skeleton king had chosen Sage as his first victim. She was weaponless and gripping her injured shoulder. The king seized her arm and raised his sword.

Without thinking, Draven melted into the shadows and transported himself. There was always a risk in melting into the shadows. It made it harder to resist episodes. So Draven focused his thoughts on Sage, and to his relief, he exited without struggle, appearing behind the skeletal king.

He stepped onto the king's shadow, locking him down where he stood and halting the king's swing. Draven lopped the king's raised arm clean off his torso.

Stillness hung between him, the skeletal king, and Sage for a moment. Then, with a creak, the king's head twisted all the way around and faced him, its glowing purple eyes locking onto Draven's. "Ah, Prince Draven. You came to me." Its blazing purple eyes brightened. "I've been waiting for you."

Draven furrowed his brow. Waiting for him?

An icy trickle of foreboding shot through Draven, tightening his muscles. He attempted a swing at the king's head, but his muscles didn't listen and stayed frozen. He couldn't move. The skeletal king rotated his body to face the same direction as his head and reached out his sole arm to seize Draven's shoulder. "Let me in, Draven."

Let me in. Let me in.

Everything paused—as if time had stopped—and the world grew darker. Something pressed over Draven's soul, forcing its way into his body. *No, no, no.* He had to resist. He couldn't let this *thing* in. How was it doing this?

Let me in, Prince Draven. Let me in.

Draven couldn't resist. He wasn't strong enough. The pain in his body dissolved, the sounds of battle faded, and there was only darkness. His inner darkness. He caved to the pressure, and the deepest depths of his sense released.

He had failed.

This wasn't part of the deal, the traitor hissed to the Spirit. *I thought you said you'd help protect the others.*

"*I said I can't have you all dying. I can't prevent death.*"

The traitor clenched his teeth. *Then what can you do?*

"*I can guide you. Mentor your ability. Give you your wish.*" The spirit paused. "*The deaths are merely a small price to pay for a better world. The loss will be worth it in the end.*"

The traitor's heart quavered. Was any death a price worth paying?

But when he thought of his family, his resolve solidified.

"The jewel. You must get the jewel," the spirit growled, pressing on his mind.

The traitor clenched his teeth. *It better be worth it.*

33

A Creature of Darkness

THE PLANT DRAGGED KAI THROUGH A DARK, DIRT TUNNEL, its teeth stinging as they dug into his skin and clothes. Kai twisted and writhed against the pull of the plant, a numbing sensation emanating from its bite. The plant's jaws tightened with each wriggle. "Let me go, dammit!" Kai screamed at the beast as he erupted into flames.

The plant let go of him, shrieking—as if alive—at the burn of the flames. Kai skidded and rolled along the ground. His ribs and shoulder, which still ached from the goblin fight, groaned in pain. He pushed himself up and glared at the plant beast as it drummed at the ground, squelching his flames.

But before he could set the whole plant aflame, vines sprung from the ground, walls, and ceiling of the tunnel and wrapped themselves tightly around his torso, arms, legs, and neck. Kai erupted into flames again, dragging himself from their grasp. Once he was free, he drew his sword and slashed at them. But more came, choking and pulling at him.

"Go to bloody *HELL*!" he screamed. Kai shot flames in every direction. The air in the underground tunnel was shallow and the walls seemed to close in on him. He hated enclosed spaces; he needed to find a way out. But another vine wrapped around one of his legs and hauled him deeper into the tunnel. Thrashing to get his leg free of the vines' tight grasp, Kai dug the fingers of his swordless hand into the dirt. The air suddenly became heavier.

He lugged in another breath, but it took more effort than before. What if he died here? He slashed at the vine, causing him to skid to a stop, and released a stream fire which turned the vine into ash. But Kai dripped with sweat, and his flames dwindled.

He needed air. He was suffocating. How would he resist the vines if he was weakened from the lack of oxygen and couldn't use his sense? Fire needed oxygen as much as his lungs.

More vines and roots broke free of the earth, and he scorched them, looking around wildly for an escape. There. Another tunnel headed in a different direction than the plants had been dragging him. Kai dove for the tunnel and found himself sliding down a slope.

Dots formed in his sight, and the tunnel swirled dizzily around him.

Air. Please lead to air.

Then a rush of oxygen hit him as he fell, and his lungs heaved it in. Gradually, his sight cleared more with each breath. The slope halted suddenly, shooting Kai out into a cavern. He skidded across the ground, still feeling weak and dizzy. But he didn't have time to rest. More plants slithered out of the ground and entangled him again, dragging him toward a crevice.

"Not again, you blasted twigs!"

Kai burst from their grip with a blast of fire, soared through the cavern, and landed on the other side. More plants immediately sprouted and he set them ablaze. How could he get out of here and back to the others? Were the others experiencing something like this? Jumping out of another plant's reach, Kai scanned the space. Besides the crevice and a few chutes, there didn't seem to be any escape from the cavern he was in.

Another toothy plant snapped viciously at him. He cursed and lopped off its head, focusing all his attention on surviving—one move, one breath, at a time.

Then the sound of something trickled and dripped behind him.

Turning, Kai searched the walls. The plants swarmed him and slithered around his limbs, forcing him to tear his gaze away. He toppled to the ground before he could burn them away. Kai scrambled back, burning and yanking himself from their grasps. He tossed another look over his shoulder where the drip of water seemed to be coming from and finally spotted something. A hallway leading out of the cavern.

Kai heaved a wave of flames behind him and dashed toward the small opening, shoving his sword back into its scabbard. He tripped and stumbled as plants snatched at his legs.

Finally, he staggered into the opening. The stone walls, ceiling, and floors curved off in two directions. The ceiling hung low, and water droplets seeped down from the walls, making puddles on the floor. One side of the wall had more perspiration than the other.

Kai darted to the right. However, not long later he halted and groaned. This hallway looped in one, big, blasted circle, and it wouldn't have mattered which direction he'd gone. He paused and leaned his head against the cool stone wall, glaring down at his clenched fists.

The plants slid along the stone floor toward him from both directions like snakes. Kai's muscles quivered. His shallow breath and the dulling of his flames informed him he was still far underground. He hated feeling vulnerable, feeling helpless.

It reminded him too much of a period in his childhood when he'd been stalked by assassins and regularly had to fight for his life. He hadn't learned until years after the first attack who had been sending them. Kai closed his eyes and gritted his teeth. Why did life seem so set on getting rid of him?

Drawing his sword once more, Kai opened his eyes and stepped away from the plants as they neared him. He sliced and hacked at them. While cutting through the vines, thorns, leaves, and roots that came for him, he focused on taking deep, careful breaths.

Water covered the stone floor making it slippery and when a plant succeeded in seizing his leg, Kai slipped, lost his footing, and slammed against the floor. His head hit stone.

The room immediately whirled and reeled. Wincing, Kai lay still, unable to convince himself to stand back up. His body and legs sagged uselessly.

He pleaded for his muscles to move, but his body refused to listen. Another plant seized his leg and tugged. More vines and roots wrapped around his body, but Kai couldn't find the will or strength to fight against them. He was too tired. All he wanted to do was take a nap.

The room swirled and it reminded him of gas—he could still feel the whirling sensations of lying in bed, gas surrounding him, seeing the assassins looming above him. He squirmed, just like he had that day, the plants' teeth pricking the same way the assassins' knives had. And today, just like that day, he was tired—tired of resisting the death that pursued him everywhere he went. His grandmother had rescued him that day, but there was no one to rescue him now. He wished she would burst through the stone wall now just like she'd burst into his bedroom all those years ago.

Suddenly, the earth shuddered, sending more dust and water cascading over him. Kai forced his eyes open. What was that?

The ground and walls trembled again. Cracks ran along the stone walls, and water spurted from them. There was water on the other side of that wall. Hope swelled up inside of him.

He took a deep breath as the ground and walls vibrated again. Then with all the strength he had left, Kai blasted the wall with his hottest flames. The rock cracked some more, and more water burst through it, dousing his flames.

Another tremor shook the room, and the wall crumbled to pieces, causing a wave of water to splash into the hall, washing away plant creatures as it went. Kai released his sword and gripped the rock floor to prevent himself from being swept away, but the rush of water was too strong.

Then something very strange happened. The water reversed and returned the way it had come, pulling Kai with it. Kai didn't have the strength to resist, so he allowed himself to be engulfed into a ball of water that defied gravity and rose up a large tunnel.

Kai squinted upward through the water and spotted a growing stream of light. An opening.

The water catapulted him out of the opening, and Kai sailed face first into an army of corpses. He and the moving wave of water bowled through several skeletons as he fell. The water splashed onward without Kai, leaving him drenched and heaving in as much air as he could.

Kai sat up slowly and took in his surroundings. Everywhere he looked, skeletons crawled, walked, and dragged themselves across the broken earth. They passed him—as if unable to see him at all—and headed toward a temple in the distance.

Ice ricocheted through the courtyard, freezing several creatures where they were. The others. He'd found them.

And they were being attacked. By walking dead people.

Kai pushed himself shakily to his feet and watched, stunned, as some of the skeletons he'd knocked over when landing rose up from the ground unharmed. How on earth were they still bloody moving? And why didn't they see him?

Just then, more plants burst from the ground and tangled themselves around his weak legs. "Dammit! When will you leave me *alone*?"

Kai shook his legs free and forced himself to chase after the skeletons toward the temple and away from the plants. He skidded to a stop just before the temple and stared, taking in the chaos. Luka levitated, Jovian smashed, Cassian froze, Archie splashed, and Tristan electrified. Then Kai's gaze landed on Sage. He scrambled for a sword as a crown-wearing skeleton closed its hand around Draven's neck. Draven didn't move; didn't resist at all.

Kai—temporarily forgetting about the plants and his tired, drained muscles—hurdled himself over bodies, sprinting to Draven's rescue. Then the skeleton king squeezing Draven's neck crumbled into a pile at Draven's feet. But Draven still didn't move.

Kai slid to a stop.

Sage grasped his sword and whirled around to face Draven but stopped short. Then he took a step back, and even Kai wanted to step back. Because Draven's eyes were as black as coal, his face still and emotionless.

Kai's gut knotted.

Then Draven's eyes flickered purple, and a gruesome smile twisted his face as a dark cloud rose out of him. The cloud took on the vague shape of something that was both humanoid and dragon. Elongated arms stretch out with long, curved claws. Purple eyes illuminated from its dragon-shaped head. But other than the eyes and silhouette of the beast, no other details were distinguishable. It was a black void.

A ravenous laugh rumbled from the beast. "Finally. I can feast," its gruff voice hissed. The creature turned its gaze on Sage, who was the closest. "Feast on flesh."

Kai staggered back, squeezing his fists. "Sage, *move!*" he bellowed, startling several of the others.

Sage bolted away from Draven, grabbing Cassian and pulling him back, yelling at the others to retreat.

The beast roared and Kai turned to run.

Then, everything went dark.

Kai stood still, staring into the blackness. He turned his head in every direction, but he couldn't see anything.

A deep laugh rumbled through his soul and sharp screams pierced through the darkness. Kai stumbled and slapped his hands over his ears. No matter where he turned, nothing but darkness met him. Dropping to the ground, Kai squeezed his hands against his ears so hard it hurt, desperate to block out the screams ringing through his mind and spirit.

Finally, through the emptiness, Kai made out a looming shape. The figure was different than the beast from before. This one had a skeletal face with shredded skin and tendons holding its jaw together. It reminded Kai of death.

This creature had purple eyes that flamed and wasn't a void like the previous one. Those eyes bored into him, burning him from the inside and out. Terror struck deep in his chest—terror unlike he had ever experienced before. Kai's eyes widened and he stared, petrified. All he could do was watch as the creature approached.

"Prince Kai, I see you're not dead yet." Its deep, penetrating voice was less ravenous than the voice he heard earlier. This had to be a different being altogether. "I'll just have to finish you off myself. Believe me when I say, I find this terribly unfortunate. You were one of my top choices. You have so much potential—but I can't risk it."

The creature reached for him, and something squeezed Kai's heart, burning it. He gasped in pain, and his grip slid from his ears to his chest. His scream joined the others that rang in his head.

The pain was so excruciating, he couldn't think. Couldn't move.

Then, a bright, blinding light flashed into the darkness. A light that reduced the screams. A light that chased away the darkness and dissolved the pain. Kai turned toward it, still gripping his burning chest, and saw the light move toward him—a brilliant, glowing form. Kai reached out, desperate to be saved. The glowing figure brandished a blazing sword, forced its way past Kai, and, after a brief hesitation, thrust its blade into the creature standing over Kai.

The creature wailed, and the darkness vanished as suddenly as it had come.

When Kai opened his eyes once more, the cracked marble floor of the temple lay beneath him, and the light from the dimming sky flooded the world around him. The skeletal army lay crumpled in heaps around him, littering the ground with motionless bones. No beast was in sight.

Only stillness.

Kai blinked, his chest still burning. What had happened? Was it over?

Overwhelmed with exhaustion, his muscles gave out, and he went limp. The brilliant figure standing over him dimmed and morphed into Sage's worried face.

Then Kai blacked out.

34

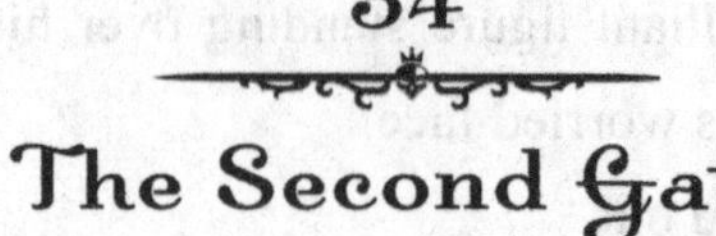

The Second Gate

SAGE PANTED, HER SHOULDER THROBBING AS SHE CLENCHED her sword tightly in her hand. She looked around anxiously, but when she did, all that met her was a black void. The darkness descended with a crushing force and she folded over, her heart speeding up as terror blended with the overwhelming force of the darkness. Her mind swirled with dizziness, queasy from the pressure on her mind and heart.

Just when she felt she would pass out, Draven's words whispered in her mind: *"I'm the opposite. I often hate light."* Sage gritted her teeth. If Draven could survive a whole month in an unshaded desert, surely she could survive a moment of darkness. She had to resist.

Light burned in her chest as Sage tightened her grip on her sword once more. Shaking, Sage rose to her feet. She would stand her ground—like Ruben stood his against the werewolves.

If he could face his fear, and Draven could face his, then she could too. She shut her eyes tight and focused on expanding her inner light, shoving away the pressure of the darkness.

Energy exploded outward.

Sizzling, pulsing power throbbed through her limbs and chest in a way she'd never felt before. When Sage opened her eyes, the temple and the courtyard lay before her. Skeletons stood frozen, as if they'd forgotten their task, staring in one direction: Draven.

Draven stood where she'd last seen him, and the terrifying, featureless creature still rose above him.

Then a terrible scream streaked through the courtyard. Sage froze. The scream emanated from *Kai*. The other six princes were cowering behind rubble or on their knees gripping their ears, but Kai gripped his chest, writhing in pain. The creature's long, dark hand reached into Kai's chest. What was it doing to him?

Her heart pushed into her throat. Trembling, Sage raised her sword. She had to stop whatever that creature was if she was going to save the others. And to save them, she had to get that *thing* out of Draven.

Sage illuminated her sword with a ray, but as she did, the strange pulsing radiated even stronger than before, energizing her. All the exhaustion and pain she'd felt a moment ago melted away. Even the aching in her shoulder dissipated. But Kai's screams didn't leave her time to think. She charged toward the shadow creature.

Its purple eyes turned toward her and it veered out an arm to knock her away, but then Draven jerked and the creature stiffened as if it was fighting against a force.

Draven was resisting.

Sage didn't hesitate to thrust her sword deep into the shadow, piercing it with her light. The creature trembled, wavered, and a loud screech penetrated her soul and echoed through the temple. Sage scrambled back, her eyes wide, as the creature dissipated like smoke.

When the last evidence of the creature was gone, Draven crumpled, along with the entire army of skeletons. Bones and various weapons clattered to the ground, reverberating through the broken temple.

Sage furrowed her brow. Had it worked? Had they won? She lowered her sword and slowly retracted her light. The pulsing drained away. A dull ache throbbed in her shoulder once more, and trembling overtook her arms and legs. She sank to the ground, pressing a hand to her head. What was that *thing*?

Sage peeled her fingers off the hilt of her sword and watched it clang to the ground. Then she faced Kai.

He lay sprawled a few feet away, unmoving.

"Kai!" Sage scrambled toward him. Small scrapes and burns could be seen along his arms and neck, and he was drenched from head to toe. She held a finger under his nose with one hand and lowered her ear to his chest. A wonderful, strong, consistent thud met her ear. Her chest eased and she released the breath she'd been holding. Alive. He was still alive. Sage straightened and looked to the others.

Luka examined the unmoving corpses around him, Archie cowered behind a column, Jovian kicked a few skeletons, and

Cassian and Tristan stared in her direction. She gave them a nod. Then she straightened.

Draven.

Jumping up, she ran back to where he lay. She pushed him onto his back and checked him. He too was still alive. She exhaled deeply, relieved. What had happened to him? Clearly, he'd been possessed by whatever had been in the skeleton king. But…where did *that* monster come from?

Draven's eyes fluttered open and focused on Sage. He moaned, gripping his head. Then he raised himself up on his elbows with a jerk, an expression of fear flashing across his face. "Did—did I hurt anyone?"

Sage stared at him. "Everyone is still alive," she reassured him. What had he meant by *I*? Did he think whatever had happened was his fault?

Lying back down, Draven gripped his face with his hand and sighed. His hand slid down his face and his eyes closed. "Good." Then he slipped out of consciousness once more.

The rest of the group circled around her, looking down at Draven. Archie, still trembling, stood a little distance away, as if too afraid to come closer. He shivered and asked hoarsely, "What in dragon's breath was *that*? What happened just now?"

Luka shook his head solemnly. "I don't know."

Sage eyed a disheveled skeleton nearby, almost expecting it to come back alive at any moment. "Do you think that *thing* is gone? Did we destroy it?"

Luka looked around. "I hope so."

Sage shivered.

A moan came from behind them, and Sage turned with everyone else. Kai sat up, rubbing his head and clutching his chest.

"I see you survived," Luka said, crossing his arms over his chest. "Even if you're a pain, I'm glad you're not dead."

Jovian chuckled. "What did I say? I told you Tomato Head would put up a fight."

Kai rubbed his chest and coughed. "A couple of annoying twigs can't kill me," he replied hoarsely. "Though, Archie, gotta say I'm glad you pulled me from the well."

Archie blinked, pausing as he fixed his ponytail. "I did?" He peered at the well and then straightened a bit taller. "I mean, sure. No problem."

Kai's gaze flickered to Sage, then dropped, his hand still rubbing his chest.

"Let's get away from here," Luka broke in, his face tense as he watched the skeletons.

Kai climbed to his feet slowly. "Good riddance. Let's get the bloody hell out of here." He picked up a skeleton's discarded sword and scabbard. He removed his empty scabbard from his belt and replaced it with the skeleton's.

Sage stared down the trail of bones left by their attackers in the direction of the gate. She hoped they didn't leap back up to slaughter them. What had happened to that skeleton king who had possessed Draven? Was it still inside him? She studied Draven's still figure. He had seemed like himself before he passed out, but who could be sure when they were in a place like this?

The group of eight, Luka levitating Draven in the air, trudged toward the gate, climbing over fallen walls and motionless skeletons. When they finally reached it, Sage peered up at a door that was very similar to the one that had led them out of the first section. Only this one had a new puzzle.

Five images created a pentagon around the image of a phoenix. Under each image was a gemstone: a green gemstone under a tree, yellow under a skull, blue under a water symbol, white under a mountain, and purple under a sun. Five small, empty holes opened at the bottom of the gate.

Sage bit her lip and her shoulders sagged.

Archie moaned. "Another dumb puzzle to figure out."

Cassian scowled at Archie, then studied the images. "The last gate was about the story of the labyrinth. I bet this one has something to do with the labyrinth as well."

"And last time Draven and Tenji helped us figure it out," Archie muttered, frowning at the sleeping body hovering beside Luka.

Cassian gestured at the gate. "This is easier than the last one though. See? Mountains, trees, water, sun, and skull. And someone did part of the work for us." He pointed to the ground in front of the gate where five gemstones matching the ones on the gate lay in a haphazard pile. "Probably the Niarien king and his army before they were killed."

Luka lowered the unconscious Draven to the ground and joined them to study the images. "Last time, the sun came first, right?"

"Oh, yeah!" Archie exclaimed, his eyes bright. "Maybe it's first again this time!" He reached for the corresponding purple gemstone.

Sage's stomach flipped, and she unconsciously lifted an arm to stop him.

Before she could, Tristan smacked Archie's hand away and shook his head. Sage allowed her suddenly tense shoulders to relax. Phew.

Jovian rolled his eyes and crossed his arms. "You've caused enough trouble with your impulsive touching, water-boy." His coy smile was empty of its usual humor. "Don't know if we can survive if you cause another catastrophe right now."

Luka agreed. "Maybe you should refrain from touching anything for a little while—for your safety and ours."

Shrinking back, Archie looked hurt. "Fine then," he said as he avoided everyone's gazes.

If the skeleton battle and creepy dark beast hadn't been so fresh in her mind, maybe Sage would feel a little sorry for Archie. But she didn't—not even a little.

"What did you do this time?" Kai asked, eyeing Archie.

"Doesn't matter." Archie waved a hand at him dismissively, still avoiding looking at anyone. "Let's focus on getting out of this horrid desert."

Kai raised his eyebrows. "Must've been pretty bad."

Sage turned her head so Archie wouldn't see her smile.

"Anyway." Cassian gave Archie a look, drawing everyone's attention back to the gate as he continued, "The skull reminds me of what we just encountered. What if these images are related to the sections of the labyrinth? There are five stones and, according to Draven, there are five sections."

"*Five* sections?" Kai blurted out, interrupting Cassian. "You're saying we haven't even made it halfway through?"

Sage winced. She'd forgotten Kai wasn't there when Draven announced that. Rubbing her aching shoulder, Sage studied the five images. There *was* an image of a tree; it reminded her of the forests in the first section.

Luka ignored Kai. "You might be onto something Cassian." He stepped closer to the gate, eyeing the jewels on the ground and then the images on the gate. "The first section was a forest— should we try the tree and find out?"

Everyone hesitated. Silence hung over them. What if they were wrong? Sage bit the inside of her cheek and squeezed her hands together in front of her.

Finally, Jovian strode through the middle of them, grabbed the green gemstone from the ground, and pushed it into the first hole. Sage flinched, but nothing happened. The green gem glowed.

Without waiting, Jovian snatched the yellow gemstone and placed it into the second hole.

Sage held her breath. Again, nothing terrible happened.

The gemstone beamed.

Luka flashed Cassian a smile. "I think it's working!"

Archie sighed as he pointed at the remaining three holes. "Now we have to figure out the three sections we've never been in."

Silence once again fell over them. Sage studied the remaining images: water, a sun, and a mountain. How would they know what came next?

An idea came to Sage. Cautiously, she spoke, "Maybe the sun is last? It was first last time. Maybe this time it's last."

No one refuted her guess and, rather, appeared quite pleased with her suggestion. Jovian inspected the group before picking up the purple gem and placing it into the last hole. It glowed, twinkling like a star.

Luka, his shoulders relaxing, looked at the two remaining. "Okay, then, what could be the next? Mountains or the water?"

When no one made a suggestion, Jovian stepped forward. "We'll never know unless we try!" Jovian snatched up the water gem and pressed it into the third hole.

Everyone lurched back.

A clatter arose behind them, and Sage whirled. Bones rolled together, forming monstrous beings, chattering and clanking once more. Sage's muscles ached and trembled as she drew her sword. Not again.

The others drew their own weapons, but none of them seemed ready for another battle, their expressions worn and tense. Luka stepped between the skeletons and Draven's sleeping body.

Archie moaned and whimpered. "Darnit, Jovian."

Jovian grimaced and yanked the blue stone from the hole and pressed it into the hole next to it instead. Then, he pressed the white stone into the remaining hole. Both gems brightened.

Once again, the pentagon on the gate shifted in a circular pattern. A rectangular box opened in the middle of the gate, and the jewels above the images slid from their places and into the box. A pedestal with a globe rose out of the ground.

Luka stepped away from the pedestal, grimacing. Sage didn't particularly want to volunteer to have her hand stuck on an orb like Luka had last time. But someone had to do it.

The skeletons skittered and crawled toward them.

Then, to her surprise, Kai rushed forward and slapped his hand on the globe. The gems in the box shifted and Kai frowned.

"Maybe try putting them in the same order," Tristan said calmly.

Kai groaned. "I hate puzzles."

Sage wasn't a fan of them either, so she kept her mouth shut and allowed the more gifted princes to help Kai. Tristan moved to stand next to the globe and with Tristan's quiet guidance, Kai shifted the stones until they lined up in the correct order. When the final gem clicked into place, the gate trembled and creaked open, revealing another tunnel.

Tears pricked in Sage's eyes at the sight. One step closer to the end. She didn't allow herself to think about the uncertainty of what they'd do once they reached the end. No. She refused to think about that.

Then, without waiting on the approaching skeletons, she and the rest of the group darted through the gate and into the tunnel, Luka levitating Draven once more.

Sage watched and waited for the gate to close behind them, but it somehow seemed slower than it had in the last section. The skeletons lurched after them, and Sage blocked their blows with her sword. She kicked and shoved, trying to keep the skeletons from passing into the tunnel with them.

Jovian manipulated the earth to create a barrier and the gates closed tight, locking the desert and the skeletons on the other side.

The second section was complete. Finally.

The traitor tucked his hand into his pocket where the jewel that had woken the skeletons nestled.

"Very good. Very good." The spirit was much louder and stronger than before. *"Now everything is in place."*

The traitor glanced back at his companions. Would they understand?

"They may not understand at first. But they will when everything is finished. They'll see our way is better and will laud the fact they helped achieve a better world for everyone. We'll show them."

35

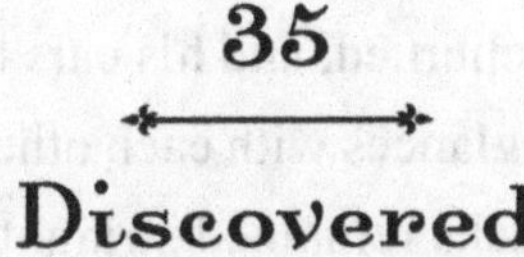

Discovered

"EVERARD," SNAPPED LORD RUFUS, HEAD OF THE HIGH council, as he slapped a stick against Everard's desk. "Do you ever use that empty head of yours?"

Everard tore his gaze from the history book lying on his desk where "Sidylla Labyrinth" was written in fine print, suddenly aware of the several pairs of eyes looking at him from around the classroom. Despite Lord Rufus' short, bent stature, his glare cut with the sharpness of a sword. Everard gulped, seizing the seat of his chair tightly with both hands. He didn't know how to respond to Lord Rufus' degrading question, nor did he fully know what the man's sudden ire concerned. He'd zoned out. Again.

Lord Rufus turned and stalked to the front of the room with quick, short strides, slapping desks of other low-ranking royals with his rod while muttering. Once he reached the front, he whirled around to face them, eyes settling on Everard once more. "Sessions for low-ranks are a blessing. You should all know this. None of you will ever come close to being king, even if someone murdered fifty or a hundred of those before you. Wouldn't that make these sessions a waste? *I* don't have to teach you any of this. But still, here I am." He slapped a desk near the front. "I expect you to at least respect my time and instruction, especially you Prince Everard, son of King Léon. To think you're related to Luka!"

Everard's stomach churned, and his ears burned. The others in the session exchanged glances with each other, but no one laughed or murmured. Their backs remained straight, their mouths shut.

"Everard, you are dismissed. I refuse to have this impudence in my session."

Ducking his head, Everard stood, grabbed his bag, and scurried out of the room without a word. Queasiness roiled in his gut, making his head swim. He didn't slow his pace until he was out of the building and in the courtyard. Then he gagged, tears stinging his eyes.

He hated his life. He hated that he had no sense. He hated the Royal Council, Valor and his friends, his father, and most of all, he hated himself. And somehow, he had sunk so low as to send ten others into the labyrinth to get *him* a sense. But the worst part was—despite not knowing what had happened to the others—he still wanted the sense he'd sent them after. The swirling emotions of guilt, shame, and yearning still made him sick when he thought too much about what he'd done, yet Everard kept his mouth shut and didn't confess a word to anyone.

What if they're dead already? Everard gripped his head and shook the thought out. No, they had to make it out alive. They had to. How could he live with himself if they didn't?

Someone whacked the back of his head, sending him stumbling forward. Everard whirled to find his dark-haired brother, Romain, wrinkling his nose at him. "Vomiting in front of the Royal Academy? Really? How pathetic are you?"

Everard hunched away from Romain, refusing to look him in the face. He sniffed and fidgeted with his bag.

"No wonder Father refuses to acknowledge you."

Tears smarted once more, and Everard's lips quivered as he struggled to hold them in. He hurried away from the Academy, but the thud of Romain's boots followed.

"If this is your way of begging for attention, Ev, then stop," Romain grumbled, his voice thick with distaste. "This behavior is disgusting."

Heat boiled in Everard's stomach. He bit his tongue to keep from snapping back. He had no reason to defend himself. Why should he?

"Oh, please," came a familiar voice, quiet but sharp. "You're one to talk, always bickering and causing trouble."

Michal. Everard looked over his shoulder to see his second oldest brother had joined them, his golden hair shining in the sunlight. Michal narrowed his eyes at Romain who scowled in return.

But before Romain retorted, another voice rose: "Well, well. If it isn't the sons of the king."

Everard's heart sank. Reluctantly, he faced forward once more to find Valor standing before them, his arms crossed, a smirk on his face, his yellow eyes piercing. Everard came to an abrupt stop. Valor wouldn't openly harass him in front of his brothers, would he? He'd become quite brazen the last few weeks.

"Valor," greeted Michal, his voice cold.

Valor didn't acknowledge the greeting. Instead, he merely leered at them. "Surprised to see you're still around. I imagine, if it *truly* was Velykov who murdered the Ten, you'd both be gone by now." For once, Valor took no notice of Everard. "Tell me, is it true the *king* is behind the disappearances?"

Everard clutched his bag tighter and shot a look in Romain and Michal's direction. Father?

"What?" Romain snarled, stepping forward, his face scrunching.

Michal tensed and his face tightened.

Valor's smile inched higher. "You haven't heard. Some rumors have been passing around that *your* father *murdered* Prince Cyprian. That his death hadn't been an accident after all."

"That's not true." Romain rolled his eyes and crossed his arms over his chest. "The rumors have been saying lots of things lately. People believe anything these days. Why would Father care about some random prince?" He nudged Michal with his shoulder as if to get him to back him up.

But Michal's lips thinned and he said nothing.

Valor shrugged and quirked his eyebrows. "They *say* he did it so Luka could be first."

Everard's eyes widened He wanted to deny it, like Romain, but…did Father kill someone so Luka could take first? Both of the princes ranking higher than Luka had disappeared within a year of each other. Prince Talon was said to be banished, but the reason why was never shared. Father had always been obsessed with Luka's ranking. Could—could his father be *that* twisted? Surely not.

"That's ridiculous," Romain retorted. But when Everard looked at him, Romain's face had paled and the look in his eyes was full of uncertainty.

Valor relaxed his crossed arms to stretch them behind his head as he continued, "If your father killed one prince, what would stop him from killing more?"

Michal still hadn't budged, but his face had relaxed, empty of emotion. "That logic is unsound. Father wouldn't do something as illogical as murdering the top ten. And he'd never lay a finger on his favorite son."

Valor's eyebrows arched at Michal's mention of a *favorite son*. He lowered his arms and nodded, his smile widening. "If you say so. I suppose the second favorite would know, huh?" He winked at Michal before striding forward, knocking Everard with his shoulder as he passed.

Everard kept his head low, watching Romain and Michal through his eyelashes until Romain stalked away, Michal following silently behind him. Everard released a slow breath of relief. At least it was over quickly.

But Valor's damage was done.

He stared at his two older brothers' tense backs. Hopefully, they'd make it back home before Romain erupted.

When they reached the royal castle, Everard followed Michal and Romain inside. They all halted simultaneously in the entryway. Everard scanned the scurrying servants and castle workers, their whispers filling the eerily silent halls. None of the workers or servants or Royal Council met his or his brothers' eyes. What was going on? What was with this odd energy?

Michal turned and darted down the hallway toward the throne room. Romain shot Everard a look before they both ran after him. Everard strained for breath as his boots pounded against the stone floors, his heart thumping in his ears. As they drew close to the throne room, something crashed from inside.

Everard skidded to a stop. Romain and Michal slowed too, and the three of them stood uneasily before the massive wooden doors carved with the image of Reudinia's soaring phoenix. No guards stood before the doors. Everard's chest squeezed. His heart thudded even louder than before and his arms trembled.

A low, angry voice rumbled from inside the throne room. "Who did you tell, you snake?"

Father.

Another voice warbled in reply, her words muffled, "...I didn't...I promise!"

Mother.

Michal's hand reached for the handle but hesitated.

"LIAR!" Something else crashed.

Michal yanked the door open.

Inside, the immense room held only a handful of people. Father. A few members of the high council. And Mother in a crouched and sobbing mess at Father's feet.

Father's gaze snapped toward them, his glare heated. "What are you doing here? Get out! I don't have time to deal with you."

Everard's eyes dropped to Mother who turned toward them, tears streaking down her face, and his blood turned to ice. Everard glanced at his older brothers, unsure what to do. Michal's face had paled, and Romain glared at their father.

Michal lifted his gaze from Mother to Father. "What's going on?"

"It's none of *your* business. Leave."

Everard's gaze darted to his mother again only to see her shooing them with her hand. He took a shaky step back.

Romain clenched his fists and stepped forward. "I'll leave when you let Mother go."

Father's face flushed deep red. "Are you defying me, you insolent boy?"

Mother shakily stood and stepped between them and Father. "No. He's just confused." She turned to face them, brushing the tears from her face. "Don't worry. He'll let you see me later. Go along." She made another shooing motion, but this time, she mouthed, *Go now*.

Romain glowered for a moment longer before he turned and stormed out of the room and back down the hall. Everard took a few more trembling steps backward, his eyes darting between Mother's tearful face, Father's sharp glare, and Michal's frozen, pale features. Then Michal turned, released his hold on the door, and walked after Romain.

Everard didn't budge until the throne doors shut in his face, and then he slowly followed after Michal. What did Father think Mother had done? Was it a mistake to leave her alone? But what could they do against their father…the king?

Everard hugged himself as he walked toward his bedroom. Occasionally, he'd tear his eyes from the floor to look at Michal before dropping them to the ground again. At least until Michal suddenly stopped walking. Everard slowed and lifted his head.

Michal's head curved forward, his fists clenched, and his shoulders slumped. To his right was Luka's door, their own rooms just ahead. Then Michal opened Luka's door and stepped inside.

Everard stared after him. What was he doing? He headed toward his own room but peered behind him. He stopped again. Then he stepped toward Luka's door and peeked inside. Michal had Luka's desk opened and papers spilled over it. Everard pushed open the door and stepped inside.

The door creaked, and Michal glanced toward him but didn't stop.

"What are you doing?" asked Everard, his nose wrinkling.

Michal didn't reply. Instead, he kept flipping through Luka's things, hurriedly scanning his journals, and making a complete mess. The longer Everard watched, the angrier he became.

"Why are you going through Luka's things?"

"Why do you care?" Michal snapped at last.

Everard squeezed his fists. "Because…because…Luka's not dead!"

Michal halted long enough to face Everard. "How do you know? You don't know what happened to him. Do you?"

Everard turned his head away, and his momentary anger went out the window like a bucket of dirty water. *He* was the reason Luka wasn't here. Not Michal. Not Romain. Not the Royal Council. Not Father. "N-no…but we can't give up on him yet! And what could be in his things that you'd want anyway?"

"Answers." Michal turned back to Luka's desk and pulled more things from the drawers. He flipped through a few more items before he paused again and faced Everard. His eyes narrowed. "You know, the day Luka and the rest of the Ten went missing, someone came into my room and shot me with a sleeping dart. Before I was knocked out, I heard a voice—one that sounded very much like you—tell the assaulter not to take me. That I was *unnecessary*." He cocked his head at Everard. "When I woke up, there was no evidence of the events from the night before. Nothing I could show to others. Since then, I've wondered and wondered what those words had meant, debating if I misheard somehow. I would tell myself that I was too drugged to understand, that I was confused and mistook the voice for yours. And other times, I'd wonder if I should be searching *your* room too."

Michal's words punched Everard in the gut. He stared at his brother in horror. He'd heard him?

Michal dropped the papers in his hands and stepped toward him. Everard took a step back.

"I've been watching you, Everard," Michal said as he drew close, thrusting a finger into his chest. "You've been *suspicious*."

He leaned in close to Everard's face, refusing to let him look away. "Just now, when you said you didn't know anything about Luka, you couldn't even look me in the eye. You know what happened to the Ten, don't you?"

Everard's stomach dropped and he stumbled back. He snapped his gaze to the door. Could he bolt? No, then Michal would know. His mind swirled, desperate to find a solution. But he struggled with his resolve. Could he keep lying like this? But it wouldn't matter now, not really. No matter what, Michal would know.

Michal stepped back, and his face slackened as he gaped at Everard. "It really was you, wasn't it?"

Everard's heart drummed in his arms and face and ears. His legs trembled beneath him, and tears threatened to spill once again. He knew. Michal *knew*. What would happen now? Was it all over? Would he turn him in?

Michal's face hardened. "Did you kill them?"

"No," Everard said, his voice cracking. Tears welled up and spilled from his eyes. He frantically wiped them away as a sob hiccupped from his chest. "I—I sent them to the Sidylla Labyrinth."

Michal's eyes widened. He stared at Everard in stony silence, and Everard's confession seemed to echo in the room that had been empty these last three and half months.

Finally, Michal seemed to find his voice. "The *Sidylla Labyrinth*? Ev, that's no better than murdering them." He placed his hand on top of his head and turned away, breath growing labored.

"I know." Everard whimpered, gripping his own head, his insides tearing him apart. The all-too-familiar nausea swam in his gut. "I—I just keep *hoping* they'll make it out, that they're still alive."

"There's no way," Michal said, tight and brusque. "Good gracious, why would you do that to them? Were you jealous? Angry?"

Everard shook his head frantically and raised his eyes, wiping tears from his eyes. "No. I just wanted a sense so Father would stop ignoring me." He released a sob. "I couldn't go through the labyrinth on my own. I'm too weak."

Michal dropped his arms to his sides. "So you sent ten others to die in your place?"

Everard's stomach reeled and the room spun. *Die in your place. Die in your place.* He bent over and vomited onto the floor, trembling as he heaved once more. The room still whirled around him, so he reached for a bedpost to steady himself and clutched his stomach. He squeezed his tearful eyes shut. "Are you going to tell Father?"

Silence buzzed between them.

Then Michal released a slow sigh. "No."

The word shot through Everard like a bolt of lightning. He opened his eyes and raised his head once more. He stared at his older brother.

Michal's back was still to him.

"Why?"

Michal's hands tightened to fists. "Because what's done is done, and if Father or anyone else finds out, you'll be beheaded."

Everard couldn't help it when his mouth dropped open. Warmth budded within his chest in a way he hadn't experienced in a long, long time. Had he heard his brother correctly? "I—I didn't think you'd care about that."

Michal sniffed and crossed his arms over his chest; his shoulders curved away from Everard. "What you did was awful—terrible—and I can't believe you actually went through with it. But…I also can't blame you for doing it either." Then he faced him. "However, if someone accuses me or Romain or anyone else innocent and you don't come clean, then I'll tell them the truth. I'm not losing my head for you."

36

A Knife in the Snow

SURROUNDED BY THE SEVEN PRINCES, SAGE STARED OUT OF the tunnel at the snowy tundra before them. Deep snow covered the ground and in the distance she could see the shadow of a treeline. Massive, snow-tipped mountains loomed above them and ran as far as she could see. She'd never seen snow before. It glittered beautifully in the sunlight, but the icy wind blew frigidly. Her shoulders sagged. They had just left a sweltering desert, and now they had to bear the cold?

Tristan pulled several cloaks from his bag. At least they would have some protection.

Cassian darted out and flopped face first into the snow. After burying his face into the powdery whiteness, he rolled onto his back, beaming from ear to ear.

"Cassian is excited," Kai muttered, an obvious distaste underlying his tone.

Cassian sat up suddenly and his smile slipped from his face as his gaze swept over the group. Sage wished his joy could've lasted a bit longer than Kai's words had allowed.

"Oh, come on!" Archie wailed, kicking some of the powdery fluff into the air. "This is too different. Whoever designed this dumb labyrinth sure knew how to make a guy miserable."

Jovian grinned and slapped Archie's shoulder. "This is the Sidylla Labyrinth, water wart." He leaned in close to Archie's face and waved a hand at the white expanse. "What did you expect to find? A field of flowers to skip through?"

Archie shoved Jovian's hand off his shoulder and clenched his hands into a fist. "Ah, shut it. I've had enough of your teasing!" He scowled and pushed Jovian roughly. "What have you done to help us anyway? You just prance around like a fairy. I get blamed for touching a gemstone, but when you do it at the gate? Everything is fine."

Jovian's easy smile slipped from his face and his gaze darkened. Despite being several years younger than Archie, Jovian shoved Archie back with surprising force, his brown braid swinging wildly.

Sage's eyes widened. This couldn't be good.

"You're sure one to talk," Jovian said, gaze hardening and body tensing. "All you've been doing the whole time we've been in the labyrinth is make trouble. You need examples? I have plenty!" He glared at Archie as he continued, "Eating poison berries, which led to the goblin attack; being inattentive, which led to Tenji's death; and, finally, as you mentioned, fiddling with the gemstone and waking an army of *skeletons*."

Luka stepped between the two, holding up his hands to stop their shoving, while somehow still levitating Draven. "Let's calm down."

Sage frowned. What had happened? Jovian and Archie always bickered, but now their snarling seemed more heated than usual. Her shoulder twinged and caused a sharp pull in her sternum. She gripped her chest.

Archie stared across Luka at Jovian, his face flushing deeper and deeper red as Jovian's words sank in. But he said nothing. Jovian turned and stalked out of the tunnel and into the snowy landscape before them.

"Let's keep moving," Luka said, watching Jovian walk off.

Tristan frowned at Sage. As the group trudged forward, he stepped toward her. "Sage."

Sage dropped her hand from her chest.

"Are you in pain?"

Sage quickly shook her head. "I'm fine. Just tired." She offered a slight smile before following the rest of the group.

Tristan kept in pace with her, looking unconvinced. He didn't bug her about it again, but Sage could feel him watching her.

The cold caused her shoulder to ache even more. She thought back to the looming shadow creature and how she'd dislodged it from Draven. The pulsating energy of her sense had been different than she'd ever experienced before. She'd felt strong, powerful, pain-free. Could tapping into that energy help with her healing?

But then, Ruben's death rose to mind, and her lips twisted. No, she shouldn't delude herself. She couldn't heal. Sage immediately shook the idea from her mind.

After a while, Archie found his voice again and complained about his feet going numb from the cold. Most of the group's bodies seemed to tremble in the frigid air. Sage herself shivered, teeth chattering uncontrollably. Only Cassian seemed unaffected, his body at ease and his demeanor calm and happy.

Kai puffed warm blasts of fire from his nostrils, which unconsciously made Sage draw closer to him. She wasn't the only one either. Soon, everyone hovered around Kai. Luckily, he seemed oblivious to them. At first.

Until Sage tripped into him.

Kai elbowed her off. "Why are you so close? Get back!" His gaze swept the group closing in around him. "Hey! Give me some room. Seriously."

Archie groaned and put his hand on Kai's shoulder. "Aw, come on, Kai!" he grumbled, waving a hand to the others as Kai tilted his body so Archie's hand slid off his shoulder. "Your fire blasts are warm, and we're cold. I'm fairly sure my feet are purple."

"Don't touch me," Kai growled. "I can't breathe with you idiots this close. Back off!"

Luka came to a stop and looked back at Kai. He seemed to debate saying something to him but changed his mind. "We should find shelter," Luka said at last. "If we can't find warmer clothing, we may not make it through."

"Obviously," Kai muttered, refusing to look at Luka as he elbowed Archie away from him again.

Sage hugged herself, trembling so violently, she couldn't think of anything else but the cold and how much her shoulder ached. She peered up at the sun, high in the cloudless sky. If it was this cold now, how much more brutal would the night be? What would it be like when storms came? It never snowed in Hallon. Oh, how she longed for the warm, breezy beaches of the coast.

Archie huffed. "Where will we get warmer clothing? It's not like we're going to magically stumble across a village. We aren't that lucky. What I'd give to be home in a warm bath, preparing for another competition, living the life."

Jovian chuckled darkly. "*Oh*, right. Because if you *had* been lucky, we wouldn't be here in the first place and everyone would be fine and dandy living a prince's dream in the kingdom, where everyone watches you and ranks you and 'loves' you. Where everything is perfect and happy. Isn't that right, Archie?" He flashed a cold smile in his direction. "Missing your mommy, little whiny baby?"

"You little twit!" Archie leapt through the snow to where Jovian stood, lifting a fist to pummel him. Luka and Tristan jumped between them, grabbing Archie's arm.

Draven's body wavered in the air then dropped out of the sky and into the snow.

"Stop!" Luka bellowed, struggling for control. "I know we haven't had an easy time since we came here. We're all on each other's nerves, but we should really focus on finding shelter. So, please, you two. Calm down."

Tristan pulled Archie back, and Archie reluctantly allowed himself to be pulled.

Sage took a few trembling steps toward Draven to check on him. She blinked. A black cloudy essence covered his body, shielding him from the snow. She leaned closer. Draven didn't even look cold. He didn't shiver and his face flushed with warmth. How could he be doing that while knocked out cold?

Someone stood beside her, and she looked up to see Luka. His brow furrowed, but he didn't say anything about Draven's peculiarity. Instead, he levitated him again and started off once more.

After several hours of marching through the bitter snow, Sage's hands, feet, legs, and arms were numb, and mist and snow particles obstructed her view. The darkened sky didn't help.

Then, Cassian ran out before them and used his sense to wave away some of the mist and snow.

A rocky, black mountain rose before them, and at the base of the mountain was a cave. Sage shivered. Finally, some shelter.

"Let's stay there for the night," Luka called, nodding in the direction of the cave, even though the group was already heading for it.

Kai clenched his fists and whirled on Luka. "Stop giving commands like some king. You're not. We're all capable of making decisions ourselves."

"I don't know why you're always so quick to get angry," replied Luka, crossing his arms over his chest. "I was just making sure everyone was on the same page."

"Oh, sure. You're always bossing everyone around, like you've been chosen to be our king. And you weren't even supposed to be in first place. Tenji was!" Kai raised a fist and shook it at him. "The entire system is messed up. And it's *your* father who allows it to be this way. Some king he is."

Luka's eyes flashed and, with a swift move of his arm, he sent Kai flying across the snow. Moving with impressive speed, Luka released a knife and it hurtled toward Kai.

Sage gasped.

The knife stopped inches from Kai's neck.

"I'm sick of your tantrums and fits of inferiority," Luka barked, glaring at Kai. "You throw tantrum after tantrum after tantrum. I don't know where all your anger comes from, but you should deal with it because it's unpleasant for everyone. Maybe if you would help out, we could get through this wretched place without losing any more lives than we have already. So, for once, *shut up*."

Kai returned his glare but didn't respond. Instead, he pulled the knife out of the air, slammed it into the ground, stood and marched off in the opposite direction of the cave. Sage bit her lip. Should she go after him? Then she shook her head. He needed alone time, and the rest of them needed to be warm.

The group reached the cave, and Luka lowered Draven carefully to the ground. Cassian and Sage joined him, and Cassian bent down to poke at Draven. "What's wrong with him?"

Luka frowned. "I don't know, but I'm sure it has something to do with whatever happened back in the desert." He sighed and ran a hand through his blond hair. "I was hoping he would have woken by now so he could answer some questions, but…"

Luka slipped out of the cave and returned some time later with wood for a fire. As he worked to set one up, the others dispersed as far away as they could get from each other and still hopefully be near the warmth. Jovian sat away from the group, and Archie hunched in a nearby corner.

Sage frowned, wincing as a dull ache ebbed in her chest. She clutched the front of her jacket. Then someone grabbed her bad shoulder.

Flinching, Sage turned.

Tristan crouched next to her, his forehead wrinkled with worry. "You're doing it again."

"Doing what?"

Tristan gestured to the hand gripping her chest. "Are you hurting?"

Cassian came to her other side, his forehead also creased.

Sage dropped her hand. "I probably just need sleep." She pulled her knees to her chest. Why was Tristan suddenly giving her so much attention?

"What about your shoulder?" Tristan nodded to it.

"I injured it a while back. It's just sensitive from the battle today." She turned her gaze to the fire. "I'll be fine."

Tristan sighed and glanced at Cassian, giving him a slight nod, before standing and returning to his place beside Archie. Cassian's lips twisted as he studied her. "You better not be lying," he said, his face serious. "Because if you lie here, you'll die. And I don't want you to die, Sage."

Her heart pinched. Sage relaxed her shoulders and her face softened. "I won't die. Don't worry." She eyed Tristan and nodded in his direction. "Do you know a lot about Tristan?"

"Quite a bit," Cassian answered. "He's good friends with my sister. She talks about him a lot."

"Does he hold grudges for a long time?"

Cassian raised his eyes thoughtfully. "Grudges? I don't think so. But I don't know for sure. Why?"

Sage shrugged, forgetting about her shoulder, and winced again. "I thought he was mad at me for a comment I made to him once, but now…I don't know. I'm just trying to figure him out." She sighed. "He's not very vocal—like some people. It makes him hard to read."

Cassian nodded. "Yeah. He doesn't share about his personal life very much. In fact, it was only two years ago that Archie discovered Tristan's father beat him and his brother, so he reported it to the Royal Council. My sister Aria was pretty upset once the news spread. She told me Tristan never once said a word to her about it."

Sage frowned again and peered in Tristan's direction once more. She remembered his face that night when she'd asked Tristan if he hated the king. She pressed her lips together.

A while later, Kai returned, but said nothing to any of them. He threw down a pile of sticks and started his own fire in the corner. Jovian joined him and Kai didn't object.

Sage turned her attention to the snowy landscape outside the cave and her eyes settled on a dead plant not too far off. Again, she thought of the pulsating power she'd experienced when she'd removed the creature from Draven. Maybe…just maybe. It couldn't hurt to try one more time.

Reaching out her fingers, careful to be as discreet as possible, Sage channeled the light energy within her. She imagined the energy pulsing through her with the steady beat of her heart. To her delight, energy throbbed within her, rolling in steady streams throughout her body. Then she focused that energy on the plant and thought of what she'd learned from the book.

"Revive," she whispered.

The plant obeyed. It sat up straighter and turned green, looking healthy and strong. Sage gaped at it. Had she just succeeded?

She blinked.

The plant still gleamed healthily. She hadn't imagined it.

She ducked her head to hide the smile that burst across her face. She glanced at the others, but none of them seemed to have noticed the now-living plant near the cave entrance. She calmed herself with quiet slow breaths. Had she finally figured out how to access her healing ability? She pressed a finger to her forehead, trying to recall what the next step was in the healing book.

She pulled back a sleeve and stared at a scrape she'd received during the skeleton battle. Again, she imagined that pulsing energy, but a wave of exhaustion draped over her, and her light energy dissolved. Brushing a shaky hand through her hair, Sage pursed her lips. She'd have to save her healing practice for another day.

Sage's body groaned as she lay down, preparing for a bitter, cold night of sleep.

Several of the others had also settled down. Their voices lulling to dull murmurs in the background.

Cassian slid closer to her. "Sage?" he whispered.

"Yes, Cass?"

"Do you think everyone back home believes we're dead?"

Sage looked at Cassian's small face. She pushed herself up onto her elbows. "Some might think we're dead, but I'm sure our families still believe we're alive. They'll keep waiting until we come home."

Cassian lowered his gaze. "But Ruben's and Tenji's families would be waiting for no one…I heard Ruben had an older sister. She's married. Due to have a baby soon. Maybe she already has. Ruben wanted to see her baby."

Sage's heart squeezed. "Ruben is in a better place. I'm sure, if she had her baby, Ruben can see them both."

Cassian nodded. "Tenji had an older brother. I've never seen him. I heard he used to be ranked quite high, but he was banished. Tenji never spoke of him."

Sage sat up and hugged her knees to her chest. Somehow, she'd forgotten everyone here had families back home. She especially forgot Tenji had one. "When we leave this place, we'll have a memorial for them both. I promise."

Cassian smiled softly and settled down once more. Sage studied him quietly, suddenly fighting the temptation to tell him about her little brother. As much as she wanted to, she couldn't. She couldn't tell him about her brother, Sage, because Sage didn't have a brother. Sage had an older sister named Faven...

Faven. How long had it been since she'd last heard someone call her by *her* name?

As she closed her eyes and lay down once more, her thoughts turned to home. Hallon's island mountains towered over her, its white sandy beaches under her bare feet. She could almost see the vibrant feathers of seaside dragons in the clouds as they darted through the bright blue sky. Her parents were there—and her brother—all ready to greet her with a smile. Tears burned her eyes and leaked from her eyelids. Would she ever make it out of this place? Or was she doomed to die here, her family waiting for someone who would never come home?

A slight tremor shook the ground. Sage's eyes flew open, and she sat up. Several others sat up too. A blast of cold, chilling air whooshed through the cave and extinguished their fires, and everything fell into darkness. Then, she heard it—the sharp, ear-splitting cry of a creature.

"Just our luck," Archie muttered, right before the cave vibrated violently.

Sage braced herself against the floor as tremors shook the cave, followed by a ricochet of crackling, snaps, and pops. Then, without warning, the floor crumbled beneath her. Sage shrieked, scrambling to hold onto something, anything to keep her from falling. Cassian grabbed her arm and Sage clung to him as he created a barricade of ice around them before they both careened into unknown darkness.

37

Jovian Versus Archie

SILENCE INDICATED IT WAS SAFE. JOVIAN DISINTEGRATED the rock barrier he'd created around himself. When he broke out, the darkness and silence continued, except for the skitter of the rocks and pebbles he'd sent reeling down the mound he now stood atop. Slowly, his eyes adjusted to the darkness. The smooth cave walls rose up around him and a dark burrow tunneled into another room on his left.

Climbing down from his mound Jovian pressed a hand to the cold, damp floor and released a minor tremor through it, listening to the vibrations it returned back. Nothing. Just to be extra sure, Jovian tossed the mounds of rock toward an empty spot in the corner of the cavern to see if anyone was buried underneath. There was no one. Where had they gone?

A cool breeze drifted down to him from above, and Jovian tipped his head back, turning his gaze upward. The others had to be up there.

Pulling at the earth around him, Jovian created a platform to push himself back up through the hole he'd fallen through. He leapt from his self-made platform and released his hold on it, allowing it to crumble back down below. When he landed securely, Jovian scanned his surroundings.

The moon lit up the cave and an icy wonderland twinkled in the night sky outside. The bright moonlight also revealed several abysses in the floor. He peered down each hole but saw no one. Great. Who knew where the others had fallen?

Jovian couldn't see a thing outside the reach of the moonlight. If he waited until morning, the sun could help him find the others, and if anyone climbed out in the meantime, he'd be there. But he also didn't want to be sitting and waiting for people if they were all dead. And they'd better not be. The thought sent a shiver of panic through him. There was no way he'd ever get out of the labyrinth without them. And even if he could make it through alone, what would he tell the others when he returned to Reudinia? No, that wouldn't be good. He couldn't have that.

With this in mind, Jovian leapt into the abyss closest to where the main fire had been.

He fell in what seemed like a bottomless pit. Quickly realizing he'd been falling too long to land without injury, he angled himself toward the cave wall and jammed his arm into it, surrounding his skin with rock to prevent the descent from ripping through his flesh.

Jovian gritted his teeth as his weight pulled at his shoulder painfully. He kicked a leg out, pulling rock from the wall into a board and, with another kick, made the rock and earth form a slope for him to slide down. Soon, he found himself sledding across a flat surface where he slowed to a stop.

For once, Jovian wished he had fire powers like Kai. Or even Sage's glowing ability. Something, anything to shed some light through the tunnel. Either would be helpful right about now.

He squinted into the dark, straining his ears to pick up a sound, a vibration, anything. He could sense someone was there, but who knew if they were friend or foe. Jovian reached down and sent another minor pulse through the floor. Two bodies, wait—three. Three of them were here.

Jovian stumbled in the direction of the closest body and knelt to feel it. He frowned. No good. This could be anyone.

Jovian checked the breathing coming from the body. Alive still, somehow. He didn't know how anyone could have survived that fall. Not unless something had slowed their descent.

Leaving the unknown body where he lay, Jovian shifted to the next. The person moaned. He tapped the person's face and roughly shook him.

The person shifted and moaned again. "Who—Who are you?"

Tristan. Jovian released a sigh of relief. Grinning, despite knowing Tristan couldn't see his smile, Jovian slapped his shoulder. "It's me, my lightning friend."

Sitting up, Tristan's shadow of a head turned one way and then another as he scanned the dark room. Then a flash of electricity buzzed to life in Tristan's hand, allowing a slight bluish flicker to illuminate the room. On one side of the cavern was a sliver of a tunnel. Jovian pulled Tristan over to the first body.

It was Draven.

Someone groaned behind them. They turned toward the groan and Tristan brightened his electric glow. Jovian frowned when he recognized the blue ponytail. Ugh, not him. Anyone but the idiotic water wart. He'd been ready to crush him earlier.

Jovian shook that thought from his head. No, as much as he disliked Archie right now, he didn't hate him that much. He'd just have to tolerate him until they could leave this place.

Pushing himself to his feet, Archie winced. "Could you make the light a little less blaring, please and thank you?"

Tristan obliged and Archie squinted at them. His face went sour at the sight of Jovian. Archie turned to Tristan instead. "Where are the others?" Then Archie pointed at the body behind them. "Is that Draven?"

Jovian chuckled and forced a smile onto his face, despite the flicker of annoyance growing within him. "Nope! It's someone who looks *exactly like* Draven."

Archie, who had come closer, kicked Jovian in the shin. The kick hurt, but Jovian chose not to react. Instead, he smiled through it.

He'd get Archie back. One day. Maybe today.

Tristan dusted some gravel off himself. "It's Draven," he said simply. "I don't know where anyone else is."

"They must've fallen through a different hole," Jovian informed them. "There were a ton of openings up there." His gaze flickered between Archie and Tristan. "How did you all survive that fall? It's quite deep. I had to use my sense to come down."

Tristan and Archie looked up. They wrinkled their foreheads as if they weren't really sure.

Finally, Tristan replied, "I feel like…Draven saved us. But that doesn't really make sense since he's still out cold."

Jovian frowned at the sleeping Draven. Somehow, he could believe it. The guy was creepy. "Maybe he can use his sense in his sleep."

"What happened up there?" asked Archie, looking agitated.

"The labyrinth happened," Jovian answered. His response was met with silence. Jovian sniffed and turned away from them. Nothing ever went as planned in this place. It was how this place was created. To keep people out and something else in.

In the beginning, Jovian had been optimistic they would all make it through alive, but he had terribly underestimated the difficulty of surviving the labyrinth. And now they had lost two princes. How many more would they lose before they were free of this place?

"Let's go before more rock falls down on us," Jovian added, rubbing the back of his hand.

"What about the others?" Archie asked, glaring at Jovian in obvious distaste. "And why, after all this time, do you feel the need to lead now? You're the youngest one here."

Jovian swallowed down the instant annoyance that rose up and smiled, forcing his voice to be brighter as he turned to face them once more. "I don't. But I don't want to die, and I'm sure you don't either. I can only feel you, Tristan, and Draven close by. The others must be somewhere else unreachable from here. It's too far to go back up, so the only choice we have is to keep progressing and hope we come across them later." Jovian pasted a smile on his face, though his stomach churned with anger. "Anyway, those guys wouldn't die from a cave in. They're too stubborn for that."

Tristan nodded. "We'll have to drag Draven with us."

Looking down at Draven's limp body, Jovian wished they didn't have to. "Maybe sleeping is part of his sense too," he joked, when really, he wanted to kick Draven awake.

Tristan pulled Draven into a sitting position, wiggling himself under Draven's limp arm. Archie helped Tristan. Soon, the two of them had Draven standing between them and the three of them turned their attention to the only tunnel Jovian could see.

Tristan spoke. "I guess we go that way."

Without a word, the four princes left the crumbling cavern behind them. They wove through the winding tunnels of the mountain cave until everyone, including Jovian, felt too drowsy to continue and they mutually agreed to rest. However, Jovian's near-empty stomach rumbled ceaselessly and made it hard for any sleep he snagged to be restful. Archie got up at some point and drifted away from them. The sound of him urinating aggravated Jovian so he got up soon after.

Tristan got up after seeing Archie and Jovian up, and they all decided to keep moving, Tristan lighting the way with his lightning energy.

Suddenly, they came to a fork in the tunnel and slowed to a stop. Jovian glanced between each new tunnel. He reached out and touched the wall of the cave and released another tremor. But both tunnels continued on, unfortunately outside of his ability to read. However, tiny, quick thuds echoed from the right. He gritted his teeth. There was never an end to the disaster. "Let's go left."

"It seems to me you *do* want to lead," Archie grumbled and eyed him distrustfully. "Why left?" He struggled to adjust Draven's weight into a more comfortable position to carry.

Heat boiled in Jovian's chest. "If you must know, there's something coming toward us from the other way," stated Jovian, calming himself with subtle breaths.

"And how do you know that?"

Jovian forced another smile and stared at the stubborn guy. "I can sense it in the wall," he answered, and pointed to himself before winking. "Earth and rock manipulator here, remember?"

"Yeah, yeah. I remember," Archie grunted, his voice sounding bitter. "How could I forget when all you do is prance and dance around using your sense like some fairy? If you're so great, why didn't you stop the cave in earlier? Now *that* would've been helpful."

Jovian waved away the frustrated thoughts that simmered within and buried them deep, deep down inside. He was used to burying emotions. He was used to pretending. Jovian forced himself to keep smiling. "That, my *friend*, is because I can't foresee the future. Can you?"

Draven moaned. "Future…she…saw…future."

Everyone stared at Draven. Jovian's eyes narrowed. What was he talking about?

Tristan stiffened. "Do you hear that?" he asked, causing the group to pause and listen.

Jovian could sense it. Whatever had been heading toward them was coming closer. Distant squeaks and flutters could be heard growing louder the longer they listened.

"What is that?" Archie asked, a look of growing alarm washing across his face in the flickering of Tristan's blue light.

Jovian pulled up a wall of rock behind them as a means of defense and lifted Draven up with another slab. "Nothing in the labyrinth is good. Let's get out of here!"

They ran as fast as they could in the direction of the left tunnel. A moment later, the rock wall Jovian had pulled up as a barrier shattered in the distance. Jovian dragged Draven along and yanked up another wall to barricade them from whatever was following them. Then he skidded to a stop, cursing. A dead end. He'd been too distracted with what was behind them to even consider what was ahead.

"It's a dead-end! A we-have-no-where-to-run dead-end!" Archie shouted, stabbing an accusatory finger at Jovian. "You led us here, you brainless jokester. And this is no time for jokes!"

Jovian blinked at Archie's finger. Brainless? His stare hardened into a glare and Jovian gritted his teeth. The idiot of the group *dared* to call *him* brainless? That was it. He clenched his hand into a fist and slugged Archie right in the face. Archie stumbled back, blood spurting from his nose.

Immediately, Archie lunged for Jovian, his hands clutching and yanking at Jovian's jacket, tunic, hair. "You scamp!"

Tristan dove between them, hands outstretched, electrocuting them both. Jovian crumpled in pain, but he wasn't done yet. He scraped his boot along the floor causing the ground Tristan was standing on to shift away from them. Then he created a rock wall barrier between Tristan and them. Archie didn't hesitate to jump Jovian.

Archie struck Jovian's face with his fist and seized his jacket with his other. Pain erupted in Jovian's lips and mouth, but that didn't slow him down. Jovian kneed Archie in the gut and shoved him to the side before popping his jaw with his fist. They rolled around, tussling like children, and Archie smacked Jovian across the face.

"Stop!" called Tristan, his voice muffled by the barrier. "Don't do this!"

Jovian ignored Tristan, his face stinging from Archie's slap, and bit Archie's arm. Archie screamed and socked Jovian in the eye. The room swirled and ringing sounded in his ears. But Jovian only grappled for Archie's tunic and pummeled him with punches. It felt good. Good to let out his frustration for once. Archie's nails dug into him before his elbow whacked the side of Jovian's face. Archie yanked on Jovian's braid, so Jovian gritted his teeth and knocked him back with a rock.

"Cheater!" Archie bellowed.

It was then the screeching became too loud to ignore and the first barrier wall thumped loudly. Then it shattered. Several huge, furry bats with long, sharp fangs swarmed the space around them. Archie scrambled for his sword which had dislodged from his scabbard at some point during their brawl. Jovian attempted to smash a few of the bats between rocks but only succeeded in catching one of them. He cursed. Pesky creatures. This was like the wyverns all over again.

The bats nipped and bit at their arms, necks, and faces. Archie swung his sword wildly at the beasts and Jovian knocked as many of them away as he could, preparing to bring the roof of the cave down around them.

But then, the room charged with such a great kinetic energy that their hair stood on end and the room glowed blue.

The air exploded around them with an electric blast. Dirt, rock, and debris scattered around the room stinging Jovian's skin and several twitching, seizure-convulsing bats rained down on top of them.

Tristan, blazing with electricity, marched through Jovian's decimated barricade and up to the two of them, zapping them both. Jovian dropped, convulsing alongside Archie. Tristan glared down at them.

"I'm sick and tired of you all!" he bellowed. "I've been patient and pleasant, but I'm tired of putting up with all this absurdity!" Tristan's eyes flashed with a ferocity Jovian had never seen from him before.

Tristan continued, seemingly too furious to stop, "How many more lives do we need to lose before you guys realize the only way we're going to survive is if we work together?"

Jovian found himself grinning, a giddy sensation rolling through his body.

"What are you grinning at?" demanded Tristan, pointing an electrified finger at him.

Jovian lifted both hands. "Sorry, sorry. You just look so cool."

He looked past Tristan's sizzling, vibrant energy at Archie.

"You're right," Archie said at last, his voice quiet and strange as he avoided looking at them. "I'm sorry, Tristan. And Jovian…"

"Apologizing is useless if you continue acting this way," Tristan stated. "This isn't the place to throw tantrums."

"I know." Archie grimaced. "I've been a nuisance." Before Tristan could respond, Archie slumped and moaned. "I've been a complete mess, haven't I? Putting everyone in danger just because I don't think."

Continuing to avoid their gazes, Archie stared down at his hands. "I'm the fifth in rank and the fourth in seniority…yet… I lack in so many ways compared to everyone else. You and Jovian, and everyone…I've seen how powerful all of you are— and how mediocre I am in comparison. Then…when Tenji died…I realized how *hopeless* I am…"

Archie covered his eyes with a hand and his voice became wet. A stifled sob escaped him. Jovian shifted uncomfortably.

"Don't deny you think it's true. I know everyone does. Even *Cassian* thinks I'm useless...*I* should've been the one to die, not Tenji. Why would he save someone as useless as me?"

Jovian scratched the back of his head, not knowing what to do, but Tristan didn't seem deterred. His sizzling energy slowly oozed away, and finally, all that was left was a small sizzle in his right hand. "Tenji's death wasn't your fault. It was his choice to step in and take the blow." He looked down at the blue energy in his palm. "You shouldn't blame yourself for his death."

Archie sniffed and roughly wiped away his tears, pretending as if he hadn't just cried. "Thanks, Tristan. You're a good friend."

Jovian stared at Archie's red eyes. Suddenly, it dawned on him: even if they made it out of here alive, there would still be scars and deaths and memories that would forever shape the rest of their lives.

Deep down in the protective cage, where he'd long since hidden his tender heart, came a small twinge of shame. But "feelings" weren't for Jovian, so he shoved them deep down again and jumped up, spreading a smile across his face.

"Well, this little heart to heart has been nice, but I think it's time to keep going." He winked, only to wince. He touched his eye, feeling the swelling. Archie had sure landed some nice hits.

Jovian glanced over at Draven who lay to the side, almost forgotten. He sighed. Why wouldn't he wake? Reluctantly, Jovian strode over to him and dragged him into a sitting position. Tristan appeared beside him to help. Grimacing from random aches and pains throbbing in his body, Jovian hefted Draven's arm over his shoulder and stood. Why was Draven so freaking heavy?

The three of them, with Draven slumped between, headed back up the tunnel. This time when they reached the fork, they took the path to the right. Eventually, they came upon a wide water current streaming by. There was no other way to go.

Jovian shot a look at Archie. "Think you can navigate us through this?"

Archie straightened and nodded.

Jovian ripped rock from the cave floor and carved it into a makeshift boat using his sense, and the three of them carefully placed Draven inside. Archie and Jovian climbed in, then Tristan pushed it into the water and hopped in after. Then down into the current they pushed themselves.

38

Beasts of the Air

KAI COUGHED THROUGH THE RISING CLOUD OF DUST, the taste filling his mouth. He waved a hand in front of his face and spat repetitively. The groans of others echoed from somewhere, but as Kai looked around, only darkness met his gaze. Climbing to his feet, Kai struck a blaze. He stood atop a pile of fallen debris. Cautiously he treaded down, sending a spur of pebbles and dirt chunks in several directions with each shift he caused.

After reaching the bottom, he held his blaze higher and squinted into the dusty darkness. A pile of ice and snow was buried in fallen rock a short distance away, Cassian wriggling amidst it. Cassian lit up when he spotted Kai. Kai sniffed but strode toward him and held out his fire-free hand. Cassian took it without hesitation and Kai pulled him free.

"Thanks, Kai," Cassian said, but turned around and began shifting the ice and snow, as if looking for something.

Kai said nothing and continued searching the cavern. He found several tunnels before he heard coughing coming from the right and climbed over a pile of rubble to peer into the darkness. There, covered in small rocks and dust, was the egotistical Snoot, Luka. Rolling his eyes, Kai left him to fend for himself. The clatter of pebbles sprayed onto the stone ground as Luka stood.

Kai circled the space they'd fallen into once more, but there was a suspicious lack of any of the others.

Where was everyone? Why had he only found Cassian and Luka?

"Kai!"

Spinning toward Cassian's voice, Kai hurried toward the boy. He found Cassian digging through the layer of rock that had amassed over the mound of snow. At his knees was a splash of purple hair. Sage.

"The rocks are too heavy," came Cassian's wavering voice.

Kai threw down his bag, dumped out the piddly number of supplies inside, and lit the bag on fire. Then, using the light from the flaming bag, he helped Cassian dig Sage out from under the rocks. Luka joined them shortly. He took one look at their digging and levitated the rest of the rocks off Sage's body and pulled him from the pile. Luckily, it seemed Cassian's barricade of snow had protected Sage from the full force of the rocks.

Sage squirmed and gasped for breath. "Thanks," he panted, wincing when Cassian pulled on his arm.

"Are you alright?" Luka asked.

Sage nodded. "It's just an older injury. My shoulder's been hit a few times. The werewolves, the skeletal fight, and now this. That's all."

Cassian sat back on his heels and looked down at his tightly closed fists. "I'm sorry, Sage. If I'd held the barrier together…"

Sage placed a hand on Cassian's shoulder and shook his head. "You did great, Cass. It would've been much worse if it wasn't for you."

Turning away, Kai tried to regulate his heavy breathing. As long as Sage wasn't dead. He was so tired of people being dead. Kai slouched and thrust a hand through his hair.

"Let's look for the others," Luka suggested.

Kai huffed some more. He was done with this labyrinth, yet it stretched on like it was never-ending. Five sections. Five, blasted-long, tiring sections.

"I didn't see any others here," Kai informed him. The fire from his bag was dying out, so he struck another blaze in his palm again.

Luka glanced back at him but kept searching. "Maybe they're buried under the rubble." He heard Luka levitating piles of stone from the ground, searching for anyone, but he found no one.

"Maybe they didn't fall?" Sage suggested as he rubbed his shoulder and winced some more.

Kai shook his head. "All I know is they aren't here. If we spend too much time calculating where they disappeared to, we'll get nowhere. And I don't know if you've noticed, but this labyrinth is already taking us a long time to get through."

Sage frowned at him. "We can't leave the others behind."

Kai lifted an arm and blasted a flame skyward, showing Sage just how far they had fallen. "We have no choice! We'll just have to assume they know how to continue on by themselves and meet up with them later."

"But—"

"Kai's right," Luka interrupted, shaking his head.

Kai blinked and stared in Luka's direction. The Snoot *agreed* with him?

"I wish he wasn't," Luka continued. "But it's better if we move on. Our best chance at finding the others will be if we continue without them."

Sage snapped his mouth closed and his shoulders sagged.

"Which way?" Cassian asked, pointing to the several tunnels.

Kai slowly stood to his feet and approached one of the tunnels. He released a stream of fire. The tunnel's height and width shrunk to an impossible size. "Not this one." Then he strode to the next. It curved and then ended abruptly. "Or this one."

Luka stopped before one of the smaller tunnels. "This one has a breeze."

Kai, Sage, and Cassian joined him. The ceiling of the tunnel came to Kai's chest. He wrinkled his nose and ducked to peer inside. A cool draft swept over his face. He resisted a groan.

Luka faced Sage. "Can you light the way?"

A flickering glow illuminated from Sage but then sputtered out. He shook his head. "I'm too exhausted from using my sense earlier."

Earlier? Kai pictured the glowing figure that saved him from the creature in the desert and snapped his gaze away. Had Kai been the cause of Sage's depletion?

Then Luka glanced at Kai, and Kai rolled his eyes and huffed. "Fine."

Crouching, Kai lit a low fire in his hand and entered the tunnel. As Kai followed the tunnel's winding curves, it continued to shrink until the others had to trail behind him in a hunched, single-file line. At one point, the ceiling got so low Kai paused and had to continue forward on his hands and knees. Would this tunnel ever end? What if it kept shrinking and they had to turn around? But at least the breeze was growing stronger and the air was fresh, if frigid.

Then his knee smacked into a small stalagmite, and his head jerked up and struck the ceiling. Kai cursed under his breath, taking in short angry breaths as the pain settled over him.

"What's wrong?" Sage's voice echoed in the tunnel.

"Nothing," Kai huffed and continued crawling. *Finally*, the tunnel elongated and widened. Kai stood and picked up speed.

Before long, the tunnel opened into a small cave that led outside. The icy chill blew around Kai as he approached the opening. The moon illuminated the quiet, untouched snow. Kai studied the mountains. They were much lower down the valley than they had been before.

Luka stepped up beside Kai and said, "Let's rest in the shade of the cave for the rest of the night." Then, without another word, he stepped outside to gather some nearby bushes and then threw them down in a pile inside the cave.

Kai kept quiet and avoided the others' gazes. He still didn't want to become the 'fire man' just because his sense was suddenly useful to them. So, he strode to the other side of the small cave and curled up away from them. They didn't bother to ask him and struggled to light the fire on their own. Eventually, the spark of a fire crackled to life and heat warmed Kai's back.

Kai wrestled with sleep the rest of the night.

When the sky outside finally lightened, he sat up, relieved to have reached the end of the hard night.

Luka sat on the other side of the cave with his back pressed against the wall. Luka looked at him, but Kai only glared back and stood. Luka turned away and peered out at the untouched snow.

Sage also sat up, shivering violently from his place near the dying fire. He looked so pale and…smooth. While it was normal for some men to struggle growing a beard when younger, it still made Kai uncomfortable how smooth Sage's jaw remained. To make it worse, Sage's hair, which had grown quite a bit during their time in the labyrinth, only accentuated how feminine his face was. No wonder he was self-conscious about his appearance. Kai grunted and turned his gaze back to the white expanse outside. Pretty boy.

Once Cassian stirred, Luka stood. "Let's keep moving."

Kai bit back a remark, suddenly wishing he had beaten Luka to it. Heading out into the early morning light, the group of four marched through the knee-deep snow. When the snow rose to their waist, Cassian created a path to walk through. He also found them a rabbit family for dinner, though Sage refused to watch the slaughter.

Kai, not wanting to waste the time it would take to build a fire, grabbed the rabbits and silently cooked them in his hands with his own blaze. The others said nothing to him and they ate as they walked. For water, Cassian created an ice bowl and had Kai melt snow into it, warning him not to boil it or it would melt his bowl. They all took turns drinking the freezing water.

In the afternoon, it snowed again and Cassian blocked them as best he could from being hit by the flurries. By the time the sky darkened, and Cassian created a burrow of ice with a hole at the top to let out the smoke of their fire, Kai decided he liked Cassian. He was thoroughly impressed with how deftly the boy controlled his sense.

The next day, they set out again, eating when they found creatures to eat and drinking when they were thirsty.

Kai hated the cold. He was used to heat and sweat and found he was beyond glad that he had his fire sense to keep him warm. A fact that was strangely ironic. When he was younger, he'd wished every day for his fire sense to disappear or morph into something that didn't destroy. Something that would cause his parents to want him back…

But Grams always told him his fire sense was a powerful gift, that the flames didn't only represent destruction. *"Fire is also meant for warmth, light, entertainment, and comfort. It truly is a gift for you to carry such a sense!"*

For once, Kai wondered if his grandmother had been right. Only since coming to the labyrinth had Kai noticed the need for fire. Coming here was the first time someone had *asked* him to use his sense for the sake of others, and though Kai refused to be used, he did notice. He held out his hand and allowed a small flame to unfurl in his palm. Fire didn't always cause destruction.

Something fluttered amidst the woods that hung between them and the labyrinth wall. Kai stopped just before Luka held up his hand. He scanned the trees and listened intently. But Kai only heard the wind, his own breath, and the shifting of the tree branches. Kai took a step forward, but then he heard the flapping again. Followed by the rustle of leaves, more strong flapping, and something squealing in terror. Then silence.

Luka dropped his arm and lowered his voice. "Probably just an owl hunting," he murmured and began walking again.

Sage shot Kai a look of alarm while rubbing his shoulder. Sage must not think it was "just" an owl hunting, and Kai agreed. Cassian and Sage followed after Luka. Kai scanned the treeline again, but, after seeing nothing, continued on. However, the loud squawks ceaselessly pierced the sky followed by a flurry of flaps.

The further the sun rose in the sky, the more tense Kai became. Sometimes the squawks were closer; other times, they were farther away. Just when Kai finally started to relax, he'd hear another one, too close for comfort.

Cassian pointed out a wild boar up ahead and the four of them lowered themselves behind a boulder near the foot of the mountain. Then, with a sharp, precise jerk of his arm, Cassian shot a large icicle through the boar. The boar squealed wildly until, finally, it stopped squirming.

None of them budged. The cry of the boar was too similar to the squeal Kai had heard earlier. If something had been hunting a *boar*…The beast must be much, much bigger than an owl.

Keeping an eye on their surroundings, Kai cooked the meat and they feasted on it. It had been a good while since they'd eaten so much. They couldn't carry the rest of the meat, so Luka cut away some for later. Cassian created a light frost on the meat to keep it from spoiling before Luka put it in his bag.

Then the strong flapping sound returned, and a large shadow passed over them. Kai jerked his gaze up. Nothing. However, a tiny spray of rocks rained down from a ledge on the mountain into the ravine below. He searched the mountain ranges for movement. He wasn't sure what he was looking for, but whatever it was could fly.

Luka waved them on wordlessly. Cassian kept eyeing the mountain ranges as if he saw something, and a little while later another shadow passed over them. Kai looked up. Again, the creature was gone.

"I think I know what it is," Cassian whispered. His gaze remained trained above him as he pulled out his sword.

"What is it?" Sage asked, his voice a quiet hiss as he pulled his own sword out.

To be on the safe side, Kai pulled his sword out, too. He eyed Luka who kept his sword sheathed and only rested a hand on its hilt. Luka's gaze darted back and forth from the trees to the mountain. Finally, his focus rested on Cassian, as if he too knew what it was. "Dragons?"

Dragons had crossed Kai's mind as well, but Cassian shook his head. Kai gave a short nod. Dragons, unless they were smaller ones, were much too large to hide and couldn't fly at the speed of whatever this thing was. He supposed it *could* be a variation of a dragon, but dragons didn't squawk.

Carried on a rush of wind, another loud cry pierced the sky above them. Looking up, Kai gripped his sword tighter. A massive creature dove toward them with blurring speed. It reached its claws toward them. Kai lurched to the side just as its claws snagged at his tunic. The creature curved upward again, preparing for another dive.

On this dive, it scraped Luka, hissing and snapping its sharp beak, flapping its immense feathered wings and digging its jagged claws into his back. Using his sense, Luka pulled the creature from his back and hurled it into the forest. The creature rolled across the snowy ground and smacked into a tree.

"Griffin!" Cassian yelled.

The massive creature rose onto its four legs and whipped its brown eagle head toward them. Large, brown wings spread out on either side as it crouched forward like a cat, its taloned front claws digging into the snow. Behind it swished a long, lithe, lion tail mixed with feathers and fur. It snapped its sharp beak.

Cassian released a swirl of ice at the griffin. The ice hit it and broke into several pieces, causing a screech from the beast. Then the griffin launched back into the air toward them, aiming for Cassian.

A rock smashed into the eagle-like head, but the griffin kept coming. Luka levitated some more rocks and logs and sent them spinning at the creature. The rocks didn't deter the griffin. It only swatted them away like pesky flies and stretched out its claws for Cassian. Kai, Sage, and Luka leapt to save him while Cassian threw a large icicle at the beast.

The griffin clawed the icicle away and closed its talons around Cassian's small body. Sage, his sword blazing, sliced through the leg that claimed Cassian and the griffin screamed. Kai took advantage of its distraction and blasted the creature's wings as Luka stabbed his sword deep into its chest. With a mighty screech, the griffin crashed to the ground.

Several other squawks reverberated against the mountains.

Kai lifted his head and muffled a groan. Four more griffins lifted from the mountain peaks and swooped toward them. He launched a ball of fire at one but missed and the griffin slammed Kai back, knocking him into Luka. They both landed in the snow. Luka shoved Kai off and jumped up, slicing at the shrieking griffin that angled and swooshed back toward them.

Kai scrambled to his feet in time to dodge another dive. He lifted a hand and released a stream of fire, but the griffins evaded. He gritted his teeth. They were too quick.

Sage sliced through a griffin's wing, and Cassian, looking a bit angry, froze an entire griffin. The frozen creature tumbled through the air and hit the ground, shattering the ice that held it. The fallen griffin lumbered to its feet and lunged at them.

Kai rained flaming balls on it. One of its wings caught fire. Sage stabbed the griffin whose wing he cut off, then ran for the flaming griffin.

But then another one dove, heading for Sage.

"Sage!" Kai and Luka cried. Squeezing his sword tightly and lifting an arm, Kai took off toward Sage and the griffin. But then Luka met his stride and ran alongside him. Kai glared at Luka and shoved him. "I've got it!"

Luka frowned, still running toward the creature. They leapt at it but smacked hard into each other instead.

"Get out of my way!" Kai bellowed, shoving Luka again. "I told you I have it!"

A *swoosh!* of cool wind rushed past Kai, ruffling his hair, and froze the griffin about to get Sage. Cassian slid past the two of them, sliding along a stream of ice, then vaulted into the air with a clean flip, landing on top of the frozen griffin and jabbing his sword through its head. Sage finished off the other griffin, leaving only one beast remaining. Luka sent his sword flying into its gut with a wave of his hand.

Everyone stood in silence for a moment. Then Luka whirled on Kai, his blue eye dark with frustration. "Your need to argue and fight almost cost Sage his life."

Kai tensed and scowled in return. "I could've taken that griffin out on my own. You got in my way."

"Or you could've failed, and Sage could be dead. But you're so stubborn that you refuse to let go of your pride. You're just like a child, blowing up about every little thing. When will you grow up?"

Kai clutched Luka's shirt, pulling his face closer, his other fist blazing. "Just because you're older doesn't make you better or stronger than me. I could've taken it."

Luka glared all the harder into Kai's eyes. "Why are you always so desperate to prove you're better than me? Why?"

"I'm not trying to prove anything, daddy's boy." Kai released his grip on Luka's shirt and shoved him back. He strode away, kicking powdery snow into the air. "You're the one acting like you're trying to prove something." But Luka's question rang in his ears. The more it rang, the more anger and frustration boiled in his chest. He wasn't trying to prove anything. He was *not*…

He heard Luka say they should head out, but Kai led the way. He wasn't going to let Luka take the lead after all of that. No way.

After a moment of silence, Kai heard Sage's voice from behind, "Do griffins travel in packs?"

"No, but they do roost together," Cassian replied. "Those of the same roost will come if one of them is crying for help. Hopefully, that was all the griffins in that roost."

"How do you know so much about griffins, Cassian?" Luka's voice asked.

"I just remember random facts. I've always found griffins fascinating."

Luka was acting like nothing had happened between him and Kai, just like he always did. Like it didn't bother him. Like Kai didn't bother him. As if nothing Kai did would ever make a difference. It only made him angrier, reminding him of Luka's father. The king and his Royal Council had only ever seen Kai as a nuisance—someone to sedate…or eliminate. Luka treated him no differently than they did. Ridiculing, humiliating, and blaming him. Dismissing him as an ignorant wild child.

Never listening to a damn word he said.

Kai closed his eyes and an image of his grandmother's figure stood before him as she faced the king. She clutched twelve-year-old Kai's arm and dragged him forward *"Look at him. Look what you have bloody done to my grandson!"*

Luka's father stared back. He arched a brow unforgivingly.

"If you ever try to kill him again, your reign will end," his grandmother continued. Kai shook the memory out of his head and glared at the snow.

He wouldn't be surprised if Luka wanted to get rid of him too.

"To accomplish your wish, you'll need to let me lead," the spirit whispered. *"You may not like all my choices, but everything I do is for a greater purpose."*

The traitor narrowed his eyes. *What are you implying?*

"That others will resist our plan, and they may need to be... removed."

The traitor tensed. Before he could retort, the spirit continued, *"If you want to create this better world, you'll need to make some painful decisions."*

The traitor tightened his lips. He didn't like the sound of that. *I don't trust you.*

Silence met his words. A moment later, the spirit hissed once more, *"Trust me or not, our plans are aligned. I'll help you achieve yours if you free me. That is the deal."*

The traitor sniffed. And just what *was* this spirit's plan?

39

Dragon

JOVIAN, ARCHIE, TRISTAN, AND DRAVEN DOCKED BESIDE THE dark stream. They had been riding it long enough for Jovian's backside to ache, so when they finally saw the large opening, they took advantage and pulled their tired, unrested bodies from the stream and spilled onto the hard, cold ground. Soon after, Jovian fell asleep.

When he awoke, exhaustion still weighed heavily on him, and for a moment, he hovered between consciousness and unconsciousness. But the hiss and sputter of fire forced him to snap out of his stupor. He sat up. To Jovian's surprise, Draven was awake. He, Archie, and Tristan huddled around a fire. How did they start a fire?

"Jovian," Tristan called, beckoning him closer. "We have some interesting news to share."

Jovian scooted closer to the group, interest piqued. He tossed a wry smile Draven's way. "I see you've finally decided to grace us with your consciousness."

Draven grunted, studying him intently.

"Draven knows the closest exits from the caves. There's one not too far from here," Tristan continued with a nod at Draven.

"How does he know that?" Jovian asked, looking pointedly at Draven.

"Apparently," Archie said, jabbing a thumb in Draven's direction. "Draven knows where pools of light are because of his shadow sense. He can sense where the shadows are and where they aren't. Or something confusing like that."

Jovian laughed. "And that's helpful?" Draven frowned at him before looking back at the fire. Jovian folded an arm over a knee and continued, "Since you're awake, I'll ask what everyone's been wondering. What happened back in the desert? Did that skeleton possess you? And what was that creature? Was it something the skeleton created or another aspect of your sense you never cared to share about?"

Draven raised his gaze back to Jovian, his eyes narrowing. "Yes."

His answer echoed in the cave and the others stared at him until the echoes faded. Jovian frowned. Which question was he responding to?

Draven held Jovian's gaze for a moment before scanning the rest of their small group. Finally, Draven pulled up the sleeves of his shirt, revealing some scars along his arms. "Shadow manipulation is only a small aspect of what I can do. I can also manipulate or create a shadow beast. Despite being a shadow, it can do whatever I ask it to do. Crush a person, tear apart a building, blind people with shadows, give people nightmares. It becomes so real, it sometimes speaks to me."

Jovian knit his eyebrows. That sounded...terrifying. Horrifying. And powerful. Immensely powerful. Jovian didn't like it at all. "If that was a shadow beast you were manipulating, why did you attack us?"

An exhausted, troubled sigh escaped Draven, and he put his head in his hands. "Shadow beasts have a mind of their own and can override my control if they're stronger than I am. However, the thing back in the desert was something else entirely. The skeleton king forced its way inside me and sent me into an episode. I fought to resist his entry, but—as you saw—I failed..." He stared back into the fire and gripped his knees. "The king was the one controlling the shadow beast. Controlling me."

Archie leaned away from Draven ever so slightly. "Why tell us this now? Why not sooner? It may have been helpful for us to know...you know, for safety purposes." His gaze swept through the darkness around them, as if expecting a shadow beast to spring out of nowhere.

Draven sighed, noticeably annoyed. "Telling others I can't control my sense and can create shadow beasts that could tear them apart doesn't usually bring people running in my direction."

Archie said nothing to this.

"I can't say I'm entirely surprised, Doom-and-Gloom," Jovian broke in, a smile teasing the corners of his mouth.

Tristan's brow furrowed. "Is that why you always slip off during the night?"

Draven nodded. "The night is the most dangerous time for others to be around me. It's better for your safety if I am as far away as possible."

Tristan looked down at the fire, jaw set. "You're remarkable to have maintained yourself with such a sense. I don't know what I'd do if I had such an ability."

Archie nodded in agreement.

Jovian hid his distaste behind a smile. He wouldn't say *remarkable*. Freaky was more like it. He forced a laugh. "If it was me, I'd find the quickest and most efficient way to get rid of that sense." He shrugged. "But that's just me."

Draven met Jovian's gaze again. "If I could, I would. You're all lucky you have senses that have never seriously hurt others around you or force you to live in the constant fear that you will."

Jovian's smile froze on his face. Nausea churned in the pit of his stomach, and he looked away from them into the dark cave. He took a deep, shaky breath through his nose and touched his braid. "Perhaps."

"I wouldn't say that exactly," Tristan broke in. "Even if I've never seriously hurt anyone, electricity isn't necessarily safe. I've made the mistake of setting small fires and electrocuting things. I've always been nervous to use it around others."

Archie kept quiet.

Jovian turned his head back to the group, spreading a refreshed grin on his face. "So…does this shadow sense help you know things?"

Draven's forehead wrinkled. "I can tell where shadows are. From that, I can make educated guesses."

"Educated guesses about…the future?" Jovian asked, his smile innocent but gaze piercing.

With a subtle jolt, Draven's eyes were back on Jovian, studying him like someone trying to read his mind. "What makes you say that?" his voice deepened and roughened.

"Well, while you were passed out, you mentioned someone seeing the future."

Draven looked back at the fire and shook his head. "I must've been dreaming. That's not possible." He avoided everyone's eyes and his forehead creased.

Jovian resisted the urge to frown, warning bells ringing in his mind. Draven was lying about something. Did he know why they were in the labyrinth? Somehow, if Draven himself couldn't see the future, he must know someone who could. Dropping the subject, Jovian mulled over this idea. Seeing the future. How could that be possible?

Draven also fell silent after Jovian's nosing, but that only made him more suspicious. Jovian needed to figure out what Draven knew. The labyrinth was tricky enough without having an untrustworthy person in the group, and he didn't trust Draven in the slightest.

Soon, they started off again, following Draven's direction. They walked for what could've been a day, or maybe two, with only Tristan's electricity as light. Time was impossible to keep track of when they walked in constant darkness. The worst part, however, was the lack of sustenance. Jovian's stomach clung to his ribs and spine and his body trembled and rumbled. Occasionally, they'd stumble upon a pool of water which kept their thirst at bay.

When Jovian's stomach gurgled loud enough for all to hear, he eyed Draven. "Not to seem doubtful of the helpfulness of your sense…" Jovian ventured, a stale smile spreading on his face. "But didn't you say this possible exit was close?"

"'Close' is a relative term," was Draven's only reply.

Then the air around Jovian steadily lightened the further they traveled, and little by little he could see with more clarity.

Archie took off in front of them. "Light!" he called as he ran.

Sure enough, the faint evidence of light gleamed up ahead.

"Archie!" Draven called, picking up speed. "Stay with us!"

The tunnel opened into a massive cavern, light filling the space from a large, jagged opening in the ceiling. Jovian winced as his eyes adjusted to the brightness. Through the opening, a cloudless sky spread. Jovian frowned. Surely this wasn't the exit Draven had been talking about, right? There was no feasible way to get out through that opening. Not unless someone could fly. He glared in Draven's direction.

Archie paused, several feet in front of them, staring up at the opening. Slowly, he turned. "Is *this* the exit?"

"Never mind that, Archie," Draven hissed, his voice tense. "You shouldn't be out there!"

Archie ignored Draven's warning and moaned. He kicked a rock that sailed across the cavern and echoed when it landed on a massive dark hill on the far side. "I hate this freaking labyrinth!" he bellowed into the space. "I want to go home already!"

Tristan sighed. "At least we have some light, I guess."

Somehow, that sentence hit Jovian and his frustration, hunger, and annoyance cracked inside. An uncontrollable tremble bubbled up within him, impossible to keep down, and he laughed. He laughed and laughed and laughed and couldn't stop. He crouched down close to the ground and pressed his palms hard against his eyes. Tears trickled out from his eyelids. He ignored the stares from the others.

"Are you alright?" Tristan asked, sounding unsure.

Jovian only laughed harder.

Draven sighed and passed him, walking down toward Archie.

Finally, Jovian regained some control of the overwhelming swells of laughter, and swallowed the rest down, down, down, locking them back inside where they belonged. Standing once more, Jovian wiped away his tears—the first tears he'd shed in a long time—and let out a breathless sigh.

"Sorry," Jovian grinned at Tristan. "This was just too much for me to handle. It's so idiotic and aggravating, it just struck me funny."

Archie huffed. "Only you would laugh in such a situation."

Suddenly, a violent tremble shook the cavern. The large hill on the other end of the space shifted and out from under the moving hill spilled piles and piles of glittering gold and jewels, their clattering echoing in Jovian's bones. In an instant, Jovian's view of his own diminutiveness was magnified by the towering creature that arose before them, unfurling its ancient, scaly wings. It blew out a blast of fire ten times hotter than any Jovian had ever felt from Kai.

Archie scrambled back up the hill toward them and away from the beast. "Dragon!" he shrieked in terror.

Fwap!

The dragon's tail swished, striking Archie and sending him flipping through open space. With a sickening *crack* Archie smashed into the wall of the cavern and crumpled in a heap.

"Archie!" Tristan and Draven yelled.

Tristan ran to where Archie lay while the ground continued to quiver and shake. Jovian lost his footing and slid down the hill toward Draven. Jovian kicked out a ledge of earth to stop his descent.

The dragon's glowing ember eyes focused on them, and Jovian's heart trembled. It opened its large mouth, exposing a slithering serpent's tongue and dagger-sharp teeth the size of Jovian's arm. An orange glow boiled up the dragon's throat and a thick stream of fire gushed out—straight toward them.

Instinct kicked in and Jovian slammed his fist into his palm, causing the ground under him and Draven to shift and send them toward the far end of the cavern, out of the reach of the flames.

When Jovian's sliding reached a halt, he vaulted himself up and behind a giant stalagmite in hopes of hiding. He needed time to gather his thoughts, to plan. He had no clue if the other three were alive and well, especially Archie. If the other four they'd lost back in the cave collapse hadn't made it, then these three were all Jovian had left. If they died, he'd be alone. Again.

Closing his eyes, Jovian took a deep breath and pressed down the feelings of anxiety rising in his gut. He didn't want to be alone.

Another shudder wracked the earth and Jovian's eyes flicked open. His hands tightened into fists and he slid from his hiding spot, throwing his arms out behind him. Jovian thrust his arms forward, tearing rock from the walls and floors, and showered the sharpened stones on the dragon. The rock slammed into its head and Jovian fired another heap into the dragon's side as he slid a foot back, causing the ground under him to shift forward and down toward the dragon.

The dragon blew a stream of flames at Jovian. Crap! He slammed his heel into the ground, causing the earth to shoot him high into the air, narrowly missing the flames. He grimaced as heat seared his skin. As he descended back to the ground, Jovian dragged his arms in front of him and down toward the dragon, pulling stalactites from the ceiling and hurling them at the beast. Jovian brought his fingertips together, sharpening the stalactites into blade-like points.

Then Jovian pulled the earth up to catch him and soften his landing. He watched as the stalactites sliced and cut at the dragon, but its scales were too thick. The dragon merely turned its glowing yellow eyes toward him once more and prepared for another blast of fire. Jovian gritted his teeth and searched the cavern. He needed a different tactic. The dragon's tail suddenly whipped toward him, and Jovian flipped back and away from its reach, cursing.

He needed help.

Then Tristan emerged from his hiding place, near an unmoving Archie. Sporadic flashes of electricity surrounded his body, illuminating a dark and furious gaze. The light from outside the cavern darkened as gray clouds formed in the sky. Tristan thrust an arm out toward the dragon and lightning rained down from the opening and out from Tristan himself.

The beast reared back and released a wild stream of flames into the cave.

From the opposite side of the cavern, Draven materialized out of the shadows, his eyes black, and a massive shadow creature wavering above him.

The shadow beast's vague clouded figure enlarged to fill the air, its glowing green eyes turning to the dragon. The dark creature formed an arm, and claw-like fingers shot out and sliced across the dragon's chest. The dragon let out a rumbling call of pain.

Jovian jumped, spun, and—with several calculative kicks—sent more rocks crashing into the dragon. Then, without hesitation, he landed and spun with one foot slicing across the ground and up, sending a large chunk of the floor at the beast while Tristan fired another jet of lightning. The dragon erupted, shooting a massive spew of lava all over the cavern. Several sparks sizzled over Jovian's clothes and skin, causing blisters to form.

"Aiyaaa! Hot!" Jovian shouted, ducking behind a stalagmite to avoid more burning sprays. Then he peeked out.

Draven's demon shadow swallowed all the fire that came his way and grasped one of the dragon's legs, crushing it in its shadow claws. Jovian's eyes widened and his lips pressed into a thin line, a sickening pang of disgust swirling in his stomach. The dragon screeched and flapped its massive wings. The flapping was so intense that the air in the cavern pushed everything away from the dragon. Jovian had to dig his hands and feet into the rock to keep from being blown away.

Another jet of electricity rained down and the dragon convulsed. Draven's shadow engulfed one of the dragon's wings and tore it from its body. The dragon's tail lashed out and knocked Draven and his demon shadow away. Then the dragon turned its head to Draven and opened his mouth as if ready to fry him.

Jovian leapt from his spot and slammed the floor, causing the ground to roll and the dragon to lose its balance. It crashed to its knees with a bellow. He needed to finish it off *now*. Jovian yanked a large stalagmite from the floor, sharpened it, and then sent it flying into the dragon's gut. The stalagmite dug deep into the side of the dragon's belly and Jovian almost cheered. But the dragon's body shook with a deafening scream of fury, swallowing Jovian's exhilaration. Tristan delivered one more explosion of lightning, making Jovian's hair stand on end.

When Tristan stopped, Jovian watched with a mixture of dread and hope. The dragon's body lay motionless amongst the broken stalagmites.

Jovian's legs buckled under him, and he fell to his hands and knees, panting. He peered over at Draven and found him sitting up and rubbing his head. They were still alive. They were all still alive. Even...

Archie.

Jovian jerked his head around, searching the destruction in the cavern for a sign of the other prince. Archie hadn't budged from where he had fallen.

Jovian stood and catapulted himself over to him using his sense. Archie was lying in a heap, crying. Tristan joined them. Neither of them spoke. All Jovian could do was stand there and stare at Archie's deformed body as Draven materialized next to them. Jovian's shock was mirrored on his face. Draven turned away.

Archie's violent, bloody coughs didn't slow his tears. "I can't...move. I...can't move," he rasped. Archie gasped for breath and sobbed. "I want...to go home."

Jovian looked away, steeling himself against the overwhelming wave of emotion swelling up inside him. Flashes of memories full of deformed bodies similar to Archie's raced through his mind. Despite his attempt to harden himself against the emotions, Jovian's chest trembled and his throat burned. Archie didn't deserve this.

Tristan knelt at Archie's side and gripped his hand. "I'm here, Archie," he whispered, voice quivering.

Amid Archie's coughs and gasps of breath, Jovian heard Tristan's quieter sniffles. Draven stood facing away, his shoulders hunched inward. Archie's shallow breaths puffed clouds of frost into the bitter air as snowflakes floated down through the opening in the ceiling. Distant clinks of water dripped from the stalactites above and a bird's song pulled Jovian's gaze up to a sparrow twittering near the edge of the opening. He crouched down near the frigid floor and seized his chest, burning with emotions he didn't want to feel.

None of them said a word, but Jovian knew. He knew. Archie wasn't going to make it. All they could do was hope he didn't suffer too long.

They didn't leave his side until he breathed his last breath.

40

Giant

CASSIAN AND THE OTHER THREE WALKED FOR SEVERAL DAYS, stopping only to eat, drink, or sleep—with occasional restroom breaks in-between. Several more griffins attacked them on their journey, leaving the four drained. Cassian lurched at every sound and struggled to rest at night, expecting a griffin to descend on them at any moment.

Worst of all, through every battle they had, Kai and Luka kept butting heads. Kai snapped at every decision Luka made or remained sullenly silent. Although Cassian really did like Kai, he was sick of his tendency to argue.

Cassian glanced in Sage's direction. Her head bent forward, and she clutched her shoulder, a slight wince in her eyes.

Though the others in their group were clueless, Cassian was not. He knew the truth. Sage was really a princess. A very brave, strong princess. She reminded him in many ways of his older sister, Aria. Aria was kind-hearted and constantly looked out for him. Aria had always been happy to see Cassian and was never too busy to spend time with him. More than anyone else, Aria was his favorite person.

When Cassian had heard the buffoon, Archie, had started dating his sister, he couldn't stand it. Archie wasn't good enough for her, and Cassian made sure he knew it. Aria deserved better. Cassian wanted his sister to be happy, and he knew there was someone else Aria preferred.

Cassian was perceptive, and although Aria would never speak of it, it wasn't hard to figure out who she'd liked more than anyone else, and Cassian had kept an eye on him ever since. Without a doubt, he believed this person would make her the happiest. More than Archie ever could.

Cassian hoped that person was still alive.

Sage reminded Cassian of Aria because of her kindness. She was quick to defend everyone and never dragged others down. And she was as transparent as a clear water stream. Cassian had realized almost immediately she was a girl, but it took him a week or two to be certain. Although he had often thought of telling her he knew, Cassian feared she would freak out and avoid him. He didn't want that. Not at all.

Cassian caught sight of strange dark clouds gathering over the mountains and the sight pulled him from his thoughts. "Do you see those clouds?" he asked, pointing.

The group turned and eyed the darkening mass around the mountain. Brilliant lightning flashed in blue strains across the gray-green sky. A dragon's roar ripped through the air. Distant smoke rose from the depths of the mountain passes.

"It's Tristan!" Cassian exclaimed, relieved.

"He's still alive!" Sage cried, a bright smile flashing across her face.

Kai crossed his arms over his chest studying the scene before them. "For now," he muttered, ignoring Luka's look. "It sounds like he's got a dragon."

Cassian stared over the mountain ridges at the clouds and lightning. There was no way they could reach the others from here. How many of the others were with Tristan? Would they be fine taking on a dragon on their own?

"They can pull through," Sage stated, biting her lip. "They have in the past."

Luka sighed and looked away from the commotion. "Mostly," he said.

Sage ducked her head and fidgeted with the oversized jacket Draven had given her. Cassian didn't like seeing her so gloomy, so he tapped her shoulder and offered her a smile. "I'm sure they'll be fine."

Nodding, Sage raised her head and stared at the clouds. "I hope so." She rubbed her shoulder once more, grimacing. Her shoulder was still bothering her. And that worried him.

As the group walked, the dark clouds gradually dispersed, and the dragon roars disappeared. Cassian hoped the silence was a good sign.

They continued their journey through the third section of the labyrinth, progressing as fast as they could.

Four days after seeing Tristan's lightning, something materialized from behind a large mountain.

Cassian's eyes widened. "The third gate!"

The other three immediately brightened at the sight. This section wasn't nearly as long as the last two had been. Were the sections becoming shorter? He hoped that was the case. If it was, they could speed through the next two sections and *finally* head home.

"Let's hurry and get the hell out of this place," Kai said.

As the group approached the mountain looming between them and the gate, they came upon a massive cave opening. Tentatively, they drew closer. Cassian half-expected a dragon to appear in front of them.

"You don't suppose we can go *over* the mountain instead, do you?" Kai asked, his gaze searching for some viable way over.

Luka followed his gaze. "It would add another few weeks to our journey—maybe even a month—depending how difficult the climb turns out to be."

Kai's expression soured and he strode onward, not responding to Luka's comment. Together, the four of them approached the opening and peered inside. A vast, dark cavern awaited them. They slipped inside and kept close to the walls, staying alert, Sage glowing gently and Kai carrying a small ball of fire in his hands. There were no sleeping dragons, treasure hoards, or nests so far—just emptiness.

The cavern shrunk the further in they went, ruling out the possibility of a large dragon being able to follow them. Maybe it was just a normal cave. Then Cassian stepped on something soft. He looked down in surprise to find a tapestry rug beneath him. Were his eyes playing tricks on him? He knelt slowly and brushed his fingers across it. The rug was soft, tightly knit, and the most comforting thing Cassian had seen in months.

When Kai looked down at the rug, his face hardened.

"How?" Sage asked as she joined Cassian and ran her hands over the knitting.

Kai lifted the fire in his palm higher and surveyed the room. A large fireplace sat in the center with huge pots, pans, and a stick hanging on hooks nearby. To the right of the fire was a massive red chair with velvet cushions. Next to the chair was a large table. Along the walls were paintings of people, monsters, and animals. Stacks of scrolls scattered in clumps along the floor. To Cassian's left lay a pile of various bones. A griffin skull sat near Sage's feet. Even further left was a giant bed with linen sheets and satin blankets. A huge, furry pillow lay at one end.

Cassian frowned. He didn't like what he was seeing, not a bit.

"What is this place?" asked Sage, rising to her feet.

Luka stepped deeper into the room. "Could a human be living in the labyrinth?"

Kai scoffed. "Human? Look how massive the furniture is." He swept an arm out, gesturing to the whole room. "I say giant."

Sage stepped back. "I have a bad feeling about this."

Cassian did too, but he didn't say so. Instead, he stepped further inside to study the room with Luka and Kai.

Clink!

The four of them froze. Cassian held his breath, listening. Approaching footsteps clicked and clattered like hooves behind them, along with an animal's snort. Kai snuffed out his flame, Sage darkened her glow, and the four of them dove behind a large basket of fur to hide.

The clinking of hooves clicked closer, followed by the scratching sound of claws against the stone floor. There was a short bark, to which another snort came in reply. Cassian couldn't even guess what was about to join them in the room, and his heart raced so quickly, he was afraid whatever was coming would hear it. Sage crouched on his right, her eyes wide and her hands clutching the hilt of her sword. Past her, Kai and Luka did the same.

Then a large, furry creature stepped into the space. It was hard to make out anything in the dark, but what Cassian saw confused him. It looked like a standing bull. When the creature lit a fire and cast an illuminating glow through the room, the glistening horns, huge furry head, human body and arms, and hoofed feet revealed a Minotaur.

When he'd been young, the older princes would sometimes tell Cassian stories about the Minotaur eating children. Cassian shot a look at the other three, eyes wide. He didn't want to be eaten.

The Minotaur heaved a deer's body into place over the fire and then grabbed a giant bag from near the bed. As the scent of roasting venison filled the space, the giant left the room. The sounds of barking and howling reverberated from the corridor. Cassian frowned deeply. Either the Minotaur had pet dogs or future dinner out there.

Shortly, the Minotaur returned and ate his meal. And after eating, he picked up a scroll to read.

As the Minotaur continued what seemed to be his evening routine, the four didn't move. Cassian's legs and back ached from crouching behind the basket, but he did his best to ignore it.

Finally, the monster placed a large gate over their only exit and crawled into his bed. Cassian clutched his knees, heart thumping painfully in his chest. Would they have to stay here all night, trapped with a monster?

Once snores rose from the bed, Kai straightened and strode to the gate. He tugged at it.

Luka leapt up after him. "What are you doing?" he hissed.

"Trying to get out of here before that thing discovers us," Kai spat back. He gave another tug and the gate barely budged.

Sage and Cassian joined them just in time to see Luka reach for Kai's arm. "That thing? That's a Minotaur!"

Kai slapped away Luka's hand, his gaze blazing. "Don't touch me, you blubbering asshole."

Sage stepped between them and pushed them away from each other. "The Minotaur is *sleeping*," she hissed, gesturing to the snoring bull-man. "Let's just move the gate and get out of here."

Still glaring at each other, Kai and Luka stepped toward the gate. Then all four of them tugged until the gate scooted over just enough for them to squeeze through, and they left the sleeping Minotaur behind.

Cassian took a deep breath. He flashed a smile of relief at the three with him as they hurried away, heading for open air. Then Cassian tripped and fell into something large and furry. He scrambled back just as a growl sounded from the heap of fur. The mound rose from the ground and Kai snapped a flame into his hand, casting a wavering light on the creature.

A werewolf. A white, snowy werewolf.

Dread and terror circled within Cassian as he stared up at the source of so many of his nightmares. He'd thought they'd seen the last of these terrifying creatures back in the forest.

Luka cursed. "Not again."

The wolf howled, the sound ripping through Cassian's soul as he scrambled toward the others. Sage reached for him and pulled him close. Following the white wolf's howl, more forms began to shift in the space around them. Teeth snapped in the semi-darkness and quiet barks and grunts answered the white wolf's call. Sage lit up the cavern, and the glints from a great many pairs of eyes stared back at them.

A massive pack of werewolves stood between them and the snowy world outside.

Cassian trembled.

41

Kai's Flaw

CASSIAN STARED AT THE WEREWOLVES. HOW WERE THEY supposed to survive this? And just when he thought it couldn't get any worse, hooves clunked and clattered behind them, drawing closer. Cassian turned to look over his shoulder, dread welling up inside him. The towering Minotaur stared back at him.

"Oh-ho!" the Minotaur said, his voice deep and rattling. "What do we have here? Humans?"

Cassian grasped the front of his tunic, heart thumping painfully in his chest. What could they do now?

When no one answered, the Minotaur continued, "It's been quite a long time since I've seen a *human* in these parts." It chuckled, gripping a coiled whip near his hip. "Quite a long time indeed…maybe two thousand years? Not since those labyrinth walls came up."

The Minotaur had been alive for two *thousand* years?

Cassian peeked back at the werewolves. They crouched and growled, as if waiting for a signal. Did the Minotaur control them? Cassian's hands trembled and he braced himself for an attack from either direction.

"Oh, don't be shy, little humans. It's been too long since I've held a conversation with anyone." The Minotaur uncoiled the whip and slashed it toward them. Cassian couldn't help staring at the big, beefy, human-like hands. The glint of an ax peeked over his furry shoulder. "I'd enjoy a little chat before I roast you all for breakfast. You do look quite tasty…. Maybe I'll eat the little one tonight. I always preferred the soft babes."

Cassian stared at the shiny horns on either side of the beast's head. Massive, round, and so sharp they could easily impale him if the Minotaur decided to charge. He swallowed the lump rising in his throat. This beast didn't seem to be in any hurry to end them. Instead, it reminded Cassian of watching house cats play with mice. The cat would bite, hit, and toss the mouse, toying with it mercilessly until the mouse could take no more and died.

Cassian didn't want to be a mouse.

"Come now!" the Minotaur said. "Tell me, where do you come from?"

Cassian kept his mouth closed. He didn't want to play games.

"Like we'd tell you, cow-horn," Kai spat. "We refuse to be your playthings."

At least Kai was on the same page as him. This might be the single reason why Cassian liked Kai. Now if only he could remain level-headed.

The Minotaur smiled. "But you *are* my playthings." Cassian had never thought a cow could smile, but seeing this one grin made him shudder. It was ugly and unnatural.

The Minotaur cracked its whip and the werewolves closed in, growling and snapping at them. One wolf leapt toward Cassian and he scrambled back as its claws dug into his chest, knocking him to the floor and holding down his arms.

"Cassian!" Sage shrieked.

Cassian couldn't help it, he whimpered. He didn't want to die. He wanted to see his mother and father again. He wanted to see Aria. His eyes burned as he strained to pull his arms free.

"Wait, wait, wait! We'll talk!" Luka called. When Cassian looked toward him, the other prince was holding up both hands, an expression of pure panic on his face.

The Minotaur snapped his whip again and the werewolves backed off, including the one now growling on top of him. Cassian trembled as he scrambled away.

Sage pulled him from the ground and hugged him against her side, her own body trembling. Cassian gripped her jacket tightly, Aria's face still flashing through his mind. His chest squeezed and he struggled to breathe. Would they make it out of this?

Kai glared at Luka. "We are *not* going to be his entertainment just so he can kill us later! I'd rather fight now than chat uselessly."

"Shut *up*!" Luka hissed. He sent a pointed look toward Sage and Cassian before turning back to the Minotaur. "What do you want to know?"

"I've already asked my question."

Luka straightened a bit taller and replied, "We're from the kingdom of Reudinia, one of the most powerful kingdoms in its area."

Kai cursed and kicked a rock. "Creature-pleaser," he muttered under his breath.

Cassian pressed his lips together and eyed the cavern around him. There *had* to be a way to escape. There *had* to. He raised his eyes to the ceiling. Several stalactites dangled above them, their edges sharp and long. Like icicles. Maybe Kai could cause some sort of explosion that would knock the stalactites down.

"Reudinia, you say?" asked the Minotaur. His dark eyes stared at them. "Never heard of it. Must be new. Kingdoms do rise and fall in time. This Reudinia will fall one day too. How and why did you come to be here?"

Luka glanced back at them, gaze searching. Cassian nodded to him, and Luka turned back to the creature. Luka cleared his throat. "We were kidnapped and brought here to free the spirit at the center of the labyrinth."

Cassian stared at Kai, hoping to catch his eye. However, Kai's gaze remained on the floor, a slight steam rising from his shoulders as he glared at it. Why did he have to be so dramatic?

"The spirit?" The Minotaur's furry forehead creased, and his gaze darkened. He scratched the back of one of his ears. "I've heard of this *spirit* from the whispers in the labyrinth, but the one at the center is of little value. Why do you wish to free it? What do you seek to gain?"

Cassian slipped to Kai's side and poked his arm. Kai frowned at him, but Cassian only nodded at the ceiling. Kai looked up.

"We want nothing. We were forced to come here and told the only way to leave the labyrinth is to release the spirit." Luka's hands tightened into fists. "We don't even know what they want with it."

The Minotaur snorted and pawed the ground with one of its hooves. "Not anything good, I'm sure. Such greedy, greedy beings humans are." His voice roughened and dropped an octave. "I'll be doing you a favor then, by disposing of you. You won't have to release the spirit if I kill you."

Sage stepped forward, bringing the creature's attention to her. Kai returned his gaze to Cassian, and Cassian mimicked the explosion with his hands. Kai's eyebrows furrowed, but he nodded.

"Why do you say the spirit at the center of the labyrinth has no value?" Sage asked.

The Minotaur's chuckle vibrated through Cassian's body. "I knew of the man who the humans feared. However, the amount of power he contained was too great for one man. I doubt the man's ghost would be a threat now, unless the ghost reconnects with the one who helped him wield that power." The Minotaur's mouth curled leeringly. "If *that* spirit were able to regain the powers held by the ghost in the center, *then* you'd have reason to worry."

Cassian creased his forehead. What was this beast saying? Was he suggesting there was another spirit?

"No one has ever ventured to my part of the labyrinth before. You four must be quite powerful. A nice challenge for me." The Minotaur grinned, snapping his whip. "Now," it said, rolling back its shoulders. "Time to play."

Kai took that as a signal. He blasted the ceiling with an explosion of flames. Stalactites crumbled down on the werewolves and Minotaur, and Luka waved away the debris that fell toward their group.

The Minotaur roared, bracing himself against the debris.

The werewolves whined and growled as they scrambled around the ruckus and attacked.

Luka forced several back with his telekinesis. "Go!"

Cassian darted toward the cave entrance. But the werewolves recovered quickly and blocked their exit.

Several pounced. Cassian jerked a hand forward and froze several of the werewolves, and Sage brandished her sword, blazing light flashing through it.

Cassian peeked back at the Minotaur who glared at them, dusting the debris off his body and pulling a large battle ax from his back. "Sense wielders," his voice boomed in the tunnel. "I should've known."

"Kai!" Luka called, levitating werewolves back and bracing himself for the Minotaur's attack. "Get us through the werewolves while we distract the Minotaur!"

Then the Minotaur swung his mighty ax. Cassian lunged away and managed to freeze four werewolves as he fell, his elbows scraping painfully across the icy ground. Cassian yanked himself up just in time to freeze several more werewolves before they reached him and used his other hand to slash each of them through the heart with an icicle. When he looked around, Cassian saw Sage cutting through the werewolves, but she was being forced back toward the Minotaur.

"Kai! The wolves!" Luka yelled again.

A whir of wind forced Cassian to duck, narrowly dodging another swing of the Minotaur's ax. A werewolf dove for him and Cassian swerved and hacked his small sword across its chest. The werewolf's claws raked his stomach. Cassian stumbled back and froze the werewolf.

Kai's voice echoed through the cave. "You're saying *you* fight the master while *I* fight the pets?" Kai slashed through a whole circle of werewolves with his flaming spear and turned to face the Minotaur. "I can take the bloody bastard."

Cassian recoiled as he froze another wolf, his stomach stinging. If Kai didn't get them through the werewolves, then how would they escape? He glanced back at the others.

The Minotaur smacked Luka away. Sage blinded and slashed at him, but her swings were stiff as she favored her shoulder. The Minotaur swung the blunt end of his ax and struck her in the side. Sage skidded across the floor and a chill went through Cassian's chest.

Luka knocked a wave of werewolves back and then flung a stalagmite at the Minotaur.

A swirl of flames knocked the Minotaur back several steps back. Cassian whirled to freeze five more wolves before searching for Sage's body among the crowd of werewolves, slicing and freezing as he searched. Not Sage. He couldn't let them kill Sage.

"Kai! This isn't about who's strongest!" Luka's voice thundered. Cassian finally spotted Sage near Luka as the other prince defended her from the onslaught of werewolves. "Stop being such a spoiled child and *listen*."

Kai didn't respond. Instead, he sailed through the air toward the Minotaur's head, releasing a blast of flame. Cassian's eyes widened as everything seemed to slow. The flames rolled outward, burning several werewolves around him and Cassian veered away from the fire's reach, trying to shoot another icicle through an approaching werewolf's chest. But he couldn't do both.

The flames seared his left arm and he yelped. Cassian yanked his scorching arm behind him, dragging in a sharp intake of breath and wincing. Using his good arm, he released a stream of ice toward the remaining werewolves. Tears stung his eyes, and he gritted his teeth as the sweltering heat continued to boil his skin. He couldn't fight like this. He looked in Sage's direction just in time to see her struggle to her feet, gripping her side.

They weren't going to make it.

Cassian turned his gaze to the snarling and snapping werewolves, the dimming light from outside barely reaching into the cave. Then he set his jaw. If Kai wasn't going to get them out, then he would.

Keeping his wounded arm close to his side, Cassian waved his good arm and covered Sage with a wall of ice. Then he whipped his good arm to the side, freezing the werewolves about to pounce. Icicles formed and pierced the werewolves and Cassian slid along the ground and spread ice across the whole floor, temporarily freezing the werewolves' feet. It didn't take long for several to break free. Slipping and skittering across the iced floor, they turned their gazes solely on him. Cassian's heart trembled, but he didn't dare stop, so he created a ramp to flip himself up into the air—and down into the center of the wolves.

Cassian slashed, froze, and pierced, but there were so many. Too many.

42

The Breaking Point

SHARP, PIERCING PAIN STABBED THROUGH SAGE'S SIDE as she struggled for breath. The room swirled around her. She gripped her side, raking in painful breaths, shaking her head in the vain hope it would clear the distorted room. Her heart pumped agonizingly loud in her chest. She couldn't focus; she could barely see. Was she going to die? Then Luka was beside her pulling her to her feet. "Breathe, Sage! We need you."

Taking in a staggering breath, Sage groaned as her chest screamed. But the revolving cave slowed its spinning, and Luka's scarred face and worried blue eye came into focus. He turned to face the Minotaur and Sage turned with him. The beast was preoccupied with Kai and an ice shelter protected her from the assault of the remaining werewolves.

"Kai, no! We need you to get us through the werewolves!" Luka shouted, but Kai continued attacking the Minotaur at full force.

Wave after wave of flames beat down on the Minotaur, forcing him further and further back, his fur charred and smoking.

"You can take care of those blasted pets!" came Kai's furious cry as he let loose a wild tornado of flames.

But Sage spun away from the scene. If she, Luka, and Kai were with the Minotaur, then who was fighting the werewolves? Sage tore around the other side of the ice wall to see the pack clambering in a circle. In the center stood little Cassian, desperately fighting off twenty werewolves on his own, slicing, cutting, stabbing, and freezing. Her chest tightened, a terrible lump swelling in her throat.

She stumbled toward him, ignoring her screaming chest. "Cassian!"

Beaming her light and igniting her sword, Sage hacked at the werewolves, fighting with all her might and ignoring the sharp twinging in her shoulder. She cut and stabbed at their thick fur and sturdy hide, killing one, killing two, but not fast enough. "Cassian!" Tears misted her eyes.

Cassian ferociously slaughtered the wolves, his white hair and clothes covered in werewolf blood. Right as he caught her eye over the chaos, one slipped past Cassian's defense and clamped its jaws around his skinny neck.

"NO!" Sage screamed, and a pulsing energy burst from her chest. Ray beams shot through the remaining werewolves. And white light blindingly filled the room.

Sage squinted and dimmed the light, her gaze slowly focusing on the scattered werewolves lying unmoving on the floor before her. Without waiting for her vision to clear further, Sage sprang over their bodies, slipping and sliding on the frozen ground until she made it to the center and threw herself down next to Cassian's small body. The werewolf who had bitten him stood frozen right above him.

Sage pulled Cassian's limp, bloody body into her arms. The child rasped for breath as she placed a hand on his cheek. "Cassian, Cassian, Cass, I'm here! I'm here, Cass!"

Blood from Cassian's neck drenched her hands and clothes and blended in with the werewolf blood that covered him. Pressing her hands against his neck, Sage channeled her pulsing energy to heal his wounds. She hadn't ever succeeded in healing a person yet, but she had to try. Cassian's eyes, hazy and distant, finally found hers. He choked, blood oozing from his mouth as he gripped her jacket sleeves, tears streaming down his face. He opened his mouth.

"Don't speak! Don't speak," whispered Sage. "I have you."

Tears spilled from her own eyes as healing energy eased away her aches and pains and seeped from her body into Cassian's. She wiped her tears away with her shoulder, which for once didn't hurt. Hardly able to believe her watery eyes, Sage watched as the holes in Cassian's throat closed. She was doing something!

Then he coughed, blood spurting from his mouth and onto her face. "Sage…"

"Don't speak!"

Cassian coughed again and swallowed. The holes in his neck vanished, but then the pulsing healing energy drained away from her chest, and an overwhelming surge of exhaustion shook her body. No…

Searching for any scrap of energy she could find inside, Sage attempted to heal Cassian's other wounds. But her sense didn't budge at her beckoning.

No.

"Aria…" gasped Cassian, coughing again, his small breaths creating fog in the frigid air.

Tears filled Sage's vision again, and this time she was unable to push them back. A sob erupted from her throat. She pressed her hands to his chest and willed some of her own life into him.

Revive!

But Cassian's heart still fluttered faintly against her palms, and he gasped for air. Sage lifted Cassian's bloody shirt up. Several deep cuts covered his stomach and chest from where the werewolves had sliced at him.

"Cass!" she shrieked. "Cassian, stay with me!"

Revive!

"Why am I so weak?" she sobbed, anger rising up inside her.

Cassian gripped Sage's sleeves tighter. "Live," he rasped, his face paling further as he struggled to breathe. Then Cassian's chest quivered and settled, and his grip on her jacket loosened.

"No, no, Cassian!" Sage sobbed, tears streaming down her face as she tapped the sides of his face and tried healing the wounds on his body once more.

Cassian didn't respond.

With an aching wail, Sage hugged his small, lifeless body to her chest and wept. She had failed. She'd told herself she would protect Cassian, but she had failed. Again. Anger swept through her and mingled with her grief. Curse whoever put him in this place!

When Sage could finally find it in her to notice someone else's presence, she found Luka standing over her, his one good eye red-rimmed as he stared down at Cassian. A bit further back stood Kai, wide-eyed and frozen. Behind him lay the lifeless body of the Minotaur.

Luka's body tensed and his fists clenched. In three long strides, Luka was next to Kai and—*smack!*—Luka's fist met Kai's face. "You," Luka gasped, his voice deep and trembling. "This is your doing. You—you—you—you just *had* to have all the glory. So much so, you let a *kid* do your fighting for you!"

Kai didn't react to the punch. He just remained frozen, eyes trained on the ground, refusing to meet Luka's gaze.

"Was it really so hard for you to work as a *team* for once? To think of others' lives over your own pride? No, really. Tell me! Was it that hard?" Luka's voice shook with fury, rising with each word. He stared at Kai's unresponsive face, then looked away. "Well, you have your Minotaur victory. Was it worth it? Was it 'bloody' worth it?"

Kai slammed his fist into a slab of ice and walked away without a word. Luka gripped his hair tightly and stood there, taking deep breaths. "I could kill him," Sage heard Luka mutter. There were more breaths and a pause of silence. Finally, Luka dropped his arms and turned back to Sage. "We should bury him," he said, his voice a whisper.

Sage nodded, silent tears still sliding down her cheeks. She turned her gaze back to Cassian, only to see the werewolf standing above him, still frozen—with Cassian's blood coating its mouth and teeth. Luka took Cassian's body from her and without a word, Sage lifted her sword, lit it with rays, and lopped off the wolf's head.

Why didn't you warn me? The traitor glared at the cave wall, a swirl of complicated emotions welling up in his chest. Emotions he had a hard time naming. He squeezed his hands into fists. *Another died, and you were no help at all. I'm done listening to you.*

"Done? I don't think so," came the sharp reply. "*If you were, then all of this would be a waste, wouldn't it? You came here for me. Do you want your wish or not?*"

The traitor lowered his eyes and glared at the ground. He still wanted what he'd come here for—but the harshness of the labyrinth and the others' deaths were getting to him. He took a slow, deep breath, and let it out. *Next time, warn me or the deal's off.*

⊚

43

The Phoenix at the Gate

TRISTAN STARED INTO THE CAVE TUNNEL, LIGHTING the way with his sense. From what he could tell, several days had passed since the battle with the dragon, but darkness still surrounded them, and it was difficult to keep track of time. Archie's death lingered over him like a storm cloud, his twisted body haunting Tristan's dreams.

If Tristan had been smarter, stronger, quicker…would any of those they'd lost have survived? He slowed to a stop and pressed his free hand to the cave wall, steadying his unstable body. He closed his eyes. In his mind's eye, he could see Archie standing defiantly before the Royal Council two years before. He could still hear Archie's voice. *"You're the Royal Council. Your job is to make sure those in line for the throne are kept in the best conditions. Especially those of us closest to the throne. Tristan is fourth in line. You can't ignore this!"*

"Our job *is to follow the king's orders,"* Lord Rufus snapped, his bent figure straining to straighten.

Archie put his hands on his hips. *"You're saying this is the king's order? If that's true, to hell with the king."* Archie turned to face a crowd that had gathered to watch their dispute and continued, *"If the king ignores this, he's playing favorites."*

Lord Rufus's face contorted. *"He's not ignoring the issue. We'll take care of it."*

"Good." Archie sniffed. He turned on his heel and marched toward Tristan. *"There, you see? You and Milo can stay with me until they do."*

Tristan opened his eyes and stared vacantly at the rocky cavern floor.

"What is it?" Draven asked, stepping up next to him, brows furrowed.

"Nothing," Tristan forced the word between his teeth, swallowing down the emotions threatening to overcome him. Archie might not have been his original first choice for a friend, but he'd somehow wedged his way into becoming Tristan's best and most loyal friend. He'd saved Tristan's and Milo's lives. And Tristan couldn't even pay him back properly.

Maybe he wasn't good enough to protect anyone. He couldn't protect his mother. He couldn't protect his little brother. He couldn't protect Ruben or Tenji. He couldn't protect Archie.

He was weak.

Tristan steeled his emotions and continued onward. Soon, a faint glow illuminated the tunnel ahead. A way out? He, Draven, and Jovian raced toward the glow, and a moment later, Tristan was squinting up at the wide-open sky, bright sun shining down on the snowy ground. As his eyes adjusted to the light, Tristan saw a beautiful, painful sight. Just before them, about half a day's walk away through a pine tree forest, stood the gate leading to the next section of the labyrinth. They'd made it.

Tristan scanned the untouched snow before him and a twinge of worry tugged at his heart. "I don't see the others." He clenched his fists and Cassian's smiling face flickered through his mind. He had to find him. For Aria. Tristan turned to face Draven and Jovian. Draven surveyed the frozen land, cringing from the light. He sighed, silent. Behind him stood Jovian, dark circles under his eyes and shoulders drooping. Ever since Archie's death, Jovian had grown quiet, and his jokes were less frequent, less effortless.

Then Draven strode out into the snow and in the direction of the gate. Tristan followed behind him. As they trudged through the calf-deep snow, Tristan kept an eye out for food to fill their growling, aching stomachs. The last thing they'd eaten, at Jovian's suggestion, had been the dragon.

Jovian lifted his head finally and a small smile teased his face. "At least we traveled through most of this section out of the bitter cold." He didn't mention the lack of food or the feeling of walking in circles or the loss of Archie.

Neither Tristan nor Draven responded.

As they hiked and wove through the forest, Jovian used sharp stones along the path to kill a few muskrats, which they cooked over a fire and then ate.

Eventually, they approached the towering white gates and Tristan squinted at them. They matched the snow almost blindingly. The gate had hundreds of rectangle-shaped iron slats covering it. There were no images or jewels or even the phoenix the last two gates had sported. Only iron slats. Tristan stepped closer and touched the cool metal. The slat he'd laid his hand over shifted to the side.

He looked back at Draven and Jovian.

Draven joined him, eyebrows raised. "It moves."

Jovian wrinkled his nose. "What are we supposed to do? Move them all? That's going to take forever."

Tristan tightened his lips against an impatient sigh. "Possibly. But the sooner we start, the sooner we'll be done." He reached out and pressed on a few more slats, but he couldn't get them to move in any direction.

Draven joined him in fidgeting with the hundreds of slats, and Jovian formed a hill of dirt with his earth sense so he could reach the ones higher up the gate. It took longer than Tristan would've liked before Draven stiffened and said, "It moved."

Tristan stepped closer to Draven and peered up at the slat in question. Behind the slab was evidence of a marking.

"They must move in a particular order," Jovian stated, crossing his arms over his chest. "Great."

Tristan surveyed the slats and his chest tightened. So many. He took a calming breath. The sooner they started, the sooner they'd be done. He fiddled with the iron surrounding the one Draven had moved, and then the others joined him. When the sky had darkened, they had only succeeded in shifting about twenty other slats.

"Let's rest for the night," Draven suggested, face worn and shoulders drooping with exhaustion.

Tristan nodded and rubbed his stiff, achy hands. How much longer would it take to solve this puzzle? As he closed his eyes, Milo's face rose to mind. Alone. His brother was all alone. He had to get back. Back to Milo. Back home. Back to...

Aria's image smiled and waved to him from across the royal courtyard.

Tristan opened his eyes and frowned. No matter how much he resisted thinking about her, his mind and heart refused to listen. He couldn't look Draven or Jovian in the eye as they started a campfire. What would they think if they knew his thoughts? Especially with Archie's death still lingering over them?

The next morning, they continued tinkering with the gate. All morning and afternoon were spent in the cold, shifting the slats; they paused only to search for food or to warm themselves by the fire. Finally, when Jovian slid a slat near the top, from his perch on a mound of rock, the slats shot away from an engraved image of a phoenix in the middle of the gate. Words glowed at the top of the gate: "If ye search for power, be warned: when toying with fire, ye shall surely be burned."

A pillar, trembling and squeaking, rose from the ground. It looked remarkably similar to the pillars they had seen at the other gates. Only this time, instead of a globe, a crystal bird with a long, flickering tail sat atop it.

"An ice phoenix?" asked Jovian, lifting an eyebrow. "I've never heard of an ice phoenix. I don't know if that's even possible."

Draven nodded. "It does look like one, but it seems rather impossible."

493

Tristan stared at the bird, then at the phrase on the door. He cocked his head. "The saying does mention fire though."

Jovian jerked his head away from the gate, back in the direction they'd come. "I hear something."

Tristan stilled and quieted his breath, listening. Sure enough, the crunch of footsteps came from somewhere in the distance. Tristan eyed the other two. "The others?" he asked, hopeful.

"Maybe," Draven breathed.

With that, they scattered and hid among the pine trees. Tristan kept his gaze trained in the direction the crunching footsteps came from. It wasn't long before three figures trudged into sight and Tristan recognized Kai's red hair. A small smile lifted his lips as he stepped out of his hiding place. "You're here," he said.

The moment Tristan spoke, Kai jolted and fired a blaze at him. Tristan stepped out of the line of shot, barely missing the flaming ball as Luka jerked back and Sage tripped.

Luka's face softened and a small smile slid onto Sage's face.

"Tristan," Luka greeted.

Draven and Jovian joined Tristan out in the open as Tristan stared at the three before him. Luka, Sage, and Kai smiled grim, sad smiles, their faces tired, drained, and depleted of all vigor. Especially Kai. Normally, he was always on edge, looking for a fight. But today he just stood there, shoulders slack, head bowed, gaze dull. Not at all like the Kai he knew.

Luka studied them. "No Archie?"

Tristan dropped his gaze to the snow. Death wasn't a pleasant thing to catch up on.

"He didn't make it," Draven replied.

His announcement was met with a heavy silence. Then Draven continued, "Where is Cassian? Have you seen him?"

As soon as Cassian's name released into the air, Tristan's gaze shot up. His chest squeezed, and a lump rose in his throat, threatening to choke him. No. It couldn't be…

Kai turned and stalked away, and Luka's fists clenched. Sage bit his lip, shoulders trembling.

"He—He's gone," Luka finally said.

Tristan stared. "No," he whispered. Then he looked up at the sky and covered his face with his hands. "No."

Aria.

Emotions rose up once more and swirled violently through him, threatening to spill. His throat burned. His chest burned. His eyes burned. His stomach burned. Cassian…How could he tell Aria? He'd not only failed to bring back her fiancé, but he also lost her little brother…

After a moment of further silence, Luka approached the gate. "A phoenix?" he asked.

Sage's voice brightened a little as he said, "I think you're right. A phoenix."

Taking a deep breath, Tristan dropped his hands from his burning eyes, desperate to hold in his emotions and eager to think of something else. He turned to face them and found Luka studying the words on the gate and Sage studying the phoenix sculpture. "Except a phoenix is made of fire, not ice," Tristan stated, voice wavering.

"This saying is clearly a warning," Luka said at last. "But what's it about? The next section?"

"Could be," Draven answered, staring up at the gate with Luka. "Or not."

Tristan stared at the phoenix in an attempt to numb his emotions, coming alongside Sage. "But how does that help open the gate?"

"How does a phoenix form?" Draven asked as he joined them.

Silence fell. Tristan frowned at him. Why was he asking?

When no one replied, Draven continued, "By rebirthing from the ashes of its ancestor. Maybe this phoenix needs a rebirth."

Luka's eye lit up and he snapped his head around in the direction Kai had disappeared. But then he just stood there staring before returning his gaze to the icy statue.

"Kai!" Draven yelled instead.

No movement or answer responded to Draven's call at first. But then, footsteps crunched through the snow toward them. Kai's figure appeared, and he stared at them blankly, eyes and nose red. Immediately, Tristan shifted and looked away. He'd never seen Kai cry before.

"We need your help," Draven informed him.

Tristan almost expected Kai to explode, but instead, Kai trudged over and stared vacantly at the ice phoenix sculpture. When he spoke, his voice was hoarse. "What do I need to do?"

"Burn it," Jovian said, his eyes sad but his smirk the same as always.

Kai scanned their faces and, after realizing Jovian wasn't joking, lit a flame and set the ice sculpture ablaze. The ice sculpture oozed away and dripped down into a hole in the pedestal.

At first, nothing happened and they stared down at it, holding their breath, waiting. Tristan clenched his jaw. Was Draven wrong?

Boom!

The pedestal exploded in flames and the group staggered back. A huge image of a flaming bird shot up into the sky and the ground and gates shuddered violently. Tristan stumbled, bracing himself as best he could, the earth's shudders vibrating deep within him as the gates creaked open. He stared into the new tunnel silently. They were one step closer to the end.

"The fourth section," Sage breathed.

Luka, Kai, Draven, and Jovian trudged into the tunnel. Sage looked at Tristan before he followed them. Pausing, Tristan took a deep breath and turned, taking a final look at the snowy mountains behind him.

Goodbye, Archie…

Goodbye, Cassian.

Two more sections to go.

◉

44

Everard's Realization

EVERARD STARED IN HORROR AT THE PIG'S HEAD HANGING from the lifted portcullis. A small scroll was bound to the spikes. Although Father would have the scroll burned before he or anyone else had a chance to see it, Everard was sure he knew what it said. The head twisted round and round on the rope, its beady eyes staring lifelessly into space. Beheaded and hung. A threat to Father. And a reminder to Everard.

Kicking a stone, Everard turned from the pig's head and raced into the royal castle. He avoided the eyes of everyone he passed and hurried to his room. The image of the pig's head swirled in his thoughts, and his mind echoed with a single word: *beheaded, beheaded, beheaded.*

A cluster of guards marched down the hall toward him. Everard stiffened and sidestepped to the wall, clutching the front of his jacket. He side-eyed them as they passed, unable to breathe until they were well behind him. Everard dragged in a deep breath. Good. Michal hadn't told anyone about what he'd done. Yet.

Once Everard reached the safety of his room, he closed his door tight and leaned against it staring blankly at the far wall. How much longer could he endure this? Would this heavy secret follow him to his grave, filling his life with more despair and anxiety?

He sank to the floor and pressed his palms to his forehead. His chest and throat burned with an all-too-familiar feeling and Everard swallowed down the lump growing in his throat and squeezed his eyes shut, cutting off his tears.

Everard dropped his arms and opened his eyes, gaze coming to rest on a dark shadow under his bed. He straightened. He'd almost forgotten about *that*. Maybe he could find an answer there. Everard crawled across the floor and pulled the case out from under his bed where he'd tucked it several months ago. He stared at it anxiously, his hands hovering over the locks. His partner had told him not to look at the contents, but Everard needed to know.

Click.

Everard tossed the lid open and peered inside. Several papers spilled from the case. He took a deep breath.

Shuffling through the papers, Everard searched the contents for clues. The papers held details about the forming of the labyrinth and the Sense Thief. Thank goodness. Maybe he could find something helpful in the materials his partner had left behind.

Two thousand years ago, a diligent cattle farmer by the name of Rupert Vilet returned to his home of two hundred people and wiped out the whole village. Nothing is known of Rupert Vilet's past before this incident. There are no previous known bouts of violence witnessed from him, nor evidence of a magical ability.

After destroying his family and village, Vilet went on to ravage other villages, towns, tribes, and, eventually, entire kingdoms. Fear of Vilet spread vastly, as well as knowledge of his ability to remove senses or magic from whoever stood against him. The people called him the Sense Thief, and since he could use the stolen senses as his own, he quickly became too powerful to be defeated by any one person.

Several prodigious leaders from various kingdoms banded together to defeat him by removing and imprisoning Vilet's spirit inside a magic stone. The elves, dwarves, and fairies aided in creating the Sidylla Labyrinth as a prison to keep others from releasing Vilet's spirit back into the world.

Since the prison was well-made, the leaders used it to trap other monsters and beasts and, over time, Sidylla grew in size. All seemed to be well, and peace returned to the land.

Then one day, about fifty years after the making of the labyrinth, a neighboring kingdom found the tribe of Kyndrie slaughtered—the men, the women, and the children. All that was left was the whisper of a vengeful demon and the rumor that Vilet hadn't acted alone.

Everard frowned. How was it that an entire tribe the size of a small kingdom was wiped out with no inkling as to who had killed them or why? If the monster had been imprisoned, then who killed the Kyndrie? Was it possible the rumors were true and Vilet had a partner?

Everard continued to search through the array of documents piled in his hands but saw nothing he didn't already know. He threw the pile back inside the case and glared at it. What was he looking for anyway? It wasn't like he could do anything to help the Ten.

Slouching, Everard fought back tears, his throat burning once more. As he stared at the documents draped haphazardly over the edges of the case, the image of the pig head spun in his mind's eye. *Beheaded, beheaded, beheaded.*

Then he noticed several papers with the royal stamp on them poking out of the edge of the case. He pulled them from the pile. The individual test scores for each of the top ten princes. His partner must've only taken their averages. This one showed how they did in each unit. Maybe this was what he didn't want Everard to see.

When they'd taken the scores from the library that day, Everard had been too ashamed by his own ranking to dare to look at his brothers' scores or any of the top ten. His partner, on the other hand, had scoured them, shocked. And ever since, Everard had wondered what on earth could have been so shocking. Now he would see for himself.

Everard scanned the sheet carefully, squinting at the lines in confusion. How could this be? Before age was added in, the order of the top ten varied greatly. Tenji placed first, then Tristan, Luka, and Cassian, who currently held tenth place. But after age was added in, they were placed in their current ranking order…except for Luka. He had actually placed second, and right above his name was an odd, unexplained addition of points, pushing him ahead of Tenji.

Everard clenched his jaw. His father and the Royal Council manipulated the ranking? If Father was willing to alter official ranking scores to make sure Luka came out on top, what else had he done? But as Everard continued to scan the individual scores on the various criteria, more shocking things surfaced.

Some of the princes scored terribly low in areas like Behavior and Emotional Stability. However, those same people ranked incredibly high—outrageously high—on their Sense Potential. Three of them passed the maximum amount a prince could achieve. Was it even possible to do that? How could you exceed a ranking system? How could the Royal Council look at these outrageously high scores and act like they didn't know? How could they remain so calm when dealing with princes whose ability potential was frighteningly high? How could they not show awe, fear, or favoritism?

Or had they?

Everard's heart chilled. All those times his father treated Everard kindly and acknowledged him were only when his friend had been around. And the Royal Council frequently held private training sessions with each of the three with the highest sense potential.

They weren't *ignoring* the scores.

They were trying to keep them hidden.

Suddenly, he remembered something his partner had said to him long ago—before all of this, before there was ever a plan. *And in case you think I'm doing too much on your behalf, let me assure you. I also have something I want. So trust me and let me worry about the labyrinth.*

Why had Everard never wondered—or cared or even *asked*—what his partner wanted? The only thing his partner ever mentioned in all of this had been how much he hated having a sense, and how good it was that Everard didn't have one.

Everard's eyes widened and his grip tightened on the papers he held as he stared at the wall. The spirit of the labyrinth was known as a *Sense Thief*. His partner had told him, over and over, but he'd gone unheard and ignored by Everard: *You're lucky you were born without a sense; all they cause is trouble.*

Was it possible his partner wanted his sense removed? He wanted it to be *taken* from him?

Then a far worse realization came over Everard, causing the papers to slip from his grasp and flutter to the ground. *The spirit.* When he'd summoned it all those months ago to ask for help, the spirit had noticed his partner. It had *known* he had a sense. If it knew that much at first glance, then surely it recognized exactly how much ability his partner had. The spirit wanted *his friend*. Because his friend's sense potential was the greatest out of all ten princes.

Everard closed his eyes. He was an idiot, a fool, and an awful friend. He had been so blinded by his own worries that he never considered asking his partner about his. And then Everard had sent him to his probable doom.

His friend never spoke about himself. He dodged questions directed at him and his past. Somehow, he had successfully evaded having anyone important know anything about him. And now, seeing his friend's scores in each criterion of the ranking revealed the very thing Everard had seen but never really noticed: He knew nothing about his closest friend.

Everard shoved all the papers back into the case, closed it, and flew from his room with the case clasped tightly in his hands. He burst into Michal's room, too overwhelmed by all of it to keep everything to himself anymore.

His eyes must've looked wild because Michal stood from his desk and asked, "What is it, Everard?"

Throwing the case on his brother's bed, Everard popped it open, causing the papers to spill out. He shoved the rankings into Michal's face, breathing hard. Pacing the room, Everard's eyes shifted back and forth from the floor to his brother's face as he looked through the pages.

Michal's eyes widened. "Where did you get these?"

"Who do you think?" Everard asked, running a hand through his brown hair. "He told me not to look at this; he told me to hide it while he was gone."

Michal stared at him, then back at the ranking. "But…" his voice trailed off as he searched for words Everard knew weren't there.

"Michal," Everard said, fidgeting with the sleeves of his jacket. "I think the Sense Thief wants him."

45

The Mire's Call

"LIGHT." TRISTAN'S VOICE BROKE THROUGH HIS MENTAL fog and Kai looked up. Sure enough, a dim light glowed in the distance. This was the shortest tunnel they had ever crossed through. Or maybe time seemed to fly by with a greater speed the longer they were here. He had no idea how long they'd been in the labyrinth. Two months? Three? Four? He had no clue, and he didn't want to ask someone who might actually know. In fact, Kai couldn't bring himself to say anything.

Kai's mind was consumed with the image of Sage holding Cassian's lifeless body in his arms. What Luka had said back in the Minotaur's cave was true and cut deeper than any wound he had ever received. If he'd released his pride for once, Cassian would still be alive. It tore Kai apart inside to have that reality and weight on his shoulders.

Cassian's blood was on his hands, and he couldn't do anything to wash it off.

Pride. It was his damn pride that caused him to fight with the others back home in Reudinia. It was pride that caused him to keep his distance from the others when they reached the labyrinth. It was pride that caused him to argue and fight with Luka. It was pride that caused him to neglect the others in his group and kill Cassian. It was time to let go of that bloody, guilty pride. No matter how long it took.

They left the tunnel behind them, pausing at the sight of a long stretch of marsh. Kai wrinkled his nose. The marsh was sticky and warm, but a hell of a lot better than the bitter cold or sizzling heat in the last two blasted labyrinth sections. He scanned the mush of ground and grimaced. Weather aside, marshes varied in depth and could be difficult to swim through. They would need to either tread carefully or somehow be blessed with a boat. And, since there wasn't a boat in sight, it seemed treading was their only option.

Over the next four days, they trudged through the soppy earth in single file. No creatures seemed to dwell in the depths as the water remained still and unmoving, and no end was in sight.

The skin around Kai's ribs squeezed, and his tongue stuck to the roof of his parched mouth. Tristan and Luka removed the vegetation as much as they could from the dense water they gathered so they could drink something and eat the vegetation for food. All of it tasted foul, but Kai needed food and water somehow, so he didn't complain.

By the fifth day, a gloom cast over them. A sinister feeling crawled into Kai's mind, and a shiver ran up his spine. The marsh was eerily quiet except for creepy echoes that almost sounded like distant voices. A thick, dense mist covered everything. A small sliver of mushy land ran through the marshes like veins. Cobwebs hung from the few dead trees found there. But the eeriest thing about the marsh was the glimmer of blue lights occasionally brushing through the fog around them. Whenever Kai passed them, it sounded like someone was breathing in his ear. They were so fast and slight he thought he'd been imagining them at first. Honestly, it spooked him more than he wanted to admit.

The blue lights continued to glimmer throughout the day and as the gray sky darkened, Luka stopped, causing the rest of the line to stop as well. "Something doesn't seem right," he muttered.

It's the bloody labyrinth, Kai thought. But he kept his mouth shut.

"When does it ever feel right here?" Jovian asked, flashing a smile in Luka's direction before turning his head to scan the area.

Suddenly, several blue lights darted through the mist and swirled wildly around them. Screaming, crying, and laughing voices circled him and filled Kai's head until unprompted flames erupted around him and the others. He opened his mouth to warn them, but they and the marsh dissolved before him, and the flames grew fierce and tall.

Kai whirled around, searching the flames for any sign of the others. What was bloody going on?

A shadow sprinted through the flames toward him. Then another. And suddenly five cloaked men with knives leapt from the flames. Kai lunged and ducked, dodging their swipes and kicks. One of their kicks landed squarely on his chest, and he stumbled back. He hit a wall. Kai's gaze darted around, taking in the familiar room that had risen around him, and he knew: he was reliving a nightmare.

The Royal Academy of Princes burned with flames Kai had created as he fought for his life. Kai's muscles strained, and his heart pounded as he blocked the assassins' blows with only his arms and legs. Their knives sliced into his skin, and the blistering heat of the flames swarmed him. He turned his head toward the door of the room. Could he reach it before the assassins killed him?

"Kai?" The flames and the Royal Academy faded as Kai turned to see Cassian looking up at him. Then one of the assassins sliced Cassian's neck, his blood spilling from the wound and drenching his clothes.

"No!" Kai dove for the assassin, but he vanished along with Cassian. Kai stumbled forward and fell until he splashed into shallow water. He glanced behind him at the place where the assassins and Cassian had vanished.

Reudinia's king rose out of the shadows holding a small, woven blade. He looked at Kai as if he were an insect needing to be squashed. "I should have killed you long ago."

King Léon sprang at him with the dagger and Kai lifted his arms to block but then sank deeper into the water. Hands seized his body and pulled him under. He jerked and looked down only to find his parents hauling him beneath the surface. His father reached for his throat and squeezed; Kai struggled for air, but his parents' grip became tighter and tighter and Kai's vision grew darker and darker.

The darkness overtook him, and he fell into an endless void. A familiar unsettling laugh reverberated through the darkness and shook Kai to the bone. Purple, blazing eyes flickered to life and a shadowy hand reached for him, closing around his heart. Piercing pain shot through Kai's entire body and he screamed.

"Die, Child of Flame. Die!"

Tristan stood in darkness until sobs and weeping broke through the silence, followed by the steady thuds of a beating. What was this? Tristan turned toward a door.

The heavy-looking door swung open on its own and inside was the familiar stairway of Tristan's childhood home. The sounds came from up the steps.

When Tristan couldn't handle it any longer, he rushed up the steps, ran down the hall, and burst into his brother's room.

"Father, that's enough!" he shouted, his voice coming out differently. It sounded more like a child's voice than his own.

His father paused mid-swing and faced Tristan. He reeked of alcohol and his doublet was ruffled and dirty. "What did you say to me, *boy*?" he bellowed. Tristan winced. "Since when did you learn to be a father?"

Slap! His father backhanded Tristan across the face. "Shut your mouth or I'll shut it for you."

Angry tears pricked Tristan's eyes and heat swirled in his gut as he glared at his father and rubbed his stinging cheek. Behind his father, Milo cowered in the corner of the room, beaten and bruised, tears streaming down his face. Milo's bed was overturned, his desk a mess, and his clothes were strewn all over the floor.

"Why are you looking at me like that?" His father picked up a vase from the desk and smashed it against the wall. "Don't you look at me like that, you fool!" *Smack!* Another slap met Tristan's face and he found himself stumbling into another memory.

"TRISTAN!"

Smash!

"Tristan, clean up this mess!"

Tristan, his heart quaking, found himself standing, looking over a mess of glass and spilled alcohol, his little brother huddled under a table nearby. Tristan bent slowly and began picking up shards of glass, accidentally cutting his fingers.

"Clean faster! Don't look up!"

He scrubbed at the floor, but the floor didn't clean, and his hands bled more and more.

"Father, I'm bleeding," he said.

"Shut your mouth! Be quiet!" A tray smacked Tristan's head, and it throbbed excruciatingly. Tears blurred his vision as Tristan rubbed his head and scrubbed the floor, keeping his eyes down. Someone knocked at the door.

Tristan turned his head. A younger version of Archie stepped into the room, and Father glared at him. "Who are *you*? What are you doing here? Get out!"

Slowly, Archie's figure morphed from child to adult.

…This was different. This wasn't from his memories. Tristan stood and searched the room. The glass faded, Milo vanished, and only Archie and his father remained. Tristan frowned in confusion and clenched his bleeding hands into fists. What was happening?

His father marched straight up to Archie and whacked him hard—just like the dragon's tail—into the farthest wall. Archie's body crumpled in a heap.

"No!" Tristan raced toward his friend, skidding to a stop and staring down at his broken body. Archie whimpered, "I want to go home…I want to go home!"

Tristan clutched his head. Archie wasn't dead. Archie couldn't be dead. He turned and ran from the house, his father's voice booming after him, "Get back here, boy! Get back here!"

Something seized his leg causing Tristan to trip and sprawl onto the ground. Water stretched out before and around him, and he twisted to see Archie's broken fingers clutching his leg. Horror spread through Tristan's chest as Archie's stared at him, hair disheveled, eyes pleading. "Don't leave me."

Tristan struggled to pull himself out of Archie's grip, but Archie was strong, too strong. Archie's face darkened. "I said don't leave me," he growled. And then, with a snarl, he pulled Tristan into water.

Thrashing and kicking violently, Tristan fought to get out of Archie's tight grip and back above water. But he couldn't shake Archie off. His heart thudded in his ears as he stared up at the surface of the water drifting further and further away. His lungs stung and burned. He couldn't breathe.

I'm sorry, Archie. I'm sorry.

Luka stared down a corridor in the castle he knew as home. He blinked. How did he get here? Voices echoed down the hall, so he walked in that direction until he found the room they emanated from. He reached for the handle, but the door opened on its own and he stepped inside.

The door opened into the dining room and his family—minus Everard and his mother—was eating around the table.

His father stopped eating and looked up at Luka from across the room. "Luka, be the best. You must always be the best."

Luka glowered at him, anger rising in his chest. "But I wasn't the best. Tenji was."

The image of his father contorted into Tenji. His family and the dining room faded away, and Tenji and Luka stood together in darkness. Tenji stared at Luka before he stalked closer. "How are you always ahead of me? I study, work hard, and seem to be better than you in every area, yet you always come out on top. How?"

Luka's voice floated through the air even though he hadn't opened his mouth. "I don't know, Tenji. Why are you so determined to beat me?"

Tenji's expression darkened. "I need to prove someone wrong," he replied and looked away.

"I'm sorry, Tenji," Luka whispered at last. "I'm sorry I never knew. I'm sorry I took the place you deserved."

Kai's voice filled the dark atmosphere around Luka, sharp and snarling. "You're always bossing everyone around like you've been chosen to be our king. You're not even supposed to be in first place. Tenji was!"

Luka turned to find Kai glaring at him, red hair blazing. Behind him stood a faded image of his grandfather, King Darian.

"The entire system is messed up. And it's *your* father who allows it to be this way. Some king he is."

Luka gritted his teeth, hands curling into fists. "I know. You're right. Your grandfather was the better king. I'm nothing."

Tenji stepped back into view. "You never were the best, Luka. You're only at the top because your father made sure of it."

Archie appeared out of smoke. "The one time I back you up, you chicken out just because Tenji is a better leader than you."

"He's just afraid if he stands against Tenji, no one will follow him." Kai strode closer. "Your father being a king doesn't instantly make you a leader, daddy's boy. You're more like a flower trying to stand tall but shifting whichever direction the wind blows. A weakling who does whatever gets him the most attention." Kai's voice echoed around him.

Tenji leaned closer to Luka. "I died to keep the others alive. What did *you* do? Three have died since you took leadership."

Luka turned away from him, desperately trying to escape the words. But as he turned, Cassian, Archie, and Ruben appeared. Luka stumbled back, and Tenji and Kai seized his arms. Before he could react, they yanked him toward a pool of water. Luka struggled in their impossibly tight grasps, unable to wrench himself free.

"Let me go!"

Tenji and Kai dove into the pool, dragging him in after. Water closed around Luka's body, locking him away from air. He fought against Tenji and Kai as they dragged him deeper and deeper down, but they were too strong.

They were drowning him.

One moment, Sage paused to look around; the next, blue lights surrounded them, and a sweet song rose from the swamp. Almost immediately, Draven dropped to his knees and squeezed his head as if he was being tortured. Luka stumbled farther into the swamp away from them and Jovian screamed, his face contorting with a fear she had never seen on him before he fell into the water.

"Jovian!" she rushed to help him. What in the world was going on? But before she could pull Jovian out of the water, something began pulling him down. Something long and flickering twisted below the surface. "No!" Sage flashed light at whatever was in the water and it screeched, releasing Jovian. Sage dragged him back onto the mushy earth, but he clutched his head and kept screaming.

What was happening?

"No!" Kai cried out from somewhere behind her. Sage turned back to see Kai stumble into the water, green, humanoid hands pulling him down into the water.

Sage ran for Kai just as she heard several more splashes. She turned to see Tristan and Draven being dragged into the water, and Luka was gone. Looking around for Luka, Sage came eye to eye with a beautiful girl. A girl with long, green hair; green eyes; and green skin. Despite the odd color of her skin, the girl was beautiful. Stunning. The girl stared at her and cocked her head, her lips moving with the song echoing loud and clear around them. A fish tail flickered behind her.

Sirens.

What could she do? Sage knew sirens' songs drew men in, so this song would incapacitate the princes...which left only Sage to save them. Her heart sped and her chest squeezed. She took a deep breath. *Think, Sage, think!*

Her eyes focused on Jovian's writhing figure, and she set her jaw. She wasn't going to fail them. She darted toward Jovian, dropped to his side, and slapped him across the face. The haze in Jovian's eyes cleared and his face smoothed. Then his gaze met hers. The squeeze in Sage's chest eased.

"Jovian, we're being attacked by sirens. They're trying to drown everyone."

Jovian jerked up and looked around.

"Luka disappeared somewhere over there, and Draven and Tristan went under there." Sage gestured vaguely, pulling off her boots and throwing her sword to the ground. "I'm going after Kai," she informed him before she turned and dove into the water. Cool water swept against her skin as she swam deeper and deeper, fighting against the force resisting her dive. She searched the murky water frantically until she spotted Kai's bright hair. Sirens swarmed him.

Sage released her light, causing several hisses and a siren darted toward her, sharp teeth bared. Sage thrust a palm at the siren and released a ray. It shot through the siren's body, and the siren screamed. Sage dove deeper, shining her light brighter.

Her lungs screamed, desperate for air. Would she make it in time? Was Kai even still alive?

When she reached Kai, the sirens jerked away from him, too blinded by her light. Sage wrapped her arms around Kai's body, pushing against the marsh floor and using her light speed to flash up to the surface. She gasped for air as she burst through the surface of the water and hauled Kai onto land before searching for the others. Jovian dragged Draven back to land, shooting muddy clumps of rock and land at the sirens coming for him. Sage turned her attention back to Kai.

Kai coughed out spurts of water and raked in air, his gaze still dazed and unseeing.

Sage smacked him across the face, partially to wake him up, partially out of relief he was still alive, but also partially to release her pent-up anger at him for the stiff headedness which led to Cassian's death. His brown eyes cleared, then found her as he gripped the cheek she'd slapped.

"Sirens!" she yelled at Kai, before taking off and diving into the water where Tristan had disappeared.

A swarm of sirens circled toward her. She flashed her bright light at them and kept swimming. Then she spotted Tristan, struggling against their pull.

Shooting her rays at the sirens holding him down, Sage grabbed Tristan and yanked him upward, but a siren's hand grasped her leg and dragged her back down. Sage lost her grip on Tristan.

Sage fought to hold in her breath as Tristan and the surface drifted above her. She looked down at the siren hauling her down and kicked at the creature with her free leg, releasing more light. The siren hissed but didn't let go.

Sage's lungs burned for air, making her more desperate. Would she drown down here? Was it her turn to die? She peered up at the distant surface and her gaze focused on Tristan. No. If she died, so did Tristan.

Sage aimed a hand at the siren, forcing herself to focus, and shot a ray through the siren's head. With one more mighty kick at the siren's face, Sage was released.

Sage swam upward, seized Tristan, and dragged him after her with all the strength left in her body. She exploded from the water, gasping for breath, and Draven helped pull her and Tristan out. But Tristan didn't respond when he was laid out on the ground. Sage stared at him as Draven pressed hard on Tristan's chest in several short pulses. Still, Tristan didn't respond.

Draven's face tensed.

Sage pressed her palms to her cheeks, her heart speeding up

and tears burning her eyes. Was she too late? Was he dead?

Then water splashed out of Tristan's mouth, and he hacked.

Sage dropped her arms and sagged. Alive. He was alive.

But the sirens' song pulled Sage's attention back to their battle. Jovian strained, dragging a soaking Luka back on land, and Kai blasted any siren that showed her head above water. Draven turned and threw out an arm. Shadows seized several sirens and swallowed them.

Thank goodness. Everyone was out.

Sage pulled on her boots, grabbed her sword, and jumped up. "Run!" she shouted.

Without hesitation, the other princes raced down the mushy strain of earth and away from the hundreds of sirens swimming after them. Blue lights flickered around Sage, the voices coming from them strangely familiar—her brother, her parents, Cassian…

But Sage didn't stop. She didn't dare. Instead, she kept running after Luka, her eyes focused on his back. The group didn't stop running until they reached a large, solid-looking piece of land where they collapsed in a heap.

"What happened back there?" Luka asked, rubbing his head. "I knew sirens could pull men into a trance, but that was nothing like I've ever imagined."

No one replied.

Blue lights flickered through the foggy marshes. Sage eyed them. She vaguely remembered reading something about marsh fairies as a child; maybe they had something to do with this too. "Maybe the sirens and those blue fairies were working together?" she suggested. "The fairies make odd sounds."

Everyone watched the blue lights swirling through the marsh.

"Perhaps you're right," Luka muttered, before he ran a hand through his hair, an uneasy expression on his face. "What did you see?"

Again, no one spoke.

Draven turned his sharp gaze to Jovian and broke the silence. "How did you break your trance? It felt so real. I couldn't see a way out."

Jovian nodded to her. "Sage woke me."

Everyone's gaze turned to Sage, and she watched as they mentally calculated who had woken them, and finally all seemed to reach the same realization: Sage had been the first to break the trance. A trance she'd never had. Jovian leaned toward her and grinned. "How did you break your trance, Sage?"

She fidgeted with her jacket. Not sure what they had experienced, she panicked, unable to think of a reason for how she *woke* as they said. "I—I just…" but the words failed to come. She could think of nothing. All she could do was stare at the five men before her.

Realization swept over Draven's face. But he couldn't help her this time.

"Why aren't you answering?" asked Jovian again, his eyes narrowing.

Sage dropped her gaze. "I—I just used my sense. It helped clear my mind," she lied, knowing it was a bad one.

"Well, that sounds like the absolute truth," Jovian said sarcastically. His chuckle echoed in the empty marsh. "It's almost as if you didn't experience the trance at all…"

Sage tensed as she racked her brain for a response. But she had never been gifted at lying. She hadn't meant to be pretending to be someone she wasn't, especially this long. She hadn't meant to be in this situation at all.

"Wait," Luka said, his voice genuinely surprised. "Did you really not fall into a trance in the first place?"

Looking back up at them, Sage still struggled to find words. Why couldn't she think of anything? Why couldn't she answer them?

Luka searched her eyes, as if trying to read her response for himself. "You didn't, did you? But how?"

"You're hiding something," Jovian said.

Her gaze found Draven again, but he only mouthed, *Tell them.*

Sage clutched her jacket, her heart pounding in her ears, but she couldn't bring herself to say it. Staring at their faces she felt the gravity of having lied to them for *months*. How would they react? Would they hate her for it?

Then Jovian jumped up, his eyes wide, pointing at her. "No way! I know what it is!"

Sage squeezed her jacket so hard her hands hurt, and her breath stilled in her chest. Had he figured her out?

Luka, Tristan, Draven, and Kai eyed Jovian, as if unsure whether he was serious or about to crack a joke.

Jovian laughed hard. "I can't be-*lieve* I didn't figure this out months ago. It's so obvious."

"What?" asked Kai, harshly. "Just spit it out already."

Sage couldn't breathe. Her secret was out. Would they hate her? Desert her? Mistreat her?

But then Jovian shook his head and put his hands on his hips. "Oh, no, this is too funny. I want to see if you can figure it out yourselves."

Holding up a fist, Kai scowled. "Tell us or I'll pummel you."

Laughing, Jovian waved a dismissive hand at Kai. "Fine, fine, I'll give you a hint. All you have to do is think about all we know about Sage." Jovian turned his mischievous smile on her, eyes glinting. "He avoids undressing to any degree, goes on long adventures when taking a restroom break, never has to shave, behaves strangely—and he's unaffected by sirens, which really only affect *men*."

Luka's eye widened, and he and Tristan jerked their attention to Sage, as if truly seeing her for the first time.

Nausea churned in Sage's gut, and she forgot to breathe. She was found out. Her body went rigid and her mind blank. All she could do was watch Luka slowly rise to his feet. Sage braced herself for the worst.

"Sage," Luka's voice was quiet, solemn. "Are you a woman?"

46

Faven

KAI STARED AT LUKA AS IF HE'D SPOKEN A FOREIGN
language. What had he just said? Did he just ask Sage if he was a
woman? Kai couldn't help but laugh. This had to be a joke.

"He may be pretty, but he's not a girl," he said as he smiled
at the others, expecting them to laugh with him. But no one did.
Instead, they all watched Sage, as if they thought Luka was
serious. As if they thought Sage might actually be a girl.

"Is it true?" Tristan asked.

Kai's smile melted, and he shifted his gaze to Sage, expecting
to see his face filled with offense. But what he saw wasn't anger.
Instead, Sage's face was pale, his eyes wide, his body unmoving.
Kai waited for Sage to say something. Anything. But he didn't.

Why was Sage reacting as if what Luka said was true?

"Wait—wait, wait, wait, *wait*!" he exploded, jumping up. He stared at Sage. "Is he bloody *right*?"

Sage dropped his—or her—gaze, and his—or her—face flushed. He or she fidgeted with his or her jacket. This was too confusing, too shocking. No—this was infuriating! Kai clenched his fists and his face heated.

"Why aren't you saying anything?" Kai demanded.

"It must be true then," Luka answered, crossing his arms over his chest.

Jovian fell to the ground, laughing hysterically. "The pretty boy is pretty because he's actually a she." He continued to cackle, rolling on the ground.

Tristan's expression was unreadable, and Draven sat, looking undisturbed by this revelation.

Steam lifted from Kai's head, arms, and shoulders. He couldn't contain it. He exploded. "A girl? A bloody girl? How can you be a girl?" he exclaimed. How did he miss it? How could he have been so foolishly blind? "This whole time…all these months… you were a woman?"

Sage dropped to her knees and clasped hands over her heart. Her face strained and she avoided their eyes. "I'm sorry. Please understand, I didn't mean for all this to happen or for me to be in this situation. And when it did happen, I didn't know what to do other than keep pretending. I'm sorry."

Silence rested among the group as the gravity of what she said sank in. Sage was a woman. Sage was a woman. Sage was a—Kai couldn't make himself believe it, even though he could see, and always had seen, her femininity. It was too weird. Too different. He had believed for too long that she was someone else.

Finally, Luka broke the silence. "Why?"

Part of Kai wanted to march off. He didn't want to hear any explanations. The other part of him kept him where he was, listening. But he was on edge. Ready to shut her down at any moment.

Sage sighed and dropped her clasped hands to her lap. She scanned the group before she began. "Prince Sage is my younger brother. I'm his older sister, Princess Faven. My family serves as envoys for Reudinia in the kingdom of Hallon, so I had never been ranked like my brother had. Thus, I came to Reudinia to be assessed."

Sage, or Faven—whatever her name was—shifted and pressed a hand to her cheek.

"How I came to pretend to be my brother is hard to explain." She pressed her other hand to her cheek and took a deep breath. "I wanted to find out some information," she said hesitantly. "The information was in the Royal Academy for Princes, so I dressed up as a boy to sneak in, but accidentally ran into Luka who directed me to the assessments. Unsure what to do, I ended up taking the assessment in my brother's place. And that's how I ended up here?" she finished as if it were a question before looking at them, as if waiting to see if they'd approve of her explanation. "I got kidnapped with the lot of you, and I was afraid you would leave me behind if you found out the truth, so I decided it would be best to keep pretending. I really am sorry."

That was her explanation? Kai wasn't sure if knowing the story helped at all. For some reason, it made him angrier. Even though he couldn't place the anger, it was there, burning deep inside him. But he didn't know what to do with his anger either. As much as he would like to erupt, the memory of Cassian kept him in check. To be more precise, the image of Cassian's lifeless body in Sage's arms. So, instead, he sat down and clasped his left hand over his right fist and squeezed as hard as he could.

"So, you're saying you had no part in our abduction?" Jovian clarified. It was a good question, one everyone else was probably wondering. Kai knew he was. After all, if she'd lied about being a boy, then maybe she was lying about everything else. Tenji could've been right to suspect her. And whoever was the traitor would be the one to blame for all the deaths they'd suffered so far.

For a moment, a familiar glint glimmered in Sage's eyes. She stood up. "No. I'd never use other people as stepping stones to get what I want. It's cruel and selfish. I would never take a child—" her voice broke and her eyes watered. She paused to compose herself. "I just want to go home like everyone else."

No one replied. Even though Kai knew this woman could just be a talented liar, he found himself believing every word. No one could argue with what she said either. It was selfish to use others as tools to get through the labyrinth. Kai's eyes swept the group. If the traitor wasn't Sage, then who could it be?

No one spoke for the rest of the evening.

Kai couldn't sleep that night. He stared up at the night sky, taking in the new knowledge of Sage being a woman. He rehearsed every memory of their interactions: how she'd chased after him in the beginning. How flustered and determined she'd been about keeping her clothes on when he stripped by the river to wash the forest dragon sludge off. How she'd fought with him against the goblins. How she'd waited until night had fallen to wash in the desert spring. How she'd saved him from the skeletal shadow creature. How she'd held Cassian and wept… Kai gritted his teeth, anger and frustration building in his chest. It was so obvious in hindsight. How had he missed it before?

And in a small place in the back of his mind, Kai felt an immense sense of relief. A relief that freaked him out more than any other thought or emotion.

That night, Sage fidgeted restlessly, lying wide awake. The princes' reactions to her secret lingered in her mind and the silence that had followed still echoed deep within her. After a while, Sage got up and slipped away from camp. She sat facing the gloomy swamp that stretched before them. Mist and blue flickering lights filled the air around her. What would happen to her now?

She hadn't been able to bring herself to tell them the whole story. Partially for Luka's sake, knowing Everard was his younger brother, and partially because she still didn't know who his partner was.

A shadow cast over her, blocking the light of the moon. When Sage glanced over her shoulder, she found Draven standing over her. She turned away from him and said nothing. Silently, he crouched next to her.

"How are you doing?" Draven asked quietly.

Sage bit the inside of her cheek and looked down at her boots. "They hate me, don't they?"

Draven shifted and took a deep breath. "They're shocked. Once it's settled in, I'm sure they'll cool down." He paused. "Do you feel relieved at all? Weren't you tired of pretending?"

Yes. Sage couldn't deny that. She *had* been tired of pretending. Almost to the point of wishing the others could find out on their own. So why was she so upset now? "To be honest, I do feel a little relieved the secret is out."

Draven nodded. "It's nice. To no longer hide a secret you were guarding with your life."

"Are you referring to what happened back in the desert?"

Nodding again, Draven sighed. "My sense isn't the easiest for me to manage. It's dangerous. Even for me." He lifted his sleeves, exposing more scars along his arms. "I dreaded others finding out about it, but now I'm glad they know."

Sage sniffed. Maybe the others finding out about her wasn't such an awful thing. At least now she could really be herself.

"You said your real name is Faven, right?" Draven looked over her, scars highlighted by the moonlight, black hair falling over his forehead. She stared at him, her eyes watering. This was the first time she'd heard her name in months. She could be Faven again…

Finally, she nodded.

"Well, Faven, hopefully we'll be leaving the labyrinth soon, and you can see your brother."

Offering him a small smile, Faven turned to stare out over the swamp once more. "And I hope you can see the girl who is precious to you." Her gaze followed a blue light swirling over the water. "May I ask her name?"

Shifting in place, Draven hesitated. "Zinnia. Her name is Zinnia."

"Zinnia," Faven whispered. "Such a pretty name."

A small smile lifted Draven's face. "She's like a little sister to me. I'd protect her with my life." His smile faltered for a moment, and he looked down at Faven. "Can I ask something of you?"

Faven blinked. Draven never asked for help, much less from her. But as she looked into his sad eyes, she knew it was important. "What is it?"

"If—If I don't make it out of the labyrinth alive…would you watch over her for me?"

"You'll make it through. We all will."

Draven looked away. "But if I don't, will you?"

Studying Draven's sad profile, Faven slowly nodded. "I will. I promise."

"Thanks, Faven," Draven said, flashing her a small, relieved smile. "She should be with my butler, Birkett, at my house near Wilmight Drop." He leaned closer. "Please remember that."

Faven didn't see the point. They all would make it out. But since she'd made a promise, Faven chanted the information in her head until she finally fell asleep: Birkett, Draven's house, Wilmight Drop, Zinnia.

The next morning, they set off through the marsh once more. Faven kept her head low and followed the princes. No one shooed her away. No one told her to leave.

However, despite the stress of the situation, what Draven had said was true. She was done hiding, done lying. They knew. Whether or not they'd ever forgive her was another matter, but she didn't have to hide who she was anymore.

Silence hovered over them as the day wore on. Faven kept a vigilant eye on the water—searching for any movement, listening to distant splashes, waiting for the sirens to resurface. But there was nothing. Maybe they'd seen the last of the sirens.

Then, suddenly, a few heads bobbled out of the water and smiled sweetly at them. Taking a deep breath, Faven eyed the men around her, but they ignored the sirens' innocent appearances and steered clear of them. She released the breath she was holding. She'd rather not have to save them all—again.

The sirens sang more enchanting songs and Faven tensed, but the princes still showed no signs of being entranced. As the sirens realized the princes weren't responding to their songs, they reached their long, pale green arms up along the path. But the princes avoided their grasps, kicking and slapping away the sirens' arms.

Then, something shifted in the sirens' attention. More and more were turning their glaring gazes on Faven. She swallowed the growing lump in her throat. Did they know she was a woman? Did they know it was *she* who saved the others yesterday? She shot a look at the line of princes ahead of her. Did they notice the sirens' change of attention? Faven bit her lip and pulled at the collar of her jacket.

Suddenly, a siren sprung from the water and, before Faven could block her, tackled Faven into the water on the other side of the walkway.

Cool water embraced her as the siren's tight grasp pulled her farther away from the surface. Muffled bellows called out from above but seemed too distant already. Faven struggled and twisted in the siren's grasp, pulling at the siren's hair and kneeing her in the stomach. The siren's hold only tightened.

Faven flashed a blinding light, then fired a ray into the siren's chest. The siren released her, hissing and screaming, and Faven kicked her away and swam for the surface.

But then hundreds of other sirens blocked out the light that filtered into the water, enveloping her. Faven's gaze darted over the writhing mass of siren bodies around her, keeping her away from the surface as she swam in place. There was no way out.

Faven's heart drummed in her ears and her lungs screamed for air. She released another blast of light and fired rays in every direction. Several sirens screeched, but there were still so many. Images of Tenji's, Ruben's, and Cassian's dead bodies flickered in her mind. She didn't want to die.

A distant splash reverberated through the water, and just as Faven thought she couldn't hold her breath any longer, several sirens hissed and recoiled, mud reaching up from the ground and seizing them. More sirens scattered at the sight of a large shadow chasing them. Then a hand clenched Faven's arm—but this time it pulled her upward.

The surface shimmered above her, drawing closer and closer as someone pulled her up. Hope rose in her chest.

Finally, Faven's head broke the surface, and she sucked in a desperate heave of air. Luka and Tristan reached from the edge of the water and pulled her up onto the soft land. Jovian and Draven were standing along the edge, focusing on the water as Kai pulled himself out of the water after her.

Had he jumped in after her?

Once Kai exited the water, Tristan electrocuted the surface. Several muffled cries rose from the marsh.

"Are you okay?" Luka asked, crouching next to her when she didn't speak.

Faven just nodded and stared at them, heaving in air.

"You all…you…saved me." She couldn't believe it. Even though she'd lied to them about being a prince, even though she'd thought they would leave her behind given the chance.

They'd saved her life instead.

"Well, you've saved our lives before," Luka responded. Tristan offered her a small smile, and Jovian winked at her. Kai remained quiet, his focus on squeezing the water from his clothes, red hair dripping.

Luka straightened from where he crouched, his gaze resting on Kai as well. "Good to see you working as part of the *team* for once instead of deciding to chase after the sirens over saving Faven's life."

Kai froze mid-squeeze. He turned his head in Luka's direction, his brown eyes finding Luka's blue one. "I'm not an idiot, and I'm not as heartless as you make me out to be. Yes, it was my fault Cassian died. If I could go back and trade my life for his, I'd do it in a bloody heartbeat. I'm not letting anyone else die on my watch, got it?"

Tristan, Jovian, and Draven glanced between the two of them, wordless, and Jovian arched an eyebrow.

Luka stared at Kai with his hands on his hips, face serious. "Finally, something we can agree on."

Kai said nothing and turned away.

Turning back to the others, Luka strode on down the thin path. "Let's keep moving."

Faven bit her lip, her eyes lingering on Kai. He kept his head turned away from them, his shoulders curved, and his fists clenched so tightly his knuckles paled. While she agreed Kai had acted selfishly and foolishly in the Minotaur's cave, she didn't blame Cassian's death on him. She blamed it on herself and her inability to heal him. Just like Ruben. But Faven couldn't bring herself to say a single thing to Kai or Luka. Instead, she dropped her gaze and followed the line of princes ahead of her.

But that didn't stop her from worrying about Kai. She'd seen how dismal and quiet he'd become since Cassian's death. And she didn't like it.

The sirens must've decided to stay away after Tristan electrocuted them because they didn't appear again. And as it grew darker, Faven glowed to help light the path through the mist. Kai lit some wood from a dead tree on fire to carry as torches while they continued their trek, the others accepting them with silent accession.

A little while later, something loomed ahead of them. Faven's eyes widened and her heart lifted. The gate leading to the fifth and final section of the labyrinth.

"Is it just me, or do the sections feel like they've been getting shorter?" Jovian asked.

"It does seem to be that way," Luka agreed, his gaze remaining on the gate. "Let's keep moving."

No one protested. In fact, Faven quickened her pace. They were so close.

Before long, she stood at the foot of the gate, staring at a spoked wheel standing horizontally on the ground. Faven's gaze lifted to the levers, pipes, wheels, and waterways that were intricately built around the gate.

"Another puzzle," Jovian murmured with a grimace. "What a surprise."

The traitor stared into the mirky waters of the marsh. The illusions from the siren's enchantment and Sage's—or Faven's—words buzzed in his brain. Cruel and selfish, she'd called him. But she wasn't wrong. He'd done all of this. He'd brought them here. He'd killed Tenji, Ruben, Cassian, and Archie. All to get rid of his sense. Was it really as worthwhile as he'd thought it would be?

"Maybe not if removing your sense was the ultimate objective. But our overall plan will be worth it, don't you think?"

The traitor's face contorted in the darkness. Suddenly, he wasn't so sure. All the suffering, all the deaths just didn't seem worthwhile anymore. No matter how much he wanted to be rid of his sense.

47
The One who Sees

AS LUKA AND THE OTHERS EXAMINED THE NEW PUZZLE, Draven found he could hardly focus. Instead, he stared at the menacing gate, dreading what was in store for them on the other side of those doors. Now that he was only a gate away, any determination or courage he'd had before melted away. Fear made his head swim. Draven winced and shook his head.

The shadows were loud. So loud. Deafening. And the shadow beast's voice drowned out the words and noises of the people around him once again. *Run*, it hissed. *Leave the others behind. Let them die.*

Gripping his head, Draven gritted his teeth. *No, I can't do that. I won't.* He was tired of living in constant fear. He wanted to be free.

Desert the others, the shadow beast growled. *If you don't, you'll never see her again.*

Zinnia. His heart ached at the thought of her. But…Draven glanced around at Luka, Jovian, Faven, Kai, and Tristan. He *couldn't* do nothing; he couldn't let them die. Even if it meant never seeing Zinnia again.

After all, that's why he'd allowed himself to be captured and brought to the labyrinth. Draven closed his eyes, his mind drawn back to a night three years ago. A night when Zinnia had stepped into his lonely life like the moon on a dark night and changed him forever. His moon, his Zinnia. Gentle. Bright.

Twenty-year-old Draven sat in the rattling carriage with the curtains drawn tightly shut to keep the light from filtering through. He stared into the gloom of the empty carriage; it was only him and his shadows, and the darkness swarmed around him as he wallowed. Draven was running away again. That's what this was. Running away.

After seeing so many people run from him in fear or seeing the shadow beast overtake him and hurt people he cared about, Draven had decided it was best if he kept away from people. At least, until he could learn how to control his sense. Or that was what he had told himself. Draven's face darkened. Easier said than done.

He'd had such insignificant progress in his sense control that he'd almost given up all hope of ever overcoming it. Whenever episodes drowned out everything else, he would retreat to the shadows. For only the shadows loved him.

The carriage came to a stop, and the door opened. A royal guard stood outside and Draven stepped out into the light, flinching at the brightness. As his eyes adjusted, he found himself at the front doors of their country house. It was blindingly white with a blue-tiled rooftop and white pillars. Flowers decorated the lawn in front. Draven hated it.

An older manservant rushed from the house and gathered Draven's luggage, but he didn't wait. Draven plunged into the dark, cool house, relieved to be free from the light of the sun. He hurried up the steps and down the hall, closing curtains as he went, until he reached his room. Inside was a neat bed, open curtains, a desk, and a wardrobe. He went to the windows first and shut the curtains there too. The manservant, who turned out to be the butler, followed Draven inside with his bags.

"No! Take those to the room next door," Draven barked. Then he waved to the furniture in the room. "Get rid of all this and have someone barricade the windows. Tell them I want to be locked in my room each night."

Without an explanation, Draven marched back out of the room, ignoring the butler's stare.

It had been more than ten years since Draven had spent time in this house, so he moved silently through the rooms and halls, stopping to look at portraits of his family when they'd all been clueless and young. Even he had been naïve back then. Before his abilities took form. Before the first incident.

When Draven returned to his room, he found it stripped of furniture with the windows boarded shut. He offered the butler a pleased smile and nodded as the butler closed the door and locked him in. Draven approached the back wall slowly and leaned against it as he sank to the floor of the empty room. Alone again.

The next morning, Draven surveyed the scrapes along the floorboards and the walls and sighed. He stared at the stream of light peeping through a crack in the boards over the windows in silence, wishing for a similar light to squeeze through any cracks he had inside and dissipate his inner darkness.

A tentative knock rapped at the door.

"It's safe," Draven called. For now.

The door was unlocked, and the butler pushed it open. There was a moment of silence as the butler took in the room. However, instead of running in fear, the butler stepped aside, and a few maids entered with Draven's luggage.

Over the next few days, the same routine happened every morning and evening. Between the two, Draven walked along the fields and returned the greetings of those brave enough to meet him. He ignored the people who were too afraid to speak to him.

On the fifth day, a disturbance rose outside while he was eating breakfast. Draven faced the butler, Birkett. "What's the meaning of that ruckus?"

"Some hunters from the kingdom of Velykov," was his simple reply.

"Velykov? What are they doing so far into Reudinia? Are they even allowed to be on Reudinian land?"

Birkett shook his head.

Ah, hence the commotion. This peaked Draven's hard-to-win interest. Nothing was interesting when a shadow beast whispered to you on the daily. He stood and headed for the door.

Draven walked by a storage room on his way out.

Bang!

He paused and stared at the door of the storage room where the sound had come from. Creaking the door open, Draven peered inside. A large table stood in the center and piles of oddities were scattered throughout the room. As Draven stepped inside, a bucket rolled across the floor. He sidestepped more buckets and eased toward a wardrobe in the corner of the room. Then he yanked it open, jumping back. Nothing inside. Draven picked up a shovel that leaned against the wardrobe and poked the blankets stashed at the bottom. Nothing.

The bucket must've fallen on its own. Draven stepped back in the way he'd come and accidentally kicked the fallen bucket, inadvertently knocking over the pile of buckets by the door. Draven paused in surprise as a tiny fox pup sprawled out of one of them and onto the floor in front of him. A Fennec fox.

The fox squeaked and dashed under a chair in the corner, trembling as it tucked its large ears back. Draven slowly crouched down near the chair and stared into the pup's big brown eyes. The fox didn't hiss. It just quivered and stared back at him.

Just down the hall, someone pounded on the servants' door. Draven glanced up at the partially open doorway to see Birkett heading for the entrance. Birkett paused by the storage room and peered at him before continuing toward the pounding. Flicking another look at the fox, Draven stood and followed after Birkett, standing back as the butler opened the door. Eight large men stood in the door frame. Their tan and black clothing declared they were Velykovian. They loved their muted colors, and Draven didn't blame them.

"Our game went through your window," the shortest and stockiest of the bunch said, his accent thick with 'ee's instead of 'i's and 'v's instead of 'w's. "May we come in to retrieve it?"

Game? Were they referring to the small fox? Draven frowned. All this for a fox pup?

"I'm afraid you can't come in," Birkett replied sharply.

"We only want our game, then we'll be on our way. We promise we aren't here to loot or steal."

"No," Birkett said tightly.

They murmured amongst themselves, and one tall, beefy man stalked closer, but the stocky one stopped him. "Is it possible for only one of us to retrieve it? You can choose who it is. Or bring us the game yourself. We've been chasing this particular game for a while. It's mighty quick, and we would prefer not to lose it now."

Draven stepped into view, his blood boiling under his skin. "This is Reudinian territory. You lost your game the moment it crossed onto our land. Now leave and stop pestering my servants."

Three of the eight stepped back at the sight of him, their eyes darting to the stocky prick. The other five straightened, as if ready to battle.

"We aren't leaving without our game," spat the leader. "You're just a kid. Did your parents give you this place?"

Draven wasn't a kid, but he was at least twenty years younger than this pudge, so he guessed it probably counted.

"Yes," he answered, undeterred by the smiles they gave at his admittance. "However, my home in the capital I gave to my parents. I suppose that makes up for it."

The man's smile melted into a glare. "You think you're special, huh?"

"No," Draven said as he stared into the other man's eyes. "I think I'm dangerous."

A few of them chuckled weakly, but others stepped back and exchanged nervous glances. One of them leaned toward their leader. In hushed tones, he spoke in Velykovian, and since higher-ranked princes were required to learn the languages and customs of other kingdoms, Draven understood every word.

"Vern, we're in Reudinia, remember? They're known for their many royals with strong senses. What if he's one of them? You promised we would avoid higher-ups. Look at his clothes."

Draven glanced down at himself self-consciously. His jacket had golden buttons running down the middle with intricately woven phoenixes along each side of the buttons. Twisted, golden accents lined the edges of his black jacket and the cuffs of his sleeves. It was undoubtedly a regal jacket.

The Velykovians must've realized he understood them when he looked down because they exchanged unsettled glances.

Vern's nose wrinkled, but he stepped away. "You a prince?" he asked.

Draven appreciated the man's straight-forward attitude. He straightened and bowed. "I apologize. I forgot to introduce myself. Bad manners," he quipped in Velykovian. He wasn't one to smile, so Draven held out a hand. "Prince Draven of the Sihan line, third in line for the throne."

At this, all eight stepped away apparently realizing they couldn't win this time. Not here. Not against a highly ranked Reudinian royal. Any attack they made or trouble they caused would result in war between the two kingdoms, and the Velykovians were well-aware Reudinia would squash them.

Vern bowed, grimacing. "I apologize for our trespassing. We'll leave."

Draven cracked a smile as he watched them walk away. Maybe being ranked third had its benefits. He turned and retreated as Birkett closed the door. Draven returned to the storage room. The fox no longer hid under the chair, but instead of searching for it, he retrieved some food from the kitchen and placed it on the floor of the storage room.

Draven lifted the tablecloth on the table. The fox cowered in the middle, its ears back and its tail tucked between its hind legs. He set his jaw and released a long, deep breath.

Draven couldn't blame the poor creature for being afraid, especially if those Velykovians had been chasing it all the way from Velykov as they said they had. With another sigh, Draven pushed the food a bit closer, then left the animal alone.

Over the next few days, Draven went to the storage room several times a day, bringing food and sitting with the fox. After five days, it sat next to him while it ate but would flee if he reached for it. Draven only managed to catch the fox once, long enough to wrap and splint its broken leg during one of his visits to the storage room. After two weeks, the pup followed him around the room and ate out of his hand. After another week, he was allowed to pet her. Finally, the fox let him carry it, and soon she followed him everywhere. He called her Nuri, and when he allowed her into his bedroom, Draven found he slept more soundly and stopped having episodes entirely.

One morning, a week before he headed back to Phoebus, Draven woke to find a small child sleeping on his bed instead of his fox. Draven scrambled out of bed, gaping down at the yawning little girl. A girl with long blonde hair and brown eyes sat up and looked at him. She wore a dirty brown dress with a green draping wrap twisting around it. It must be elven-made. Her big brown eyes were strangely familiar…and so was her small, pointed nose. It wasn't until two large fox ears sprung from her head and a bushy tail swished behind her that Draven realized what he was seeing: a shapeshifter.

"You're a girl?" he gasped. "A human girl?"

The girl hugged her knees to her chest and cocked her head at him. Maybe she didn't understand him. The Velykovians had mentioned chasing her from Velykov. Maybe she spoke Velykovian instead. So, in Velykovian, Draven asked, "You can shapeshift?"

The girl's eyes brightened and she nodded. Her fox ears and tail vanished. "But just into a fox," she squeaked.

"Why were those men chasing you?"

The girl looked down. "They wanted to use me for awful things," she whispered.

"Why?"

Her teary, brown eyes found his. "Mama said King Yusuf wants to gather people with senses so he can create an army."

Draven frowned. He was pretty sure Yusuf was the name of the current Velykovian king. "You're Velykovian?"

She nodded.

"What's your name?"

"Zinnia."

Draven nodded and strode toward the door. Then he paused and said, "Don't worry, Zinnia. I'll keep you safe."

A smile flashed across her face and Zinnia trotted after him as he left the room. The servants gasped at the sight of her and whispered amongst themselves.

Draven ignored their whispers and frowned to himself. Now that Zinnia was a girl, he couldn't bring her back to Phoebus with him. But the hunters might come back for her, so he couldn't return her to Velykov yet either. What could he do with her?

"Birkett!" Draven called.

The butler appeared in the hallway just outside the kitchen. "Yes, Your Highness?"

"Zinnia cannot come to Phoebus with me. Begin preparations for her to stay here." Draven gestured toward Zinnia. Birkett stared at the girl but then bowed his head in acknowledgment. "Whatever you wish, Your Highness."

On the day Draven left to return to Phoebus, Zinnia pulled him aside. "Shapeshifting isn't the only thing I can do," she told him. She bit her lip and her gaze flicked around before looking down and fidgeting with her fingers anxiously. Draven scanned the hallway, seeing nothing, but pointed down the hallway and offered, "We can speak in my study."

Zinnia nodded emphatically, her eyes wide.

Draven led her to the study and, after a final check around the hallway, closed the door. "It should be safe here."

Zinnia's forehead creased, and she took a deep breath.

"I can also see the future."

Draven stared at her. No wonder the hunters had been so persistent as to chase her so far into Reudinia. "You—can see the future?"

Zinnia nodded again and wrung her hands. "My mama made me promise not to tell others."

Draven nodded slowly. "Yes, let's keep that between the two of us."

No more was said about her ability that day, and Draven returned to Phoebus, leaving her comfortably in his home. He wrote to her often when he stayed in Phoebus and visited her as often as he could get away.

The last time he'd visited her had been about a week before his kidnapping. It was then Zinnia received the first glimpses of his future. She told him about the labyrinth, teary-eyed, "It's awful! The labyrinth, everything! So many people die…"

Unable to put what she saw into words, Zinnia reached out, touched his forehead, and showed him visions of his future. There he saw the Ten—struggling through the labyrinth, dying gruesome deaths, their appearances worsening with each vision. He saw the werewolves, the goblins, the skeletons, the sirens. And he saw this strange boy he didn't know among them, a boy with the sense of light. Through these scenes he came to understand that the boy was not a prince after all.

"You can't go to that awful place, Draven!" Zinnia had sobbed. And for a moment, Draven considered avoiding the assessment, walking away from his kidnapping, changing his future. But he couldn't shake the others from his mind. He couldn't abandon the other princes, and he couldn't forget about the girl with the light sense.

Draven placed a hand on Zinnia's head. "I must return. I need to try to find out who is planning this. If I can't do that, then maybe I can prevent the deaths I saw in those visions. Maybe with the visions, I can help them get through alive."

"But if you go..." Tears streamed down Zinnia's face as she clung to him. "If you go, you might die!"

Draven gritted his teeth. Yes, he'd seen that too. "I can't do nothing. I have to try."

Draven stared up at the gate to the next section of the labyrinth. The final section of Zinnia's visions. Dread settled in his stomach and fear trembled in his chest, but he clenched his fists against it. He wouldn't run from this.

If you go, you'll all die, the shadow beast hissed in his head.

Not on my watch, he whispered back.

48

Waterways

STARING BLANKLY AT THE PUZZLE, LUKA QUAKED INSIDE. He knew better than to be too hopeful about being so close to the end. He didn't know what was on the other side of this gate, nor did he know what awaited them when they returned home. He was cracking. From the dread of facing his father, from the pressure of Tenji's shadow, from the weight of leading this group.

The image of Cassian's bloodied, limp body seared his mind. If he'd done things differently, would Cassian still be alive?

"Luka?"

Turning to the voice, Luka found Tristan looking at him, then back at the puzzle before them.

"Any thoughts?" Tristan continued.

Luka blinked, then focused on the puzzle before them. The pipes and waterways were turned in odd directions, none of them lining up with the others, and they were empty of water. There was a lever on the gate and two pedestals of three levers each in front of the gate on either side. The water wheels hung still on the labyrinth wall, no running water to make them turn.

Nodding slowly, Luka replied, "I think we're supposed to make the pipes and waterways line up."

"No kidding," muttered Kai under his breath.

"Maybe using these levers," Tristan suggested, pointing.

Jovian strode over to one. "Only one way to find out!" he quipped and used both hands to force the lever down, grunting.

Luka tensed, gripping his sword, expecting monsters to descend. But instead, one of the pipes on the wall turned. Jovian pushed it up slowly, and the pipe aligned with those next to it.

"Hey, it actually worked!" Jovian exclaimed, flashing them a grin. "Totally thought it might kill us all."

"Good," Luka said, relaxing his shoulders. He pushed down his fear and focused on the task at hand. "Then let's try aligning the rest."

Jovian released his grip on the lever to reach for another, but the lever snapped back to its original position and the pipe became unaligned once again. "What the…?" Jovian pushed the lever and pipe back into place, then released the lever again. Once again it reset.

He grimaced as he turned to Luka. "It won't stay. We may need to hold them in place."

"Great," Kai groaned. "They *had* to make it difficult on us."

"It wouldn't be the labyrinth if they didn't," Jovian joked.

Luka clenched his teeth. What could they do? There had to be a way. What would Tenji have done if he was there? And how could Luka emulate him?

What if he couldn't figure it out?

"This shouldn't be too hard," Draven said, grounding Luka once more. "We can have two people per pedestal, one person to handle the lever on the gate, and still have one person free if we need them."

Luka took a deep breath. Right. He shouldn't complicate things. "Very well. Jovian, can you manage two levers?"

Instead of replying, Jovian carefully lifted the first lever to its position, before he strained to navigate a second. Grunting, Jovian nodded. "Yes, but man are they heavy!"

Tristan joined Jovian and pulled the third lever into position.

Steeling himself, Luka nodded. "Let's hurry then. We need two people on the other side and one person at the gate."

Everyone moved into place at his direction. Kai and Faven pulled the levers on the second pedestal, and Draven strode forward to pull the last lever.

After all the levers were pulled and the waterways and pipes were all aligned, they waited for something to happen, but nothing did.

"What now?" asked Kai, grimacing as he held two heavy levers in place.

Luka frowned. "Not sure." He turned and looked around, scanning the contraption. What could be missing?

Struggling to hold his lever in place, Draven nodded his head at the wheel in the middle. "What about that? Do we need to turn it?"

At the mention of the wheel, Luka inspected it. Gripping a spoke, he pushed but it only budged an inch.

"Would you hurry up?" Kai grunted.

"Oh, no. Take your sweet time," Jovian said through gritted teeth. "My arms are only *slightly* burning right now."

Luka grunted and puffed some more before he gave up. "It's too heavy. I can't do it alone."

The crack of a lever snapping back into place ricocheted through the quiet swamp, and Faven jerked away, rubbing her palm. Her piece reset. She grimaced. "Sorry, it's just so heavy."

Luka nodded and waved a hand at them. "It's fine. Everyone rest for a moment."

With groans, the rest of them released their grip on their levers and watched the pieces reset.

Kai sighed, rubbing his hands together and glaring at the gate. "What an annoying puzzle."

"Can someone help me see if we can turn this wheel?" Luka asked.

Draven joined him at the wheel. Together, they pushed, and the wheel turned, slowly. As the wheel turned, water poured from the top of the water mechanic and flowed down. Luka and Draven stopped pushing.

Straightening, Luka stared at the gate. "It appears we have to turn this wheel while holding the levers in place in order for it to work."

"But we don't have enough people for all of that," Tristan said, gesturing back at the levers.

Luka studied the levers, searching for a solution. "Can someone hold three levers at the same time?"

Tristan, Kai, and Jovian exchanged looks.

Jovian chuckled. "Psh, I wish."

Luka approached one the levers and strained to shift it. "They are pretty heavy. I wonder if I can use my telekinesis to lift one." Holding one lever up, Luka turned to focus on the lever near the gate. The lever twitched, then slowly shifted, clicking into place. Luka released both levers. "I can. But only briefly." He faced the others. "Could someone help Draven push the wheel? I can do this lever and the gate lever, if two people can lift two levers each. Sa—uh, Faven can lift one lever."

Luka waited for volunteers.

Then, to his shock, Kai huffed. "I'll help push the wheel. Tristan, you can take my place on the pedestal."

Nodding, Tristan approached the pedestal. Faven joined him, and Jovian joined Luka. They all stood, looking at each other. Then their gazes turned to Luka. Waiting. Waiting for his guidance.

Luka took another deep breath. "Let's do it on the count of three. One...two...three!"

Lifting the lever by the gate with his telekinesis, Luka heaved the one near him up with his arms. Draven and Kai pushed the wheel. It creaked and turned, and the water rushed. The pipes and waterways slowly clicked into place as the rest of the group pushed their heavy levers. The water rushed down the pipes and waterways, turning the water wheels. And as the wheels turned, the gate vibrated open.

With each moment, Luka grew increasingly tired, but he held on. The others were looking to him for guidance. He couldn't crack. Not now. Luka peered over to see Faven struggling to hold her lever in place. He turned his gaze on the gate, watching it creep open.

"That blasted gate better hurry up!" Kai hollered as he pushed the wheel, his face growing red from exertion.

Finally, the gate clicked in place, the last section in sight.

Luka's heart rose. So close. They were so close.

But before Luka could decide their next move, Faven released her grasp on her lever. The lever snapped back to neutral with a tremulous click. Her pipe spun away, breaking the waterway. The wheel stopped spinning.

Then, with a mighty tremble, the gate started to close.

I can't do this, the traitor thought to the spirit. He stared vacantly into the last section. *I thought I could, but...I can't keep hurting people like this.*

"You think you don't have what it takes?" The spirit chuckled, his voice filling the traitor's head. *"Hurting others scares you? Death scares you? Look at all you've already done. All the people you've killed. You think you can back out now?"*

The traitor squeezed his fists so tightly his nails dug into his palms. Heat burned in his chest.

"You're already a monster. Why not delve in and get rid of everything you hate? Let go of your meddlesome guilt and give in fully to me."

The traitor glowered. Monster? He supposed that was a good word to describe him now. After all, like the spirit said, he was already a killer. He couldn't bring any of the ones they'd lost back from the dead.

Something inside of him snapped.

If he was a monster, then he might as well use that monstrous side to destroy what had made him one in the first place.

49

The Confession

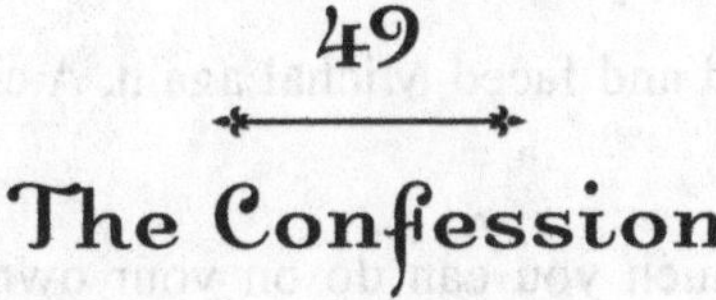

EVERARD SAT AT HIS DESK, PAPERS SPILLING OVER IT AND the floors around him. He was searching sleeplessly through books and scrolls that had recorded known information about the Sidylla Labyrinth and the spirit at the center.

He paused for a brief moment to look out a nearby window, mind racing. It had been only a week since he'd spoken with Michal about the possible danger his partner was in. Since then, he had been searching for a way—any way—to save them. To reverse the damage he had done.

But so far, he had found nothing.

At the sound of footsteps, Everard scrambled to shove the papers into drawers or to kick them under his bed. Then he flipped open a random book on his desk, pretending to read from it.

Someone opened his door, and he looked over his shoulder to find Michal. He released a relieved sigh. "Oh, it's you. I thought it might be someone else."

"Have you found anything?"

Everard shook his head. "No, not yet." He turned back to his desk and stared blankly at the book he'd opened. "Surely there's information out there that can help them. There has to be."

His murmur was met with silence.

"Everard…I think you should tell Father," Michal said finally.

Everard paused and faced Michal again. A chill ran down his back. "Why?"

"There isn't much you can do on your own. But if you tell Father, at least he'll know where they are and might be able to figure something out." Michal shifted his stance uneasily. "Maybe if you confess the right way, he won't have you beheaded."

Everard wrinkled his forehead and turned away, stomach churning. "You think that's the best thing to do?"

Michal sighed. "I don't know, Everard, but the Sense Thief isn't something you should've ever messed with. If they actually succeed somehow and release it…" He paused, but Everard refused to look at him. Then Michal continued, "It could endanger more than just the Ten."

Everard eyes blurred over with unshed tears. "You're right. If I hadn't gone through with it, Luka and the others would still be here, and we wouldn't have to worry about the Sense Thief at all." He took a shaky breath. "If only I hadn't sent them to the labyrinth."

He lifted his head, finally ready to look at Michal, only to see a figure standing in the doorway behind him.

Everard lurched to his feet, a chill running through him. "Romain."

Michal spun to face their brother.

Romain stared at Everard, eyes wide and fists clenched so tightly his knuckles seemed to be on the verge of bursting. "It was *you*? This whole time?" Romain's voice shook. His gaze darkened, and he shouted, "It was you? You—you stupid, selfish, idiot!" He lunged across the room at Everard.

Falling backward over his chair, Everard raised his arms in defense.

"No, Romain! Don't!" Michal commanded, wrenching Romain's hands from Everard's hair, ears, and throat. "Romain! Stop!"

The scurry of feet pounded down the hallway and Everard's stomach plunged. Their screams were drawing more people.

The next thing he knew, more arms were pulling Romain away. Past them were several maids, butlers, and servants. Mother stood at the back, a hand over her mouth. A strong manservant restrained the seething Romain, and Father loomed above them all, looking back and forth between the three of them, furious.

"What in dragon's breath is going on here? What has gotten into you all? This isn't how royals should act!"

Romain calmed immediately at the sound of their father's voice, but his gaze still burned with hatred. Everard looked to Michal instead, but Michal only shook his head.

Everard scrambled to his feet, searching for the words he needed to say. "Father..." His own voice cracked, then he spilled into tears, the emotions of the last several months overwhelming him.

"My goodness," Mother gasped, stepping closer. "Whatever is the matter? Why are you like this?"

Father narrowed his eyes, then waved away the servants and maids. Once they were alone, Everard stared at Romain through his tears. He was surprised Romain hadn't turned him in yet. Instead, Romain stood there—steaming, glaring, and fuming... but keeping his mouth shut.

Finally, Everard found the words. "It was me!" he wailed, bursting into sobs. "It was me!"

Michal's eyes widened and he froze.

"What do you mean it was you? What on earth is going on?" their mother demanded. "You're scaring me with all this nonsense."

"Luka...the Ten...it was me!" Everard hiccupped and continued to cry uncontrollably. It was out. He'd said it.

Silence swallowed the room and Everard stared up at his parents. Father's face turned as hard as stone.

"What are you talking about, Everard?" Father asked. His voice was terse, sharp, too quiet. It was the first time in years since Father had said his name...and it was because of this.

All Mother did was stare, shaking her head in warning.

Everard hiccupped again and sniffed, swallowing back his sobs. "I—it was my...fault...they're...in Sidylla...Labyrinth... seeking the...Sense Spirit."

"Sidylla?" Mother whispered, horror coating her voice.

Father didn't move. He just stared at Everard. "How…"

Mother turned to Father, fear in her eyes. "Is there a way to get them out of the labyrinth?"

Father shook his head. "No," he said, his voice still sharp. "Even if any of them are still alive, there is only one way in and one way out. Once you go in…." His frown deepened and he stepped toward Everard. "Do you know what you've done? Don't you realize these things aren't just fairytales?"

Everard trembled and sniffed. "I wanted to tell you the first day…but I was so scared."

Father slammed his fist on a bedpost. "Scared? You sent Reudinia on the verge of a full-on war with another kingdom and put ten lives in jeopardy by placing them in a labyrinth filled with monsters and an evil spirit. A spirit who has a long history of killing hundreds of people and stealing senses! If the spirit gets the chance, it will use *any* means to secure its freedom. It will take advantage of anyone who happens to survive long enough to reach the labyrinth's center. If freed, it could end our kingdom— and others—in a heartbeat. And yet, you were too *scared*?"

Everard stared at his father, speechless.

His father straightened, shifting out of the role of father and fully into the role of the king. "On account of the princes, the top ten in line for the throne, your act will be seen as treason. By our laws, anyone who commits treason must be executed. In two weeks, we will have your trial." King Léon's face was cool and unemotional as he turned away and opened the bedroom door. "Guards! Arrest the traitor, Everard."

The room seemed to swirl as guards entered the room and seized him. Everard stumbled and spewed vomit all over the stone floor, his throat and eyes burning as the guards dragged him toward the door.

His mother cried out and hurled herself between Everard and the door. She pressed her hands together and stared pleadingly at the king. "No, Léon, please! He is your son. You can't do this to your own son."

King Léon glared at Mother. "Don't call me Léon, woman. He's like this because of you." The king waved a dismissive hand in Everard's direction, never once turning to look at him. "He's no son of mine. Never has been."

Pain pierced Everard's heart like a hot knife. He'd always thought being ignored by his father was the most painful thing he could experience in life, but he was wrong. The words hurt more.

50

The Sense Thief

FROM THE WHEEL, DRAVEN STARED AT THE DARK SPACE ON the other side of the gate. The gate juddered and shivered, grating stone on stone, ready to shut them back out.

"Go!" Luka yelled.

But Draven didn't budge. Zinnia's visions whirled in his brain, turning his muscles to stone.

Jovian darted between the doors as they slid toward each other. He dug his feet into the ground and pressed his back against one of the gates. Earth rose and braced the other.

"Hurry!" Jovian called, his face twisting.

Faven and Tristan zipped through, followed by Luka. Kai leapt over the wheel and raced toward the gate.

Jovian grunted and strained against the gates.

"Draven!" Luka called.

Draven flinched. Luka waved him toward them, his face intent, while Tristan and Faven stared at him from their place behind the gate. Draven closed his fists. Shutting his eyes, he melted into the shadows and pulled himself into the last section just as Kai slid in through the gate behind him. Once they were all through, Jovian released his hold and tumbled inside.

The gates slammed shut behind him.

Draven stared at the closed gate. Its boom echoed through the space, sounding a bit too final. He drew in a slow breath and turned away, grounding himself in the sounds of Tristan's panting breaths. Faven stood near his side, rubbing her wrist.

Slowly, Draven shifted his attention to the dim, empty, round room surrounding them. A room with no doors except the one they'd come through. On one wall, there was an etching of the labyrinth, and in the center of the room, a stone hovered in the air where a lone light seeped down.

Exactly as it had looked in Zinnia's visions.

"The fifth section," Luka confirmed.

"It's just a room," Jovian said, wrinkling his nose.

Draven strode toward the wall, studying the words engraved above the labyrinth etching.

Luka joined him. "This labyrinth imprisons the Sense Thief. Only the one who can destroy the creature may escape alive." He paused, and his brows furrowed. "All other trespassers will be killed or trapped here forever. If the labyrinth perceives a trespasser is trying to escape, the labyrinth will bury all within it." He fell silent.

Tristan finished the reading for him: "Do not free the Sense Thief."

Draven stared at the shape of the words, unseeing. No escape? He turned away and approached the floating stone. He bent close to it and paused as the other five joined him in his examination of the stone. It was a muddy red color. Nothing spectacular. Nothing terrifying or beautiful about it.

"Is this where they keep the spirit?" Kai asked.

"Well, either way—" Jovian teased, drawing Draven's attention to his sharp smile, "—as we saw in the desert, touching random jewels in the labyrinth doesn't seem like the wisest thing to do."

"How do we get out?" asked Faven. "The engraving makes it seem like there is no escape."

Tristan shook his head. "Not necessarily. It's a warning."

"Why don't we destroy the spirit?" Kai blurted out. "It said we can leave if we destroy it."

Draven ignored the others and turned his gaze back to the stone, his chest squeezing painfully tight.

You shouldn't have entered this section, the shadow beast hissed. *Now you'll all die.*

Luka crossed his arms over his chest. "But if the spirit could be destroyed, why didn't they do so in the first place? Why build this prison if they could end the spirit instead?" His one blue eye glowered darkly. "They must not have been able to, so how can we?"

Closing his eyes, Draven took a deep breath, his fists clenched by his sides. No, he wouldn't let this happen. He opened his eyes once more. "There's only one probable way to leave."

"And what's that?" Luka asked.

Draven glowered at the stone. "We free the spirit."

"But we don't want to release the spirit," Faven pointed out.

Silence fell as everyone stared blankly at the stone. Draven didn't want to release the spirit any more than the rest of them. Dread lingered over him, numbing his thoughts.

Luka shook his head slowly. "Maybe we can prevent the spirit from leaving the labyrinth."

Again, the others stood still, as if afraid to move.

Draven looked at Faven, then eyed Tristan, Kai, Jovian, and Luka. The longer they prolonged this, the hungrier and weaker they'd become. They shouldn't delay any longer.

"So…" Tristan said, breaking the silence. His eyebrows pressed together uncertainly. "You're suggesting we release a dangerous spirit back into the world…just so we can live?"

Draven drew in a deep breath, scraped together some of his courage, then he reached out and touched the stone. Everyone jerked back as if expecting the room to cave in on them. Nothing happened.

"Why'd you bloody do that?" Kai snarled.

Was something wrong? Draven frowned at the stone, ignoring Kai's question. He'd done exactly what he'd seen himself do in the vision. Was he supposed to do something else now? Something Zinnia hadn't shown him?

Then a blue light burst forth from the stone, and a swirl of white smoke pooled above them. Draven lurched back and seized the hilt of his sword. He gritted his teeth.

So, it had begun.

The smoke formed into the shape of a man of average height and build with blue flickering eyes. The figure examined his hands and then looked around. "I'm free? Two thousand years of being trapped and I'm free?" Then he laughed incredulously.

Draven narrowed his eyes. Was *this* the spirit they'd heard about?

"Sigeberht really thought this place could stop him. Rupert Vilet is back!" the ghost bellowed, laughing again.

Stop who? Draven frowned. He braced himself for something, though he wasn't quite sure what.

Then the ghost paused, staring through his hand. "I don't have a body." He turned his head and peered down at them, finally acknowledging their presence. He shrugged. "I guess one of you will have to do." Then, before Draven could process his words, the ghost spiraled and shot inside Luka's body like a bolt of lightning.

Faven cried out and Draven yanked out his sword, staring at Luka as the other prince doubled over, his face hidden from them. Then, as Luka straightened, Draven's eyes widened. Luka's entire eyeball was bright, inhuman blue, no pupil to be seen. Luka opened his mouth, but instead of his voice it was Rupert Vilet's that came out. "Ah, much better. Though he only has one eye. What a bother."

"Did—did he just go into Luka?" Kai asked.

The spirit lifted a hand, levitating some pieces of dust and dirt around him. "Telekinesis. Not too bad. Though this one is underdeveloped. But I can fix that." He smiled and turned to the others, still swirling the cloud of dust around him. "I'm sorry to reward you with death now that I'm free, but it must be done. Goodbye."

Suddenly, stones from the floor cracked away and joined the dirt and dust in the air, filling the whole space. The stones fired toward them with such speed that all Draven could do was hold his arms over his face and take the small cuts he received from the debris.

Immediately, Kai burst into flames, ready to attack.

Faven jumped forward to block him, her arms raised. "No! We can't hurt Luka!"

Draven clenched his sword, lowering his arms slowly. If they couldn't hurt him, how would they fight him?

Luka smiled a dark smile and lifted his hand once more. "Your worry for your friend will only result in your downfall." Then the ceiling trembled above them.

Kai grunted at Faven as Luka raised his arms and a part of the ceiling crumbled. "Luka can take it. Let's just beat this guy!"

Jovian shifted his feet and kicked up a wall of rock before sending it sailing at Luka, the force of it sending their friend sprawling.

"No!" Faven cried. "If we do this, we're hurting Luka. Not the spirit!"

Draven jumped forward, yanking Faven out of the way of Luka's crossfire. Then something strange happened. Luka shot a stream of ice in each of their directions. Draven called to the hand of his shadow beast and swatted the ice away before it reached them. How was Luka using senses he didn't have? As Draven leapt back against the wall, he remembered what Tenji had said about this spirit. This wasn't just any spirit. It was known as the Sense Thief.

This wasn't good. How many senses did this 'Rupert Vilet' have?

As if to answer him, a sharp wind picked up, whistling past his ears with such speed Draven could hear nothing else. Luka dove for Kai, plants and wood erupting from the ground and encircling the redhead. But Kai burned through all of it and rained a torrent of flames back. Luka merely waved a hand and doused the fire with water. Tristan threw bolts of lightning at Luka, only to be deflected when Luka's arm turned to stone. Jovian jumped and danced around, firing rock and earth.

Draven lurched forward, attempting to catch the edge of Luka's shadow, but Luka sidestepped out of reach. Using her light speed, Faven lunged against the current of the wind, blinding Luka with her light. She punched him hard in the chest, eyebrows pressed tightly together in a picture of deep regret.

The spirit soared from Luka's back as Luka slid across the ground. Without hesitating, the spirit spun, looped, and flashed toward Tristan, dissolving almost instantly into his body.

Electricity danced and sparked across the room. Draven's hair rose on end and he gritted his teeth. Where could they hide from bolts of lightning?

Then Tristan released streams of electricity toward all five of them. One bolt zapped Draven and shocking pain coursed through his body. He dropped to the ground and convulsed, gritting his teeth.

How would they defeat the spirit if he continued to dance from one person to another?

Draven forced his focus back on Tristan despite the constant, painful tingling and twitching in his body. Tristan grinned and zapped them once more. Then he strolled over to the stone in the center of the room and picked it up. It glowed.

"I'm sorry you went through this place only to die now," Rupert Vilet said. "How sad it must be to die knowing you released such hellish creatures back into the world." As he spoke, a golden oval-shaped glow spiraled in the middle of the room where the stone had been. A portal.

Jovian lunged at Tristan, his eyes lit with ferocious anger. Rocks formed around his fist, and he punched Tristan across the face. Tristan stumbled back, the gem fell from his grasp, and the portal dissolved.

Then Jovian slammed his foot on the floor, making the floor underneath Tristan waver and crumble. He pulled up a strip of earth as if it were no more than a hall carpet and snapped Tristan into the air. The ground cracked and shuddered, vibrating

Draven's bones and teeth. Crevices opened in the floor as rock flew up and struck Tristan's chest. Blood spurted from his mouth, and Tristan stumbled to the ground.

The ghost in Tristan stared at Jovian, his blue eyes bright. "You're on another level." Then he surged out of Tristan and toward Jovian.

Jovian's eyes widened.

Without stopping to think, Draven dropped into the shadows, transported himself into Jovian's shadow. He emerged with a rush, placing himself between Vilet and Jovian. Vilet sailed into Draven, and everything went black.

The shadows in the room grew as Vilet laughed in Draven's body. "Now *this* is an interesting sense!"

Faven's eyes widened and she clutched the hilt of her sword. She tensed, her eyes sweeping the room. What now? The last time Draven had been controlled…it hadn't been pleasant. She stepped further back.

Draven's eyes widened. "Wait…" Vilet's voice came roughly from Draven's mouth. "I can't control…"

Black smoke unfurled behind Draven, and the shadow beast formed. Its vague, shadowy, humanoid figure towered over them and darkened the room. A gruff, hoarse voice very unlike Vilet's filtered through the darkness: "I'm hungry for flesh. Let me eat!"

Kai dove for Draven, but the beast slashed one of its massive shadow hands toward him and knocked Kai into the wall. Tristan, gripping his chest, scrambled backward while Jovian tossed large pieces of ground at Draven. But the shadow only seized whatever Jovian threw and ate it. Luka forced Draven back with his telekinesis, but then the shadow reached out and snatched Luka off the ground. The shadow brought Luka to his mouth.

"No!" Faven screamed and released a burst of light, her legs quaking beneath her.

The shadow winced back and dropped Luka to the ground. Luka wheezed and scrambled back, his face pale and sweaty.

Then the shadow turned its gaze to her. "You…light creature. You must die."

Darkness swarmed and covered her eyes. Faven stumbled and released her light, but this time the light didn't dispel the shadows. Her chest tightened. She still couldn't see. She shut her eyes and gripped her head.

Cries, grunts, and clatters from the others filled her ears. At least she could still hear. Faven bit the inside of her cheek and forced in a deep breath of air. She refused to die now. Not when they were so close to the end. She *had* to get that ghost out of Draven.

Faven lowered her hands, keeping her eyes tightly shut and focused on the ruckus around her. She reached for her sword and drew it from her scabbard. Pointing it in the general direction of the beast's voice, she ignited her rays, and then just as quickly dissolved them. No, she couldn't use her rays; she might hurt the others. Faven grimaced and, instead, released a beam of light as bright as she could manage.

The beast howled furiously. "I will snuff you out, light creature!"

The crushing weight of shadows descended on her, crumpling her painfully to the uneven floor. The weight grounded her into the stone floor and Faven strained in the darkness.

"Draven!" she called.

The weight stifled her lungs, cracked her ribs. Her skin scraped across the rough ground as she struggled to drag herself out from under it.

"Draven!" she cried once more. Her head and ears buzzed.

Somewhere in the smothering darkness, she heard Tristan shouting with her. "Draven, you need to fight it!"

51

The End of the Labyrinth

A NUMBNESS SWALLOWED DRAVEN. DARKNESS AND silence filled him. Once again, he'd failed. When he regained consciousness, would the others be dead? Would he have killed them?

His life had been consumed by the darkness. He'd let it overtake him, again and again, pushing away family and potential friends in fear that his sense would hurt them. He'd lived, constantly listening to the lies the shadow beast whispered to him.

A failure. He was a failure. He had failed to save Ruben. He couldn't save Tenji, despite his attempt to warn the man. He hadn't resisted the creature in the desert or prevented the separation in the snow section. And, on top of all of that, he had been unable to prevent Archie and Cassian's deaths. Must he fail here too?

"Draven!"

Was that Faven?

"Draven, you need to fight it!"

Another voice. Tristan.

Draven searched the darkness around him and found a small pool of light, but immediately shrunk back at the sight of it.

How often had he run away from the light? Retreated from its blaring brightness? If he hid from it then, would the others die?

Draven clenched his fists. He hadn't spent his whole life resisting being controlled by his sense to allow some ghost to overtake him now.

Draven faced the light. He thought of all the times he'd been afraid of the light, all the times he'd hidden from it. All the times he'd been so afraid of hurting others that he refused to step into the light and face the destruction he had caused.

Not anymore.

He wasn't going to fail this time. He wasn't going to let the shadows dictate his life anymore.

Draven pushed through the dense darkness toward the light, his footsteps heavy. He would fight the ghost's control. He would resist. He took another step.

As Draven crept closer to the light, the steps became easier.

Vilet's voice sizzled his mind. *"No!"*

"This ends now," Draven hissed as he reached for the light. "You won't control me anymore."

Then a slippery, slimy sensation filled Draven and he knew— Vilet's spirit was trying to leave his body. Draven tensed. If Vilet's ghost left, he'd go right into Jovian and that would be the end. He couldn't allow that either.

Draven manipulated the shadow beast back into himself and created a cage around Vilet's spirit, trapping the ghost inside his body.

He pictured himself in a dark room, and Vilet's figure formed before him.

Vilet glared at him. *"You think you can keep me here?"*

A force pushed at Draven's mental prison. He winced. For a ghost, Vilet was pretty strong. Draven struggled to maintain his hold on Vilet. "I'm going to do my best."

"I've stolen hundreds of senses. I can kill you if you keep me here."

"I know."

Vilet's image crossed his arms over a flickering chest. *"Very well."* He reached out a hand and snapped his fingers.

Sharp heat stabbed through Draven's body. His grip on the mental prison slipped. Draven grunted, turning all his concentrating on regaining his hold instead of on the pain. He had to keep that ghost here as long as he could.

"I just injected you with a lethal poison," Vilet hissed. *"You only have a short while left to live, and the weaker you become, the easier it will be for me to leave."*

Draven grimaced, images of Zinnia and his parents flickering through his mind. He quickly knocked them away. He had to focus on keeping Vilet inside him. He couldn't afford to be distracted, not even by the ones he loved.

"When you're dead, I'll continue to unlock the labyrinth, taking all those dastardly monsters with me."

"You will never leave this place," Draven said through gritted teeth. A slight haziness drooped over him, and his gaze became unfocused.

"You can't stop me." Vilet's ghost laughed. *"And even if you could manage to stop me, you'll still be trapped in the labyrinth. It traps the holder of the gemstone—meaning someone will have to stay behind. The only way for everyone to leave the labyrinth is to unlock it and free all those monsters. So, give up."*

Draven's body trembled, and nausea rose like acid in his throat. Someone needed to stay behind?

He glared at Vilet. "Unfortunately for you, I have a hard time giving up."

Vilet scoffed.

Draven felt his strength continuing to slip away and he stumbled. The ghost's eyebrows flickered, and he smiled at him before turning away. *"Time for me to go."*

Draven reached out with his shadow beast and seized Vilet, holding him still. His grip on the mental prison trembled.

Vilet frowned at him. *"You forget—I have the ability to remove senses. You're nothing without this sense."*

"Sense or not, I'll find a way to hold you here."

Vilet held up a hand. A strange, painful sensation streamed through Draven's body as dark smoke filtered out of Draven and into Vilet. The shadow beast faded, and Draven lost his grip.

Vilet smirked, then left Draven's body without another word.

Darkness dissipated, and the others came back into sight. Draven stumbled, his head swimming as the room swirled. He shook his head and focused on the ghost rising above them. He'd failed again.

What now?

Searching the ground, Draven spotted the gemstone. If Vilet had been trapped in it before, then maybe he could be trapped in it again. It was worth a try.

Vilet darted toward Jovian and Draven dove for the stone. He snatched it up and faced Vilet, holding it up despite his trembling arms and legs just as Vilet disappeared into Jovian's body.

"Return," Draven commanded.

A second later, Vilet oozed back out of Jovian and his eyes widened as an unseen force dragged him back toward the gemstone. He strained against the pull of the stone, but Draven held on firmly.

"No!" Vilet roared. But it was too late. Vilet's ghost spiraled into the gemstone and vanished from sight.

Stunned, Faven blinked. The crushing force had dissolved, and she could see once more. She carefully picked herself up off the ground, searching the room, bracing herself for a surprise attack. But nothing came.

Was the spirit gone?

Her gaze fell on Draven. He stood in the center of the room, just in front of Jovian, holding the stone and staring at it. Had the spirit gone back inside the stone? Faven relaxed and lowered her gaze to her bruised and worn body.

Then something rumbled. She whirled toward the source of the vibrations. In the middle of the room, where the gemstone had been, a portal began to glow. A bright, shining light fell through the opening, and a cool breeze sifted into the room. Faven exchanged glances with the others. Could it be?

"The—the exit?" Luka asked, his face full of anxious hope.

Kai looked at them and a smile spread on his face. "Are we really done? We can leave?"

Faven's chest quivered and tears burned in her eyes. Would they finally be able to leave this dreadful place behind? It seemed too good to be true. She followed Luka, Kai, Tristan, and Jovian closer.

"I think it is," Luka said, his voice trembling with excitement.

"Well, then let's leave this damned place!" Kai said.

Faven flashed a smile at Draven only to see him stumble and drop to his knees. Her excitement vanished in an instant. "Draven?" She hurried to his side and gripped his arm, holding him steady. "What's wrong?"

The others came a moment behind her.

Shaking his head, Draven gripped the stone. "Go," he whispered. "Leave."

"Not until we get you through."

Again, Draven shook his head. "I can't."

Luka tensed. "Why can't you?" he asked, his voice tight.

"The only way to leave the labyrinth is for someone to hold this gemstone. The labyrinth won't let whoever holds the gemstone leave—someone has to stay behind."

Faven tightened her grip on Draven's arm. No.

"I should be the one who stays," Draven continued. "Vilet injected me with poison. I don't have much longer to live. So, go. Now. Before I'm too weak to hold this anymore."

No one spoke; no one moved.

Tears pricked Faven's eyes once more, and words spilled from her. "No, you can't be dying. I'm sure we can figure out a way to get us all out." Maybe she could heal him. Maybe her sense would finally work.

Draven pushed her arms off him.

"Don't," he said, his voice gruff. "The only other way to leave the labyrinth is to free all the monsters back into the world. We don't want that." He paused and pulled a multicolored thread from his pocket. The one he'd been braiding and re-braiding throughout their trip. Faven had almost forgotten about it. He held it out to her. "Don't forget your promise. Give this to her, will you?"

Zinnia. Tears blurred Faven's vision and her throat burned as she pulled the tiny, neatly braided thread from his hand.

Draven suddenly bent over and groaned. "Go! Go now, dammit!"

Then nodding, Luka grabbed Faven's arm and waved the others toward the gate. "Hurry." Luka turned to face Draven. "Your sacrifice will never be forgotten."

Draven looked up at them, his eyes red.

"No, we can't leave him!" Faven cried, tears sliding down her face. But Luka's hold on her tightened, and Tristan seized her other arm. Jovian stepped through the portal first, then Kai, who nodded to Draven. Tristan and Luka waved to Draven with their free arms and stepped through, dragging her with them.

Faven struggled but couldn't pull herself from their strong grasps. Just before she disappeared into the gel-like substance of the portal, she met Draven's gaze, and a sob escaped her.

"I'll take care of her, Draven!" she called. "I promise."

Draven stared after the five royals as they disappeared through the portal, Faven's words ringing in his ears. As soon as the portal closed, the room shook violently, sending tremors through his weakened body. The labyrinth was self-destructing.

Unable to hold himself up anymore, Draven crumpled to the broken floor and rolled onto his back. Draven squeezed the dark thread tied to his belt as tight as he could and gritted his teeth. In his mind's eye, he could see Zinnia smiling at him. Then Birkett. He saw his father's calm eyes and heard his mother's happy laugh. He wished he could say goodbye to them or thank them for staying by his side even when his sense had been at its worst.

Draven sucked in a sharp breath of air.

His shadow sense. The shadow beast.

It was gone.

He was free.

Tears swelled in the corners of his eyes, and a short, breathless laugh burst from him despite the room fracturing and tumbling down around him.

He was finally free.

52

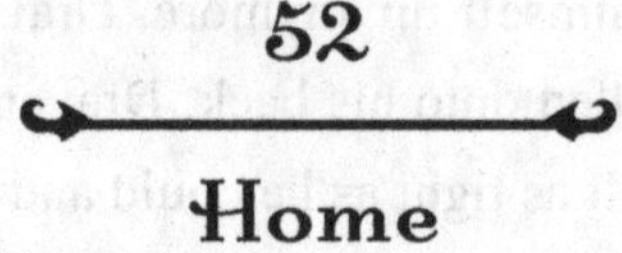

Home

FAVEN EXITED THE GLOWING PORTAL ONTO GREEN GRASS. Orange, yellow, and pink splashed in a sunset across a widespread sky. No walls barred their escape or guided them on their way.

No more labyrinth.

Another sob hiccupped from her, and Luka and Tristan released her. She wiped tears from her face, then faced the portal, but it had already dissolved and vanished, leaving only a tall, stone wall—the labyrinth's entrance.

Draven.

A deep rumble rolled from far behind the wall. Then the wall trembled, clattered, and cracked. Faven and the others scrambled back as the labyrinth crumbled to the ground and explosions erupted from inside. No one spoke until the entire labyrinth lay crackling on the ground.

Faven looked at the four men on either side of her, all of them staring silently at the labyrinth. Tears rushed down her cheeks and another sob bubbled up in her throat. Unable to hold her emotions back anymore, Faven turned away from the labyrinth and wept until her chest ached, her throat burned, and her body trembled.

As she cried, she stared at the setting sun. The green grass waved, and the trees shifted to yellows, reds, and oranges and glimmered in the sunlight. Faven breathed in the cool, autumn air and stared over the wide-open fields. She'd thought they would never leave that terrible place. Yet here they were.

She peered back at the ruins of the labyrinth and fresh tears spilled for the ones who would never leave.

Finally, Tristan spoke. "He saved our lives."

Faven clenched her jacket sleeves tightly. Tattered as it was, it was still the jacket Draven had given her. He'd helped her so many times and had been so kind to her…and in the end, she couldn't even help him once.

Luka stared at the ground. "I thought he was the traitor most of the time in the labyrinth," he whispered. "And I think he knew it. Yet, he still put his life on the line to save us."

Kai and Jovian were silent.

After a long pause, Tristan asked, "Who do you think was the traitor?"

The other four looked at him.

Faven sniffed and returned her gaze to Draven's grave. Who was it? Could it have been someone who had died in the labyrinth? But for some reason, she couldn't shake the sudden uneasiness that rose with the question. If Everard had been one of the ones behind their kidnapping, then could Luka be the traitor? She studied Luka quietly, watching as he ran a hand through his long, blond hair and sighed.

"I'm not sure," Luka answered.

Tristan's frown deepened. "What do you think the traitor wanted with the spirit?"

Kai's gaze hardened and he gestured to Draven's grave, glaring. "Who cares? Nothing is worth all the lives we lost and the torture we went through."

Faven brushed a strand of hair from her face. Did whoever the traitor was really die? Or was he one of the four standing by her? Kai with his hot temper, Tristan with his gentle kindness, Luka with his determination, and Jovian with his jokes.

After another long silence, Luka turned and stared out across the plains. "Should we head home?"

Faven took a deep breath, wiped her face, and reached up to clutch the front of her jacket.

Home.

What a beautiful word that was.

◎

53

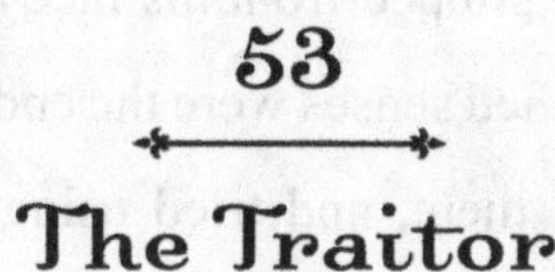

The Traitor

THE TRAITOR LEANED BACK AGAINST THE DARK COOL WALL AND picked at his fingers as Everard shrank away from the dark figure of the Sense Spirit.

"I need a prince," the Sense Spirit's coarse voice echoed through the empty cell. The traitor flickered his gaze up to the spirit. So far, this summoning was going exactly like he expected it would.

"I *am* a prince," Everard replied, his voice wobbling. "I am Prince Everard, fourth son of King Léon of Reudinia."

The deep voice chuckled and drew closer, illuminating a skull face with pieces of shredded skin clinging desperately to the bones in the firelight. Its empty sockets flickered with flaming purple eyes. Its chuckles died as he spoke once more, "Ah, but you are mistaken, young one. I need a *real* prince."

The traitor smirked and rolled his eyes. A real prince? What even counted as a *real* prince anyway?

"*You* do not carry a sense," the spirit hissed, its words sharp and unforgiving. "I see no potential in you."

The traitor's smile slipped from his face and his eyes narrowed. Once again, it seemed senses were the end all, be all. Everyone wanted them, sought them, and tried using them for their own benefit. In his experience, senses only brought misery. However, despite having told his friend this, Everard still thought having one was the only thing that would make him happy.

Everard stood in silence as the words settled in. His small frame looked lonely standing before the spirit, and the traitor could only imagine the pain the spirit's words inflicted. Yet, he had no remorse for his friend. Everard needed to know a sense wasn't worth all this madness.

It was, however, worth it to get rid of one.

The Sense Spirit shifted its focus from Everard to the traitor. "*He*, however, is a different story."

The traitor adjusted his position against the wall and scowled at the spirit. The way the spirit referred to him reminded him very much of how someone else had once spoken to him—seeing him as a tool, nothing else. And he hated that.

But before he could respond, Everard stepped into the spirit's line of sight. "*He* isn't the one who called you. This concerns only me."

The traitor lifted his eyebrows. Everard *really* wanted a sense, didn't he?

"Is that so?" The bony face retreated. "How unfortunate. Then what you ask of me is impossible."

Silence draped over the room. The traitor's forehead creased as the spirit's words sank in. He swallowed down a laugh. Everything revolved around sense wielders. Wouldn't the world be better without them?

Everard broke the silence. "Is there anything I can do?"

The shadow's purple eyes flickered to the traitor once again. "If the one you brought with you is to have no part in this plan, then you must find another to take your place. Bring him to me in the labyrinth. Then—and only then—can you have your wish."

"Bring a prince to the *Sidylla Labyrinth*? I can't—"

The spirit's figure enlarged into the space before them, causing Everard's torch to dim and his words to die out. "This is the only way!" it bellowed. Its figure shrunk again, and its voice softened. "The prince must be able to survive the labyrinth. Choose wisely and bring him to me within six months."

The room lightened and the creature vanished.

Then—and only then—can you have your wish. The traitor stilled, his heart picking up speed in his chest. An idea tugged at his brain. Maybe he could get what he wanted after all. It would be a reckless plan, but the traitor was willing to do just about anything to rid himself of the curse of his sense.

Everard moaned and kicked a nearby chain. Throwing down the book of spells, he stomped on its cover.

"Damn it," Everard hissed.

So, the spirit's words weren't what Everard had been hoping to hear. But the traitor couldn't allow him to get discouraged. Not if he wanted his plan to work.

"What are your thoughts, Everard?"

Everard turned to face him. "It's no use. There's no way I can lead anyone through that cursed labyrinth." His shoulders slumped. "Not even the king of Niaria and his army could do it. How could I outlast an entire army? It's impossible."

The traitor sighed. "Not impossible. Just incredibly difficult." He hesitated, guilt creeping in. The traitor forced his focus onto Everard's father instead. "Do you really need a sense to be happy?"

Everard paused. "Yes, I think I do."

The traitor sighed again. "Having a sense is nothing special. There's nothing good about it. But..."

"But what?"

"You're certain you want one." The traitor's conscience twinged. Over the years he'd grown very practiced at pretending, but maybe now that practice was serving him too well.

"Yes."

"And you will do whatever it takes to make this happen?"

"I will."

The traitor studied Everard's thin, weak figure. If he genuinely wanted a sense, it was going to cost him. So, for Everard's sake, he added, "I really mean whatever it takes. Think this through carefully."

Everard looked down at the spell book that lay by his feet. Raising to meet the traitor's eyes, Everard set his shoulders. "I'll do whatever it takes."

The traitor nodded. Success. "Very well. Then I will go into the labyrinth in your place."

"What?" Everard's eyes widened, and he struggled to find words. "What do you mean? No! I won't let you. The Sidylla Labyrinth is too dangerous!" he exclaimed, his words spilling from his mouth. "No one has ever succeeded in completing the labyrinth. Going there is suicide. How would you get through it? What if you lost your sense? What if you died?"

The traitor straightened from the wall, towering a head taller than Everard.

"I thought you said you would do whatever it takes." His voice came out gruff, agitated. He closed his eyes and relaxed his shoulders, taking in a breath to calm himself. "If you really mean that, then you must be willing to do anything. We both know you will die if you enter the labyrinth." Reaching out a hand, the traitor pressed it onto Everard's thin shoulder. "Don't worry about me. I'll make sure I get through alive, and you get what you want. But you can't object to my plans, whatever they may be, understood?"

Everard swallowed and nodded.

"Good." The traitor released his grip and turned toward the exit of the dungeon. He paused in the doorway and looked back at Everard, his sole braid swinging at the side of his head. He smiled coldly. "And in case you think I'm doing too much on your behalf, let me assure you. I also have something I want. So, trust me and let me worry about the labyrinth."

54

The Execution

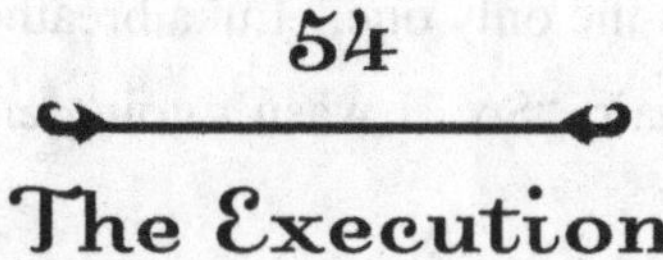

FAVEN AND THE FOUR PRINCES CAME ACROSS THEIR FIRST civilization after two weeks of traveling on foot. They trudged into the village looking like a gang of bandits with their ragged clothing, wounded bodies, untrimmed hair, and bearded faces. Luka wanted to catch a ride to Phoebus to cut down their travel time, but none of them carried any coins, having left what they had in the labyrinth. None of them had decent clothing to sell, so they traded in their swords. Despite being dirty and dull, the swords still showed excellent craftsmanship and that was enough to earn them some food and a ride on the back of a cart.

During one of their many stops on the way, Kai, Tristan, and Jovian shaved their faces while Luka merely trimmed his beard. Luka also bought a patch to place over his scarred and unseeing eye.

Most of their travel was in silence. With Cassian, Draven, and Ruben constantly on Faven's mind, words failed to come.

One day, while they were sitting quietly in the cart full of hay, Tristan sighed and put a hand on his forehead. "It's so nice to be able to think without having a random voice whispering to me."

Faven jerked her gaze toward him. Draven had mentioned something similar while in the labyrinth. "You heard a voice?"

Luka, Kai, and Jovian also turned to stare at Tristan.

Tristan glanced between them. "You didn't?"

"I thought I was the only one," Luka breathed as he combed a hand through his hair. "So…I wasn't going crazy? It really was just the labyrinth?"

Kai crossed his arms. "Huh, I didn't know the labyrinth was whispering to several of us."

"Draven mentioned hearing a voice once too," Faven added. How could so many of them have heard the same thing?

"At least we know we were all going crazy together," Jovian added with a smirk.

"I didn't hear anything," she said quietly.

The four princes turned to look at Faven. "You didn't?"

Faven shook her head.

Luka frowned and looked up at the blue sky. "I wonder why."

"What—what did the voice say?" she asked.

Luka leaned back against the side of the cart. "It would give me suggestions or ask me to rely on it. But why would I rely on a random, unknown voice?"

Tristan nodded. "Yes, and it knew things about me. Not sure how."

"That's unsettling." Faven drew her knees up to her chest and hugged them. Why hadn't she heard anything? Was it because she was a princess? Did Ruben, Cassian, Tenji, and Archie hear whispers too? "Where do you think the voice was coming from? Rupert Vilet?"

Kai jerked forward suddenly. "Didn't the Minotaur mention whispers as well?"

Faven widened her eyes. Yes. Yes, he had mentioned whispers. When he'd spoken about Rupert Vilet…and the fact that he'd had some sort of partner. "He did," she confirmed.

"It couldn't be Rupert Vilet. He didn't seem to know anything about us, yet the voice that spoke to me knew too much." Tristan frowned. "Could it be a side effect of the magic used to create the labyrinth?"

Jovian shrugged. "Maybe. Or it could've been something else."

Faven didn't like this. She didn't like it at all. And the reminder only strengthened the uneasiness that had been weighing on her ever since they'd left the labyrinth. Whatever it was—whatever had helped Ruper Vilet—she hoped it was destroyed along with the labyrinth.

After two more weeks of travel, their driver stopped a short distance away from the gates of Phoebus to let them off. "Good luck on your journey, lads!" the elderly driver said, smiling a gaping grin. "Hope you find whatever you're looking for."

"Thank you," Tristan and Luka said in unison.

As the man's cart rolled away, Faven turned her attention to the city before her.

The walled city of Phoebus looked as beautiful as it had before, with the royal castle standing tall on the mountain, the waterfall descending into the center of the city. The sun hit the orange-tiled roofs and illuminated them like the flames of a fire. It was a strange sight to see. The last time she'd seen this view, she'd been arriving from Hallon with Trent to take the princesses' ranking assessment. So much had happened since then.

Luka glanced at their small group, and after a slight pause, cleared his throat. "Shall we?"

Only Tristan responded with a nod. Faven peeked at Kai, who had been especially silent the last several weeks. He didn't erupt into as many angry bursts and listened without protest to whatever Luka said. Honestly, she didn't like it, and wished he'd go back to his usual, passionate self. She bit the inside of her cheek. Cassian's death must've been a huge blow to him. Maybe she should talk to him about it.

As if sensing her stare, Kai's eyes flickered to her. Faven jerked her head away and instead looked over at Tristan and Jovian.

Jovian didn't seem quite the same either. He didn't joke as much as he used to and spoke less frequently. Tristan actually spoke more than before, but whenever Faven happened to look in his direction during their long silences, his eyes were often red and raw from tears. Finally, her gaze turned to Luka's back. His shoulders sagged and his head bent forward.

Luka came to a stop once they approached the gates. There were guards questioning each person who passed through and checking all belongings. Luka turned to face the group, frowning thoughtfully. "They won't let us in, not while looking like this. And we have nothing to prove our identities."

Jovian tapped Luka's shoulder. "I can get us through the wall," he said with a gesture toward a spot further out from the gate. Luka nodded and Jovian led the way.

When they were out of sight of the people coming and going from the city, Jovian stopped, faced the wall, and slammed his foot into the ground. He pressed his hands together like he was praying but then shot them toward the ground like an arrow. Then he rotated his arms to the right. The ground caved before them and rolled away, leaving a tunnel under the thick wall. Without hesitating, Jovian entered the darkness.

The tunnel was small and narrow, causing Faven and the others to need to crouch down as they entered. When the last of the group was inside, the tunnel closed behind them. The journey through the dark tunnel was short, thankfully, though it still seemed like forever before Faven finally exited the tunnel and found herself standing inside Phoebus. Once more the tunnel closed behind them, but they didn't stop—Luka leading them straight up the mountain toward the castle.

People gave them double-takes, their faces contorting in disgust, but no one stopped them—probably because they looked pretty intimidating, despite being weaponless. When they finally reached the royal castle, Luka strode up to the gates with the confidence of someone returning home. The guards, however, found this threatening.

Unsheathing their swords, the guards stood prepared for an attack. "Who are you?" called one. "Stay back. Don't take another step!"

Luka stopped, holding up his hands. "We're not here to harm anyone. I am Prince Luka, first son of King Léon, and we are what is left of the Ten. We wish to speak to my father, the king."

The four guards standing between them and the castle chuckled. "You?" laughed another guard. "Prince Luka? You look nothing like him."

The first guard to speak to them was older and clearly more experienced because his laughter was short-lived. "We've had plenty of people come pretending to be one or several of the missing Ten. We aren't as easily fooled as people think." The guard pointed his sword at them. "The king is busy. He's currently engaged in a trial regarding the missing princes who, from what I've heard, were put in the Sidylla Labyrinth. There is no chance for their survival."

Faven frowned. How did the king know where they had been? Did the Velykovian tell them?

"Trial?" Luka asked.

Another guard, not much older than Luka, nodded. "Yes, the king's youngest son, Prince Everard, confessed to organizing the kidnapping of the Ten. I'm surprised you haven't heard."

Luka stepped back, Tristan took a sharp intake of breath, and Jovian stiffened.

"Everard?" Kai exploded, eyes blazing as he glared at Luka, the first show of true anger Faven had seen from him since the labyrinth, since Cassian. "Isn't that that puny brother of yours who's ranked in the three hundreds? He bloody did this to us? He's the cause? How do we know you didn't have a part in this too?"

But then Kai's anger cooled drastically. When Faven saw Luka, she could see why. Luka stared at the gate over the guards' heads as if he couldn't see anything. "Everard?" he asked, sounding shocked. Then a slow anger shifted through his eye. He pointed to the older guard. "You. You said they are having the trial now?"

The guards tensed and exchanged uncertain glances with each other. The elder eyed Luka. "Yes."

"Since this trial pertains to us, we deserve to be there." Luka shifted forward and thrust his hand at the guards, sending them soaring back. The guards landed hard, still and stunned. "Let's go," Luka commanded, and none of the four argued.

The five of them hurried through the courtyard and into the royal castle, following Luka's lead. Several guards scrambled to stop them, but with ease the five—who had been fighting terrible monsters for several months, after all—fought their way through. Jovian knocked guards out of the way with his earth sense, Tristan electrocuted any who came close, Kai set fire to the clothes and armor of several guards, and Luka levitated them out of his way. Faven illuminated the hallway behind them, blinding any who followed.

Finally, Luka raced toward the large doors that led to the throne room. With a jerk of his hand, Luka yanked the guards standing outside out of his way and launched the throne room doors open. The doors banged against the wall. Together, they burst into the room and for once, Faven didn't feel the tiniest bit winded.

Everyone in the room twisted to stare at them and low murmurs filled the space. Several people in dark clothing stood between them and the front, but they sidestepped out of the way. At the front stood the royal family, and to Faven's right a few guards held a chained Everard who stood next to a slab of stone. Next to the stone stood a masked man with an ax. To her left stood a large mass of the Royal Council.

The heavy, thudding footsteps of approaching guards echoed from behind them. Jovian turned and heaved up his arms, effortlessly forming a wall of stone from the ground and walls, protecting them from the guards on the other side.

The king stood. "What is the meaning of this? Who are you?"

Instead of answering his father's question, Luka strode forward, his gaze focused only on Everard. The guards in the room raced to stop him, but he threw them back with a wave of his hand and grabbed Everard by the front of his jacket. "Why, Everard?" Luka thundered, his voice echoing loudly through the room. "Why did you do this?"

Everard stared in bewildered horror at the man before him, no sign of recognition in his eyes. He struggled to find the words to respond to this stranger. Guards scrambled to their feet and raced to knock Luka back, but Jovian reached out a hand and twisted his fingers, causing the floor to rise and trap the guards' feet.

Faven approached Luka carefully and placed a hand on his shoulder. "Luka, calm down," she whispered.

Luka didn't acknowledge her, but Everard stared at Faven then turned his gaze back to his brother, his gaze confused, searching. "Luka?" he whispered.

Silence hovered over the room.

"Are you really, Luka?" Everard asked again, a bit louder this time. Even though his voice was quieter than Luka's, it echoed in the silent room.

Luka shoved Everard back. "You can't even recognize the brother you sentenced to death?" he asked through gritted teeth. "How could you, Everard? Half of the Ten died because of you…" Luka's voice broke, and angry tears slipped down his face. "Why?"

Everard trembled violently and dropped to his knees, tears filling his own eyes. "I'm sorry. I'm sorry, Luka. I'm so sorry… I didn't want any of this. I didn't want them to die…" Everard doubled over, and his voice shook. "I just…I just wanted to belong."

Luka stared down at his weeping brother, shaking, before scrubbing the tears from his face with the back of a hand. He stepped away from Everard. "You have five lives on your shoulders. All because of your selfishness."

Tears stung Faven's eyes and she stepped back. The room remained still, too still, as if it were holding its breath. The first to break the silence was the king. He strode closer and demanded, "Are you really my son?"

Luka said nothing as his father drew closer. His father reached a hand up to Luka's face and grazed a finger around his patched eye. "You're alive?"

Luka pulled away, avoiding his father's gaze. His mother, the queen, rushed toward her son. "Oh, Luka!" she exclaimed, touching his face briefly before embracing him. "It's really you."

Then Luka wrapped his own arms around his mother, burying his face in her shoulder. And he wept.

Faven turned away. Luka and his family deserved some privacy after…everything. When she looked up, Faven saw several of the people in black clothing shuffling closer. Sniffling, they stared at the others who had returned. A young woman with strawberry blonde hair pushed her way to the front, searching the group.

"Tristan!" The girl ran up and gripped his arm, her eyes searching his. "Cassian?"

Tristan seemed unable to say the words. Instead, he shook his head and looked away. The girl dropped his arm and stepped back. She crouched low to the ground, shaking. Then she began to wail. Aria.

Tristan raised a hand toward her head, but then dropped it back to his side. An older man and woman joined the girl and hugged her tightly, protectively. Cassian's parents. Unable to look at them, Faven turned to the rest of the black-clothed group. A young boy around Cassian's age raced through the crowd yelling, "Tristan!"

The boy leapt into Tristan's outstretched arms. Tristan held the boy tightly. The boy wept loudly as he clung to him. And that's when she knew. These people…they were the families of the Ten. Her heart plunged into her stomach.

Faven couldn't help but search the crowd for her own family. When she didn't find them, her shoulders dropped. Were they still in Hallon? Did they even know she was one of the missing Ten? She peered at Kai and Jovian and hesitated. No one was rushing forward to greet them. Where were their families?

"Where are the others?" the king's voice rang out from behind her and Faven turned to face him. The king looked back and forth between the remaining five and finally caught Faven's gaze. "Where are the other five?"

Luka, having calmed down and stepped away from his mother's hug, faced his father. He spoke loud enough for all to hear: "We're all that's left."

Several more wails erupted from the crowd of people behind them, but Faven couldn't bring herself to face the people. Tenji, Ruben, Archie, Cassian, and Draven—they all had families who would never see them again.

An elder Royal Council member approached the king, interrupting the reunion. "Shall we proceed with the trial?"

Faven recognized him as the same one who had caught her before she could escape the princes' assessment. The king nodded. "You may carry on."

Everard shot a look of panic in the remaining five's direction, as if pleading for help. Why would he think any of them would help him?

The Royal Council member nodded. "On account of the disappearances of the top ten in line for the throne, we have decided, with consideration of all we have discussed, and all the evidence provided, Everard is indeed guilty of treason.

"The evidence is as follows: several documents were discovered including the detailed ranking of each of the ten princes from last year's assessment. The rest of the documents pertained to the Sidylla Labyrinth, where the princes were sent. All the documents were found in the prince's possession. The most condemning evidence is the confession which came from the mouth of Prince Everard, fourth son to King Léon. Prince Everard himself admitted to organizing the kidnapping of the ten princes to send them into the depths of the Sidylla Labyrinth to retrieve the spirit found at its center. As only five of the princes have returned, Everard is now also charged with the murder of five royals."

The council member paused and faced Everard. "Prince Everard of the Remy line, son of King Léon, you have been found guilty of treason for the kidnapping of ten royals in line for the throne and the murders of five. The penalty for treason is death."

Everard whimpered and the guards on each side forced him to kneel. They shoved his head over a slab of stone as the man swathed in black stepped forward bearing his ax. Faven jerked to stare at the Royal Council member, and then at the king. The king didn't speak or move, and the queen only turned away and pressed a hand to her mouth. Were they really going to let him be executed?

Luka stepped forward. "Wait! You're going to execute him?"

King Léon looked at his eldest, his expression cold. "It's the law. If any commits treason, they must be executed immediately. I can't give special favors just because he's my son."

Luka stared at his father; his fists clenched. For a moment, Faven thought he might stand up to his father, but instead, he dropped his gaze and stepped down. She heard Kai grunt his disappointment. Luka shifted to stand next to Faven and the others. He refused to look at anyone, especially his father or Everard.

Looking over at Everard, Faven watched as the executioner raised his ax. Everard trembled and tears slipped from his eyes. He shot another panicked look at them, but this time, Faven realized it was directed at someone in particular.

He was expecting one of them to act.

She glanced at the others next to her, searching for the traitor among them, but she didn't see any sign of acknowledgement of Everard's plea for help on any of their faces. At least not until she saw Jovian's steady gaze move from Everard to the king, and a purple glint flickered in his eyes. Before Faven could react, Jovian's hands tightened into fists and his body moved.

The earth rose, breaking through the floors, and whacked the executioner and his ax away before he could take a swing at Everard's head and Everard's chains snapped off with a flick of Jovian's finger. The ground trembled and crumbled like an earthquake, causing everybody except the king to slide back. Then Jovian flipped through the air and landed before the king. The earth seized the king's arms.

"Everard won't be the one being executed today," Jovian said in a voice Faven had never heard him use before. Her eyes widened and her stomach wrung. She recognized that voice, and suddenly, everything clicked within her.

One thing had always bothered her about the traitor—she could never recognize the voice she'd heard in the library. None of the Ten had had the same cold, calculating, yet cocky tone she'd heard. Tenji had sounded the closest to that voice, but even his wasn't the same. Tenji's voice had been deeper, older. And at some point, Faven had given up trying to match the voice to one of them. She had even started believing the person she heard in the library with Everard had been someone else entirely. Until now.

The king's eyes widened and Jovian smiled grimly.

"This is for my family," Jovian said. "For my family who you pretended never existed." Jovian brushed his foot along the ground and flicked his toes up at a sharp angle. A jagged boulder sliced through the floor and plunged into the king's chest.

55

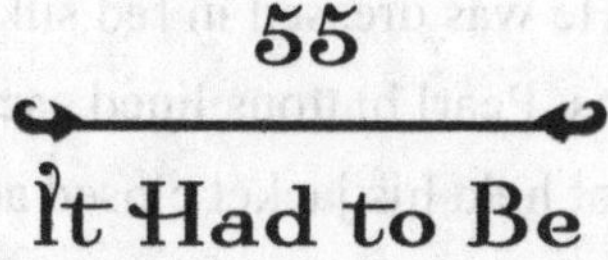

It Had to Be

A SEVEN-YEAR-OLD BOY WITH WILD BROWN HAIR AND A small braid on the side of his head sat silently in a dark room with his back pressed against a cool, stone wall. His skin and the peasant rags that clothed him were covered in layers of dirt. The room he sat in had no window, just a door that was tightly shut. And the boy, called Jovian, stared off into the distance, too tired to cry anymore.

He hadn't moved an inch since he'd been put there, and it wasn't until he heard movement outside that he turned his head to the door. Low, hushed voices murmured on the other side, seeping in. He wondered, briefly, fleetingly, if they were aware he could hear what they were saying.

"The boy you told me about, he's in here?"

"Yes, Your Majesty."

"Have you told him anything yet?"

"No, Your Majesty."

"I want to talk to him before I decide what to do with him."

"Yes, Your Majesty."

With the jangle of keys, the lock clicked and the door squeaked open. Jovian flinched at the bright light that poured into the room from the lanterns outside. A large shadow stepped into the room and Jovian's eyes focused on a tall, broad man with graying blond hair and blue eyes. He was dressed in red silks embroidered with flames and phoenixes. Pearl buttons lined each side of his jacket, while the buttons that held his jacket closed across his body were pure gold. A frilly bit of lace puffed from his neck and from under his sleeves. His black boots fell heavy against the stone floor. However, the most terrifying thing about this man was the greedy curl of his eyebrows and the curious gleam in his eyes.

"Hello, little one. I am your ruler, King Léon." The man offered him a smile as he crouched down to see Jovian face to face. "Do you mind answering a few questions for me? Then we can get you out of this dreadful room."

Jovian had seen enough fake smiles in his life to recognize one when he saw it. But somehow, he knew if he didn't answer this man's questions, something not so good would happen to him. He said nothing to this king and just continued to stare at him, waiting.

"Did you know you had a sense?"

Jovian nodded.

The king returned a nod, looking pleased by Jovian's compliance. "Did your family know?"

Jovian nodded again.

"Are you able to control your sense? Do you find it easy to use?"

Jovian blinked, unsure how to answer that question. Images of rumbling, cracking streets and crumbling buildings flashed through his mind. He clutched his head, gritted his teeth, and rocked back and forth.

"You don't need to answer. Forget I even asked. I didn't mean to bring up painful memories," the king said, his voice a strange sort of pacifying. Jovian's rocking slowly stopped and he looked up. The king turned to another, older man in a long white robe who stood by the door. "Have you tested his ability control?"

The old man nodded hesitantly. "We have," he answered, peering down at Jovian. "He has a high ability to manipulate his sense. However, we believe he didn't realize the full magnitude of his potential. This resulted in the...incident."

The king turned to Jovian. "Did you know how strong your sense was?"

Jovian shook his head.

The king nodded thoughtfully. Then he focused on Jovian again. "How about we make a little deal? I'll get you out of here, give you a lovely place to live, give you anything you ever want or need, and we can offer you training so you can better control your ability. I'll do all of this for you if you do one thing for me." The king waved his arm toward the open door. "All you need to do is comply with the rules of our royalty. Do you think you can do that?"

Jovian stared at the king, his face blank, but his survival instincts kicked in. He nodded.

"Good." The king smiled as he stood. "I'll send someone to come fetch you and take you to your new quarters. A much more comfortable home, I promise. They will get you settled and fill you in on all the rules and requirements. From now on, you will be a prince. Welcome to Phoebus, Prince Jovian."

The king and the old man exited the room and closed it behind them, locking it tight once more. Jovian wondered if someone really would return for him or if they'd forget about him, leave him alone in this dark room, and move on with life.

"Your Majesty, I hope you don't mind me asking, but are you sure this is wise? If his emotional state was stable, he could be a great asset for the kingdom. However, we fear he'll just become another troublemaker."

"That's why I decided to speak with him first. If he doesn't obey, we'll terminate him. He doesn't have anyone to stand up for him like the other one does—the wife of King Darian has proven quite impossible to control." The king paused. "Unless…does the child have someone? Did anyone survive?"

"No, none from his family survived."

"Very well. Bury this incident. I doubt the boy will talk. We can even hire someone to act as his parents to help cover the whole ordeal if we need."

Footsteps clicked away and faded, leaving Jovian alone with his spinning thoughts. None from his family survived. They were all gone. And the king wanted to pretend they never existed.

Anger and pain swirled inside him. If they were going to erase his family's existence, Jovian would try just as hard to remember them. This was all the king's fault, the Royal Council's fault. It had to be. It had to be.

Jovian gripped his head again and rocked back and forth.

It had to be.

56

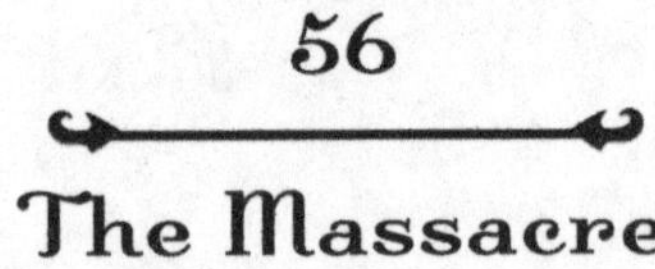

The Massacre

KAI COULDN'T BELIEVE HIS EYES. THE BODY OF THE KING he hated was hanging lifeless before him. Luka dropped to his knees, stunned, and a freed Everard screamed and ran to his father's feet, cupping the blood that poured from his chest as if that would stop the bleeding. Before Kai had a chance to react, Romain, Luka's younger brother, yelled and lunged for Jovian.

Without a single glance in Romain's direction, Jovian flicked his hand and knocked the other prince back with a rock. The floor rose up with the twisting of Jovian's fingers and seized Romain. More people dove to attack him, but with another wave of Jovian's hand, they were also seized. He stared at the king's body a moment longer before he turned his focus on the white clad Royal Council. He wasn't smiling now.

"Your turn."

Several screams rose as the floor caved and cracked all around the room. The Royal Council slid all into one place, and broken pieces of earth whirled around Jovian in a chaotic mess. Sharp, jagged rocks shot forward and struck down every last one of the Royal Council. Kai fell to the ground with the tilt and clawed at the floor to keep from sliding into the crossfire of the rocks.

"What in the bloody hell are you doing, Jovian?" Kai yelled over the screams, reaching out to catch someone who had been sliding toward the massacre of the Royal Council.

Jovian's gaze turned toward the rest of the crowd: the families of the Ten, the royal family, the guards, and those who survived the labyrinth. The ground stopped trembling for a moment and a familiar smirk spread across Jovian's face. "Kai, you of all people should understand. This is for the best. The best for the world."

Kai stared at the kid standing before him. Was he insane? Jovian's eyes were calm and his face registered the same clever, thoughtful humor it always had. He seemed awfully undisturbed despite having murdered several people.

"What do you bloody mean it's for the best?" Kai cried, standing and glaring at him.

Next to Kai, Tristan rose to his feet, clinging to his younger brother. Kai scanned around the room. How many innocent were dead? Some people clung to the wall, while others clawed at the earthen caves Jovian had formed around them. The royal family— including Luka—seemed oblivious to Jovian, their focus still on the punctured king. Faven stood a step behind them, frozen.

Jovian eyed Kai and Tristan. "The entire system is twisted. They choose who they want to succeed, and you know it. If they don't like someone, they dispose of them. Like I'm sure they did with Tenji's older brother. Like they almost did to you, Kai."

Kai took a step back. How did Jovian know that? No one ever acted like they did, and he knew for a fact that the king had taken careful measures to keep the fact hidden.

Jovian didn't wait for a response before he continued, "They're power-hungry; they see themselves no less than gods. They do as they please. They glorify senses like they're worthy of being praised. But they aren't." Jovian's gaze hardened. "Senses only bring destruction. Leaving those without them weak and defenseless, unable to protect themselves."

Jovian paused to point at Kai. "You almost killed your whole family in a fire." He shifted his gaze to Tristan. "You said you worried about hurting those around you with your lightning sense." Then he dropped his hand. "We've all seen the destruction Draven's sense had on those around him."

Nothing Jovian said was wrong. In fact, he was right. King Léon and the Royal Council really *did* make things go the way they wanted. He was right when he said that some senses could be dangerous and harmful. But Kai could only think of his grandmother and the words she had said to him. He shook his head, his anger feeling different than it had before.

"Senses can hurt when they're hard to control or used in the wrong ways," Kai argued. "But you can't blame senses for all that's wrong in the world. And murdering the king and the Royal Council won't solve anything."

Jovian's hands tightened into white-knuckled fists as he heaved in short, aggressive breaths. "Senses are evil. They must be eradicated. And with the help of the Sense Thief, I could rid the entire world of them."

Tristan frowned, pushing his brother behind him. "But we defeated the Sense Thief in the labyrinth."

A smile inched onto Jovian's face. Instantly, a chill seeped into the air and the room darkened. A dark, deep, vibrating laugh erupted all around them. A black mist crawled out of Jovian's side and his eyes flashed purple. Above him rose a creature with the face of a skull. Its sockets held flaming purple eyes. He wore a dark garment and had a shredded hood over his head.

A shiver of fear ran down Kai's back. He recognized those purple eyes.

"Defeated me?" The laugh continued. "Not even those of Kyndrie could defeat me. Rupert Vilet, the 'spirit' at the end of the labyrinth, was merely my puppet. The reason that man became so powerful was because I possessed him. It is I, Kazimir, god of the dead, who made him into who he became. I am the true Sense Thief."

The creature from the desert. The one who possessed Draven. The one who had tried to kill him. Kai pressed his lips together tightly and lifted a hand to his chest, clutching it as if he could still feel the pain.

"How?" Faven asked, coming to stand next to Kai, her heart quaking in her chest. "How did you get here?"

The purple blazing eyes shifted to her. "Ah, yes…Prince Sage. Or should I say Princess Faven? Your light sense may be good at keeping me out of your head, but it's not strong enough to vanquish me. All you did was dislodge me from Draven's body. Did you really think you could defeat me so easily?"

Faven glared at the monster and turned her focus to Jovian. "Jovian, the spirit is using you to get what he wants. You'll only be aiding him in his own goal!"

Jovian smiled at her. "Maybe. But if he can help me rid the world of senses, then it will all be worth it."

The spirit, Kazimir, floated closer to her. "You think you can do something?" The creature chuckled. "You couldn't even save the other princes, despite having the power to do so. Do you really think you could stop me?"

Faven stared into Kazimir's flaming purple eyes, her chest tightening. How dare he.

Kazimir retreated to his place above Jovian. "You won't even be able to keep that promise of yours to Draven. That little girl he cared so much about—that one who sees the future—will eventually fall into my hands. She will be mine."

Faven stiffened. Zinnia could see the future?

"Jovian!" a broken voice interrupted their conversation. "Jovian, why?"

Everard was covered in his father's blood. He clenched his hands and stared at his partner. This was all his fault. This blood was his fault, as well as the deaths of all those princes who hadn't survived the labyrinth.

The room spun around him as he stared at his father's murderer, the only person he had trusted. The person he'd called his friend. "You—you said you would help me," Everard stuttered, unable to gather his thoughts. He gripped his shirt as if his own heart was bleeding and not his father's. "I thought you were my friend. But you killed my father!"

The spirit and Jovian turned their gazes to Everard. The spirit's deep cackle made Everard step back. "I remember you! You're the weakling I spoke with all those months ago. You thought you were summoning Vilet, but your summons was so vague that I was able to answer instead. Thank you, weakling."

Everard fell to his knees as more hot tears flooded down his face. "I didn't want this. I didn't want this!"

Jovian's tall, lanky figure towered above him and he stared down at Everard. "I know you may hate me for this, Everard," Jovian said slowly. "But your father wasn't a good man. He had to go."

"But he was my father! You promised! You told me to trust you, and I did!"

Jovian straightened, his braid swinging with the movement, and put a hand on his hip. His gaze hardened. "You're right, and I did. I promised I'd keep Luka alive, and I did. And I promised I'd help you achieve the ability to have a sense…I do my best to keep my promises, Everard, even though I explained to you that senses are evil. So, until I can eradicate every sense, you may have your wish." Jovian raised his hand toward the king. "Here's me—keeping my promise. You can finally have what you always wanted. To have a sense like your father."

The Sense Thief sunk down into Jovian's body and molded into one being with him. As Everard watched, burgundy mist sifted from the king's lifeless form into a pile floating above him.

Jovian's demon-self shifted toward Everard and Everard's eyes widened as he realized what Jovian was doing. "Wait! No, Jovian! No!"

The burgundy mist raced toward him and drilled into him through his eyes, nose, mouth, and ears. Pain raked through every fiber of Everard's body, and the room whirled and blurred around him. Everard screamed.

57

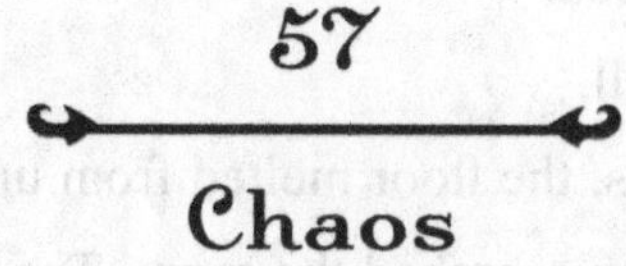

Chaos

FAVEN SLAPPED HER HANDS OVER HER EARS AS EVERARD'S scream reverberated through the room and through her body. She stared, her eyes wide and her mouth gaping as Everard writhed on the ground. More screams erupted around her and Faven turned to see people scrambling toward the throne room doors, still blocked by Jovian's rock wall. Those held in the earth's grasp struggled to free themselves. Senses of the people in the room beat at walls or doors or earth prisons.

Near her, Tristan clutched his wide-eyed brother. "We need to get everyone out!"

"There's no way out." Faven dug her nails into her palms. "Unless we break through the walls."

Luka, his gaze on Everard, jumped up and raced toward him. But before he reached Everard, Jovian swept his hand out and a rock shot from the ground, knocking Luka back.

Tristan grimaced and his eyes snapped toward a wall. "Leave that to me!" He grabbed his brother's arm and rushed to the side of the wall while Jovian and the demon spirit were distracted.

Faven took a step toward the fallen Luka when, suddenly, the room converged. The floors and walls shifted, swirling and spinning around her. She stumbled, then lost her balance and toppled to the hard floor. She clutched at the ground and stared in horror as the floor melted from under her hands. She squeezed her eyes shut and shrieked.

But she didn't fall.

Opening her eyes, the floor melted from under her, but again, she didn't fall. Faven searched the room. The walls wavered like water and the people morphed into deformed figures. Repetitive images of the king's death sprang up all around them, and oozing monsters lifted from the ground. A massive, beheaded pig dangled from the ceiling, turning its black lifeless eyes to the people below it. Screams and shrieking filled the room.

Faven didn't know what was going on, but it was terrifying and bewildering at the same time. She couldn't move or stand without feeling overwhelmingly dizzy and nausea churned in her stomach as she braced herself as best she could against the melting ground. Looking around, she spotted Kai on the ground, not too far from her.

"What's going on?" she shouted over the noise.

"Everard!" Kai shouted in reply. "He has the king's sense—illusion—but he doesn't know how to control it. He's sharing his nightmares with us."

Faven followed his pointing finger to Everard where the boy crouched on the floor, clutching his head. Faven glanced between Kai and Everard. It was a logical conclusion. Everard had never had a sense before. He hadn't grown up with learning how to maintain and control one. Then suddenly, one was dumped full force on him. Of course he wouldn't be able to control it.

An explosion rocked the room. Faven jerked her gaze toward where it had originated. Through the illusions spinning around them, the sun cast rays through a massive hole in the wall, and the royal courtyard lay on the other side. Tristan crouched near it, pushing his brother through and waving for others to escape.

Faven pointed, looking back at Kai. "Tristan!"

Kai nodded and together, they crawled in that direction. Dragging herself over to a crying lady, Faven called out, "Move toward the light! Get out of here!" She pointed toward the hole. "Tell more people on your way!"

The lady nodded and wriggled in that direction, gesturing to others. Faven turned and looked for other people close by, but instead, familiar boots stood between her and Kai. She raised her eyes.

Jovian and his half demon-self looked down, first at Faven then Kai, seemingly unaffected by the bizarre dizzying effect of the illusions. "Where do you think you're going?" he asked, his grin teasing.

Kai ignited a flame and blasted a stream at Jovian, but the younger boy dodged. Faven jerked a leg out and swiped at Jovian's legs, but he merely jumped over. He clucked his tongue at them. "And I hoped the spirit would be wrong, that you would understand and help me."

Kai roared as he delivered another blast. Jovian dodged again and kicked Kai's hand back. A cluster of rock encased Kai's hand and buried it into the ground beside him. Kai winced and grunted before he glared at Jovian and said, "All this time, you were the one that put us in that damn labyrinth!"

Faven channeled light to blind Jovian, but he merely closed his hand and the earth swallowed her, caging her body tightly, leaving only her head above ground.

"I never wanted to hurt anyone if that is what you're implying," Jovian answered. "I did try to prevent deaths from happening, but I underestimated just how difficult the labyrinth would be. Originally my plan was to only remove my own sense…but Kazimir was right. It's better if the entire world is without them. Please understand." He lifted a hand toward them. "Soon you'll see how wonderful it is to be without a sense. You'll no longer have to worry about hurting others. You can live life, unpressured. And this way, children with senses too strong to control won't accidentally wipe out their whole family ever again."

Again?

Faven looked up into Jovian's eyes, and, for the first time, she saw a heavy loneliness and deep sorrow weighing him down. A weight he had carried in silence, unknown to others. He had carried it and carried it until he had grown to hate himself and his own sense. Now he was finally releasing his fury.

"Jovian," Faven pleaded. "You can't rid the world of evil. It's impossible. But you still have a choice in who you will become; we all do. Please stop this!"

"Maybe I can't rid the world of evil, but I still think it's worth trying." Jovian raised his hand toward her, smirking. "And I have decided to give you two the pleasure of being the first to experience this new world."

He was going to take her sense. She had to do something before he did.

Faven radiated her light out with all her strength. At first, nothing happened, and panic bubbled up inside her, but she willed her sense to work.

Finally, the earth exploded around her, releasing her from its grasp. Without hesitation, she released a light at Jovian, blinding him. He lurched backward and sent the earth rolling toward her. A boulder shot from the ground, striking her in the chest and sending her soaring back. Faven skidded painfully along the ground.

Faven clutched her screaming chest and pushed herself up, coughing. Jovian frowned as he stared down at her from across the space. But while he was distracted, Kai kicked Jovian's legs out from under him before he blasted his hand free of the rock trapping it. Kai tackled Jovian, but the demon hand instantly whacked him away. Then the demon half of Jovian spread to both sides of his body.

"Prince Kai," boomed Kazimir's voice. "I won't let you get away this time."

A black shadow beast rose from Kazimir's figure. Faven's stomach dropped. How did he have Draven's sense? Did he take it before they left the labyrinth?

Terror flashed across Kai's face. Faven forced herself to stand and stumbled toward them, staggering through the dizzying illusions. Nausea swelled in her stomach, but she couldn't stop. The shadow's hand reached into Kai's chest, and he screamed in pain. Faven stared at them. Could she dislodge Kazimir from Jovian like she had in the desert with Draven? Maybe, maybe. If she could just get there in time.

Faven tripped, her entire world spinning end over end. She wasn't going to make it!

Then, out of nowhere, a strong wind pushed Jovian back as Luka's brothers, Michal and Romain, appeared through the illusions, sliding into place. Romain's tree roots shot out of the ground and twisted around Jovian's body, but Kazimir sliced through the branches with ease and returned Michal's wind power with his own. Kazimir pulled back into only Jovian's left side and Jovian slammed the ground with his foot, causing the earth to rise. The shadow beast released Kai and dissolved. With two jerks of his arms, Jovian smacked the princes away.

Jovian frowned at Romain. "Since you're deciding to give me so much trouble, I'll just start with you." With a wave of his hand, brown mist rose from Romain.

Romain jerked a hand toward Jovian, but nothing happened. Faven pressed her lips together. Jovian had taken his sense. She crawled closer, moving as fast as she could. Kai was still clutching his chest. Faven jolted as Jovian spun around, but his gaze was focused on the people escaping. He raised his demon hand again and colored mist streamed from several of them. The mist floated into the demon side of Jovian.

Michal, using his wind sense, shoved several people from the room, including Romain and the queen. Michal whisked another wave of wind at Jovian and ran toward him.

Jovian glided along the floor just as the last of the people slipped through the hole. He scowled. Michal lunged for Jovian, and Jovian encased his fist with rock and punched Michal in the face. Blood spurted from Michal's nose and mouth and he stumbled back. Jovian followed after him and kneed him in the gut, before sucking his wind sense from him with no more than a twitch of his demon fingers. Michal clutched his face with one hand, clenched his other into a fist, and swung it at Jovian. Jovian dodged and his face hardened. Jerking a hand forward, Jovian yanked a rock from the ground and heaved it at the prince. There was a sick cracking sound as it connected with Michal's head. Faven gasped.

Jovian watched as Michal dropped to the ground and a strange look of shock flickered on his face.

Taking advantage of his distraction, Faven released her light with all the strength she could manage. And when the light faded, she found Jovian splayed out on the ground with no evidence of the spirit on him. But she couldn't wait for him to recover. She released a large ray at him just as Jovian opened his eyes and met her gaze. Jovian yanked the ground over himself and disappeared, the ray beam exploding the ground and leaving a crater. But when she looked into the blackened remains of his hiding place, Jovian wasn't there. Where did he go?

The crackle of earth crumbling made her spin to face the sound. Jovian rose from the ground inches from her and slammed a rock-covered palm into her gut. She stumbled back and smacked down hard against the uneven, broken floor. Struggling to breathe, Faven could only watch as a ball of fire crashed into Jovian's body. Kazimir crawled back out of Jovian and swallowed the flames, turning to face Kai.

58

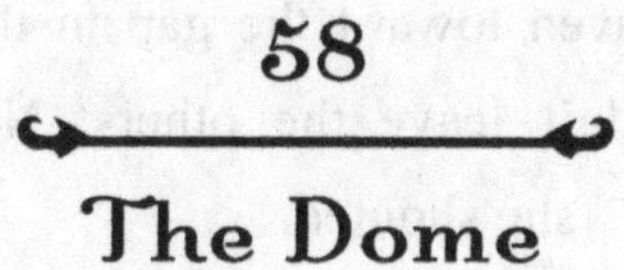

The Dome

SEARING PAIN RAKED THROUGH FAVEN'S CHEST. SHE dragged in breath, but her lungs squeezed. Princess Aria appeared at Faven's side. "Are you alright?" she gasped, her blue eyes wide as she pulled Faven up.

But Faven only turned toward Kai. "I've got to help…"

Aria's grip on her arm tightened. "Jovian's too powerful with that demon. We need to escape."

Allowing herself to be pulled up, Faven shook her head. "Kai."

"Don't worry about Kai," Aria answered, nodding toward him. Faven looked. Lightning rippled across the room and struck Jovian at full blast. Tristan ran at him, holding what looked like a lightning bolt. He released it and the lightning bolt flew out of his hand and struck the demon, who reverted back to one side. Jovian, gritting his teeth, jabbed a fist in Tristan's direction and a large rock smacked into Tristan's side.

However, while Tristan was distracting Jovian, Luka appeared behind him, Everard in tow. Luka waved a hand and tossed Jovian into a wall. Jerking his hands down, Luka pulled the ceiling down over Jovian and turned, pushing Kai toward the exit. "Go, everyone, go!"

Aria dragged Faven toward the gap in the wall, but Faven resisted. She couldn't leave the others. Not now. Not after everything. "Hurry!" she shouted.

Tristan climbed to his feet, clutching his right arm, and stared at the buried Jovian before racing toward them. Kai glared at the pile of rubble, then ran toward the exit. But Luka stood frozen over Michal, his eye wide. He bent down and seized his face. "Michal!"

An explosion from the pile Jovian had been buried under shook the room. Rocks spun around him, and the ground trembled. A shadow beast rose out of Jovian, and its eyes glowed purple. At the wave of Jovian's hand, an entire wall crumbled and shot toward them. Luka blocked the shards of stone with his telekinesis and returned them to Jovian. He and a tearful Everard lugged Michal away.

Then a shadow hand seized Everard and Jovian's voice rang out from the dust and debris, "He's staying with me."

"Everard!" Luka called, but he didn't reach out, still holding onto Michal, who didn't seem like he'd ever stir again.

The rest of the ceiling crumbled and splintered around them. Kai whirled around and grabbed Luka, dragging the other prince toward the opening. "Bloody run, idiots!" he yelled.

Luka levitated Michal and heaved him over his shoulder as he ran.

Tristan appeared next to Faven and Aria. "Aria! What are you doing here?" he exclaimed, pushing her toward the opening. He looked back at Faven.

Faven pressed her lips together tightly and followed after him, with Luka and Kai a step behind. Faven left the swirling room behind, her chest squeezing painfully and her heart thumping in her ears. She glanced back.

A growing shadow beast rose over them with Everard in one of its hands. Jovian darted after them with terrifying speed. The ground shuddered, and Faven struggled to keep her feet under her. She leapt over broken earth and blocked her head from the tumbling of bricks of a shattering house. Flames erupted all over the city, and it looked like it was turning to ash as formless writhing monsters rose from the ground. Faven couldn't tell what was real and what was Everard's illusions.

People fled the palace and city around her, their screams and cries rising high in the dusty air as an impossibly large shadow beast rose from the crumbling castle.

Faven tossed another look back. Jovian slid down the hill after them, standing on a board-like sliver of rock.

Suddenly, a girl with pink hair jumped between them and Jovian and multiplied herself into several bodies. Jovian skidded to a stop as all the versions of the girl attacked. Another girl flew in and slammed into Jovian, knocking him back.

Faven shot a bewildered expression to the others.

"The top ten princesses," Aria answered her unspoken question breathlessly.

The five of them reached the gate leading out of the town, but there were so many people crowded by the gate, shoving their way out, that none of them could move. Faven frowned. What now?

Then Aria waved them over to the side. "Follow me!" she called and ran away from the entrance. Faven glanced back toward the royal castle before she trailed after Aria and the others. Once Aria reached the wall surrounding the city, she pressed her hand to it and faced them. "I made it so we can move through. Hurry!"

Tristan, Kai, and Luka offered no further explanation and ran through the wall as if it were water.

Faven only stared.

"Come on!" called Aria.

Faven stepped toward the wall and reached for it. But her hand went right through, touching nothing but air. "How?"

"No questions!"

Faven nodded and darted through with Aria following closely behind.

On the other side, a young dark-haired boy waved them over to a small, horse-drawn cart. It was Tristan's little brother. It couldn't be anyone else. Despite his dark hair, he looked just like Tristan.

"Jump on!" the boy yelled.

Tristan helped Aria and Faven into the cart and hopped in after them with Luka close behind. Luka lowered Michal to the ground, his face grave. Kai, wincing and gripping his chest, stared at the cart as if unsure he could manage to hoist himself inside. Luka flicked his hand and Kai lifted into the air and flew into the cart. Kai grunted and the cart took off as fast as the little boy could make the horses go.

"Good work, Milo!" Tristan called to his brother. The little boy smiled back. Luka checked Michal's pulse then put his face in his hands and didn't move again. He didn't speak.

Faven studied him. His brother had betrayed him, and his father had been murdered before his eyes. Michal lay dead near his side. His world probably felt like it was falling apart.

"I'm sure your mother and Romain made it somewhere safe," she assured him. "They know the city just as well as you do."

Luka didn't move or respond.

Tristan pressed back against the side of the wagon. "Jovian wouldn't have let us get away with Everard."

Again, Luka didn't budge. Tristan's brow furrowed and Faven bit her lip. What else was there to say?

A violent cough from Kai interrupted their forced conversation. He wheezed, gripping his chest.

"Are you alright, Kai?" Aria asked, expression worried.

With a grunt, Kai shifted. "I'm fine," he muttered, refusing to look at them.

Faven crawled over to him. "I don't believe you. Let me check." She tugged at his shirt.

Kai shoved her back. "I said I'm fine."

A loud boom echoed through the valley. Faven straightened quickly and looked back toward Phoebus, clutching the side of the cart to keep her balance. A purple dome curved over the city, trapping whatever people were still inside from escaping. A large shadowy creature loomed over the mountain; its outline only illuminated by occasional flashes of lightning in the darkening sky. A multicolored mist rose from the city, filling the air with screams.

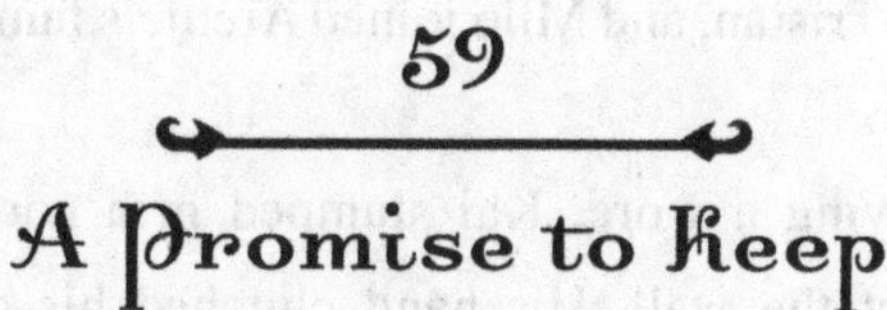

59

A Promise to Keep

FAVEN SHIFTED POSITIONS, EASING HER ACHING RIBS AS best she could, as the cart rattled onward. She kept a watchful eye out the back in case Jovian happened to follow them, but so far, only gently shifting plains met her gaze. As darkness fell, Tristan, who had taken over driving the cart, pulled over at an old barn.

Milo leapt out from the cart and darted inside. A bit slower, the rest of them piled out and followed. Faven squinted into the dim barn and barely made out the figures of a few other people. But it wasn't until the lanterns were lit that Faven recognized any of them. Queen Osanne, looking quite bedraggled for a queen, huddled to the side with Romain. She stood and Luka trudged toward them, holding Michal.

Queen Osanne wailed.

Faven turned away.

The rest of the people in the barn seemed to be from a large family. It took a while before Faven learned they were Archie's family. She had never really bothered to talk much with Archie, so she'd never known he had three older sisters and two younger brothers. Aria, Tristan, and Milo joined Archie's family in another part of the barn.

Without saying a word, Kai slumped in a corner, his back leaning against the wall. His hand clutched his chest, and he hadn't stopped grimacing throughout the cart ride. Faven opened her mouth to offer assistance, but he held up a hand. "I'm fine," he grunted.

Faven frowned at him, but seeing as she didn't know anyone else, she sank to the ground in the middle of the barn and hugged her knees to her aching chest. If only her family could be here too. Tears stung her eyes, and she lowered her head to her knees. Before long, she lay down for a restless sleep.

Throughout the night, Kai coughed violently and even if Faven *had* been able to sleep, she couldn't with Kai's constant coughing fits.

Eventually, she saw Tristan stand and move toward Kai in the dim lantern light. Tristan paused his approach when Faven pushed herself up. "I think something's seriously wrong with Kai," he whispered to her.

"I think so too," Luka said, joining them with a lantern in hand. His one eye was swollen, no doubt from crying. "Let's go check him out."

Tristan and Luka stole across the barn to Kai's side and Faven joined them. In the glow of the light, Kai's face was terrifyingly pale, and his breath was shallow. He looked as if he was on the verge of death.

Tristan crouched down and lifted the edge of Kai's shirt, but Kai grabbed his arm. Tristan shook his hand off. "You need to let us look at you. Something's wrong."

Kai dropped his arm and didn't stop Tristan again. Tristan pulled up his shirt. Faven held in a gasp as his torso was exposed. Black and purple bruises radiated over his chest and ribs, swelling unevenly.

"What is this?" Luka asked, his voice filled with shock.

Faven fidgeted with her hands. "Kazimir did something to him earlier."

"He certainly must have." Luka crouched down with them, a worried wrinkle creasing his forehead. Faven's heart warmed at the sight, despite the situation. How the labyrinth had changed them all; Luka did care about Kai, even if only a little.

Faven turned her gaze back to Kai, biting her thumb. The way his health seemed to be rapidly declining scared her. What if he died? Memories of Ruben, Draven, Cassian, and Tenji flashed through her mind and the weight of their deaths and Kazimir's words pressed heavily over her. Could she have saved any of them? Could she save Kai? She didn't think she could bear another death.

"Do you think...?" But Faven couldn't bring herself to say the words.

Neither Luka nor Tristan answered.

Kai winced and leaned his head back against the barn wall. Then he coughed again, violently. Faven squeezed her hands into fists to steel herself, then knelt beside him. Kai turned his head away, kept his eyes closed, his eyebrows drawn.

"I know you don't want help, but I won't sit by and watch you suffer," she told him as he wheezed. "Those bruises looked pretty bad, and I won't have another person dying on me." Faven paused, hesitant.

Kai shifted slightly but said nothing. His eyes remained closed and he kept his face turned away from her. She took that as compliance. Taking a deep breath, Faven reached out to press her hand on his chest. He winced and opened his eyes to look at her.

"That doesn't help," he hissed.

Faven didn't move her hand. "Just let me try something," she said.

Kai opened his mouth, then closed it again.

Choosing to ignore him, Faven focused her light into her hands, feeling them warm with the heat. The directions in the healing book she'd lost rose to mind and her thoughts turned to Ruben, to Cassian, to her grandfather. Would she fail again? Her heart pounded in her chest as Kai's coughing became more frequent and his breath shallower.

Kazimir's voice penetrated her mind: *"You couldn't even save the other princes despite having the power to do so."* She couldn't do it. Tears pricked her eyes and her chest tightened, causing her breath to rattle.

"I—I can't do it," Faven whispered, withdrawing her hand. She clutched her chest as if that would help hold her together.

Luka shifted closer to her. "Faven…can you heal?"

Tears spilling from her eyes, she nodded, a sob escaping her. "I was told I could, but I haven't been successful yet. I tried so hard with Cassian and Ruben, but—" Another sob leaked out.

Luka lowered his gaze. "Kazimir said…"

"That must mean you can!" Tristan crouched on her other side, and even through her tears she could see the hope in his eyes. "If Kazimir mentioned it, that must mean you do have the ability. You can do this, Faven. If you don't believe in yourself, then how can your sense respond?"

Staring at Tristan through the blur of her tears, Faven considered his words. Slowly, she turned her gaze back to Kai's heaving body. Believe she could. Maybe Tristan was right. She would try again.

Taking a deep breath, Faven focused on what she knew she could do. She focused on the memories and sensations of what it felt like to revive the dead plant, to heal the wounds in Cassian's neck. She could heal. She'd done it before, so she could do it again. Wiping away her tears, Faven pressed her hands to Kai's body again.

Kai kept quiet, his gaze low as he dragged in haggard breaths. Then he whispered, "Why help me when I caused Cassian's death?"

As she pressed her fingers against his wounds and imagined healing his body, Faven lifted her gaze to his face. He stared up at the ceiling, regret thick and heavy in his brown eyes, and seeing that only strengthened Faven's resolve to heal him.

"Because, Hothead, you care. Yes, your pride can blind you and cause you to make stupid decisions, but at least you're willing to admit your wrongs and learn from them." Pushing a bit harder against his chest, Faven felt Kai tense. "And whether you believe it or not, I actually like you for some odd reason."

Kai's gaze flickered to hers, and suddenly, she remembered she was a girl again. He might take those words differently now. She widened her eyes and shook her head at him. "I didn't mean anything weird."

A tilt of a smile lifted on his face. Yes, he looked better when he smiled. He should do it more often. Shaking the thought from her mind, Faven forced herself to refocus on the wound.

His injury was different from the wounds she healed on Cassian's body. The injury seemed to be resisting her light and energy. What did Kazimir do to him? Faven put more power behind her healing, ignoring the tremble of exhaustion settling over her. Kai grimaced but stayed quiet. What if she failed again?

Then some sort of energy gave in his chest, and Faven drew the force out of him. A bright light flashed in the room and knocked out all the lanterns that had been lit. She stilled and held her breath. What was that? No one spoke until Luka lit one of the lanterns again.

"Did it work?" Luka asked, raising the lantern over Kai.

Faven's eyes widened. Golden swirls of light swooped across his body like a bird and disappeared. She gaped, not sure what she had just seen. Kai took a few deep breaths and touched his chest. Opening his eyes, he slowly sat up.

"It's better," he said, a small smile lighting his face. Then he looked up at them and his smile slipped. "What?"

Luka shifted to a different spot, as if to see Kai from another angle. Then he did it again.

Tristan tapped his chin. "You look…different, Kai."

"Faven, did you do this?" Luka asked. "Is this an aspect of your healing sense?"

Faven bit the inside of her cheek before replying, "I don't know. This is my first time successfully healing someone. I'm not really sure what happened…" She continued to stare at Kai. He did look different. His red hair had slight golden streaks in it, and his eyes seemed more reddish-brown rather than plain brown, and his teeth were white and fresh. All his features were sharper.

Kai looked down at himself. "What? I don't see anything wrong." Then he paused. "Hey, wait a minute! All my scars are gone!"

As he said that, something strange began to happen.

"Uh, Kai's glowing," Tristan informed them, as if it wasn't obvious.

Sure enough, Kai glowed with a warm, golden light. He looked down at himself and jumped up. "What the bloody hell is going on? How do I turn this off?" he patted himself down as if that would help snuff the glowing out. When that didn't work, he lifted his eyes to Faven. "You. What did you do to me?"

Faven raised her shoulders defensively. "I don't know. Maybe it's just a side effect of the healing I did. I'm sure it'll go away with time."

"It better," Kai said with a scowl. "I don't want to be a lantern like you." Then, before their very eyes, as if cowed by his displeasure, his glow gradually faded.

Aria chose that moment to appear behind them, bringing their attention to her and the rising sun. "The others are talking about going to a neighboring kingdom to find shelter. They can't decide where the safest place to go might be. Any ideas?"

Thoughtfully, Luka crossed his arms. "Velykov should be avoided at all costs. I don't think they would take pity on anyone from Reudinia."

"Hallon is on an island," Faven said quietly. "It's full of kind people. The Hallonese would gladly welcome any refugees. And my parents will be there to help smooth over any problems." She shrugged.

Aria smiled at her, eyes bright. "That actually sounds really great!"

Luka nodded. "Good thinking, Sa-uh—excuse me—Faven."

"Actually," Aria added. "I've been curious about several odd statements that have been said. And by the fact they call you by different names."

Faven sighed, nodding. "I'm not Prince Sage. I'm his older sister, Princess Faven. It's a long story."

Giving a giddy little jump, Aria smiled again. "I knew it! I knew you were a princess!" Then her smile dissolved and a sad expression settled over her face. She looked away.

Luka glanced back toward his mother and brother, then looked back and forth between them all. "We're all going to Hallon then?"

"I don't think I can go to Hallon," Faven said after a moment, Kazimir's disturbing words playing on loop in her mind.

"What? Why?" Aria asked.

Looking out the door of the barn, Faven wrung her hands. "I promised Draven I'd watch out for a young girl he cared for. Kazimir mentioned her during the battle at the castle. He said something about her being able to see the future. I can't let him take her."

"See the future?" Luka's eye widened.

"That's why."

Everyone turned to Tristan who sounded unsurprised. "I mean…Draven always seemed to know so much, and I honestly wondered if he was the traitor…but now I know why."

Kai slammed his fist on the wall of the barn. "Jovian…how did I miss it? That prick…I should've realized it was him from the beginning, but I was fooled all the bloody way through! That joking bastard."

"We all were," Luka said, looking away. He was silent for a while. Then he faced them again. "If this girl can see the future, we can't let her fall into Jovian's hands. I'll go with you, Faven."

Faven gave Luka a relieved smile. "Thanks, Luka."

"I'll go as well," Tristan said, looking over his shoulder at his brother. "If I can find someone to take Milo to Hallon."

"I'll take him," Aria whispered. "But I hope you'll all join me there soon."

Tristan smiled gratefully at Aria and everyone turned to Kai. He groaned and leaned against the barn wall once more.

"Fine," he muttered. "Count me in."

Faven couldn't help but smile.

Several months ago, these three men had been strangers to her. But now, it would almost seem strange to be apart from them. The events of the last few months had connected them in an irrevocable way. The deaths they'd experienced, the monsters they'd encountered, and the hopelessness they'd felt—all these things had changed them, had changed her. Her perspective of the world and being a royal had shifted a great deal since she entered the labyrinth all those months ago. And, honestly, it seemed as if they never truly left the labyrinth at all. Life was still uncertain and dangerous.

She didn't know what the next several months held in store for her. But one thing was certain: she would keep her promise.

Royals of Reudinia

Prince Luka
1st

Prince Tenji
2nd

Prince Draven
3rd

Prince Tristan
4th

Prince Archie
5th

Prince Ruben
6th

"Prince Sage"
7th

Prince Kai
8th

Prince Jovian
9th

Prince Cassian
10th

Prince Everard
307th

Princess Faven
Unranked

Acknowledgments

When I started drafting this book back in 2020 during quarantine, I really didn't expect it to come this far. I started it merely to reawaken my passion for writing. It still blows my mind how effortlessly this story flowed out. It only took three months to write the first draft, and it was just under 100,000 words. Not only was this the quickest I've ever written a first draft, but it was also the longest book I'd ever written at the time. I don't think it would've been so easy if I hadn't had my brother Jace. He listened to me talk about my story for hours and let me bounce ideas off him. He was my first fan, so I must acknowledge him first.

As he was also my illustrator for the map and character illustrations, I must commend him once more! I don't think anyone else could've captured each of their characters quite as well since he knew them *almost* as well as I did. I'm grateful for the passion and attention to detail he put into each illustration.

To my beta readers Courtney, Kali, Kalea, my aunt Kim, Roni, and Jace for bringing me joy with your reactions and for all your helpful feedback. I couldn't have done it without you!

To my editors Courtney Kleefeld and Mariella Taylor, I *definitely* couldn't have done it without you. Courtney, not only were you the biggest encourager and the most enthusiastic about this story, but you were the very first person to read the book! I think if you hadn't stayed up all night finishing it and sharing your reactions, this book might not be published today. You taught me so much and helped me more than any other person; I don't think I could ever thank you enough!

Mariella, your feedback forced and challenged me to really dig in and grow as a writer. Thank you for seeing the potential in my story and showing me where I could grow.

Kalea, Kali, and Courtney, thank you so much for helping with the marketing posts! Without your feedback on the design and text, they wouldn't have looked as great as they did. And thank you for proofreading everything!

I'd also like to thank Roni and several other various editors for helping through the grapevine, even though you didn't even know me! It blessed my heart a great deal.

To my parents, my husband Naheun, and my other two brothers—Josiah and Ben—thank you for supporting me every step of the way. All of you contributed in one small way or another and I haven't forgotten any of them!

Finally, thanks to all my friends and family who have encouraged or rooted for me along the way—even when fantasy wasn't your thing. Each and every one of you are the best!

Kaitlyn Rose Hong was born and raised in Oklahoma and has traveled to Australia, Thailand, and Japan as well as all over the United States. She lived and worked for a year in South Korea, and also lived briefly in Oregon. Her stories are deeply inspired by nature, fairytales, and the Japanese and Korean cultures. Other than reading and writing stories, Kaitlyn enjoys fiddling around with art, dancing, and watching Studio Ghibli films. She currently lives with her husband and their two cats.